THE CITY

A CYBERFUNK ANTHOLOGY

Edited by

Milton J. Davis

THE CITY

A CYBERFUNK ANTHOLOGY

Edited by

Milton J. Davis

Cover Art by Edison Moody
Cover Design by URAEUS
Copy Editing by Milton J. Davis
Manufactured in the United States of America

First Edition

Welcome to the City

By
Milton J. Davis

The City. No one knows how it began or when it will end. No one knows how we came to be here, 20 million souls, 1500 different species all crammed together in plascrete and biosteel. No one's been in or out of the city in 20 centuries. Some have their theories why, some don't care. But no matter whom you are, or what you are, you have a story, don't you? The trick is finding someone who cares to listen...'

And that's how it began, as a random idea in the middle of the day. I'm sure there are underlying concepts that sparked these words, and a closer examination of those concepts would bring forth a deeper discussion but at the time it was just a statement. Soon afterwards I posted these words on the State of Black Science Fiction, a group dedicated to the creation, support and distribution of science fiction and fantasy by and about people of African descent. The response was immediate and amazing. Other writers added their own ideas and linked them with images that helped convey their thoughts. Soon we had a continuous thread of ideas and concepts orbiting the central theme. Balogun Ojetade combined these ideas then created a City Manifesto, a guideline for stories based on this new creation. The next step was inevitable; the creation of an anthology.

The City anthology is a unique creation. It's a concept anthology, a collection of stories where eighteen different authors share their vision of a single idea. It's Cyberfunk, stories that play with future concepts from an Afrocentric perspective. Most of all it's engaging, exciting, thought provoking and fun.

Like the inhabitants, the City is perceived in different ways by different writers. The result is a journey into a unique world describe by unique and engaging voices. I hope you enjoy your visit to The City.

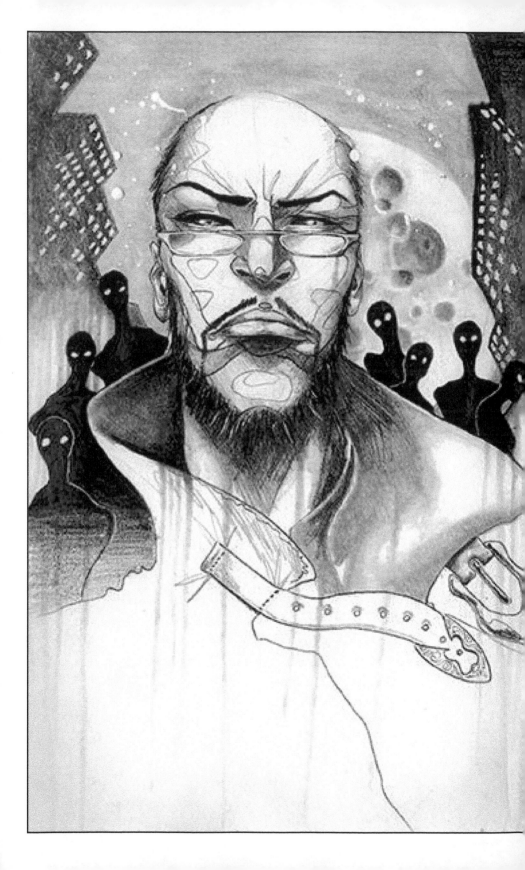

Knowledge

You say something to me? Yeah, I'm Knowledge Lateef. What is The City? That's a dangerous question. No one knows how it began or when it will end. No one knows how we came to be here, 20 million souls, 1500 different species all crammed together in plascrete and biosteel. No one's been in or out of the city in 20 centuries. Some have their theories why, some don't care. But no matter whom you are, or what you are, you have a story, don't you? The trick is finding someone who cares to listen. Now keep moving, and be careful what you think, or what you say. There are no secrets in The City, no secrets to The City. The City is always Watching. Now move on. I ain't time for you...

Watch out! Who were they? Runners. The eyes, ears and mouth of The City. What you say? We don't need messengers? Everything is in the Wave? That's exactly why the Runners exist. You keep forgetting what I told you. Nothing is secret to the City...unless it's not on the Wave. If it's on the Wave, The City knows. Want to send a message? Give it to a Runner. They are honest, trustworthy, loyal...and literate. What does that mean? Ha! They can read and write! In any form. Cityzens don't have need to read or write these days. Everybody jacked to the Wave. Oh yeah, they can take care of themselves pretty good, too. How do I know? I used to be a Runner before I found Street Wisdom. Now I spend my time schoolin' folks like you, trying to keep you out of the River. The River? That's another subject.

Who? His name was Jamal. Yeah, I know you probably heard of him. He was a Runner. Jamal knew The City. Some say he'd been from one End to the the Other. That's a lie; The City never ends. But he had a vision to make it better. Not just for humans, but for everything. The Runners spread the word and some actually believed he could to it. But what did I say? They are always watching, and they began to pay attention. Then Jamal and every single one of his followers disappeared and everyone forgot, just like that. Everyone except the Runners. Runners never forget.

You just won't go away will you? How do they watch us? We all have Tells, every one of us. Not tails, Tells. Reach behind you head. Now touch the back of your neck. Right there, that's where it is; or rather that's where it starts. The old books...I mean the old vids say The City used to implant them right after we were created. But it figured how to make it a part of us, just like your heart, you lungs, your brain. It automatically connects you to the Wave...and to The City. Can it be removed? Yeah. You can have it surgically removed, if you can find a Scalper brave enough to do it. But even the best Scalper can't get it all. It grows back. But you can Purge it. Purging will scour your brain of every bit of the Tell. If you survive it, you'll most likely go crazy. Most do. Those that don't become Runners. But then most folks think Runners are crazy, just controlled crazy. Now that's it. No more questions. You're going to get us snatched. Keep it up and the only place we'll be safe is in The Lush.

The Lush? No, it's not a myth. It's real, as real as you and me. The one place where the City can't reach you, where the Watchers can't watch you. Where is it? If I knew I wouldn't be talking to you. I'd be there. People are always looking for it though I'm I'm sure a few have found it. But since they ain't coming back to tell nobody, it stays hidden. Now stop asking questions. They're going to start paying attention.

What? You still asking questions? Okay, last answer, one way or another. The River is the Soul of the City. They say everything comes from it, and everything eventually goes back to it. You ever been to it? Smells like perfection, doesn't it? Water as clear as glass. Makes you want to jump in and swim with fishes, doesn't it? Don't. And never accept an invitation to go for a walk by the River. As a matter of fact, just stay away from it all together. Hey, did you see that? Shit! I knew it! Walk fast and get the hell away from me. They're paying attention! Watchers are coming. Run!!!

Glitch

By
Brandee Laird

I

"Inhale for a full-body stretch, letting your hands meet." She takes an audible inhalation, her lithe form elongating, hands gracefully touching palm-to-palm above her head. I mimic the movement, looking up at my own arms--shorter, more muscular than hers--letting out a great sigh as I fold forward at her bidding. Those around me follow suit, building an ensemble of soft exhales.

"Clasp hands behind your back, rising up with a great breath, opening your heart." I do, feeling my sternum shifting with an inaudible *pop*, clavicles settling into place. My hands and forearms are mad sore from yesterday's trainings, shoulders aching from hours of crawling and climbing.

We exhale as one, allowing our hands to stay locked as we fold once more, arms falling toward relaxed heads. I inhale, allowing my chest to expand, stretching my shoulders with an inner grimace. *Good morning hot mess, it's grappling day.* I try to focus only on my breath, my body, and the woody scent of the asana room, but the murmurs are louder again today. Each slow inhale brings the distant susurrations ever closer, exhales ending with high-pitched ringing through my head.

"Exhale and release." Madame Ghiri's tranquil voice makes its way through the din. "With your next inhale, ground your palms, shoulders shifting forward over wrists." She demonstrates, ankle bangles chiming as she tucks her knees to her chest, feet hovering above the ground. She maintains a balance on her hands for a long moment before smoothly extending legs behind her into a high plank. We follow, all strong enough that after our moment's balance the sound of feet alighting is less heard than subtly felt vibrating beneath our hands.

"Exhale, lower down."

My Tell jerks and twitches inside me, screaming all too quietly. My head aches with the sensation, half-seen phantoms pushing through me. I clench my jaw, trying to will it still as I slowly lower my chest. Watching my sweat dripping steadily onto the floor, I listen to my comrades breathing consciously, trying to push myself to physical pain just to have more to focus on.

Struggling to keep my breath, I continue the session diligently mimicking Madame Ghiri's peace, hoping to vicariously win some for myself. I anticipate the last position with dread, remembering when laying supine meant relaxation and wellbeing. Now it's the most painful to endure, the lack of distraction allowing my Tell to screech and wail, sending me disturbing, disjointed images--bloated bodies floating The River, children trapped within burning homes, my own death from a thousand violent ends. Each day it worsens, feels more alien, like an invasion of my very soul. *What good is the fucking thing if it's all glitch?*

Madame Ghiri calls for our final pose. I lay down; glad the dim room and my sweat conceal my tears as I wait for whichever terrible visions will happen today. I try anyway, taking deep, full breaths. I will my eyes to relax, sinking down into my body, hoping that today it'll be as it's supposed to. Another full inhale fills my lungs, expanding my chest, muscles yielding as I exhale.

My next breath is labored, like drawing air through an obstructed respirator. I try to sit up yet cannot move--am I sleeping? I can hear my comrades breathing around me, can feel the hot, humid air of the asana room. I am not asleep. I can barely breathe. I will my fingers to twitch, toes or neck to curl--anything.

Nothing.

A panic builds in my chest, throat loose and mind tight with the need to scream, "Someone help me, I'm not sleeping!" *My eyes are closed, but I can somehow see, no longer in the room but in a cold, damp alleyway. Two men lift me, carrying my body unceremoniously between them. They joke and laugh as they haul me down a tunnel of switch-backing stairs, dropping me as so much meat onto a cart at the bottom.*

I'm atop a pile of cold bodies, some rigid beneath me, the cloying scent of decay thick in my nostrils. My mind is crying out for anyone, Anyone! Wake me, so I can move again. *I know I'm alive but have no control, body static with a lucid soul. I know I'm me but cannot speak.* Please! Somebody wake me...*I try to shift, kick, turn, begging myself to just* Move! *Sure for an eternity that I never will, hysteria building to no avail, I struggle against the invisible bonds of at rest in-body while terribly alert in-mind: Trapped within myself.*

Not again.

The cart moves, smoothly propelled just above the ground. The domed ceiling bends blue light coming from electronic sconces every five meters, telling me we're in a subterranean transit way, City built and abandoned.

The cart stops, another two bodies thrown atop my own. I can feel swollen flesh soft and cool against my face. My body hurts with the need to scream, but I can hardly take a breath, fingers not so much as twitching.

We begin movement again, accelerating. The cart flies forward along its invisible track until brought to a sudden halt, tilted upward so we are hurled forward. I hear splashes from the upper corpses before feeling the water slap against my back then envelop me, filling my nostrils and my ears. I fight against my bonds, willing myself to move. So futile. *I watch the dim blue light of the tunnel fade as I sink until I can see no light at all, sure I'll never break free. So I die with a silent, powerless scream...*

A single, clear bell breaks through my vision. I jerk upward, whimpering softly from relief. Madame Ghiri holds her chimes apart while the tone falls, looking on at me calmly. I don't wait for the prompt to take a full-bodied stretch, to roll gently onto my side or slowly sit. I'm shaking, heart battering frantic lungs. My comrades don't outwardly acknowledge me, though I know they're all hyper-aware--there're enough mods in the room to read my elevated heart-rate and smell my fear. I seek eye-contact with Madame Ghiri, placing my palms together in a brief, apologetic acknowledgement before silently padding to the door and through, sprinting as soon as it closes.

I make it to my locker on the other side of campus just before the breakdown, slamming both fists against the nearby wall with a hoarse scream. I know the three other women in this chamber won't intervene. Emotional mastery is recognized as an essential part of a warrior's training, and no one in all of The Spear would fault anyone else for a controlled expulsion of rage. As expected, the other women simply finish their tasks then go, leaving me to my fit. I scream again, ripping my locker open violently, tears falling freely.

My integrity avoids it during the training day, but if I'm still to grapple and then study I will need to be better than this. *I cannot fucking do this.* I reach for an unmarked, opaque bottle, opening and downing its contents. The Ooze takes effect almost immediately, heart-rate slowing, Tell shutting the fuck up. I sag against the wall, slipping down it until I'm on my ass, head propped on my bent knees. *It must stop.* I take slow, deep breaths, clinging to this feeling, remembering what it is to be normal.

The soft chiming and the light scent of Jasmine alerts me to Ghiri's approach well before she turns the corner and clears her throat. I steel myself before looking up, taking a deep inhale and relaxing my face from a grimace to something more neutral. She smiles, though concern is clear in her tightly held eyes.

"Perhaps you are over-training?" Efficiency as usual. It would insult us both had she asked, "Are you okay?" because obviously I am not. This way she expresses her interest in my well-being while also seeking a solution.

I nod minutely, "Perhaps."

Two Risings ago I'd have been offended by her inviting herself into my troubles this way, righteous pup that I was. Lately I've been so desperate and lonely that, even though I know I will not explain it to her, I welcome her attention.

She studies me, no outward sign of her assessment other than a minute tracking of her pupils. I'm sure of what she sees--shadows hanging below lackluster grey eyes, the deep bronze of my skin flattened by the pallor of malnutrition and sleep deprivation, hair let grown long enough to become a hazard. *No one should ever be able to hold me by my hair.* I've done well to keep my armor and rig in shape, but I'm still in my loose, sweat-soaked asana garments so I don't even have that to help my case. *If I look half the shit I feel like...*

"If I may," Ghiri says, dropping gracefully into a cross-legged sit before me. I look on at her, unable to call even a semblance of warmth. When she's not instructing, we're friends. We've gone out for drinks, events, train together. I'd take her as a partner any day. *How can I trust her with my life but not my thoughts?* She settles into her seat and takes a deep breath, *seeing* me.

"Oh, girl," she sighs it, awed and vaguely pitying, "You gotta change somethin'. Sabbatical." She holds my gaze, weighing her own with a gravity she rarely possesses. "Or see a shaman." She reaches a hand toward my forehead, presumably to get a better look. I raise a hand to halt her.

"I know, Ghiri, but I have shit to do. I can't go nutter before my next rank eval. I need two weeks."

She sighs, shaking her head. She sees right through me, but is too polite to say so.

Her eyes are ruby today, lace-like facial tattoos

glimmering deep magenta to highlight her ebony skin. I realize that I'm still envious of her, having seemingly effortlessly achieved perfect balance of feminine and masculine, a true warrior as alluring as a goddess. No matter what anyone's said, I feel too bulky to be lovely, would never have my tats show anything other than dark, thick bands on my arms and across both eyes. Where Ghiri lets her locks grow long down her back, I trim my scalp neatly every week. *When I'm not full fucking glitch.* Looking at her poise, her peace and acceptance so authentic, I'm disgusted with myself. *You don't belong here.*

I take a deep breath, making the effort to look like I'm collecting myself as I sit taller. "Thank you for your concern, Ghiri. I apologize for disrupting your class."

She hears the dismissal, sighing deeply in return. "Just keep yourself together, woman." She hesitates. "If you need my shaman, you have his info." With a thought to access my messages, I do indeed have the address and available hours of Ungarif Ashtan. *In the Night Market District.* I nod a thank you as she swiftly rises, turning to leave without another word or shielded glance.

I rise slowly, feeling thick and distant. Changing from my damp clothing into fresh undergarments happens mechanically. I've donned my armor and rig enough times that checking and re-checking are done unconsciously, eyes closed. The most awareness I have is when I carefully tuck loaded capsules of Ooze into my inner chest pocket, hand held over them briefly for comfort. My current dose is already waning, and in the next two hours will be completely gone.

I finally take a moment to stare myself down in the mirror, trying to imagine what my comrades see. Comfortable--if shabby--light armor in shades of grey, S11 holstered at right thigh, Dillo pack secured tightly around my waist and chest, supple boots well broken-in. I don't have any obvious enhancements, light 'weave armor impossible to see. I don't look fancy, interesting, or particularly useful. *I look like another mediocre human cadet, barely fit to guard a child's trinkets.* I snarl at my reflection, bearing all ten claws in a flash, mimicking ripping into my own throat and stomach.

"Get your shit together or get the hell out."

I retract, take a deep breath, and disembark into the rest of my day.

May it pass rapidly.

II

The East Yard is all but empty, one veteran Breather moving through a longsword kata fluidly in the north corner, two human cadets knife sparring nearby. I'm early enough that I have time to warm-up with ground crawls and sprints, reinvigorating my aching limbs before the rest of the cell shows.

When my comrades begin to trickle into the yard, I take the moment to stow my S11 in my Dillo, holstering a simulator in its place. Others do the same, locking their live weapons into packs and cases to replace with training props from the shelves and lockers near the entrance.

As usual, Master Clyde is the last to arrive, shuffling in as if he don't give a fuck and wants us all to know it. He won't bother to address anyone until we're an hour into independently reviewing our last lesson. He never does.

Scanning the yard, I choose Ayrn Oakheart to partner with. He's got 58 kilos on me and more strength than I'd ever know what to do with, but I'm faster, have better technique, and need the challenge. *Be honest, you welcome the pain's distraction.* Watching him calmly load charges into two scopeless sim BFG1s, I consider dosing again for good measure. As keenly as I know my menstruation cycle, I feel the glitch coming on again, head pulsing and vision just slightly too bright, halos surrounding everything the late sun touches.

I can make it through.

I send Ayrn the request to spar. He looks up toward me, accepting with a lopsided grin. I interpret it as arrogance, already examining his posture to discern imbalances and plan my strongest attacks. He's wide as a house, heavy 'Weave shimmering iridescent green as he moves. If I have the nerve to go for submission it'll have to be a single joint, as his dark and heavily scarred arms are nearly the size of each of my legs, his own legs larger than my torso. *Wrists, fingers, possibly ankles.* We haven't sparred since stealth takedowns--at which I owned him--and I can already see his hamstring flexibility has barely improved. *Single-leg attacks, bring it high.* As he approaches, I see he's favoring his left shoulder, arm held just slightly tighter to his body and elevated like he's unconsciously guarding. *He'll draw left first for security.*

We meet near the north corner, the meditating veteran having already slipped away. I try to recall all his known enhancements--adrenal boost, muscle fortifications, and emotional control. Compared to my light 'weave, combat useless tattoos, and claws I can't use per regulations, I'm theoretically screwed.

With no words, we set in a clenched position as drilled last session. We press the right sides of our heads tightly together, his left hand encompassing everything from the base of my skull to my windpipe, mine barely able to cover just the back of his neck. He smells like cinnamon and sweat, breath slow and deep. *I wonder if he holds a grudge...*

I feel his neck contract just before he moves, sweeping my right elbow outward to make room for him to enter on a hip throw. I let him do it, waiting until I'm airborne but not yet over to tuck my legs hard, kicking my feet back out into his lower neck. It startles him, already committed enough that the change sets us off balance. I'm glad he chooses to release my arm in order to guard his face to fall, rather than twisting me down to the right. I ride him down, jarred as I draw my sim S11 close to my torso. Once grounded, I place it against the base of his skull. I have every right to stun him, "The reinforcement," Clyde says. I choose to taunt instead.

"Point."

He grumbles, standing.

We reset.

Now that he knows better than to let me get too far from him as he throws, I can see him re-thinking his approach, watery reptilian eyes flicking back and forth as he reviews me. He's not a handsome man, not particularly smart. But as a mostly-human tank, he excels.

He could literally tear my arms off.

I have a moment's imagining he's truly out to kill me. The one feeling triggers a visceral panic that overtakes my thoughts, rupturing my calm as the glitch takes over. Ayrn tenses to make another attack as my Tell initiates a full battle response, heart suddenly painful with its tripled effort. Infinite scenarios play through my mind in a blink, all designed to maintain my life, to end the threat.

No!

I react, eyes pulsing with clarity as I focus enough for my perception of time to slow. I take a sharp inhale, already aware that his new goal is brute force. It is his way.

He shifts his hand down and clamps my lower neck, moving to lift me by it. Even through the barrier of my Tell, I have the thought that it might feel like a nice massage were I not preparing to end him.

His right arm continues pulling up, lifting me as he crouches slightly, and his other arm reaching toward my low calf. I jump, harnessing his violent pull while dodging the grab to my legs, pressing one foot into his chest to guide me up his torso. He realizes my plan just too late, releasing me as I hook one, then two legs around his thick neck, squeezing tightly between my thighs. He stays standing, hands working to find purchase around my waist to pull me off. My Tell flushes me with more epinephrine, and before I've made any conscious decisions I've deployed my two strongest claws on each hand, sinking them into his eyes as I scream.

By The River, no!

His bellow shakes the yard, and though I can feel the attention of the others, my response is not finished. I withdraw, wrapping my arms around his head and releasing my legs, throwing my hips up and behind me to twist him down. *Where the head goes, the body follows.* He moans as we both slam into the ground. My Tell doesn't care that I've lost my air with the impact, so I'm quickly on my feet, panting as I assess. Ayrn's shrieking with rage and pain, both big palms covering his eyes, blood and other leaking out beneath them. I look down at my arms and hands, the sight of his blood ending the battle response. Looking up from my hands, I automatically seek Clyde, who looks on at me with an expression I cannot read. He's not angry, startled, or baffled, but this...

This ends my career. No sane detachment will take a fighter who cannot control herself during sparring.

Ayrn's screams have subsided, curses cascading out of him as he fumbles around the ground trying to find me.

"You gonna die now, little bitch. You gonna fuckin' die!"

I look from him back up to Clyde, devastated. I don't see judgement there, or reprimand. I read concern--or maybe just hope for it--as he mouths a single word to me.

"Run."

I pivot and go; throwing my sim to the ground as I spot then grab my Dillo, listening for the feet of my comrades-- *previous comrades*-- in pursuit as I turn out of the East Yard, sprinting toward the gate that will let me out into the greater City. My eyes burn but it would be cowardly to cry, not when this is my fault. The East guards don't take two looks at me hurtling past them. *Bloody uniforms on sprinting failures are just that commonplace.* I run south toward the train, still no sign of pursuit. My head pulses, too much shame and panic to stay on any one thought. I default to mission-mode, referencing the address Ghiri gave me while slamming the entire pocketful of capsules into my mouth, swallowing some and biting others open. I slow to a jog as I calm then walk into the station as if I'm not fleeing from myself.

The train is already arriving, wobbling and rocking as it slows. Doors hiss open, a motley assortment of beings shuffling off and on. I can't care to study any one of them very closely, can't even say how many just disembarked and boarded. The details I'd normally attune to are trivial distractions in comparison to my current status. I sit, turning briefly to see if anyone I recognize has followed me onto the train. No marshals, guards, or even other cadets. I look down at my hands and arms, still spotted with Ayrn Oakheart's blood.

I carefully deploy my pointer claws, cutting away the forearm sleeves of my jacket to ball up and stuff into my pack. I'll discard them somewhere later, for now relieved to see my unmarked skin rather than the proof of my failure. The rough sway and rhythmic *cachunk-cachunk* of the train is soothing as I focus on breathing slowly, staring at my calloused palms. I methodically review the route to Ungarif Ashtan, angry, mournful, and resolute. I tried to fight it but knew from the start I'd lose. Had hoped I could work it through but proved too weak.

Now, I must Purge.

III

Deep South District. The streets smell terrible, feces, piss, and decrepit wood wafting through the corridors. Though night, the way is illuminated by low streetlamps and scattered light from surrounding windows. Two young boys are still playing on a stoop, their conversation audible as I pass.

"You ain neva gonna do it."

"Ah will so!"

"Ain neva! You too chicken ooze. No Tell you be Runner food!"

The smaller boy balls his fists, face contorted in the helpless rage of any child under-trusted. His antagonist taunts him singingly, offering a silly face of bugged-out eyes, a finger in each nostril.

"Chicken ooze! Runner food!" Initiating a furious chase, the small boy sprints forward with a set jaw and tears streaming, the older boy laughing maniacally in what he perceives is all good fun.

Hold your ground, Young Warrior, I think, passing their engagement with but a moment's glance their way. *Walk your talk,* my heart whispers to me. I shuck off my own nagging conscience as I trudge forward, the shrieking of the boys at play-war fading into the distance. I clasp the tag around my neck, having already loaded it with every credit to my name. I have no nerve to lose, but seek reassurance anyway.

Six blocks of holding and I can hear the distant din of the Night Market. I'm already starting to see more beings on the stoops and in the street. I let go of my tag, set my shoulders back and down, and pretend I'm not full nutter.

The Night Market is just one of many of its kind, a darkened and dense place to buy and sell anything to anyone. Around here, everyone walks like they own the street, chests high, bodies and mods on display. I feel like I'm in a city of armored peacocks, most hoping the bluff is strong enough that no-one's going to test it. I do the same, aiming for the brooding, quiet-dangerous rather than bold-and-buff. This is where you don't ask questions beyond what you want or need to get rid of.

This is where people get lost.

Ungarif's place is adjacent to a cybernetics shop, one of the few businesses with a solid storefront rather than the temporary tarp-topped booths. The entrance is an unassuming steel gated door, the initials "UA" discretely stamped at its left edge. No one outwardly pays me attention as I test the door--unlocked. I step through it into the darkness.

Spicy incense ride the cool air. The narrow hallway winds right and then down, coming to a barred wooden door with no handle. An archaic buzzer on the wall is the only outstanding feature. I push the worn metal button.

After two breaths, a low voice crackles out of the speaker. "Do you have an appointment?"

I have a moment of panic, fearing I'll have to wait. "No," I say, "I was referred by Madam Ghiri Rosenbalm."

Another two breaths and I hear three latches disengage. The door creaks open, revealing a shrunken old human with black eyes. Incensed air pours from the room into the hall.

"Ghiri alerted me to your visit. I am Ungarif Ashtan. Come in."

I mask my surprise. *She must've seen the severity of the glitch.* Passing the threshold feels like stepping out of myself, into a world I'm not sure I'm ready for but must encounter.

"Would you like some tea?" Ungarif has already busied himself puttering at the counter near the back of the room.

I consider. No, I don't want tea. "Yes, thank you," I say.

The room is lit by a few dim flame lamps along the walls, the thick smoke causing its entirety to glow and flicker. There's not much here, just a low, damaged coffee table between two over-stuffed, threadbare chairs. Ungarif carries a small tray to the table, setting it and then himself down.

"Sit," he invites, waving me toward the other chair.

I comply, arranging myself on the edge, the balls of my feet set firmly in case I need to quickly up and go.

Ungarif heaves a deep, whistling sigh. "Are you fully committed to the Purge?"

I start, unused to blunt dialogue and overly sensitive to my plight. "I am," I whisper. I realize he's making it easier for me, taking the responsibility of initiation.

"Do you know all that it implies?"

Every citizen knows of Purging. Children hear the horror stories to encourage their complacency, adults whisper over drinks about its mystery. Runners dart from all ends of The City, proof that some do make it through.

"I understand the risks." I pause. "It's worth the attempt. I can't live like this, with this…" I look down at my hands, then up to stare woefully at him, pleading to help me understand. He nods, gesturing me toward the tea. I take it, sipping politely.

"Some call it the Curse. We don't know why it happens. There are theories--bad genetics for integration, underdeveloped neural pathways, and bad luck. Most go nutter and never look back. Some die from the strain, others die from bein' put down."

He sighs, finally opening the case that's rested in his lap since he sat. He turns it toward me, showing eight silver vials and covered hypobases.

"Some attempt the Purge."

I inhale slowly, no true thoughts, only a wash of emotions moving through me. My traitorous Tell is quiet for now, so much Ooze already in my system that I feel more drone than human.

"How much?" I ask, already removing my cred tag, prepared to transfer it all if necessary.

"One mill deposit."

I exhale, having expected it to be three times as much. He continues, voice steady.

"Should you survive, I will reimburse it all in return for a favor, to be called in at any time."

I narrow my eyes, wondering why the policy would be such. How would he contact me at any time if my Tell is gone? What could the favor possibly be?

I nod, extending my tag to him.

He takes it, and then reaches forward suddenly to grab my wrist. His grasp is firm and warm, black eyes reflective slits buried by wrinkles. Whether it's my vulnerability or his sincerity, I trust him, so do not struggle.

"If you wake, you must move. They will be searching for you."

I nod. Of course they will come. Watchers seek anyone who's recently left the Wave.

Ungarif releases my wrist, taps my cred tag with his thumb, and then returns it with a vial and hypobase. I tuck them all into my inner chest pocket, strangely unable to speak. Thankfully, he seems to know what to say when I do not.

"Few are brave or nutter enough to attempt such a journey--and you do not seem wack to me. Fight hard, and return when you make it through."

I nod and stand deftly, precious package resting over my heart. "Many thanks, Ungarif Ashtan."

"For this?" He shakes his head sadly. "Don't thank me."

IV

I make way further south, toward a sprawl of run-down apartments and abandoned factories. With the Ooze already fading, my anxiety begins to take over. A cold sweat trickles down my spine, shoulders held tense, breathing shallow. I second-glance every being I pass, wondering if any of them are Watchers, my previous comrades, or Ayrn himself coming to end me.

I have the urge to run, knowing it would only draw suspicion. Instead, I slow my pace, remembering to stroll like I don't give two fucks. It takes longer than I'd like to wind through the apartments and into the old warehouse district, some buildings let completely crumble under the seasons.

I left into a honeycomb of infrastructure that folds in on itself at every turn, a maze of ramshackle walls. It's hard to tell what may have been produced here--kitchenware, home mods, medical supplies. The hallways are littered with caches of squatters' existence; blankets, cans, and old shit buckets abound. My Tell doesn't pick up on any other presences, nor do I see or hear more than rodents scrambling about. I tell myself that I need to find the perfect place, that each dank room is not *the* one, stalling out of fear.

Fuck it.

I turn into the next room I pass, a larger open space with exposed beams above, slick concrete for flooring. There's no concealment, no alcoves. Back against the nearest wall, I take a few deep breaths. *There are no other options.* I'm already committed.

I look down at the vial in my hand, holding it gently. With shaking fingers I twist it securely into the hypobase, uncap it, and carefully insert the tip into my most accessible arm vein, known well from epinephrine training. I depress the button as I slowly pull out; making sure every drop of liquid goes in.

The familiar electric rush spreads from deep in my stomach, tickling out toward my limbs in long, luxurious waves. I take a shaking inhale, loving how the lights above me jump and dance with the strumming of my soul as I settle into balance. I have a moment of perfect clarity, the layers and shadows of the dilapidated walls surrounding me all cut in sharp relief, breath slow-motion, my own steady heartbeat felt as a strong war drum in divine cadence. I inhale slowly and let out a long sigh.

Peace.

An acute and painful trembling starts within my toes, vibrating up my legs and into my groin, then up through my belly and chest, to my head. I have the sense to sit, legs folded carefully beneath me. *This is gonna be a bad trip.* My stomach lurches, the tea I drank rushing up, out. I vomit explosively before me, palms grounded. My eyes burst with light, blinded from the inside, the violent heaving sending fierce lances of pain through my limbs. I retch until there's nothing left to expel, diaphragm spasms so hard I cannot draw full breath.

I panic as I imagine this being my last moment. This

torment, my last experience of life.

My body thrashes as it takes my nervous system, hurled forward onto my chest and face. I can barely feel the cold hardness of the ground, my concept of things like temperature or texture--of anything--fading behind the focus of remembering my life:

I was a soldier. By choice, because of too few options...

I was curious and naturally brave, so often afraid to be it.

I fought well. Very well.

I had so much left to learn about humility and grace.

The light around me fades to grey and then black as I think my final thought--

Better death that live fucking glitched.

*   *   *

Silence.

I groan, shifting from my back onto my right side.

I'm alive.

My veins pulse painfully, muscles jumping. My entire body feels full, heavy, chest and head burning like I've got acid for blood.

I am alive!

"'Runnas.' Cleva name, doncha tink?"

The voice startles me, epinephrine flushing away some of my haze. I spin upward onto my feet, the world wavering in a swirling, colorless swash as I fall back to the ground, too disoriented to pinpoint the speaker. Though glad I had the unconscious reflex to draw claws, I curse myself for nearly opening my own hide, barely having rolled to the side before falling onto them. I close my eyes and take a deep, shuddering breath, holding my hands in ready guard, relying on my hearing until I can function normally. *If I ever will...*

"Oho! What rush Warria? Feelin' vulned? Ya tinkin'

dis may not be da tightest box ta Purge sick, hey?" With the strange sing-song tone, I cannot tell whether the speaker is male or female, human or Helium Breather. I do hear them take a soft, two-footed drop, indicating they'd been watching from the exposed I-beams above me. Eyes still closed, I sheath my right claws, palming my primary pistol.

"Whoa Warria, I ain gonna hurtcha. Naw. I's gonna scavenge ya, butcha survive, hey? Ya joinin' da ranks o' Runnas, yah, if dem Watchas don getcha first? Dun look strong nuff ta make Lush, naw..."

Watchers. Another wave of panic forces my eyes open. *Get your shit together.* I inhale, trying to ground myself. I'm dizzy and sick, but my headache is already fading, no buzzing or whispering to replace it. I automatically move to view my map, check the date and time, but there's nothing. No messages. No stats. No controls.

I'm alone.

I carefully turn my head right, spotting the rag-clad individual immediately. They're crouched three yards away, head tilted sideways in interest. *Human? Probably. Unlikely gendered.* I stare at the individual and have no sense of how to contact them, no systems beyond my own human thought to asses them. Straggled and hunched, I get an impression of their general enjoyment of life. Like another sense, I can tell that they seem like a crafty person, someone who'd accepted themselves long ago. It seems like they knows their place, their power, and own it. *Who else would be heckling a stranger freshly free?*

I laugh a soft, quick exhale of air.

Unceremoniously in this decrepit and shadowed place, I've freed myself, fought my toughest battle unsure of my continued existence and sure as hell worried about its importance. I can't Tell where the hell I am and barely remember, but I am astoundingly and refreshingly alone. I cannot return to my previous "home." But oh! How I laugh. The sound of it fills the room, cascading out of me. My voice is hoarse from apparent screaming, body exhausted from its fight. But I'm alive and completely free. Even were the watchers to capture me, I'll have known it.

I pivot around carefully, finally remembering to clear the rest of the room but already sure no-one else is here. I can *feel* it. No more twice-damned Tell, but I can *feel* like I didn't know possible. Like my perception is a nimbus expanding around me, mapping out my vicinity. It may just be the Purge haze but I don't care. I turn to my ragged guardian, grinning fiercely.

"Thanks for looking over me." I take a deep inhale, pleased to see seriousness has taken them, and they finally think to see me. I rotate my neck; roll my shoulders and hips, getting a general sense of my body. It sucks, but it'll move for me.

"Hey Raggedy, be sure to tell the Watchers which way I went." I laugh again, a joy like I've never known filling me.

And I run.

First out the door, over the debris scattered throughout the first hall, the next, them all, finally cutting out into the narrow alleyway.

I chose this maze of old industry because I thought it'd be less likely that someone would stumble upon me. *I'll bet ol' Raggedy don't just stumble onto anything...*Now I sprint all-out, forced to meet corner after corner, hands up in front of me to absorb the moment's shock and re-direct myself. Right, right, left. My boots slip on the slick pavement, hands touching down onto the ground only enough to push me back up, forward. I need to make as much distance between me and the point I went off wave. I don't know how long I'd been out--perhaps Raggedy was a watcher pretending. *No matter, they're seeking already.* I run to secure my freedom.

Purge high or not, Watchers fucking scare me. Their ability to completely control us. The fact that they are not who but what, mysterious in their very existence. Cognizant extensions of The City--*the* most powerful thing in life. They have no identity, no will individually, and are the embodiments of The City's will itself, omnipotent. *To a point.* They'll have already been dispatched to find me, subdue me and…

I speed up, arms pumping rhythmically as I lean around the last corner and into the main avenue. I stop briefly, eyes scanning for all life around me. No pests, no people. I look up, the moon a bright sliver within the otherwise dull grey sky. I grin, barely resisting my urge to howl with glee.

Safety then celebration. I don't know where to go, soon but not yet onto Ghiri's. *They'll look for me at home.* The Night Market is the most logical, being relatively close and full of activity I can disappear into. The pain in my body is subsiding, but my senses haven't yet diminished. I can feel the edges of others nearby as I pass, sometimes just beyond me. It's freaky but not disturbing, my trust in it allowing it to feel helpful, natural. Like there's always been this much of me.

It's what tells me that the Watcher is up ahead, sensed as a voided space amid the otherwise intricate environment. I review my engagement possibilities--do I try to take it out? Do I continue to maneuver around it? You can shoot Watchers, they say. They won't stay down unless it's all brains, but it'll slow them. Enough damage incapacitates their vessel and they'll have to compose anew. *I wonder it feels me like void, too, if it's already noticed my presence.*

Combat right now sounds far too tedious, undesirable, and my guilt over Ayrn washes through me suddenly. *I lost control.* I reverse, the new plan to make a wide berth around the Watcher, hitting the market at its North end rather than somewhere in its center. In seconds it will know my new plan, moving to pass through the market to catch me at the end. *We will see.*

I look around but mostly forward, assessing all walls and windows in the block before me. *Too sketchy. Actively occupied. Too technical.* I finally see the sequence that was all but made for my ascension, the opposing wall close enough and first deep-set window placed perfectly.

I direct myself at the right wall, loading lower as I approach. I sink into my left hip before launching diagonally and upward to the right, at the wall. My right foot intercepts it, leg bent and immediately pushing off, up. I twist my head to the left, spotting my ledge. My torso, arms, and legs follow my gaze, left leg already extended to ease the catch just before my hands grab. I land quietly, controlled, feet slipping down just enough to absorb impact. With a strong pull and the driving of one knee upward, I gain height, pull transitioned smoothly into a push, palms flat with the edge of the window at my hips. Pushing off the wall with my toes, I pop my hips back and up, making time to tuck my legs beneath and in front of me. Crouched in the window, I turn and look across to the other side. There's a less deep but equally catchable window a torso length up and slightly to the left.

I rock to the balls of my feet then jump, extending my legs in front of me to intercept the wall before catching with my hands. Pulling up, I reach for the next viable hold, a bar cage bolted securely over the next highest window. Once caught, I use it to climb to the next, then to the rooftop.

I take a moment to stretch, arms reaching up and out. The next inhale is the sweetest I've had for years, regardless of the smoky stench of the Night Market on the breeze. Though exhausted and hurting, I feel joyful and calm. *I feel real.* I have the reflex to check the map that's no longer there, laughing at myself for doing so. *Memory from here on out.* I run the rooftop toward where I know the market to be, bridging the gap to the next building with a casual push, both legs tucked in front of me to intercept the next surface, falling easily into a roll. Pushing up to my feet, I run ahead to the next edge, slide into a crouch to study the Night Market below.

It's busier now, more alive. My new sense is overwhelmed by personalities and emotions, felt as a great wall of mortality before me. *No way can a Watcher make me in that crowd.* Getting low on the edge, I belly-down and rotate to grab and slide along the nearest drainpipe, boots *shushing* against the wall. At the bottom I stand swiftly, eyesight soft for anyone giving me extra attention. I dare not return to Ungarif yet; sure my last mapped hours are still being re-traced and guarded.

It occurs to me to change my appearance, if only superficially. *I should secure an intelicloak.* I've dropped by the armories, clothiers nearby. Meandering past the storefronts and stalls, I avoid extended eye-contact with any one person to seem confident and aloof. The murmuring of haggling customers rises from every corner, a more serious confrontation between some males heard in the distance to my east. This time through I'm awake enough to notice the age of the slick, cobbled stones beneath my feet, the dealers looming in the darkest shadows, whores positioned under every streetlight calling out and sashaying for passers-by.

It's simpler buying here. No one asks for personal information, any city checks or cred scans. All I need to do is walk into the shop, point to the intelicloak I want--the newest from Visilé--and hand over my tag. A swipe and a nod and I'm back on the street, armor and gun hidden beneath the loose fabric.

Checking my own reflection in a mirrored window stops me, causes me to back up.

Oh shit.

My tattoos have wandered, having no Tell to program them. Usually a single band across my eyes, the dark pigment has migrated to the right side of my face, around forehead and dripping down my cheekbone. I throw my cloak back to expose my arms. Sure enough, the once static bands of black are broken into fractals, the left presenting jagged vines winding round my wrist and forearm, the right busted splotches around my upper arm. If I look closely and still myself, I can see them shifting minutely, like slow boil. *Nothing to do with it now.*

Knowing I should stay in the masses for another few hours at least, I decide to wander about the market, map it out and test how crazy I really am. *Am I* actually *feeling more?* It's too early to tell. I may be imagining the wash of feelings that appear only when others pass--frustration, anticipation, and lust. Perhaps I'm fabricating the shadows of personality that brush by--sneaky, resourceful, and sullen. Maybe I just substituted one insanity for another. *Maybe just be happy you're alive.*

I've almost allowed myself to relax when I sense the void again, somewhere before me in the dense populace. It's different than the one earlier, warmer somehow. Less empty. Probably stupid, I follow my gut, pulling my hood up and weaving in-between bodies toward the feeling. It's surprisingly easy to tell which is the Watcher, exudes what I can only describe as an anti-soul, no light or vibration within it.

It's presenting as a young female Apunu, walking casually from booth to booth, one set of arms clasped behind the back, the other crossed in front confidently. It seems unaware of my presence, appears almost genuinely interested in the goods before it. Within moments of noticing it, I can feel someone else putting their focus on the Watcher as intently as I am. A quick scan of the crowd shows an older human with sharp eyes flicking toward it every few seconds. He doesn't stand out, just another fighter-type with well-worn armor, broadsword strapped across his back.

We're both four meters from where the Watcher is pretending to browse a table of exotic spices and herbs. There's something strangely real about it, eyes intent on the goods before it, small mannerisms like head tilting and frowning seeming natural. Without thought, I've been walking ever closer to it, drawn by a sense of familiarity. *Why does it fascinate me?* As I near, the void gives way to something else, equally strange and far more compelling.

I can feel it…feeling. It finally notices me, looking

over. Eyes wide, I meet the gaze of this thing, a Watcher, and feel complex emotions emanating from it. Confusion. Anger. Curiosity.

Sorrow.

In this moment I know that *this* Watcher won't try to capture me, subdue me, or kill me. It wants something; it needs me to understand--

Its head explodes sideways in a rush of matter, body collapsing heavily to the ground. The man I'd marked earlier steps out from the near crowd grinning down at his kill. I crouch next to the body, confused by the lingering sorrow I'd taken from it and angry--fucking livid--at what this man just did. "Find me again," I whisper to the body, its color already fading to match the black of the asphalt beneath.

"Hey fresh meat, 'round here that's officially a favor you owe me."

Only years of training keeps my claws sheathed, fists clenched tightly instead. I keep watching the body as I say, low and quiet. "Just because you think you tough don't make me fresh meat."

"Oh yeah? What'll I call you if not fresh meat?"

"Don't call me." I stand, the sudden loss receding in the waves of my anger. I'd like to walk away, but know better than to turn my back on a violent unknown.

"Oh, big talk comin' from Watcher bait. What's your name?" He asks like I'm obligated to tell him.

"I don't owe you my name or nothin' else."

He sneers, likely unused to getting talk back from "fresh meat." I don't give a single fuck, staring at him with a steady, heartless gaze.

"You gotta slick mouth *fresh meat*. I know I ain neva seen you before, and that mean you ain got no cred here." He makes a point to look me up and down. "You ain't got no gear, no swag, no crew. You betta check what you say to dangerous strangers."

I drop the lazy talk, finished with his game.

"Strangers that boast of their own dangerousness--how intimidating."

He makes to laugh at me, and then considers otherwise, eyes peering intelligently into mine. "Whoever you think you are, you ain nothin' here." He points to the decomposing Watcher. "Too dumb to even take a Watcher, you ain gonna last long. So dumb you talk to me like you do--oh I'll tell 'em all 'bout you. Fresh meat new girl with no riverdamned name. You ain nothin'."

"Say what you want to who you want." I walk past him, claws primed in case he tries something. I don't bother to turn back, or pause for bravado. I do speak loud enough so he and everyone near us can hear.

"Tell them my name is Glitch."

Mission: Surreality

By
K. Ceres Wright

Rain pattered the empty street, almost washing away the plumes of fetid odor from the piles of trash that heralded the unresolved garbage collector's strike. Despite the rain, the smell rose up like thin tentacles to the upper floors of the Four Seasons building, which had to open its windows to the night because the air conditioning was off—a result of the City's electricity rationing. I stood in front of my open freezer, wondering which was worse—the heat or the smell. Voices wafted in from the lower floors.

"Oh, my god! I can't believe this shit building shut down again."

"It smells like ass up here! When are they gonna start pickin' up this trash?"

As an organic building, the Four Seasons itself decided when to turn off people's air and water—when it had the electricity to do so. Sometimes residents loudly cursed the building's decisions, their yelling echoing in the hallway, but they could do nothing to reverse the decision. Some said the building was going insane, turning on the heat in 90-degree weather, or turning off the hot water when it was 20 degrees, but I knew better. She—I called it a she—was punishing wayward parents and cheating spouses with her own brand of justice. People were just too stupid, or stubborn, to figure it out.

My peripheral lit up purple, signaling an incoming call. I tapped my temple, opening the line. A high-pitched keening sounded and I straightened, staring at frozen hamburger next to a half-eaten popsicle.

*   *   *

A snap and Vivian's rat-like face hovered above me. I jerked in surprise and then froze at the sight of the syringe.

"I'll never get used to this," I said.

Vivian laughed, her face creasing into a razor-sharp grin. "A pinch, and then…"

I slipped into a twilight state, aware of my surroundings, but not quite sure if it was a dream or sleep-like reality. I sat in an overstuffed chair in a narrow living room while a single lamp threw out dim light on the proceedings. Vivian sat on her haunches in a matching chair directly in front of me and a man with grey dreads and skeptical eyes watched from the corner. He smoked a cigarette as if he'd been born to it, twirling it around long slender fingers between exhales of languid smoke.

"The hell kinda name is Concordat?" he said.

"Formally, a concordat is an agreement between the Holy See and some sovereign government relating to matters of mutual interest. But she…" Vivian pointed to me with a taloned paw. "…thought the Holy See abandoned its True Purpose, and took it upon herself to carry it out."

"Seriously? You sound like a narrator from some fantasy movie. So what's she supposed to be? Our white knight? So to speak, I mean…her being black and all. With machine parts in her head."

Vivian paused. "Being black and all? Shut the fuck up and learn something."

The man fell silent.

"Who?" I said.

Vivian flicked her head in the man's direction. "Valmar. He's one of the Lords, a runner, and says a tinkerer has a way of defeating the Tell. But she needs money for equipment. We need you to procure funds for this venture, about three thousand credits. It's not like we can issue an IPO."

Business. IPO had something to do with business, which is what Vivian frequently spoke of. I wracked my brain to figure out who she was...again. Seems I forgot at each meeting. Hell, it was getting to the point where I was forgetting who *I* was. But Vivian used to be human, a successful hedge fund manager. That was it. And she was pushed into the River by a jealous wife. The River's toxins ate her flesh until there was little left except bone, patches of skin and muscle, and a hard-bitten determination to survive. The doctors had to rebuild her immune system from scratch, adding genes from another species: rat. Apparently, rats have a gene diversity that makes them resistant to many poisons and diseases. Or at least, that's how Vivian explained it to me. She showed me some "before" pictures—long black hair, smooth cocoa skin, hourglass figure. Afterward, she looked like a large brown rat woman with a ponytail. But the thing was, due to her dire physical state, and with the doctors replacing many of her genes, the Tell had been eliminated from her body. The doctors were supposed to have reinserted it, but after Vivian performed trial hypnosis, they forgot her procedure and lost her records.

The Tell consisted of subdermal organs, implanted at birth, which grew alongside other organs. The Tell connected people to the Wave, which monitored everyone, listening to what they said, seeing what they saw. At least at the conscious level. At the subconscious level, things became...murky. Oh, sure, the Watchers who maintained the Wave perceived plots to overthrow the City, but they didn't know if the plots were real or dreams. And after an injection or two, a hypnotic state or two, I wasn't quite sure myself.

"Let's hypnotize you to program this information at the subconscious level. You'll have an overwhelming drive to complete your mission, but you won't know why," Vivian said.

I nodded in reply, and then woke up to a view of frozen hamburger next to a half-eaten popsicle.

*   *   *

The 'hood didn't have banks; they had loan sharks, pimps, hustlers, and drug dealers. If you needed extra money, you chose one of them. Loan sharks and drug dealers were the worst, but had the most money to lend. Pimps and hustlers wouldn't harass you too much if you were only a week or so late. But after three weeks, all bets were off.

Three thousand credits wasn't a huge sum, so I went with a local hustler, Same-Same, who was always looking to make money from the odd con, theft, or back-room deal. Oh, there were the real hustlers, but they hung out with the rich, hoping to peel a few hundred thousand from their marks. But Same-Same couldn't hope to make it to the big time. He lacked the sophistication.

I walked through the magfield into his store-front office that doubled as a used-office-equipment shop. He was sitting at a three-legged table fixing an adding machine. I used to wonder who in the hell would buy a used adding machine, but with the Watchers monitoring everything connected to the Wave, pre-Tell machines had become popular. The Watcher could still track you through your subdermals, but using a typewriter or even an abacus was one less way of letting them into your life.

"Zhappenin'?" I said. The odor of dust motes, a fried circuit board, and pastrami rose up to greet me. Somehow, I found the smell comforting.

Same-Same looked up from his work and smiled. "Concordat! Same ol', same ol'. What brings you to the lower west side?"

I pulled up a wire chair, turned it around, and sat, folding my arms over the back. Same-Same reminded me of my father, who used to fix things around our house at his workbench in the basement. My older sister and I would watch him in between cartoons on the holovid. My mother would bring him a dinner plate and place it next to him on his workbench. Sometimes a thin layer of wood dust would settle on the food, but he would eat it anyway. My sister and I wondered if he crapped out dowels.

"Credits," I said in reply. "Not much, just three Js."

Same-Same paused, then put down the screwdriver and snapped the cover back onto the adding machine. He plugged it in and tested it, and it hummed as it spat out a tongue of white paper.

"You usually have something to sell *me*. Things you pick up on your travels. Now you need a loan? What's with that?"

I opened my mouth to speak, but couldn't find the words to say. Nothing pushed past my lips. After several minutes of gaping, frustration set in.

"None of your business why I need it," I said. "I just do. That a problem?"

Same-Same tilted his head as he regarded me with a new-found wariness. His eyes narrowed. "No," he said quietly.

"Good. I don't need an ex street preacher telling me what to do." A pang of guilt cut through me as the words left my mouth, but Same-Same said nothing. He simply got up from the table, crossed over to his back office behind an old black-and-white magfield, and returned with three thousand credits. He placed it on the table in front of me. I met his gaze.

"Have it back in two weeks, fifteen percent interest," he said.

I couldn't believe my luck. He usually charged twenty-five percent. I grabbed it up and shoved it into my cleavage where I had a resealable flap.

"Thanks," I muttered, then headed for the exit.

"And tell Vivian I said hello," he called after me.

I froze. "Vivian?" The name sounded familiar, but I didn't know whom he meant, and I turned, puzzled.

Same-Same just smiled and waved, then disappeared behind the magfield.

*   *   *

The frozen hamburger and another syringe. It was all starting to become a blur. I sat in the same overstuffed chair, but instead of the man with dreads standing behind Vivian, it was a woman with a closely cropped afro, dyed bright pink and large inquisitive eyes. Vivian spoke before I had a chance to ask.

"Shai Gea. She's the tinkerer we spoke about earlier. Works for The City helping to manufacture Ooze. Do you have the money?"

I reached into my cleavage and pulled out the credits. I handed them to Vivian, who nodded in appreciation.

"Ya done good, kid. Now, Shai here's going to explain what we're doing."

Shai replaced Vivian in the matching chair and smiled as she tapped her fingernails on her knees. Her voice shook a bit as she spoke.

"Hurry up, kid. I don't know if you were followed," Vivian said. She poured herself a whiskey from the bar against the wall, and then raised a glass in salute.

"I've been experimenting with variations of Ooze, trying to define the properties that allow it to purge the Tell when taken intravenously. Taken in capsule or liquid form, it's merely a narcotic. I finally discovered that the hydrolyzed molecules bind to the walls of blood vessels and the body's connective tissues. They convert the Tell's synthetic proteins into a waste product that the body ejects through urine and feces. Stomach acid destroys that ability to convert. Once I knew the process, I replicated it first in the lab, then in my body. That's right. I'm Tell free. And once I get the proper equipment, I can replicate more, enough for everyone--"

Shai must have seen my face, because she whipped around, and then screamed. Two figures emerged from the wall behind her—3D pieces of forevercrete that began to take on bodily shape. *Watchers!*

"Get out!" I said.

Shai and Vivian scrambled and left through the front door. I stayed, waiting the full two minutes before the shapes assumed discernible faces. Two men, one short, one tall. I recognized them.

"Watcher Dan and Watcher Trell. I don't want to say, 'We meet again,' but we do," I said.

"Concordat. We thought we'd lost you," Watcher Trell said.

"You did. I'm self-aware now. I make my own decisions, my own choices," I said.

"Do you really think that hunk of metal sticking out of your head gives you consciousness?" Watcher Dan said. "Makes you one of them?"

"It's worked this long," I said. "But I know you didn't come here to chat so…why don't we dance instead?"

I balanced on my back foot as I snatched up the lamp to my left. I stepped forward, swinging it upward. It caught Watcher Dan's chin, snapping his head backward. The shade bent and the bulb broke, but I used the base to block Watcher Dan's arm chop. I caught Watcher Trell's kick to my back, which propelled me forward. I crashed into Dan, pinning him against the wall. Trell's right jab missed my head and punched a hole in the forevercrete as I ducked left. I grabbed Dan by the collar and swung him around, into Trell. They both fell over the back of the chair. I ran toward the kitchen, visions of the butcher's block running through my head. As Dan rounded the corner, I hurled a carving knife at his chest. He grunted and stopped, watching the red blossom on his shirt as he fell to the floor. As the blood leached from his body, the linoleum swallowed him up like expensive paper towels, until he was gone.

Trell pulled a gun and fired blindly toward the stove. The bullet went wide, but I dove for the pantry. It was narrow, stacked on both sides with shelves stocked with provisions, so I pocketed a few cans and shimmied up the walls, spread eagle, arms outstretched. *Death from above!*

Trell hurried to the wall beside the pantry door and performed a quick sight check. The darkness played to my advantage. He ducked and brought his gun around, then squeezed off several shots, low and fast, figuring I was hiding behind the bag of dog food, which spilled onto the floor. I beaned him in the head with a can of French peas. Imported. He fell back, the gun dangling from his hand. I jumped down and relieved him of his weapon, then fired three shots into his skull. His head lolled, eyes open, mouth agape, until he, too, melted into the floor.

I unloaded the rest of the canned goods from my pockets, slid the gun into the back of my jeans, and went in search of Vivian and Shai, wondering where they could be. But they found me.

*   *   *

They drugged me in the van on the way to the safe house, and my world spiraled into lemon drop flowers and ethereal faraway voices as we lumbered along a dirt road. Someone's face faded in and out of my field of vision, almost rat-like, giving me instructions, but her voice came and went, like a radio station approaching its airwave limits.

"...weeks away...total purge...if...go...normal life until we...summon. I'll...Lola is a...octopus...sewer... Shai's work...almost complete."

*   *   *

I stared at the frozen hamburger and half-eaten popsicle, wondering why my back hurt.

KEEP RUNNING

Free your mind
(Journal of Iset: The Protector)

By
Kai Leakes

Entry 1.0

Where can I go? Where can I hide? All I do is run. Running has become so common that it scares me when there is a moment, no, a fleeting second of peace.

See in this world, in this place, are only good as our body parts. If you're like me, with gifts to bring change, you're as good as dead. That's why I was a protector and also why the Watchers are after me so hard.

Well that's not true. The Watchers want the disk I carry with the coordinates to the refugee camp hidden under the catacombs of my place of operation, my motel. This is where my people hide if that is what they want.

Anyway, the enemy can't have it. I won't allow it!

The City will breathe with life again separated from the constant brainwashing and mind jacking occurring through the Tell. My people, as the Street Priest teach and as us Runners shout:

Free, your mind!

Don't be a slave to the technology that is meant to help us, not enslave us!

This is why I run, why I protect and why I fight.

Screaming with the angst of my people through these shifting labyrinth based streets, the Watchers and the City can't have me.

Soon they will understand and feel the reason why they will never be able to touch me.

I am Iset. The Protector.

"*End journal entry Orion*," rushed from Iset's lips in weary fervor, while looking around in a fluster.

Someone followed her. She was in a rush from dropping off another highly sensitive package while holding on to another missive, an object of high importance to not only her but to others who lived in and under the Heap. Iset flicked her wrist and charged up her body, pushing forward and faster, heading to her stomping grounds/slums, the Southside Heap. The district sequestered a mishmash of people, usually the rejects, castoffs of society or poor who the rich deemed invisible. It was her home and its people her family.

Iset skated across the smooth metal ramps under her Kicks, the stylish black and white metal belted foot guards encasing her calves and feet around her wedge sneakers. Transportation in the City came in many forms, and Kicks were one of a thousand means to move swiftly through the populace. With mental reflex, her jets sparked and pushed her in a gust of air, allowing her to somersault then land and skate across the roof of a towering building then back onto the busy mental ramps.

Encrypted symbols in the form of integrated lettering swirled across a curved visor nestled within her *Tech-Gogs* then disappeared. Though the words scrolled across the screen she could still see her surroundings. The great area bellowed out, 'The City, a home to vast unique and not so unique beings.

The scent of sulfuric gas saturated the atmosphere within the haven. It wasn't uncommon for such fumes to make their way into the ozone and overtake the breathable air of the people who lived in the lowest level of the multilayered, multifaceted refuge, in inner gothic barrio many describe as the Heap. To describe the makeup of the City would take many, many hours, so those who lived and survived in its hold described it as a nucleus with many walls and buildings curving and rising near the River.

The River. Heart of 'The City,' its watery depths

was known to offer sustenance, spirituality, and death to the diverse enigmatic populace living around it. The murky dissonance of life, death, and rebirth caused Iset's nose to wrinkle in thought and annoyance while she jetted by. She had lost many friends to death, only to find them dumped into the River by a sect of people, Watchers, known to terrorize and stalk Runners like herself. Runners were messengers of sorts, people chosen to send missives, products, or other sensitive information. What she had hidden in an intricately designed tube locket -an infinity box- around her neck like jewelry, held a small beacon of hope to the Slum and its people.

Lost in thought about the grave responsibility hidden against her chest, an instant panic sliced through her like a paper cut against the side of a person's palm. Not that people in The City used paper much anymore. This pain caused a stinging hurt that traveled through her whole body, a signal to pay attention to her health levels. Iset fisted her black gloves and sent a charge through her T.G. to check her stats and load up her journal.

"Orion, open journal...new entry. Record," she spat out in a huff before she spoke to the melodic molasses smooth deep voice of her TG's operating A.I., which she named Orion.

"I'm running too hard again. Feeling all eyes on me but also not on me while I use The City as my invisibility cloak."

Her stomach cramped, a sign that she needed to slow down. Her wretched tech suit was putting too much strain on her body. Nevertheless, she couldn't stop. She had to keep going, not only for herself but for her people.

"I was almost caught in the Marketplace today by a Watcher. Had it not been for the future Bone Collector and her trusty friend, I would not have made it too far, which would have turned into a problem. Why? Because then I'd have to kill. I don't want to kill. Runners don't always have to kill. But if I'm to protect myself and this precious cargo then I'd do it

in the name of The City," she explained to her digital journal.

Iset listened to Orion record her message. This was a ritual of hers, something she did to make notes so that if she ever disappeared, one of the new Runners she trusted and trained would have her most precious thoughts.

"*Orion, pause journal entry for now*," she stated, watching her journal flicker to off on her goggles.

"*As you wish, Iset*," Orion responded in kind.

Whipping through the wind, flying by her jets this time, Iset saw the seedy lights of the Heap beckoning her to move hastily through the business district and make it to the Southside. Heat spread through her body, perspiration beading at her temples and catching in the twisted ropes of her slim Marley braids. The sound of thumping hip-hop with a rapper spitting out energetic lyrics in a rushed manic manner had her mentally dancing while seeking out a place to rest. She was running on fumes, a bad habit of hers. However, habit and her long history as a Runner taught Iset that she needed to listen to her body. Her favorite café was too far so she opted to hide in a street-level rail station depot.

Hand pressed against a wall scrolling advertisements and other media worthy intelligence about 'The City, Iset paused for a moment then dug into her pocket. Taking out two silver tablets of Murk, energy tab the opposite of Ooze, she tossed them in her mouth then closed her eyes to let the surge hit her. Heavy footsteps splashing on the scummy wet street way drew her immediate attention.

Tapping on her info cuff again – a stylish metal stud bracelet – several digital maps appeared. It was a festival and the streets swarmed with boisterous city people dancing. Steel drums played in time to ebbing dub music. Street and festival lights gave a seductive and seedy allure in the midst of the falling confetti, flower petals, and colored smoke. People swayed to the infectious beat, covered or partially covered in various costumes. Some wore biotech; others wore electric glowing body paint – possibly dried Ooze – over their naked bodies that contrasted against the midnight surroundings. She waved a hand in the air and looked over her shoulder. Those thumping footsteps were getting closer and had her heart rate rising in fervor.

Using the tips of her fingers to scroll through the floating maps, Iset paused when the sound stopped. Several revelers danced by then stomping continued. Glancing down the dark wet city streets, she glimpsed a massive cloaked form several blocks away.

Sequestering in the terminal, she turned in a panic pacing thought, *"Damn! I have to move out!"*

"My best bet would be to stick to the sewers catacombs," she muttered. "Not sure if I can get their fast enough."

Negative fifty HP flashed red across her digital shades and tightness in her chest caused her to have a headache. If she did not get far enough away people would die shortly. The clueless carefree people, partying in the streets of the business district would soon meet nothing but darkness if she stuck around. Iset had to go. Had to run. Had to protect what she held around her neck but she was just so damned tired.

"Crap!" she said, slamming her fist again the depot wall.

"Warning! Warning! Blood level rising. Please stay calm Iset," her A.I. pleaded.

The force of her punch caused a threading against the screen that webbed under her fist as the digital images glitched then corrected. She hated this. Iset had been running for thirty-two, almost thirty-three years hiding from the Watchers. Moving those people who sought her help to her motel where they could hide as best as they could from the Watchers, as a means to hide the fact that they all went through the 'Purge from the 'Tell. She had done so much through the years and neglected her own life that she currently felt how she did when she was just sixteen years old. Already tired of being a Runner. Iset just wished that she and her people could live in peace without the 'Tell. So that she didn't have to be a Runner and so that she could be free and live like an ordinary person. Nevertheless, she wasn't normal was she? The ever-growing power within her, and years of survival could attest to that.

"It's all good Orion. Just calculate the Murk I took. I have to keep running," Iset explained.

Orion acted instantly. A spurt of cool then surging energy pumped through Iset's veins. Eyes rolling and her body slightly trembling, she gave a pleasured sigh then exhaled. The result of the Murk would only be minimal, but it should be enough to get her to a safe zone, she hoped.

In this life she chose, there was no time for pity parties. This was for her people. She'd be damned if she failed. Another jarring thump of those haunting feet had Iset shaking off her emotions. She had to get what was around her neck to her safe haven Refuge, an old rundown motel. Not only was the Refuge a place for refugees of the 'Tell Purge', it was also a place for her River Rat friends. The future Bone Collector, a young girl who was one of the many Slum kids always were in awe of Iset, needed this. Iset saved the teen when the girl was just eight years old running from the Watchers who had killed her mother. The girl's life consisted of snatching and scrapping for herself, and her pet octopod monster. Tiny's seventeenth birthday was coming, and soon the girl would need the coordinates to lead more refugees to safety as a top level Runner right along with Iset.

Therefore, she had to keep moving.

"*Alert! You are being tracked, please find safety.*" Orion automatically responded to Iset's stress levels rising.

"No shit Orion!" Iset uttered.

Slapping her palm against her TG, Iset glanced behind her and gave a mischievous grin towards her stalker.

"Catch me if you can ass wat."

With that Iset jetted off, attaching to the side of the nearby building. A speeding rail curved nearby; Iset figured that it might be the fastest route to the Heap. Painfully winded and feeling woozy, she contorted her body suit to trigger the suctions on her gear-gloves which allowed her to climb against flat surfaces.

The mysterious anomaly continued to hunt her. Sweat blurred Iset's vision. Her partial tech-suit alerted her of her low blood pressure due to fatigue. The sudden chattering of her teeth had her dizzy; her hand slipped from the side of the wall and she went sailing into the wind. Her mind blurted as she fell backwards into the bowls of the glorious illuminated city. *Stupid wet spot. Stupid exhaustion.*

"Warning! Health Priority is level thirty and dropping. Danger level breaching." echoed in Iset's ears.

Memories of Iset's past flashed in her mind. The faint heartbeat of an infant within her womb. A young privileged teen she knew as an ingenious hacker and carefree man. *So many regrets. So many choices that I had to make to protect those close to me.* The vision shifted to a grimy clothed young girl named Tiny with big innocent, scared eyes snow-white locs, beautiful dark toffee skin, and a growling monster reaching out from the sewers. Within that same image flickered the girl's mother, Iset's own best friend, Mira-Lola.

Iset watched her friend die in the Heap marketplace at the hands of Watchers. Her body later discarded into the River, only to come back to life as the octopod monster that protected the little girl and ate their enemies. The little girl named Tiny, who was Iset's goddaughter, would grow into the future Bone Collector -a title given due to her mother snatching bodies- and train up to become a protector as she was.

As for her best friend's death, Iset saw it all. The forced scanning for the 'Tell,' only to fail it. Beaten, assaulted, and then kidnapped by the Watcher's henchmen before Iset could get to her. Tears spilled down Iset's cheeks. She was the one who took Tiny off the streets, shielding her from the harsh truth of her mother's death. She also was the one who eventually told Tiny that the monster that protected the little girl whenever she ran the streets in search of safe lodging or stealing food had the name Lola.

In her fall, Iset recalled the past. She saw all the battles she had ever fought. Saw the future ones she still had to battle and she gave a weary cry in her fall. This was her doom. This was her fault. So many were going to die.

A shrill scream shot through Iset, triggering the voice box or 'vox' implanted in her throat. Used as a means of communicating in various languages, and as well as a weapon of protection, it shattered the glass in the nearby buildings. Arms flailing, Iset grunted with wide eyes. Her right arm came over her in an attempt to shield her face from the glass shards and other debris following her in the fall. Her ears filled with the sounds of passing jet cars, bikes, skating transporters, and regular city-goers walking below her.

"Ey, little bee. I gotcha kid."

Iset looked up then gasped. A large beefy hand gripped her braids, the spicy smoky scent of a cigar hitting her senses. Her running had failed. Everything changed around her. She hung in the wind like a guppy, her legs dangling with no hope of escape. She had been caught, foolishly trapped by a huge masked goon with a menacing hat, blacked out goggles and a long trench coat with huge feet. This was not her life.

"Don't fight kid. I hate fighters," the voice demanded.

"Danger level breached!" Flashing red appeared on her visor.

Oh, crap! Iset thought.

Fighting Battling against her swallowing black out, Iset pushed away from her stalker. *Like hell won't fight!* Reaching behind her, she gripped a speeding rail near the building she had previously scaled. It twisted and curved in its grand beauty. Various transport vehicles, bikers and skaters traveled on it, though it was not congested.

With a hard grunt she pulled away, using the railing as a flipping board. She sailed in the air and then landed in a crouch. Isis pushed up, ready to run. Swiping her hand in the air, her GPS pointed her to a transport portal. She pulled out her only gun tucked into the side of her boot then fell into defense mode.

Iset pointed her Zentec 9110 11mm combat magnum. The flashing laser sight zoned in on him then allowed her to squeeze the trigger. Iset usually had a decent aim. However, her body was shutting down and the bullet only met brick near the side of her stalker's head. Annoyed and acting quickly, Iset tapped in the hidden codes she often used in emergency for portal travel on her bracelet. Light swelled from the portal opening behind her.

"Danger! Danger! Find a medic! Move your ass, as you say Iset," Orion said.

Weary triumph and relief hit her with an amused chuckle at Orion's words. Iset programmed him to learn her lingo and after all these years it still made her smile when her A.I. showed off. Exhausted to her bones, she glanced back to the hulking figure who stared at her in the distance, shrouded in all black. His cloak whipped around him, his scanning goggles lit up in an attempt to lock on her.

There was no way that she would allow him to get her. She'd fight to the death before that happened. Determination was her resolve and had her holding a hand to her chest as she felt herself faint backwards into the portal. Middle finger to the law was her goodbye, before blacking out from her HP crash.

The life of a runner was never dull.

Entry 2.0

Many hours later Iset jerked back to life. Silken threads of heaven brushed against her flesh. She knew she had nothing on under it due to how every nerve in her body tingled with a cooling sensation that occasionally shift to cozy warmth. Eyes closed, she used her other senses to gauge her center. The sweet smell of vanilla mixing with that of a slight astringent scent let her know that she was home in her bunker hidden under Motel Refuge. She was in her simple little room, its environment lights washing the room white.

She felt the touch of hands upon her body causing her to turn on her side, those hands shifting to skim over her bare hip.

"Have the Rat's partied too hard again in my bar Orion?" Iset muttered. Her eyes still closed in half-slumber she flinched as the hands caressed a tender spot.

"Woi! You're pressing too hard man!"

Those seeking, firm, yet gentle hands continued to travel her body, leaving goose bumps in their wake. After all these years, it still amazed her how human-like Orion's touch could be. Iset paused in thought and had to laugh to herself. Truly, her trusty friend was at one time or other human. She had found his body on the side of the river in torn pieces. Before her was Orion. He had been a young man who was older by a mere year at that time. Twenty he told her. Rah'bel had been his real name.

His body had been in chaos. Pieces of him were strewn everywhere like a rag doll ripped into pieces that had once been his human body. From what she had seen, he had been in a horrible fight. Built like a stocky boxer, Iset knew that if he could stand next to her he would tower over her by several inches while in her boots. However, what interested her was the mark of a Runner on his chest. He was literally bleeding to death, one bandaged hand and arm ripped from him and resting near her feet, while his leg was missing, Iset knew without a doubt that the Watchers had done this. Half of his skull was open exposing his brain to the world. Yet there he laid still fighting, rapidly blinking, muttering strange words, muddled with, "Runner…free…your…mind…"

Free your mind? That was runner code for supporting Purge. Yeah, she was familiar with that personally and survived it. She actually was very skilled in performing the procedure. Through the years of practice she developed unique techniques that resulted in a higher percent rate of survivors. It was a rewarding gift of hers, even though it wasn't a perfect process. Too many still died in her opinion.

In the City everyone was born with a 'Tell,' a unique organ linking their minds to the Wave. This allowed all living beings to live every day traced, monitored and sometimes brained washed. To remove it, a person had to go through the painful and often deathly process of 'The Purge.' Only sixty percent typically survived and out of that seventy-eight succumbed to madness. However if a person survived then they were liberated, no longer brainwashed or insane. Well, maybe just a little crazy.

Iset chuckled as she recalled the past. Rah'bel recited the Runner's motto, resulting in her gathering him up as best as she could and bringing him to safety. Iset remembered her then basic level 'Tell' free operating system chattering to her in its computer lingo as it scanned Rah'bel's torn body. Diagnostics results ran over her TG and she saw that there was only a twenty-five percent chance in saving him. At that moment, Iset made a choice, one that changed her whole life as a Runner. She saved a man who set her on the path of preventing the brainwashing of millions and building a secret refugee under her business.

In saving Rah'bel, she turned him into a half-android by fusing his brain with her computer system. Renaming him Orion, she pieced him back together using sanitized discarded Pleasure borg bits and other robotic parts from which she bargained, stole, and made deals for. It took her years, to piece him together. After that, the rest was blessed.

Rah'bel became Orion after the system reboot and merging. Whoever he was in his past was gone or so she thought until Orion began to display habits that she hadn't put in his programming system. Computer and man evolved into something human and less computer like in the later years. Eyes once emotionless became soft and caring, reflecting intelligence unlike that of a typical android.

Shifting in her bed, Iset let those memories lead her back to consciousness. Finally opening her eyes, she stared into the umber eyes of her friend. His brown sugar toned jaw was flawlessly line with a simple goatee beard which tapered into a lone wisp of long cotton soft kinky hair from his chin. Familiar smile lines crinkled near his eyes, each contour reflecting how her friend still aged where his human flesh remained despite her efforts to stall the process. Dark hair cropped into a dreadlock Mohawk, the way he tilted his head to the side made her chuckle. Something that she realized transferred from his human past. Those large fighter hands traveling up her body to check her pulse by her neck reminded her how much more human he had become over the time he spent by her side.

"Huh? What did you say Orion?" she asked, realizing that she had not listened to him giving her the rundown.

"Apologies, Iset. Your levels are still balancing. The motel is filling with civilians seeking your help in Purging them. Indeed, this is a good thing my friend. As for the Rats, they played their music too loud and filled the motel lounge with smoke. They furthermore tried to go through your Ooze supply again, and libations. As usual, I broke several Rats noses and dumped them back on the street."

Iset gave a relieved laughed. Nothing changed with those Rats. Her gaze roamed over her companion. Stocky, built like a boxer, Orion, had he wanted, would be a prized pick as a pleasure 'borg, especially since he still carried human parts enhanced by tech. However, he was a fighter. He had given her the first seed of rebellion against the brainwashing of the 'Tell.'

In his ramblings during his surgery, he taught her the wisdom of a Street Priest, a group of individuals gifted with the ability of spiritual divination, minor psychic and physical healing ability as well as a gift of spiritual cleansing. It was rumored that Street Priest power only worked if their feet touch the plascrete ground of the City. However, she never knew if that was true or not.

It made sense as to why the Watchers had torn Rah'bel apart as they did. This knowledge about him caused her to meet up with her old mentor, former Runner and powerful leader of the Learned Order of Street Priests, Knowledge Lateef. In the end, Orion had sat with her through her worst times and darkest of secrets. He was a true friend and confidant. He also was an annoying android forgetting she was one hundred percent human.

"Orion! Watch how you take my blood, godblind man! That stung worse than fighting an Apunu," she hissed once the prick of a sharp needle pierced her flesh. She swatted at him.

"I was gentle Iset. Relax with that drama, as you say…no…as I once said," Orion replied. He chuckled then a brooding expression filled his face. "I am what you made me."

Sitting up from the bed, her twisted braids swung over her shoulder and breast, Iset carefully took in her friend's appearance. He wore his typical white tent pants, a belt of weapons, Tech-gear hanging low on his narrow hips and a medic sling bag over his shoulder. Since Orion was in the comfort of their shared home, he wore an open linen shirt, showing his bare chest with a smock around his hips covered in speckles of what she assumed was her blood. His gorgeous rum brown skin showed scarring from his battles as well as where his android parts fused with his human flesh.

There was weariness to him and it worried her. But

more so, the way he was speaking, had her staring at him strongly in thought.

"Wait a minute; you say that as if I harmed you. As if this life is a curse my friend," wrapping the healing sheets around her, Iset brushed her braids off her shoulder.

Orion's body seemed to tense as he turned his back on her to fiddle with his medic kit.

Nervous concern had Iset laughing in trying to understand her companion, "Are you upset about last night? This is work. This is what we do. I run. I gather the information for us all, but also for some really jacked up clients. I can't help the nature this battle Orion."

"Affirmative. It is what it is, as you say."

"Grrr! I hate when you say that! I never say that. You say that, Rah'bel!" she spat out in frustration.

She couldn't believe she was fighting with a freaking android.

"What is wrong with you? I hate when you're like this. It happens every time you use the link chair and synchronize back into your body. Am I overworking you?"

"Negative. I am but an android. I do not compute. There is no wrong. My work is yours Iset." Orion curtly stated.

Here we go.

That heart of his was still very much human, though his biotech kept it beating. Just by his emotionless words, Iset knew that he was trying to push her into a reaction, into blasting him for being insensitive to his existence. He was more than android and right now, he was proving that point. The longer they were together, the more memories of his past he gained. However, after her mission from last night, Iset could tell that something major must have clicked in that unique brain of his.

"Stop being an ass. You are more than that and you know it. Please…tell me what happened," Iset pleaded. She shifted to the edge of her soft bed.

"As you wish, mistress. Your fall. Your near death caused a system outage. Once I came back online, I quickly returned to my body and let the general Orion system handle the business. It was then that I grabbed you at the district and brought you home. Afterwards I gathered all the data you complied and it was then that my system froze then restarted again. In that quick second," Orion snapped his fingers then came closer to the bed then knelt in front of her.

"I suddenly remembered everything. I am Rah'bel. I am a Runner. I am a Street Priest and I am your companion. This work is yours, but it's also mine, feel me? This game out here isn't only yours anymore. Stop killing yourself and let me be more than your eyes. We hold each other's secrets, but you hold me back."

Shock jettisoned into Iset's body. She couldn't believe he was saying all of this in the manner he was. Previously he spoke in cold, straight to the point computer lingo. However now it flowed like that of a human, with slang, and the slight dialect of a man from The Heap. This was not like the android, but very much like the man had she helped years ago. This was pure human emotion. Not fabricated or programmed by her. This was free-will speaking and it stunned her to her core.

"I hold you back? I do not!"

Pushing up from the bed, she took two steps forward then fell backwards on her bed in fatigue.

"Indeed you do. Stop reacting and stop tripping. This is my work. Lay back so that I may heal you mistress."

Caring hands tucked Iset back into the bed, and then changed everything by caging her to it. "My objective is to protect you and care for you. I always will do my job."

Eyes locked on each other, Orion gazed down at her as if there was more between them than their vast years of friendship. Yes, he had been privy to scratch her private itches from time to time but there was never an intimate connection. Just a machine giving her quick pleasure to help her through the need she had. She never was into Pleasure 'Borgs and never really saw the android body of Orion as one due to his parts coming from different machines. However, what was happening between them now was different. This was not a trivial moment of desire. This was more.

"I know that you're scared, but this is what you aimed to do in saving me, correct? Heal me by any means necessary for the fight. Well, it took years but the robotics and your 'Purge' has healed my brain, my heart, my body, and every nerve in me. When we train to fight, I hurt, I tire, and I sweat, just like you. These parts are just enhancements now. Don't discriminate against me. Listen when I suggest things. I'm your partner. We can handle whatever comes, even whoever it is that is tracking you. Okay?"

Orion whispered against her lips. "Don't be scared of me…Iset."

A flush of heat spreading through her body turned her upside down. She hadn't felt heat like this since her last lover long ago. This was madness. She had a mission and she was a fighter. Yet, Orion's words were true. So was he. So much so, that he managed to defeat death by the hands of the Watchers. She had only aided in his healing. The rest was all him.

Just like the smooth brush of his skin sliding over hers, the weight of his thick body covering hers sent a natural chemical response through her body, a sudden craving to mate. Quieting her mind, she let him have control, something she had never experienced with him before. Her body moved in kinetic respond to his. The simple heady, yet gentle, entry of him with the feel of his tongue against her toffee-toned skin caused her to bloom.

It also caused her to tremble in need for him to go deeper while her long legs wrapped around his narrow waist. Her lips brushed the lone jagged scar near his temple, which ran behind his ear. She skimmed her teeth over the side of his warm tattooed flesh, hitting angles of soft human flesh with that of android flesh. They both appeared the same yet she could feel the difference.

Iset was stunned. She was very pleased and she wanted more of this healing connection given to her to make her understand that life was fragile, but life was also healing. Sighing in deep contentment as the time passed on, Iset turned on her side hours later. She took her gentle time to slide over Orion's warm slick body and snatched open his medic kit. Searching through it, she pulled out a hand scanner then ran it over Orion's face while he slept, focusing on his skull. Silver tracking light skimmed over Orion's features revealing a 3-D image of his skull then his brain, She was flabbergasted but the scientist in her was fascinated.

"Oh, my goddess!" she whispered against the hand that covered her mouth. "It's fully intact."

Just several days before it was half-electronic and half-surviving brain matter. Now it was Orion's once human pumping brain flashing on the projection screen. Iset could see flashing neurons fusing together and knitting his brain together. She did not know what triggered the change, but she had to find out.

This could help not only Orion, but also many of the people she assisted. It would be her main goal to speak with the backstreet doctors she once employed to help save Orion. She'd have to ask them to help her understand what was happening and if she should worry. Until then Orion was right. With his memories back they had to work as a team to fulfill their secret goal, to Purge the City of the Tell.

The map of the camps and the partial plan had to be safeguarded from the Watchers. With Orion well, he could leave the motel front desk and get out there too. The countdown to disconnect the link that too many people in the City were dependent was on. Unplug the tech, and free your mind, was Iset's motto.

Clicking the scanner off, she tossed the metal stick back into the bag and jumped at the feel of Orion's hand squeezing the lobe of her rear.

"Check everything Iset?"

Nervously laughing, she shifted to straddle him and smiled as he played with the ends of her braids.

"You know me too well. I'll have to change the journal system since everything had changed."

"Why? I do not understand," he asked with a blank look on his face. His lush lips formed a straight line.

For a fleeting moment, she thought Orion was back to the android aspect of himself until he flashed his pearly whites and slipped her hips down to take him back inside of her,

"Oh...you play too much."

Orion chuckled, "It feels nice to be able too. One last round and then we get back to business as usual my friend."

With a curving slow erotic roll of her hips, she nodded, and then planted her palms against her lover's chest.

"Hmmhmm...we have people to train and find out who that man is hunting me..."

Entry 3.0

Sweat lined Iset's brows and dripped into Iset's eyes while she skated on the transit rails.

"Damn it! Orion, I'm being followed again. Give me a quick route out of here."

"*Make a right on to Hallow Drive, then a quick left on State Street. Traffic ahead,*" he responded.

She bit her lower lip. She knew Orion was sending her into traffic to hide but at the same time she had to be careful otherwise people could be hurt. Iset chewed on her bottom lip and tapped her TG's.

"*Communication call: The Bone Collector.*"

A melodic chime of a hip-hop track sounded then a click.

"Hey, mum!"

The jovial voice on the other end had Iset shaking her

head while she ran.

"Tiny are you at a safe checkpoint?"

"No, ma'am! But I am safe, ya taught me well. But I do see you."

Tiny sent a video image, revealing her location. Her god-daughter was flitting in the air, dangerously surfboarding over flying transport cars. The teenager's wild, dark mane danced in the wind behind her. The purple and black jumpsuit she wore, with her hip cut, split purple skirt and skull lined belt marked her style. She too wore Kicks and TG's, with headphones. On her back was a backpack. Her protector trailed behind her hidden in the sewers but shaking the streets below.

"Good, you're blocks away from me," Iset said. "Keep guard. The Watchers are monitoring us, but they are not a problem. Do you see who is trailing me? Does he look familiar to you?"

Iset could hear Tiny chewing on her gum, humming in thought before the girl gasped.

"Oh…yeah! I see him. That's him mum. That's the dude. I swore I saw him talking to one of the Rats. Same mista that Rat Queen Vivian saw some months back bumped into Orion."

Panic hit her hard. She had so forgotten that Vivian had told her that. People whispered about a man in all black who moved like a shadow. No one knew who he was or where he came from, which is why people labeled the masked man Noname.

Clasping the encrypted tubed locket around her neck, Iset put the pieces together. Since she progressed into the next stage of her plan, more Watchers started showing up. Some of the refugees went missing, her contacts began to ignore her, and she now she was being followed. She was positive that the whispers of her plan had leaked. Someone knew she planned citywide Purge. All eyes were on her, but she had no proof until now.

Now with what Tiny shared, fear trembled through Iset. She had been compromised, but she was not exactly sure how deep it was yet.

"Tiny, call Lola and have her knock him off my trail. Keep your key close to your heart, baby girl."

"Okay mum. You be careful, okay?" Tiny said.

"I will sweetheart. Free your mind and keep your eyes open."

"Switch communication. Dial Orion main."

Iset closed the link. Zipping between flying transport and civilian cars, a loud bang then a plume of dust erupted in the airway behind her. Turning her body to see better, Iset laughed then grinned when she saw a long octopus tentacle break through the smoke and wrap around a building. In it, she could see the small form of Tiny flitting in the air then doing an aerial backflip in joy.

"Those two are a saving grace," Iset muttered to herself then tapped the nitrate boost to her Kicks and sped off.

Iset's sensory monitor scrambled and she almost lost her balance. It was him again.

"Orion answer!" she screamed at the same time fisting her gloved hands. She didn't have time for this. Today they obtained a major piece to the puzzle that would help them in their fight to start the 'Purge.' Vivian, the Rat Queen, sent her word from a top official in Ooze Inc. to meet with her about a new coordinate locket. It was another encrypted message holding a gift that would change the game in how the 'Purge' was administered to the populace citywide. She was on her way to meet a man she hadn't spoken to in years. However, that meeting now had to be rescheduled due to a possible breach in her camp and the mother-trucker still tracking her.

"I am here Iset," Orion finally answered. "Your HP stress levels are rising. What is wrong?"

"I don't need you to read me. Where are you?" she demanded, trying to keep her tone level.

Orion appeared on her screen, dressed in an all-black

Runner suit with matching goggles. His hands stretched behind him as he skated in the air.

"I'm transporting the package to the Street Priests as agreed. South Avenue is where I am. Tell me what's wrong."

"Have you been compromised?"

"Why do you think I am compromised?" Iset heard Orion chime in her ear.

"Because that freaky looking bloodclaat is trailing me!"

"I don't know who you're talking about Iset. Watch your levels," Orion said with a slight patronizing tone.

"You don't know?" shooting him an image, Iset grounded herself. "This fool is rushing me!"

Silence came from Orion then muttering, "I...I don't understand. Watch out Iset!"

As soon as Iset turned around a large hand swiped across her vision.

She attempted to scream but that large hand sent a punch directly into her throat, sending her gagging backwards from the forceful blow. Iset hands came up to her throat in defense and disbelief while she locked watery eyes on the man in black. She tried to activate her 'vox', but nothing came from it. The bastard had blocked it.

How had the fool made it past Lola?

Light glared behind his hulking form while he followed her fall, a Zentec gun in his hand. His big hat flapped in the wind and Iset imaging that behind those dark goggles was nothing but evil and malice. Today he was not about saving her. Today he was about killing her and she could not allow that for anything.

She twisted her body and felt herself land then skid across the rooftop of a building,

Losing communication with Orion, her gun appeared in her hands and she faced down the man who was intent on taking her down, "What do you want!"

"Nothing," the man stated. "Just doing a job, kid."

A Gods damn bounty hunter! That's who and what he is? Oh hell no! Iset was officially pissed.

"Then let's have some fun then because you either kill me or you let me go. Capture is not an option," she said.

Two steps forward had her stopping in her tracks.

Orion dropped from the sky, landing between her and the bounty hunter. Twin pistols were in his hands and pointed from her to the Hunter.

Confusion had Iset slacked jawed. A booming dark laugh came from the hunter. Iset noticed a blinking yellow light on his wrist. She watched its flashing rhythm then noticed an identical light blinking near Orion's temple.

"What did you...?"

"Let the fun begin kid." Noname began shooting. "Kill her Orion."

Iset didn't know what to do in that second. However, once bullets, then grenades flew her way from his Zentec 'Combo' Assault Rifle, she had no choice but to act. Plumes of orange smoke attempted to invade her nostrils, but she was quicker than the bounty hunter. Silver nostril plugs designed to filter gas, toxins, and other obnoxious clouds snapped into her nose while she dodged the attack then ran right into her once sane friend.

Orion shifted his stand in tandem. Tracking beams jettison from his once soulful irises and locked on her. He sent several rounds her way with a blank expression upon his handsome face.

"*Target Threat! Target Threat!*" Orion chattered while squeezing off rounds.

Iset realized Orion was still linked to her operating system.

"Damn it! Orion don't do this!" Iset pleaded.

Each time she tried to pull up her shields, she was denied. Red lights flickered as Orion threw up firewalls that blocked her commands. Frustration caused her lips to curl in a snarl as she ran and thought of another way to get back her security system.

"System manual override!" Iset screamed. She swiped her hands in front of her then frantically typed on the holo-board that appeared, hacking her way through her system until the red faded away,

"Shields up!"

Multiple light shields clocked her as she back flipped into a crouch. She aimed at her former confidante and her stalker.

"You did this! You messed with his bio-tech and turned him!" she shrieked with tears in her eyes.

"Yes ma'am, it was simple too," the stranger answered. "One hit with an injection serum and he was my friend. Nothing against you, kid. Just doing my job."

Iset made a beeline toward the bounty hunter but Orion only blocked her way. Arms up, she stretched out her leg, kicking Orion in the face. Orion's head snapped back and he stumbled away. Iset dropped low then spun to sweep Orion. He dodged her leg then sent his large booted foot into her ankle.

Iset screamed as her ankle snapped. She pulled her leg back. There was no way that she could move on her leg unless she bound it. She quickly pulled the straps of her boot to tighten around her ankle to turn it into a makeshift brace.

"Orion! Don't let that asshole control you. Please! You're compromised!"

Orion tilted his head. "Compromised? Negative." He rushed her, knocking her goggles away from her face with his palm knives.

Iset rolled behind Orion then sprang to her feet before Noname, punching him in the face several times before he could react. Orion turned and attacked before she could finish off the bounty hunter. Despite her skills, she couldn't fight them both.

Tiny's voice rang in her earpiece.

"Mum, are you alright?"

"Stay away, Tiny!" she blurted. "Stay away!"

Sweat dripped down her battered face and her body ached. Orion attempted to snatch at her gear, but she dodged as best as she could. Her former ally fell into a ginga before attacking again, battering her body with vicious blows. The bounty hunter tried to shoot her; Iset managed to press her wrist set, releasing a directional EMP which disarmed his weapons. Standing on the edge of death, she knew she could not keep this up.

The men circled her, cautious yet relentless. Watching her old friend, regret filled her spirit. There was no way that she would let him be this man's puppet.

"Orion...it's me and you, always friend. I'll never desert a friend."

"But I am not a threat to you," Orion said, his voice void of the emotion of his words.

"Whatever he did, I'll fix it, I promise. Forgive me," she muttered.

"Always Iset," Orion said. He reached behind his head, pulling his spare gun free. He aimed at her skull.

"Whatever you do kid, don't run. That's boring," Noname taunted.

"Everyone in this City is lost to the Wave! Dependent on the 'Tell'! Don't you get it? Don't you care? I'm only a piece to the whole game,"

Iset pulled out a pulse gun hidden in her jumper. "You can't stop progress but you can't let it enslave you either! Screw you!"

Two charges of energy flew past Orion's shoulder and into the bounty hunter stunning him. The next went into Orion, sending into system shock. Orion fired in reflex; several rounds grazed Iset's leg and shoulder. Iset crouched then activated her Kicks. She rocketed toward Orion, dodging his grasping limbs then wrapped her arm around Orion's head and neck. Biting her lower lip, she used every ounce of power in her to squeeze and then snap his neck apart. A mixture of bio-fluid, human blood, broken bone and metal tore through his skin. Orion collapsed to his knees, dragging Iset with him.

Fire burned her lungs, exhaustion wanted to claim her but she wasn't done. She needed to know who hunted her and why. Crawling to the knocked out bounty hunter, she pulled off his blinking gun, and then smashed it into pieces, pocketing the bits.

"Thanks for the pieces, I'm going to figure out what you did to Orion and reverse it," she barked. She emphasized her words by slapping the man hard.

The man's big hand snatched out, gripping her neck and squeezed tight. Gasping for air, she clawed then wheezed.

"Whatever the bounty price is on my head, I'll pay you triple to kill who is after me plus extra to keep me off the list, deal?" she managed to say. "If you agree, show yourself in the market."

Noname loosened his grip. Iset huffed, gripped tight then flung her hand free, "That is all I'll need to see. Until then…"

Iset slammed her fist into his face, knocking the bounty hunter out,

"Sweet dreams!"

Never piss off a woman with a mission, let alone a woman who is a Runner and who has a backing like no other, Iset mused.

She sighed, relief flooded her senses. Iset scrambled back from the unconscious brute then limped toward Orion. She moved as fast as she could to get as far away from that crazy man.

She gazed at her broken companion. "Orion…"

Wiping the muck of sweat, dirt, and blood from her battle worn face, she cupped her forehead while looking on and holding in her rising emotion. Orion lay twitching in a pool of blood and bio-liquid. His head was askew, exposing his tendon, bone, and bio-parts. Orion's arm stretched out frozen in the act of trying to grab her. She swore that she saw softness return to his eyes, swore she heard him mutter thanks, but she wasn't sure. Once again, he lay in a compromised position, death ready to take him and yet again she was standing over him, hoping to save his life.

A whistle from afar alerted Iset that Tiny and Lola was nearby and that was a blessing because her Kicks were shot. Looking down at her smoking skates, Iset slammed her good foot down to try to fix them but came up with nothing. She'd have to repair them later, just like Orion. Whatever the bounty hunter injected into Orion had healed her friend's mind, but also made him a slave to whatever tech pumped into his brain grid. Iset had a feeling that her friend was under the influence of the 'Tell' again. However, she would not know until she ran some tests.

Everything they had both worked on was in danger. She was scared all her thoughts and journals were in the hands of the enemy, but again, she had to be sure. Iset always saved everything to the encrypted system of Orion's mainframe but not the android component. She could only hope that only small bits of her plans were exposed. Crouching near her friend, Lola swooped them both up in her tentacle hold carrying them into the sewers of the city. Watching the City fade away, quiet was Iset's solitude.

"Is he…like dead-dead?" Tiny said from her spot on top of Lola's head, her curly dark hair blowing in the wind.

"No, he is just wounded and in a coma," she explained looking down at the mess that was Orion. "It was the only way I could stop him.

Secretly she hoped he wasn't dead, that the human part of him that came back and the brain were undamaged. She wouldn't know until her team examined him. For now, all she could do was hope.

She would continue to prepare to act on her plan to purge the City, taking in people who want to be free or were free of the Tell.

"Let's go home Orion and lay low for a while. I promise you, we'll get you back. This is what we do. We live. Fight and die, all for this City and the refugees."

Holstering her gun, Iset tenderly reached out to touch Orion's shocked face then rest her hand on his chest, where she could feel his slow beating heart. She closed his twitching eyes and then sighed, "Free your mind my friend. The Purge will happen, trust in me Rah'bel."

The Man with No Name

by
D K Gaston

A glint from the ceiling lights reflected off the dark spherical visors as he stepped out of the shadows to reveal himself to the four patrons sitting at the table. Wearing black from head to toe, the stranger looked totally out of place in the bright cyber café. Cladded in a Stetson hat, long leather trench coat, armor-plated vest, a utility belt draped around his waist equipped to the hilt with gadgets, and an assault Zentec rifle slung over his right shoulder; he knew he made an impression on folks. But what stood out most about him was the full face mask with mirror lenses. When people gazed into his glass eyes of his, all they could perceive were their own stares. The effect chilled most and he reveled in knowing that.

"You must be him?" one of the four asked. She was also, one of two women, among them, though there might be room for debate of the true sexual category of the second woman. Garbed in a two-piece business suit, she stank of being a member of the Cartel—one of the four gangs occupying Ward 215.

"I must be," the new arrival answered. An empty chair was shoved out for him, but he remained standing. "Why am I here?"

The debatable woman was big, bald, and muscular, with facial hair. Her exposed body parts were covered in tattoos. She answered, "We wanna hire ya." She wasn't in a suit, but instead wore a dark blue tank top. Dead giveaway she was a member of the Soors.

"Sit down," one of the men ordered, "You're making me nervous hovering over us like that." Dreadlocks ran down to his shoulders and he smelled foul like a sewer. There was

CYBERFUNK ANTHOLOGY 73

no mistaking that he was a member of the Lords.

The stranger turned his attention to the last man who carried this air of leadership about him--likely the one making all the decisions. The fact he let the others do all the talking while he sat in mock silence said it all. Though he was smallest of the quartet, his arrogant expression and posture could only come from a member of the York.

"You the one in charge here?" the stranger asked.

"Have a seat, please," the small man replied, gesturing toward the empty chair. He slipped on a pair of glasses that hid his eyes. "I'm Mondo Savage." A mighty powerful name for such a tiny bite sized package. Obviously, the man felt he needed to compensate for his vertically challenged stature.

Unslinging the rifle from over his shoulder, the stranger sat, still keeping his reflective gaze on the small man.

Savage continued with his introductions gesturing toward the well-dressed woman at the table, "This lady is Numara Pinnacle, the larger, ah, woman with the tattoos calls herself Edge, and the smelly fellow is Omari Caesar."

Caesar shot out of his chair, gun raised. "No one disrespects me! No one!"

Savage laughed. "Be calm, friend. I was only poking fun at your expense."

"Don't disrespect me," Caesar retorted before settling back into his seat.

The stranger noted the alliance between the four gangs was a fragile one. The wrong word or gesture and whatever thread that bind them mutually at the table would fall apart in seconds. He nearly hadn't shown up at the café, but they dangled a carrot he couldn't ignore. When he first received word of the meeting he thought it was to ambush him. On occasion he'd been hired to make some of the gang members disappear and they've been longing to return the favor. Now he was glad he came, because whatever had them working together may be used to his advantage.

"Why am I here?" the stranger demanded.

"We want you to find someone," Pinnacle answered.

The stranger didn't bother looking her way. A digital readout appeared in front of him alerting him that a facial recognition scan was being performed. Counter-measure automatically kicked in to thwart the scan.

After long seconds Savage frowned. He ripped off his Scanner glasses and tossed it to the floor. "Totally useless piece of—" Taking a deep breath, he leaned back in his seat, scrutinizing the stranger. "You really don't want anyone to know who you are."

"Who I am is not important," the stranger said. "What I can do is."

Edge stabbed the tip of a large knife into the table to gain everyone's attention. Folds of knobby flesh, where eyebrows should be, creased. "Dere's ah rumor you can pass through da Vertigo-Gate without bein' affected. Is dis true?"

The stranger said nothing.

"It's true," Caesar answered. "Some of my crew spotted him from the tunnels."

"But how do you go through the Vertigo-Gate without being detected? The Watchers should know your every movement. You're way too stable to have removed your..." Savage eyed him suspiciously, "Tell."

The stranger said nothing.

Savage snapped his fingers breaking the silence, and then held out an open palm toward the middle of the table. Pinnacle's hand disappeared as she reached below the tabletop fumbling for something.

The stranger's fingers tensed around the rifle resting in his lap. He watched her intensely searching for any telltale signs that she planned some type of attack against him.

Her hand resurfaced clutching a tan folder. With brows furled, nostrils flared and a tightened jaw, she sighed heavily. Pinnacle slapped the file hard into Savage's palm, obviously not happy playing secretary to a rival.

"Gratitude," Savage said to her with a hint of a

mocking grin.

He placed the folder on the table and flipped it open to the first page to reveal a photograph of a black female with long dreadlocks. She wore a yellow, tight-fitting leather shirt, baggy black pants and rocket boots. Savage poked a skeletal index finger on the photo directly between the woman's breasts. "We want you to find her."

The stranger's optics zoomed in on the picture. *Not a woman*, he thought, *a child.*

"Her name is Iset. She calls herself, da Protector or some jazz like dat," explained Edge. "She ah runner."

"She has something we want," said Caesar. "We need someone like you with practiced tracking skills. If half the rumors about you are true she should be no problem for you to catch."

"A runner," the stranger said, thinking out loud.

The remark must have been misinterpreted as a question, because Edge took it upon herself to answer. "Dat's right. We can't find da runt 'cause she can do some weird sh—"

"Enough," Savage interrupted. "I'm sure our visitor doesn't need to know every little detail."

That caught the stranger's full attention. They were hiding something about the girl from him. "Why?"

"Why what?" Pinnacle asked.

The stranger leaned in. "Why do you want her?"

Pinnacle shrank in her seat. "Ah, it's not her, we're interested in. It's what she possesses."

"That being?"

Savage slid the photograph closer to the stranger. "A package. Its contents aren't important--at least, not to you. We want you to find her and retrieve the package."

"Easy enough," the stranger replied. He slowly traversed his gaze to everyone seated at the table. "But I didn't accept your invitation here to talk about a girl. I was told this would be about Nubian King."

"In a way, it is," Pinnacle offered.

"How so?"

Pinnacle's gaze seemed to stare past the stranger's mirrored lenses finding the eyes beneath. She had the look of someone obsessed. "What she holds, Nubian King wants. If he wants it, so do we."

There was the answer to the question. The stranger now knew what would bring the four gangs together—power. If they obtained anything Nubian King sought they could bargain with him and conceivably extend their criminal empires beyond Ward 215. If that was their goal, more power to them. Anything that hurt the crime lord he saw as a plus.

"I don't come cheap."

"Find her, get what she has and we'll pay you enough creds to retire," Caesar said, grinning confidently.

Savage slid the folder and all its contents toward the stranger. "The information contain here will tell you Iset's last known whereabouts and some of the places she frequently been seen."

The stranger took possession of the folder and flipped it closed.

"Now that you're in our employ, perhaps you can supply us with your name," Savage insisted.

The stranger said nothing. Standing, he was underway to turn.

"One mo' thing," Edge said, "We can't be connected to dis. Once you take da package from the Protector. Kill her."

"She's just a child," the stranger said his voice betraying no emotion.

Savage cocked an eyebrow. "Child? She's an ambiguity. We must be certain what you do cannot lead back to us four."

The stranger faced the quartet. "You four won't have to worry about that." In a flash, he reached inside the folds of his leather coat and withdrew a pistol. Before any of them could react, the gun spat. The blast of the gun drowned out the café's music. One round for each person left gaping holes squarely in their foreheads.

The music went silent as everyone observed what he had been done, but the stranger knew no one would dare interfere. Ward 215 was a penitentiary without walls, where the law was ran by the gangs. Murder, theft, assault, rape and corruption were as commonplace as taking a breath. What he had done wasn't out of the ordinary--it was everyday business in 215. The music, the dancing and drinking resumed as if nothing transpired.

What happened next added to the folklore of the stranger everyone came to called, Noname. He took a small amount, but not all the creds from the people he'd just killed, leaving the remaining creds to be stolen by others.

Someone was brave enough to ask him, "Why didn't you take all their creds?"

"I'm not a thief, but bullets aren't free," the stranger answered before melting back into the shadows.

*   *   *

From the mezzanine Cutthroat watched with cold calculation at what had transpired at the booth. The faceless man had been fast and efficient in offing the four individuals-- too much so in fact. Cutthroat wondered if he wore cybernetic enhancements or took Bio-neural supplements. Regardless of whether the stranger did or not, didn't matter. He had done the assassin a favor.

Climbing on top of the balcony ledge, he jumped from the second floor of the club to the first nearly crushing a couple on the dance floor. He split the pair apart, the man to his front and the woman to his rear. The music once again came to an abrupt halt.

The male dancer was lean and fit, sweat poured down his face. After getting over his initial shock his surprise turned into anger and he closed in on Cutthroat.

"What th—"

His words were cut off mid-sentence by the assassin's powerful hand. Gripping the man by his throat, he closed his steely fingers around it.

The man fought back as Cutthroat drew him in with a suitable amount of tension and slack until they stood eye to eye. The man struggled like a flailing fish against a hook commanded by the more formidable hunter. The assassin measured his prey and then asked, "Are you a sinner, boy?"

The man's eyes danced around in his sockets. "What?"

"Are you seeking salvation?" the assassin asked.

"All I've come to do was dance, mister. I'm not looking for trouble."

"Yet you found trouble anyway." Cutthroat's fingers tightened around the man's neck. "Salvation awaits you brother and I shall pave the way for you."

A female's voice in his earpiece interrupted him. "Stay vigilant and on mission. Let the sinner be."

Though saddened, Cutthroat didn't hesitate to follow the order and released the man. "Your salvation will have to wait. I'll see you again soon, brother."

The dancers cleared a path for the assassin as he made his way to the booth where the four bodies remained. He stared down at the spilled contents on the table. The photograph of the Protector lay prominent in its center.

"The targets have been eliminated," he said aloud.

The voice answered, "Excellent work."

Cutthroat shrugged. "It wasn't by my hands. The man with no face killed them."

There was a long pause, and then she asked, "Do you know why?"

He stared down at the table focusing on the picture. It was an old photograph. "I think he has a soft spot for children."

"Iset is no child," she shot back, irritation in her voice.

"They showed him a photo at least twenty years old.

That would have put the Protector in her teens. Guess they should have found a more recent picture," he explained. "Their mistake is our fortune, sister. The stranger did us a favor by eliminating these obstacles."

"Or he has created yet another stumbling block," she countered. "Without knowing his true intentions for executing the four miscreants we must assume he will go after the Protector."

Cutthroat shook his head. "Even so, he's as trapped on this side of the barrier as I am. There's no way he could interfere."

"I have heard rumblings about the man with no name. They say he can cross the barrier freely. I suspect this was the reason the four sought him."

He hesitated, rethinking the event of the killings. Perhaps the stranger had slaughtered the gang members to obtain the Protector for himself. It made more sense than his theory. Someone so accustomed to spilling blood wouldn't give a second thought to kill a child.

"Shall I convert the sinner?" he asked eagerly.

"Yes, if possible. If he does not join the fold, then send his soul into the river of flame. But first, remove any evidence of Iset from the club."

He grinned. "It will be done."

"The Edict shines his light around you, brother." The communication ended.

Cutthroat looked down at the sprawled bodies admiring the immaculate work and then turned his thoughts to the man with no name. "You will see the light or I will have you burned in the river of flames."

*   *   *

Noir Gray worked feverishly on the modifications of his invention. He'd been tinkering with the device to improve the power output by twenty-five percent. If he made one miscalculation he'd end up blowing himself up along with half of Ward 215. That was his reason for choosing to work a mile underground. He'd spent years modifying a bunker, a remnant of the great Transunion Conflict, into a laboratory that met all his needs. Well, he and his solitary friend's needs.

Gray was just finishing up the final adjustment when he became aware of being watched. He looked up from his work, catching the dark silhouette hovering nearby. With a start, he gasped, "Stop doing that! You're going to give me a heart attack one of these days."

The visitor said nothing.

"How the hell do you keep sneaking in here without being detected by my sensors?"

Silence.

Gray straightened. "Oh, you're in one of your moods today, I see. That's fine by me I'm too busy to be socializing anyway." He held up the power pack he'd been working on. "By the way I've upgraded the power cell by fifteen percent."

Rounding his workbench, he approached his friend, palming the device in one hand. "Don't think just because you're wearing a mask I don't see you frowning underneath. Oh don't give me that look. It's easy for you to complain but I'm the one risking my life every time I make an adjustment on these toys I build for you. I'm the one who's potentially being exposed to dangerously high levels of radiation, not you."

No response.

"If we didn't have the same goals I swear I wouldn't put up with you." He laughed more to himself than to his friend, and then he turned serious. "These people, I tell you, they've blinded themselves to the true nature of the City. All they see are structures of steel and concrete erected to protect them from the elements and the cruelty outside their walls. They don't understand that the City is alive. It's a succubus draining those trapped within of their very life's energy. The City manifests itself in the guise of great beauty and shelter, ensnaring the weak-willed into its womb."

Curling his hands into fist, Gray shook them in rage at the ceiling as if communicating to the world itself. "I am not weak! I am resolute! I am your champion! And I will open your eyes to the truth!" Taking several breaths to calm himself, he glanced at his quiet friend. "Sorry, I got carried away again--I meant us. We're doing this together, right?"

He said nothing.

Gray cleared his throat and looked down at his shoes. "I've tapped remotely into your ocular and auditory sensors. I saw what happened in the café." He stared up from the floor. "That could have gone better. Did you have to kill them?"

A shoulder shrug was his answer.

"The girl in the photo, the one called, Iset. . . You have to help her you know?"

Another shoulder shrug.

"Come on. You saw how young she was. If Nubian King is after this girl, you know what he's capable of doing. What he'll eventually do to her if she doesn't cooperate with him. If she's lucky, she'll be killed quickly, if not, well, you know what first hand... Don't you?"

Gray didn't wait for an answer, circled back to the front of his desk and lifted up a handful of silver marble sized metal spheres. "These are Ogles. They will be your eyes and ears throughout the City." He tossed the twelve objects up in the air. They silently hovered in place. "They have adaptive camouflage to conceal themselves from being spotted. And best of all, they are already linked to your suit's internal circuitry."

His friend flinched involuntarily.

"Oh sorry," Gray said holding his palms out

apologetically. "It'll take a moment for you to get used to the sensation you're experiencing. It's not easy to see in every direction at once. Give it a second to calibrate with your neural uplink and then you'll be able to control what you see."

His friend straightened, fully recovered from the experience.

"I've already preprogrammed them to find Iset before you arrived. Something told me you wouldn't want her being taken by King or the rival gangs." The Ogles streaked through the air and shot into a ventilation shaft leading to the surface. "I've also put out the word that you've been hired to kill her. Can't let anyone know you have a heart under that tough exterior of yours. Not good for your rep if that happens."

Turning, his friend headed silently for the exit.

Gray waved to his back. "Stay in touch."

*   *   *

The Edict's network was widespread throughout the wards of the City. As stealthy as the stranger thought of himself, his mask and hat might as well have been a bright beacon. Sooner or later, Cutthroat would be alerted to the man with no name's movements.

In the interim, he occupied his time by questioning inmates regarding the whereabouts of the stranger. The man struggling for air under his boot clawed desperately at the leg pinning him to the ground.

Cutthroat added more weight. "I was told by a reliable source you know something about the man with no name." He let up on the pressure to allow his prisoner to speak.

Gasping for air, the man groaned, "I... don't know... where he... is."

"I didn't ask you for his location."

Squatting down beside him, Cutthroat placed the flat of his palm on the man's chest. His hand glowed blue and the air surrounding it crackled like electricity. Kinetic energy coursed through his arm. The prisoner began convulsing, his eyes going wide with shock, fear and pain. As blood drizzled out of the man's nostrils and ears, Cutthroat pulled his palm away.

"Tell me what you know of Noname."

The man said much without saying anything at all, that was until he spoke of rumors about a hermit who lived under the ground that supplied Noname with tech. It sounded like the beginnings of a fairytale but had a ring of truth. The hermit's whereabouts were as elusive as Cutthroat's prey, except that those few spotting's were centralized to the eastern section of Ward 215. He would have the Edict's followers concentrate their search there.

*   *   *

He'd always been overly cautious, skeptical of the offer of someone's help, doubtful of his or her true intentions. Now he was supposed to freely offer his services to save a total stranger. He didn't owe the girl a thing. Why should he care if she lived or died? And what did it say about him if Noir Gray knew him well enough to know he would help?

He had always counted his skepticism of the world and his unpredictability to stay alive all these years. Had he let his alliance with Gray compromise everything he'd worked so hard to become? If it wasn't for the fact he and Gray were of like-minds regarding the City's hold on its people, he would have broken their association long ago. The man who supplied him with weapons, technology and comradeship was his Achilles' heel. The City was harsh and pitiless place, sentimentality was a weakness he couldn't afford.

"Screw the girl," he said aloud. He flattened his hat, settling it tightly on top of his head, then yanked on his collars pulling them in close and walked against the wind. "Screw you too, Gray."

He hadn't gone more than fifty yards when he noticed the pair, a man and a woman, walking parallel to him on the opposite side of the road. He cursed inwardly for allowing himself to be distracted enough to have picked up a tail.

Are they gang members looking for revenge for the four I murdered tonight? he wondered as he zoomed in on them with his optical. Neither wore the typical tattoo gang markings but rather writings that ran the length of their arms. It appeared to be lines of religious scriptures. Focusing on the woman, he silently mouthed the words from her limb, "The Edict's will is eternal. His intellect is omniscient. Deny Him and be plunged into the River of Flame."

Who the hell is the Edict? Tapping into the web link, data that only he could see appeared in the air in front of him. *Not gang members...cult members.*

Although unsubstantiated, it was believe that the Edict was once the City's librarian, a 600-year old Ni'carion named Vetigo Druro, who disappeared almost two decades ago. Word was that he resurfaced five years ago to form a religious group based on all the knowledge he collected during his long stint as the librarian.

He'd seen enough. The text faded from view. He had been pursued by many in his time: The military, bounty hunters, mercenaries, law enforcers, and criminals, but he couldn't recall ever by hunted by a religious cult. Staring at the dubious pair once again, he suspected their intentions weren't to preach about saving his immortal soul.

Turning to face them, he stared the man and woman down through glass eyes to see what they would do. The pair froze in their tracks but didn't try to hide the fact they were watching him. He reached across his shoulder and drew the rifle slung on his back making it clear he didn't want them there. Still, they stayed in place showing no fear.

"Can't take a hint I see," he said, "Guess I do this the hard way."

He started to cross the road when he caught movement

in his peripheral. A crowd was moving in fast from the east. All of them bore similar tattoos to the pair tracking him, who by the way was heading in his direction.

"Great."

He fired a warning shot inches in front of the feet of the couple. They didn't even slow their pace as if they didn't fear death. He admired their bravery. Then he shot them both in the chest. They laid flat and bloodied on the asphalt, their empty opened eyes staring up at the dark sky above.

Whirling on feet, he faced the oncoming crowd, which appeared to have grown. He reseated the rifle into its holster on his back and then reached inside the folds of his leather coat. His hands came out gripping two mini-machine guns. They wouldn't be getting a warning shot. The darkened road lit up as guns blazed taking down those in front. As bodies crumbled to the ground the cultists stepped over their fallen comrades and continued pouring forward.

He fired until nothing came out of his guns but smoke rising from the barrels. The crowd closed in. Placing the weapons back into his coat, he snatched a sonic grenade from his utility belt and quickly tossed it at the cultists. There came a deafening wailed. The crowd's inner ear were being bombarded with both sound and vibration traveling through their canal, disturbing the inner hair cells, tectorial membrane, basilar fiber, spiral ganglion and cochlear nerve. Clutching at their ears a massive wave of vertigo brought them all down to their knees, backs, and stomach.

"Chew on that," he said, as he turned west to walk away. He stopped dead after spotting a large man standing in the middle of the road directly in front of him. Like him, he carried an assortment of weapons. "Are you going to be a problem for me too?"

"I suppose I am," the man said, "You can call me, Cutthroat. What do I call you stranger?"

"Death."

Cutthroat laughed and then extracted two large blades

from scabbards sewn into his pants legs. "Let's do this like the men of old, true warriors, brother."

It has been a long time since the man with no name fought with blades but a challenge was a challenge. "What is this about?"

"Iset the Protector," Cutthroat answered without hesitation. "I've been told to convince you first to voluntarily join our brotherhood but I know I'd be wasting my time."

"Yep."

Cutthroat charged without fear or favor. The man with no name met him halfway. The pair stopped short of colliding. His opponent made a vertical strike, coming straight down trying to slice him from shoulder to hip.

Backpedaling, the attack was dodged with no trouble. The man with no name executed a forward thrust with his own knife, aiming directly at the man's chest. Metal clattered as the maneuvered was easily parried. It went back and forth like that for a long time with forward horizontal strikes, reverse diagonal swipes, and so on and so forth. They seemed equally matched in the art of knife combat.

The crowds of cultists were starting to recover from their bout of vertical, rising up to their feet. Some moved in closer readying to throw themselves into the fight. Cutthroat didn't appeared bother by that fact, so much for fighting like true warriors.

So the man with no name did the unthinkable in an honorable fight...he cheated. He faked an above strike by swinging down with one knife.

Cutthroat responded predictably to block, raising one weapon.

While his opponent was distracted, an inch-long blade flitted out the toe of the man with no name's right boot. He sent his foot up hard with enough force into Cutthroat's groin to displace the man's feet from the ground. A choked scream tried to escape but all he could mustard was a high-pitched whimper. Cutthroat's knives clattered to the surface, followed immediately by the moaning man. Despite his obviously pain he tried to clasp a weak hand that glowed blue around the man with no name's leg.

Batting it away, he reached down to his sprawled opponent. He inserted his fingers into two hoops and ripped out the pins of the grenades attached to Cutthroat's belt harness. He had about five seconds before detonation. Without preamble the man with no name ran.

The cultists pursued, leaping over Cutthroat's prone body in the road. They didn't make it far. The explosive made night into day, the blast masked the shrieks of those caught up in its wake.

He stopped running but continued to walk not even bothering to look back. Before the cultists came after him, he'd been resolved to let the girl fend for herself but he didn't like to be threaten and he had to teach Edict's cult they'd messed with the wrong man.

*   *   *

Eden Night tried to reach Cutthroat to no avail and began to worry. When she couldn't communicate with any of her sisters and brothers within Ward 215 she could no longer deny the truth. They were all dead, wiped out by the man with no name.

Night's eyes glowed scarlet. She screamed in rage at the loss of so many. Those close by moved away not daring to even look in her direction. After a full minute of righteous indignation she decided to change the perimeters of her mission. "The Edict is the light. The Edict is the way. None may defy the Edict. I will hunt the stranger with no name. There is no place in the City where he may hide. The stranger will give in to the bliss of the light or else be granted the agony of eternal darkness and flame," she swore.

Night knew that to find her prey she must first find Iset the Protector.

*   *   *

After his encounter with the cultists, he decided it was time to leave Ward 215. Gray had concocted some kind of electronic thingamabob for him that effectively made him undetectable by the Vertigo-Gate or the Watchers. The device had been broken into two parts--both were surgically implanted into the flexor carpi ulnaris muscle of his right and left arms. To activate, he had to place his wrists together to form a connection.

The sensation of pins and needles coursed throughout his entire being. Gray called the affect: Fragmented. He'd gone on to explain that every molecule was being fluctuated to such speed it no longer coexisted in time and space. The explanation didn't make much sense to him--science wasn't his thing, his expertise was in tracking and warfare.

The world around him slowed to a crawl. Fully immersed into the Fragmented jump, he crossed through the Vertigo-Gate without incident and stopped walking once he was on the opposite side of detention perimeter. The sensation ended abruptly. He crumbled to his knees breathless and completely drained of energy. The experience took a toll on the body and likely stole a few of his precious years of life each time he operated the device, but it was a trade well worth its value.

After regaining his breath, he stood to his full height, ignoring the wave of nausea brewing in his stomach. People stayed cleared of the Vertigo-Gate because of its affects, so he knew he was alone. He raised his mask up to the bridge of his nose revealing his dark brown skin. He plucked a cigar out of one of his pockets, placed it in his mouth and lit the tip. Smoking always helped ease the queasiness faster and it was one of his few vices he actually enjoyed these days.

A voice spoke into his ear. "Time to go to work, one of the Ogles has detected the girl," Gray said.

He pitched the cigar away no longer finding pleasure in

it. "I don't like you invading my space."

"Calm down, friend, I'm here to help."

"Whatever," he said shrugging. "How'd you find her so fast?"

"The Ogles utilizes Fragmented tech. They scanned most of the surface of the City in…"

"Okay, I got it," he interrupted. He pulled down his mask to fully cover his face. Accessing the Ogle a high-def visual appeared in front of him. He watched a woman streaking through the City on black and silver kicks. She looked like an older version of the girl in the photograph. "Who's this?"

"It's Iset," Gray answered hesitantly. "Apparently the four gang members had supplied you with an outdated picture."

She moved with the grace of a dancer and the speed of a demon. Nestled in her arm was a package. The man with no name wondered if it was the bundle and not the girl, Nubian King, the gangs, and perhaps the Edict wanted from her. She appeared strong and confident, not as vulnerable as she had in the photo. He watched her, his expression imperceptible beneath his mask. Maybe he wouldn't need to intervene.

"She still needs your help," Gray said as if reading his thoughts.

"Helping her was your idea, not mine," he countered. "I like to be paid for the work I do."

"If she's killed it'll eat at your conscience."

"I'll manage."

"Will you?"

The man with no name shrugged considering all the things that could go wrong by involving himself in someone else's business. Still, there were the cultist's who'd tried killing him and King's connection to the woman. Could he let the opportunity past to get under their skin?

"I'll do this but you owe me a box of cigars."

He could almost see the grin on Gray's face. "You got it, friend."

Pulling up the coordinates of the woman, he prepared

to Fragmented jump once again. It would be the fastest way for him to travel to her location. It wasn't wise to utilize the tech in such a short space of time, doing so would leave him weak a great deal longer than he liked but he had little other choice.

He slapped his wrists together.

The moment he came out of the Fragmented jump he doubled-over in pain and couldn't catch a breath. He lay on the rain-soaked street in the fetal position in the middle of the business district, surrounded by the crush of people staring down at him. His gut felt like the cold steel of a knife had been slammed hard into it. Despite the pain, he rolled onto his stomach and pushed himself up to his knees. He wanted to rip off his mask and suck in large gulps of air but restrained himself--too many witnesses around to see his face.

Struggling up to his feet, he tried to get his bearings. He turned south and staggered off, shoving people out of his way. Several of them called out, "It's Noname. He's real," but he ignored them. All that mattered was protecting a woman who strangely enough referred to herself as the Protector.

Catching his breath, he picked up his pace, but was far from recovered. He was slow and clumsy. His boots pounded heavily against puddles of water and concrete. Because of the speed the woman was moving, there would be no chance of him relying on his usual stealthiest or staying in the shadows.

The heat from the woman's jet boot repulsors left an invisible trajectory in the sky that his sensors easily detected. He followed her trail closely at the expense of anyone who got in his way. The crowd finally got the message and spread apart making a huge hole for him to pass through. Unfortunately, it made it easier for someone to spot him.

After several minutes of pursuing the woman, he realized he couldn't keep up his pace. He would have to depend on an Ogle to keep track of her until he could catch up. Her image appeared ahead of him. She moved in a panicked state. Had she spotted him? All the grace in her movement that she exhibited before had faded away. She moved erratically in the air and then she started to fall.

He slammed his wrists together and became a blur. The woman's descent turned into a slow motion free dive. Some kind of high-pitched shrill had been released by her, causing glass in nearby buildings to burst out. He avoided colliding into those walking the streets, bikes, and jet cars. Scaling up a thick pipe on the side of a building, he climbed high enough to push himself off and catch hold of a suspension support for a rail. Her descent sped up. The effect of the Fragmented tech was wearing off.

Holding on to support with one hand, he reached out with the other in a desperate attempt. Even if he did manage to catch her, there was a good chance he wouldn't be able to keep hold of her because of the Fragmented jump aftereffects. The world spun and excruciating stomach-cramping nausea once again overtook him, but he held fast to her leg and the suspension support.

"Ey, little bee..." he said gruffly, realizing how stupid that sounded, shook his head and tried again, "I gotcha kid."

She struggled in his hand, not realizing how much danger she was placing them both in. "Don't fight kid. I hate fighters." He couldn't think straight and forced himself to remember she wasn't a kid.

Hanging completely upside down, she stretched her arms downward, grabbed a speeding rail and with a grunt wrenched herself free of his grasp. Too exhausted to move he could do nothing but watch her fall. Her gracefulness returned, she performed some acrobatics and landed safely on her feet. She spun around to face him holding a Zentec 9110 11mm combat magnum. Before he could react she fired. Her aim was off and hadn't even come close. She disappeared into the shadows.

"You're doing a great job by the way," Gray said.

"Stay out of my head," he shot back.

He somehow managed the strength to slide down the beam, and immediately collapsed to the wet pavement.

He stared up at passing jet cars and hover bikes wondering how many more years he'd shaved off his life with three fragmented jumps. He sensed more than heard someone close to his position. Leaning his head to the side, the silhouette of a woman slowly approached.

"Iset?" he whispered.

"No," the stranger answered. A six-foot tall woman stood over him and placed the blade of a sword to one side of his neck. "I am the Light Bringer, Eden Night." Draped over her head was a thick hood and in its center was beauty itself: Crimson eyes, smooth light brown skin, full lips, and long flowing hair as black as the large cloak she was dressed in.

"Wonderful," he said, too exhausted to do anything. His tech immediately pulled up any information regarding her and displayed in front of him. "You're one of Edict's, right?"

She nodded curtly. "I am his most loyal servant. You are the one known as Noname." It was a statement, not a question.

"I take it you saw everything that happened? Why didn't you grab the package from her while you had the chance?" He hoped Night was a talker. He was not only fishing for information, he needed to stall her long enough to regain some of his strength.

"I've been following her for weeks waiting to collect the very information she now carries. It contains the location of many sinners whose *will* can be bent to follow my master. It would have been a great gift to present to him but that no longer matters to me. You have killed many of my faithful brethren. That cannot go unpunished."

"What about forgive and forget?"

She grinned. "That will come after you're burning in the river of flame." Placing one foot on his chest she raised the sword straight up readying to plunge it down into his face. "Guide my hand Edict, so that I may smite down this demon with my rapier of justice," she shouted.

She brought the blade down.

Her head snapped back, sending the cloaked woman

backpedaling, and grunting in pain. The sword clattered to the pavement mere inches from his face. He looked around confused. It took a moment for him to realize that one of the Ogles had descended out of the darkness and attacked Night before she could strike him down. Bringing himself up to a sitting position, he pulled out his pistol at the same time, but she was already gone. The only evidence she had been there at all was the sword beside him.

"This day just keeps getting better," he groaned, as he worked his way up to his feet. He scooped up the blade and used it as a crutch.

The Ogle hovered around him. It was not the same one that tracked Iset. He debated whether to let the woman fend for herself since Night admitted that he was her new focus. Still, she might have sent others from her cult to go after the Protector. Hobbling off, the Ogle on his tail, he'd make another attempt to explain to Iset he was trying to help her and hope he didn't get himself killed while doing it.

"I need specifics on the Protector, Gray. I need to know what she's up to so I can get ahead of her."

Gray responded immediately. "I've already been working on that very thing. She appears to have a network she's working with. They communicate through a secured data transmission."

"A group of runners?"

"Likely, but I can't confirm that since I didn't have time to decrypt the communications. However, I had one of my Ogles follow the data stream to one of the sources."

"This better be good news, Gray, because I'm having a really bad night." Before he finished speaking a visual appeared in front of him of man with micro circuitry strewn throughout his body. "A cyborg? Who is he?"

"I'm running a facial recognition program now. I'll have that answer in…Have it. His name is…or rather was… Rah'bel. Records indicate he's dead. Hmm, seems somebody needs to update their records. He's called Orion these days."

"Good work, Gray," the man with no name said, "I'll take it from here. For the time being I won't go after the woman because I have a tail on my butt." His fingers unconsciously gripped the hilt of the sword.

"Your bio-readings are off the chart. Are you sure you're in any shape to continue?" Gray asked with concern in his voice.

"I'll manage."

"Good. Stay in touch," Gray said.

"Stop saying that!"

Gray laughed.

The man with no name had a serious problem. He had to help the Protector without looking as if that was his intention. If it became known to Eden Night, she might use Iset to get to him. Luckily, Gray had already established the fictitious background for him by putting out the word he was working a bounty to capture Iset. He'd have to play the role of a ruthless pursuer until she delivers her mysterious package.

Regaining some strength, he lifted the sword up and carefully examined the blade. It was as beautiful and dangerous as the woman who'd almost killed him. He'd have to give the weapon back to her and return the favor. He glanced around. Somewhere hiding in the shadows she watched him.

"Let's see if you can keep up," he said, as he himself disappeared into the darkness.

*   *   *

Night observed him inspecting her sword, before he sank into the shadows. She nursed the bruise on her forehead feeling warm moisture—her blood. It stung with her touch and she grinned. It had been a long time since she'd felt the sensation of pain. She had underestimated Noname, a mistake she wouldn't repeat. "I will have my sword back bounty hunter and then I'll slay you as you deserve," she whispered.

*   *   *

With the passage of hours came a magnificent morning, making it difficult for him but not impossible to keep to the shadows. Positioning himself far from any internal detection sensors Orion might possess, he waited for him to line up with the sight of his tranq gun. The Ogle had led the man with no name directly to the cyborg. Despite himself he had to admit that without Gray's tech, the job of finding Orion would have been much harder.

Like him, the cyborg was dressed in all black, bore dark goggles and had a backpack strapped over his shoulders. He wondered briefly if Orion now transported the package he had seen in Iset's hands hours ago. *Smart*, he thought, while everyone is in search of the girl, her toy playmate carried out the real mission. In the meantime he had a mission of his own.

Earlier, he'd loaded a dart filled with a cocktail of specialized psychotropic drugs and Nano-Rectifiers. Gray had explained the former had been designed to make someone suggestible to commands while the latter temporarily overwrote the CPU integrated circuits. Perfect for controlling someone who's half-human and half-machine.

Orion, to the man with no name's fortune, had been travelling the streets as if in search of something or someone. Tranqing the cyborg at the apartment where he'd found him a few hours ago would have been problematic with someone hot on his tail. However Orion now being out in the open was perfect. By the time the gun made a puff sound, the dart had already hit its mark. The cyborg froze in his tracks as the serum worked its way into his nervous system.

Pressing a device attached to his wrist, the man with no name said, "Lift up your right leg." Orion bent his right limb raising his knee level to his stomach. The serum had done its job the cyborg was under his full control. He didn't like that he had to do, but the woman with the crimson eyes left little choice. He had a role to play and he'd see it all the way through.

After ordering Orion to continue with whatever mission he was doing, the man with no name set out to find Iset. He'd worked hard to give the appearance of someone trying to lose a stalker since his encounter with Night and hoped she caught sight of his actions with Orion.

*   *   *

Iset bounced around the City rarely staying in one place long. It took him a great deal of time before he caught up to her. That was a good thing because if he had difficulties so would anyone else who might be after her. The Protector sailed through the air propelled by her boots headed toward South Avenue.

The Ogle's 360 degree aerial view had pinpointed Night's hiding position. She observed him while he observed Iset. He pressed the command unit on his wrist summoning Orion to his current position. The deception he was about to be performed had to be perfect.

"Showtime," he whispered.

"About time, friend," Gray said.

"Get out of my head." The man with no name bolted into action, leaping from one rooftop to the next closing in on Iset's flight path. He avoided the shadows wanting to be spotted by anyone who could see. Because he was still fighting off the effects of the Fragmented jumps he'd gotten winded by the time he came up behind the Protector.

She yelled, "Trailed," and whirled around to face him.

He balled his hand and took an exaggerated swing connecting with her throat, pulling his blow to avoid doing any serious damage to the girl. There he was thinking of her as a girl again.

The sun beat on his back putting her in the wake of his looming shadow. She clutched at her neck staring at him with wet eyes filled with fear and pain. He slowly drew his pistol attempting to impart even more terror in her. He needed Iset to believe he was there to kill her.

She twisted away, falling against the skid of the rooftop. "Because the asshole who is trailing me has been watching us for months," she said obviously talking to someone on her comm.

Trailing her for months? He recalled Night saying something about tracking the girl for weeks. He guessed that Iset and her network of friends had mistaken the tall woman for him. As she retreated, rambling on with someone on her comm, he said nothing, taking occasional steps forward to ensure she didn't move too far away.

Finally, she directed her attention toward him. "What do you want?"

"Nothing," the man with no name whispered. "Just doing my job." *A job I'm not being paid for*, he thought, scowling.

She got to her feet and back away slowly. "Then let's have some fun then, because you either kill me or you let me go. Capture is not an option."

He was starting to like her. He took another two steps in her direction and she froze in place, her gaze focusing on something above him. Orion hovered in the air pointing two pistols, one trained on Iset, the other on him. She looked totally baffled as she stared down the barrel of the weapon held by her friend.

The man with no name laughed, he purposely let the blinking control panel on his wrist be seen by the girl.

"What did you...?" she said before he cut her off.

"Let the fun begin kid," he said, thinking how corny that must have sounded. He fired a wild shot at her and then yelled, "Kill her, Orion!"

The cyborg opened up with the pistols. He'd been programmed to make his shots come as close as possible without actually harming his friend. The man with no name tossed a few marble sized stun grenades into the fray for extra measures. It would give a light show, some smoke and make a lot of noise but not much else. His intentions weren't to harm the girl after all.

Eventually he decided to take a step back and let Iset and Orion duke it out, allowing himself time to assess whether Eden Night would try to take advantage of the situation while he was distracted. He doubted it, but he couldn't exactly tell himself why.

After a short tussle, Iset turned to him. "You did this! You messed with his bio-tech and turned him!"

"Yes ma'am, it was simple too. One hit with an injection serum and he's my friend now."

"Wow, that was over the top," Gray chimed in.

Ignoring him, he went on. "No foul to you kid. Just doing my job."

She made a play to come after him but was blocked by her friend. Iset screamed in pain as Orion stomped down on her booted ankle.

The man with no name grimaced. Gray's tech must have malfunctioned, the cyborg wasn't supposed to harm her in any way. He wanted to put a stop to the struggle, yet as long as Night watched him he couldn't. The cultist image appeared as he accessed the Ogle shadowing her. Her hood and cloak fluttering in the wind like a malevolent phantom. He tried not to notice her ample breasts, small waist, wide hips, and muscular physique but not too hard.

Distracted, he hadn't notice that Iset dodged her cyborg friend until after she had closed in on him. She'd been slowed to a certain extent by her bad leg, though she was still fast. Her first blow to his face couldn't be avoided, the impact of the punch lessened by the durable micro-filaments of his mask. It could withstand a bullet striking it from ten feet away. He feigned shock. Again he was impressed with her skill as she disarmed him of his gun sending it flying to the other end of the roof.

The man with no name hastily retrieved another gun. Orion in the meantime came up behind Iset walloping her with a series of blows. Thankfully whatever programming glitch the cyborg had suffered earlier seemed to have corrected itself, because his hits were causing little damage.

Again, she slapped his second weapon out of his hand and then moved away to face her friend in combat. Woman and cyborg circled each other until she shouted, "Orion... it's me and you, always friend. I'll never desert a friend."

"But I am not a threat to you," the cyborg responded all the while continuing his assault on her.

"Whatever he did, I'll fix it, I promise, just forgive me for this," she pleaded.

"Always Iset," Orion replied warmly, simultaneously raising his pistol, aiming the weapon directly at her face. The glitch obviously hadn't righted itself or another one had taken its place.

Pressing a button on his wrist control panel, the man with no name stopped the cyborg from pulling the trigger at the last second, freezing him in place. To get her attention back to him before she understood what he had done, he said, "Whatever you do kid, don't run. That's boring."

"Well that's a smug thing to say," Gray offered.

"Screw you," she barked, and then she surprised him by revealing a Pulse gun she had pulled out of the folds of her jumper suit.

Two bolts of energy were emitted from her weapon. Instead of doing the logical thing which should have been taking down the immediate threat standing before her--the blasts from her gun whizzed by Orion's shoulder and stuck the man with no name in the chest.

Knocked off his feet he tumbled to the ground with a grunt of pain. All the air had been forced out of his lungs. Two patches of smoke rose up from his upper torso where he'd been hit. If he hadn't been wearing protective armor he wouldn't be alive.

With him out of the way she concentrated on her frozen friend still not realizing the cyborg had been temporarily immobilized. She opened fired on him, tears pouring down her face as she done so. The blast's impact caused the cyborg's finger around the trigger of his gun to jerk.

Superficial pulse burns appeared on Iset's leg and shoulder as a result. Ignoring her pain she expertly bobbed and weaved around. Her Kicks propulsion jettisoned her forward toward Orion. She coiled her body around his, grabbing hold of the cyborg's head and neck. His skull was torn away from the rest of his body spewing a fusion of bio-fluid and blood. His body remained standing still holding the gun firing wildly. She performed a backflip landing smoothly on her feet in front of him, then lifted a leg and swirled. Her foot slammed into Orion's chest. He buckled to his knees, the gun clanging to the rooftop.

Fatigued from her efforts, she crumbled to all fours beside her friend. Her gaze proceeded to Orion's motionless body, and then inclined toward the head his eyes blinked and his mouth opened and closed continually. She squeezed her own eyes tight for long seconds. When she opened them they settled on the man with no name with pure hatred.

He hoped that anger didn't translate to murder because as much as he wanted to help her he would put her down before he'd allowed himself to be killed. She crawled toward him, grabbed his arm snatching the blinking control panel from his wrist. She smashed the device down onto the concrete, busting it into smithereens.

She poked him in his chest. "Thanks for the pieces. I'm going to figure out what you did and correct it. But one thing, whatever the bounty price is on my head, I'll pay you triple to kill who is after me, plus extra to keep me off the list. Deal?"

He pricked up, thinking, *Maybe this freebie just changed into a major payday.* Then she had to ruin his good mood. Iset slapped him.

His arm shot up automatically before he realized what he'd done. He gripped his fingers around her thin neck cutting off her air. She scratched at his limb but could do no damage through his thick leather coat.

"If you agree show yourself in the market," she gasped. She added, "That is all I'll need to see of you. Until then…"

He loosened his grip enough for her to pull herself free; instead she used the opportunity to reel back and slammed her fist into his face. He was really getting tired of her hitting him. The possibility of a payday kept him from punching her back. He let his arm go limp, freeing her neck.

She backpedaled moving quickly away. When she turned to check on her cyborg friend he took that as he opportunity to make his stealthy exit. He leapt off the roof onto another.

"Did your device get it?" he asked.

"Everything has been recorded just as you requested. It'll be uploaded to the web in a few seconds. I'll edit out that bit of where she wants to meet you later," Gray answered. "Do you think everyone after her will get the point of your little performance?"

"The footage will prove Iset's moniker as the Protector is well suited. If she was tough enough to defeat the mysterious hunter, Noname, I'm sure others will have second thoughts before taking her on."

"Wow, you used a whole two sentences to explain that."

"Get out of my head, Gray. I still have one other problem to deal with."

"And that leads me to what I have to tell you next." His tone had gone serious. "The Ogle has lost track of Night. Almost as if she knew she was being watched."

"Great. That's all I needed right now."

The man with no name was midway through a jump between one rooftop to the next when Night came out of nowhere. She collided with him in the air. Both man and woman plunged downward in a spiral. They smashed heavily against passing jet cars in a tangle and legs and arms.

"You have something of mine and I want it back," she shouted.

He reached out with one arm, grabbing hold of a support beam for railcars almost dislocating his shoulder. He grunted in pain but held tight. Night clung to him with a hand and using the other to search his body.

"You're crazy," he said, "We could have both fallen to our deaths."

"Death is only another phase of our being. I have no fear of it," she shot back.

"Okay, good to know," he said, then head-butted her. Her grip was gone but not for long. She'd slipped down clinging to one of his legs. With his free arm he reached inside his coat and pulled out the item she wanted. "Were you looking for this?"

Her eyes went wide and wild. "Give it to me!"

He dropped the sword. "Oops."

Her gaze followed it all the way down to the streets below. "My rapier!"

"Guess you better go and fetch it then," he said, and then kicked her solidly in the face.

She grunted and fell.

The metal support made a loud crunch and twisted into an abnormal shape in his grasp. He glanced up in time to see it give fully away. He too plummeted toward the ground. His Stetson flew loose from his head and floated down in a slow descent while gravity had a much greater effect on him.

His vision went black and breath rushed out of his lungs once again as he thudded on top of a public air transportation bus leaving a huge man sized crater in the surface. When he finally regained his senses the first thing he noticed was a hilt of a sword pointing skyward, the metal blade rooted deeply into the bus's roof. Beyond the weapon, Eden Night, sprawled on her back, stared indignantly back at him.

"We really have to stop…meeting like this," he said. After a long intense silence she burst out into laughter and so had he. The man with no name couldn't recall the last time he genuinely laughed.

She sat up, wiping a tear from her eye. "I want you to know I didn't believe a bit of that act you put on with the Protector," she said.

He pushed himself up. "The message wasn't exactly for you. To be honest I expected to have killed you by now."

She stood upright, yanked the sword out of the bus's rooftop and examined the blade. "I believed you were after the woman for money, but it wasn't that at all. Is she a friend?"

He shook his head. "Never met her."

"Then why?"

"I thought she needed my protection," he explained, then glanced up in the general direction of where he last saw Iset. "She didn't."

"I have misjudged you. I've considered you a dishonorable man."

"You weren't wrong." He snatched the rifle off his back and pointed his weapon at her.

They stared at each other without speaking for a long time, neither showing any indication they wanted to fight. Sirens off in the distance snapped them out of their trance.

She returned her sword to its sheath. "Because I sought revenge for those you have dispatched instead fulfilling my duty of capturing the Protector, the Edict has excommunicated me. I'm now being hunted by the one I had so faithfully served." She look down at her feet, ashamed, and then back up at him. "You have nothing to fear from me."

"Well that's anti-climactic," Gray interjected.

"If we cross paths again, I cannot guarantee that you'll have nothing to fear from me," he explained without malice.

She smiled. "I'm not sure if that was meant as a threat or something else."

The sirens grew closer.

He slung the rifle on his back. "Guess there's only

one way to find out." He turned his back to her.

"Before we depart," she said, halting him. "What is your real name?"

He glanced over his shoulder. "I don't know," he answered forlornly before leaping off the side of the air bus.

*   *   *

The man with no name found a place to hold up for a couple of hours to rest. He still wasn't one hundred percent but felt better than he had since making his third Fragmented jump. Standing in front of the mirror, he pulled off his mask. Deprived of a name for years, he refused to give himself a new one. He stared into the reflective glass wondering if he'd ever remember who he really was.

Not understanding the cause of his memory loss was the worst part. Years ago he woke up in a desolate field of blood and bones where a major battle had been fought. Bodies littered the ground with skin covered with burns and deep gashes. Somehow, he avoided those same injuries, except for a small cut that ran level just above his left eyebrow. It had been surgically cleaned and stitched. He left that battlefield without knowing why he'd been there or who he was.

Bending, he scooped up water from the basin, he splashed his bruised face--Iset and Eden had done a number on his battered body. Grabbing a towel, he dried himself and then gazed into the mirror. Noir Gray's grinning reflection stared back and said, "Time to go collect your money for your good deed."

The man with no name frowned sourly. "Stay out of my head, Gray."

Street Moon's Revolution

by
Valjeanne Jeffers

*And if you ever see my shadow it'll be the last thing
you see. Believe that.*

She rose at dusk, a dark brown woman with
cropped hair, midnight eyes, and full lips a shade darker than
her face. She was a muscular young woman, tight some would
say. Her nimble muscles looked as though they were chiseled
by the hand of a skilled and loving sculptor. She dressed in
clinging black trousers, and a sleeveless black shirt.

Street Moon clipped her gear-belt around her
waist, and walked through the round enclave of her living
quarters to the lift. A laser rifle and sword hung from a mesh
holster round her waist, and she wore a thin breast-plate
designed to stop bullets . . . or at the least slow them down.
A cube was embedded in her left nostril, and the tips of her
ears were pierced, each with a chain strung through a second
earring in her lobe. On both wrists bracelets of onyx firestones
and tiger's eye glittered; the marks of the men and women
she'd killed.

She pulled the lift gate back and rode the lift to
the ground floor. The young woman got out and walked down
a long foyer of circular lights. Monitors hummed and blinked
as she headed for the exit.

Once the door slid back, the stench hit her nose
. . . the ripe funky odor of garbage, rancid cooking meat, and
unwashed bodies. Ten miles behind her the conical spirals of
the Apunu Hives rose against the sky. The River traversed the
East and Westside, more than a hundred watery tributaries
flowed from it; guarded by its ever vigilant human and Borg
acolytes: The River Rats. Further to the West lay the deadly

Ward 251, the prison without walls that even an assassin as skilled and lethal as Street Moon avoided.

I should move. I can afford better . . . Maybe to a cleaner borough on the Northside.

Yet the tall, lean steepled buildings of the Southside stretched beyond the dark clouds reaching for the twilight, kissed by the darkness with a soft ambiance. There was beauty here, a familiarity that she found comforting. Besides, she did most of her hunting on the Southside, tracking Runners. Runners, those who'd had their *tell* removed freeing them from the Wave, often chose to cut through the Southside to escape to the River and the Lush, a fabled paradise that lay outside the City, if one could survive the dreaded Beyond. . .

Damn fools! Who wants to be cut off from the Wave? It's like a baby being cut off its mama's. . .

The Southside was her home, and she would never leave. *They say the Lush is on the other side of the Beyond—that if you can survive the monsters you find yourself in a place with no filth, real air, real sun and no eyes watching you . . . no Wave. But talk is cheap. What's over there might be no better than right here. I trust biosteel, lasers, blood. That's real. Not some dream whispered in the streets. I'm staying right here.*

I met Sly here. Just one cyber-block over. He said the Lush was real. He said he'd been there, and he was gonna take me one day. Before he left me for Abeekay. She bit her lip, as the bitter memories washed over her. Sly had wooed her, not an easy thing to do, loved her, made *her* love him; and then dumped her.

I want a drink. I want to forget.

He said the Lush dwellers are still on his back for leaving, and telling other folks about it. They want him bad. . . But imma give it to him. Him and his woman.

By sheer will, she pushed her musings aside then made her way up the street. Her eyes fell upon a tall decrepit tenement across the street then shifted to the building adjacent to it. It looked brand new. Fresh biosteel shined under the cyberlights that had just flicked on.

Huh? When did they replace it? I don't remember . . . ?

A young mother wearing tattered clothing, and her two children emerged from the squalid domicile. As they stepped outside, the crumbling edifice shuddered, the outside walls stretching like a woman's belly in the last months of pregnancy.

The building vanished, along with the woman and her children.

There were screams from the window and the streets, the citizens gesticulating frantically.

"Did you *see* it?" a man beside her said, his eyes wide. "I *knew* it! I *told* my wife they did shit like this!"

Street Moon couldn't answer. She gawked at the now empty lot, her heart pounding a drumbeat, and swallowed the gorge threatening to rise in her throat. She'd heard of the City making modifications like these, but she'd never really believed it. Until that moment.

Why? Why would they do *this?*

Moon remembered the whispers. *Population control,* some said. *Genetic cleansing,* said others; purging the City's inhabitants of those who didn't meet their standards. Or perhaps, and this made her feel somehow worse than the first two, perhaps the woman had just been in the wrong place during this techno-*renovation.* What sterile, innocuous words for something so horrific.

I'm doing good. I got a place to live. There's plenty that don't. The City takes care of me. Let the rest do for themselves. . . I'm. . .I'm. . .Let them. . .Let me. . .

Linked in. Tied to The Wave. Enslaved. No choices. No options. Live the life they choose for you. Don't ask questions. Don't fight back.

"It's not my *problem!*" She turned her back to the gathering crowd. *Nothing I can do about it.*

On her belt her crystal tracker buzzed. Her target was close.

Under a violet night sky, Street Moon peered from around the side of the edifice, and then melted back into the shadows. The night was warm; it was always warm on the Southside. The lithe woman sauntered through the biosteel streets and structures, her movements as sleek and graceful as a feline. She was in her element now. Night was when she came alive with the hunt . . . becoming one with the darkness.

Street Moon's tracker buzzed again and she pulled it from her belt. A blinking arrow appeared in the center, pointing southeast.

She clipped her tracker back to her waist and followed the direction of the arrow. She passed two non-humans skulking in the shadows: a Cypeek, his long pointed head and bulging eyes glittering in the shadows; and a voluptuous cyborg, her shapely body encased in translucent red. The cyborg turned up a tin of ooze, guzzled it and then handed it to her companion. A long tongue snaked from his pucked mouth, sucking the ooze from the tin. The cyborg was half-human (she was drinking ooze after all) and half-machine. Judging from her dress, she was probably a pleasure borg. Suddenly, Street Moon longed for a taste of ooze, and for tranquility that came with it.

But she was hunting. She couldn't afford to drift away on a cloud of bliss. She needed her wits about her. Needed to be upbeat. On edge.

Later. When I 'm finished.

Just ahead music played—upbeat with a fusillade of horns, song and drums. On her right, she spotted four teenagers dancing in an alleyway. The youngsters, two boys, two girls looked to be anywhere between fifteen and sixteen. The evidence of their upgrades shimmered on their faces, heads and legs: pulsing multi-colored skin. All of them wore colorful loose clothing and favored kinky long hair.

Where they'd gotten the money for the

enhancements was anybody's guess. They might be the children of upscale citizens, who were slumming it. Or the upgrades could be homegrown—and therefore dangerous. Bootleg tech-parts were very popular among teenagers, who were too young to know better.

She watched them, her feet rooted to the biometal pavement, losing herself for a moment in the music—in the sheer beauty of their movements. Had she ever felt so free?

They're young. Too young know fear. Too young to understand the City and how it can eat you alive. But they'll learn.

The music radiated from a tall, gyrating brown boy's head . . . blasting through his dreads in the top of his head. A young girl beside him cupped her hands, sending a blast of translucent static over the other two youngsters. It suffused their wiry bodies . . . and then separated into holograms of the teenagers. Now there *were* six youngsters—two dancing in perfect unison with their human twins. The boy with music upgrade switched to slow motion-time and did a graceful back flip . . . landing in languid funky rhythm.

Sly Sincere's face suddenly appeared before her eyes. He loved to dance too. She remembered him pulling her close down in his...in their... rhythm. God she missed him . . . missed his touch, his smile. Another vision—this one of Sly and her former best friend, Abeekay, now his wife—flashed before her eyes and her lips curled back in a snarl.

Time to go. Time to hunt. Time to kill.

The two-inch screen at her waist buzzed. Her tracker had picked up the signal of Easy Rider, the runner she'd been paid to kill.

There he is!

Her target was heavily muscled and sugar-brown with dreadlocks. He was dressed in black, and wore combat boots. If she'd hazard a guess, Moon would say his boots been specially treated. He stood between the two buildings across from her. She considered using her laser, but decided against it. A dart would make a clean kill, and wouldn't disfigure the target.

She ducked inside a niche of the building next to her before Easy Rider could spot her, and peeked around the corner of the building. She loved hunting on the South-side with its high, faux wood buildings. It reminded her of something, someplace . . . or maybe an old song . . . *The Duplex.* A sizzle erupted in her ear, making her jump. *What the* hell? She hit her ear with the heel of her hand. Was it the last upgrade to her boots? Bad enhancements could infect your brain, throwing the Wave.

No time for worries now. I'll get 'em checked out later.

Her long fingers brought the dart blow-gun to her lips. The man's nostrils twitched. He'd smelled her! *Damn implants!*

She blew the dart and he fell forward— catching himself on his hands like a man about to do a set of push-ups. The dart soared over him, missing him, and continued harmlessly into the alley behind him. In the next instant, he'd leaped up, and whirled about— a running flash of black and brown—and darted into the mouth of the alleyway.

Street Moon pursued him, her own kick-boots sparking the bio-pavement, dropping her dart gun in mesh bag on her waist, and pulling her rifle from her holster in one smooth motion. With her enhanced boots and natural athletic prowess she was unstoppable. Nobody could outrun her. *Nobody.*

She cleared the alleyway and found Easy Rider standing in the middle of the alley waiting for her. *Oh, so he wants to fight?* Her full lips turned up in warrior's smile. She was skilled in a myriad of martial arts, and weapons.

Easy Rider had just committed suicide.

He began chanting in a low, bass voice: "*Sa se pou ou. Mwen prale san ou.*" Words she recognized from her Haitian grandmother: This is for you. . . I'm going without you.
. .

Oh no! He's a Bard!

The air suddenly smelled clean and fresh.

Easy Rider vanished. And a hulking shadow blocked her path.

The Indigo colored creature was hairless and had thick arms and legs. It was dressed in a white tunic and trousers. It wore a carved medallion round its neck (a neck roughly the size of small tree trunk) the symbol of its tribe and gender. This one was male. Razor sharp claws tipped the ends of its meaty hands. His single delicate feature was his green feline eyes, now glittering with intellect... and rage.

A Fudokiht. Hence the smell.

Street Moon had never seen an angry Fudokiht. They were gentle, slow-witted and plodding creatures, and only attacked if they felt threatened. If menaced, their intellect and speed tended to increase *mighty* fast.

This one looked mad as hell. If she let him get too close he would rip her head off with his bare hands.

The creature lumbered toward her. He was *big,* bigger than it should have been, and *fast.* She raised her laser rifle. The Fudokiht roared, and charged straight for her, razor claws extended for the kill. She fired at point blank range. In the same instant the creature lunged. The shot nicked the corner of its head off. It didn't even slow down. The Fudokiht roared once more and kept coming, greenish blood trickling down its face.

It's amped up on something!

She turned, and raced toward the edifice ahead with the Fudokiht on her heels reattaching her laser to her waist as she ran. Coming abreast of an edifice, Moon leaped and caught the metal banister and lifted her lower body, barely missing the thing's claws. She braced her feet against the grip and scaled it. The Fudokiht let out another ear splitting howl and its lips curled back from its razor sharp teeth. It began to scale the building. Damn thing looked to weigh 300 pounds, and it was all muscle.

In the minutes she fired once and again with her laser—hitting it in the chest and head. The Fudokiht kept on coming. *That's not possible!*

Then she did the unexpected. That's why she was the best. Five years on the South-side, a broken heart, and the name of *Street Moon* was still an urban legend.

She jerked her sword from her waist and scrambled atop the railing. Street Moon stood with her back to the Fudokiht, dropped and landed on his shoulders, her thighs around its neck. Before he had time to react, she leaned back and pulled the edge against its throat. The laser cut through his neck like butter.

The assassin leaped off Fudokiht's shoulders as it toppled to the ground, giving it a wide berth, kicking the head out of the way.

The Fudokiht vanished.

With a pounding head, the young woman stared down at the now empty space where the creature had fallen. Distractedly, she pulled a cloth out of the mesh bag on her waist and wiped her sword clean, as was her a habit. But this time there was no blood.

What the hell *just happened?*

She'd just spent the better part of an hour fighting something that wasn't even there. The night was a bust. Her target was long gone by now— probably halfway to the River. No help for it now.

I need a drink.

She was a foul mood. She cut through the alleyway, half-hoping some ill fool would start a fight so she'd have an excuse to kill something. Moon walked the half-block to *The Maniac*. A beam pulled away from the building. For an instant it was only a shaft of wood. Then the wood morphed into the shape of woman and crept into the alleyway behind the assassin.

The Maniac was a bar that doubled as pleasure unit. The front of the joint sold ooze; in a back room of the nightspot patrons could buy time with male and female pleasure Borgs. Patrons could rent one for an hour or two or for the night. But Borgs could be dangerous. You never knew where their loyalties lay.

Real don't always mean *real. Dig it?*

An image of her ex, Sly Sincere, pushed his way inside her head, and she walked a little faster, wishing with all her might she could stop thinking about him for good. The ooze helped but it was temporary fix.

Once you body him and his bitch the pain will be gone for good.

Street Moon walked into the conclave joint with its revolving crystal bar. Fiberglass tables, soft drums and bass from plasma sound system greeted her arrival. She took a seat at the bar. At the table closest to her a heavy-set mercenary, Fly Guy, glared at her. She'd taken most of his customers away. She also refused to sleep with him. Both, in his eyes, cardinal sins.

Fly Guy nodded at the mesh bag on her waist. "What you doing bringing that thing in here? You stinkin' up the place."

She met his eyes and he drew back from her assassin's smile. "Nobody would notice, dig it? 'Cause you in here." His two companions chuckled. Fly Guy scowled, but said no more. He didn't want it with Street. She killed for fun.

She turned to the bar keep. "Fresh suds." *I was walkin' barefoot down a country road . . .* out of the blue the thought thrust itself upon her mind. She rubbed her forehead with the heel of her hand, as if to scrub the thought away.

An image blossomed in her mind . . . *Of her and Sly strolling together, arms about one another's waists and him suddenly pulling her into his embrace . . . pulling her to him with those big muscled arms that always smelled like persimmons, the result of all his upgrades, lifting her up, and her throwing her arms around his neck. He would never let her go. They would make babies together . . . even though the City was no place to make babies. . .*

Street Moon thrust the vignette away and truculently pounded on the bar. "Can I get some *service?"*

The owner of *The Maniac,* MoDupe, stepped behind the bar and tapped his bar keep on shoulder, signaling that he wanted to take over. MoDupe slid a blue florescent tankard of ooze in front of Street. She picked it up, took a long swallow and breathed with relief as her pain receded to a dull ache. She could feel all her worries washing away . . . almost see them floating beneath her stool before her anxiety disappeared . . . For now.

MoDupe, a caramel-colored, slender man with a braided reddish goatee leaned on the bar. "You been busy tonight?" He watched her with eyes that changed with his mood, hazel, brown, indigo, or sometimes a combination of two.

Street sipped her ooze, savoring the calm now coursing deliciously through her veins. "I stay busy."

"What's the matter baby?"

"Who says anything's wrong?"

"It just looks like you're having a bad night."

"A Fudokiht attacked me on the way over," Moon replied.

MoDupe furrowed his brow, looking concerned, and stroked his goatee. "Wow, that's *heavy!* What did you do to it?"

Street shook her head, anger and confusion shifting on her brown face. "I didn't *do* anything. He just appeared outta nowhere and came at me."

"Then you must have wandered into his territory."

"I haven't told you the best part. After I killed him, he disappeared."

MoDupe eyebrows rose. "Come again?"

Street Moon told him what happened, and he chuckled. "You ran into a Bard with some *serious* skills. He conjured up a big old bad hologram, that's what he did." He leaned in closer. "But I'm glad to see you're alright. You should take a few days off, spend some time with me."

She sighed, suddenly she felt tired. "Look, MoDupe, you good people. We had some fun together. Let's just leave it at that, okay?"

"You still hung up on Sly?" he said softly. "Why don't you let another man be sweet to you? A man like me?"

She smiled. "You wanna tangle with me again? Last time I almost broke your back."

He grinned back. "I enjoyed every minute of it."

A howl from Fly Guy jerked her attention away. She followed his terror-stricken gaze to the shimmering wall across from her seat.

It was moving . . . growing an assortment of arms and legs.

"WATCHERS!" a voice shrilled.

"MoDupe. . .you have been found guilty. . . of selling. . . Purge," a halting non-human voice intoned. The voice was flat. Dead. It was the sound of machine coming from the fluorescent woman standing between two shimmering males. All three had emerged from the wall of the *Maniac "It is the judgement of the City that you be executed."*

Street Moon turned eyes wide with disbelief to MoDupe. *Purge.* Ooze that had been reconfigured to remove a citizen's Tell . . . to disconnect a citizen from the Wave. In the City, the sentence for making or selling Purge was death.

She shook her head and at the same time pulled her laser and leveled it at his chest.

The female Watcher honed her bone-colored eyes on the assassin. *"Citizen,"* she went on in her hideous disembodied voice, *"this is not your concern. We will deal with him. Stand aside."*

With lightning speed, the assassin whirled and put a laser bullet through one of the Watcher's multicolored eyes, and in quick succession shot the other two flanking her.

It wouldn't kill them, only slow them down. No one knew how to kill Watchers—if they *could* be killed. Screams exploded around her, folks scurrying past them out the door. When she looked back at MoDupe, his face was covered with black lenses. He threw a canister over the bar.

It spun on the floor, and huge, opaque clouds of purple smoke rose, blinding her. She felt powerful arms lifting her, pulling her across the bar . . . shoving her down into a tiny hatch she couldn't see, but she could feel the walls on either side. And there was darkness and fresh air. The young woman made out the staircase before her and hurriedly descended the stairs, MoDupe on her heels. They reached a wet leveled-out street of biostone, hemmed in by walls of cinder.

Street Moon grabbed him by his throat and shoved him up against the wall. "I oughta kill you for getting me involved in this shit! I'm on their radar now—a *hunted* woman!" *All the time I put in! All the folks I dropped! And for* what? *To wind up a splatter on the wall myself!*

"If they hadn't been so busy looking for me, they would've executed you by midnight," MoDupe said calmly.

She narrowed her dark eyes, confusion swirled about her face. "What's *that* supposed to mean?"

"I've been feeding you Purge."

She snarled and pushed her laser against his chest, curling her finger around the trigger. MoDupe kept still and searched her face. "The memories of a country road, the bursts of static . . . that's from the Purge I've been feeding you. I'm breaking you *out,* baby. *Liberating* you. If only for a moment. So, you can *see.* "

She let her hand drop and turned her back to him. "I didn't ask you for this, MoDupe! I didn't ask you for any of it! This is my life! You had no *right!* " The last word was a sob. "You knew him didn't you—Easy Rider? You knew what she did! You set me up! And I thought you were my friend!"

"I *am* your friend!" MoDupe shot back. "He wanted to kill you. Can you dig it? *Body* you, baby!"

"I ain't that easy to kill!" she snarled.

MoDupe smiled humorously. "Sho' you right, Street. You're the best out there. No doubt. But even you can't take on five or six Runners. I talked him out of it. So, Easy Rider conjured up a hologram instead, to get you off him."

"Why me? What they got against me," She turned to face him, her brown eyes shinning with something very near to hurt. "I ain't the only one hunting Runners."

"Are you for real?" MoDupe shook his head. "Baby, you been dropping Runners like cyber-insects—you take down more folks in a month than some do in a year. Ever since Sly."

"What you go bringing him into this for?"

"Ever wonder why you can't forget him?" MoDupe said softly, "why your pain has become an unnatural ache?"

Street Moon flinched. For a long moment she was silent. "It's an open wound that won't close up," she finally whispered. "No matter how much ooze I drink, his face is all I see. He's all I think about."

MoDupe held her gaze with his strange, impassioned eyes, eyes now a deep color of violet and brown. "The Wave took what you felt and magnified it a hundred times over. Because they want him dead too. He's been to Lush! He's got the City *and* the Lush dwellers pissed at him. They been using you to get to him."

A screeching rumble shook the walls. "The Watchers," she shouted, "they're *coming!*"

MoDupe held her gaze. "Let me finish what I started."

Street Moon hesitated for only a moment. She held out her arm.

He pulled a spike from his pocket, dashed forward and stuck it in her arm—mainlining the Purge through her system. Street Moon fainted and MoDupe caught her. The cement walls rippled, melting as he hurried down the passageway through a labyrinth of interconnected tunnels.

Cradling her in his arms MoDupe raced down the maze. . . Now he used the implants in his legs and feet, hidden enhancements that were only revealed through his eyes. He picked up speed . . . twenty miles per hour . . . thirty miles per hour . . . a brown Juggernaut of swiftness and flight, Street Moon bouncing in his arms as he turned left, then right.

The walls on either side of him shifted and undulated, and four Watchers stepped forth.

MoDupe cried a staccato: *"Ase-Ase-Ase!"* and an archway appeared, a doorway swung open. He leaped through it, and it shut behind him. Behind him the Watchers hissed in mechanical static of rage . . . and began their assault upon the door.

With her still in his arms, MoDupe leaped once more—booted feet pumping. He was airborne now, traversing time and space . . . passing the towering edifices of the City, the River shimmering beneath them.

He touched down before tall building calling again: *"Ase-Ase-Ase!"* A doorway appeared swung open and he entered the Temple of the Bards.

Street Moon awoke beneath a whirling fan. She turned her head to look at the room, the only part of her body she felt like moving. Multicolored strings of beads hung from an arched entrance to her left. But the room was without windows. It resembled a dim comfortable cave with woven clothes of rich mauve, greens and gold. The sweet fragrance of sandalwood floated on the air. The smell evoked memories that danced at the edge of her mind.

"Where am I?" she whispered. "Where's MoDupe?"

"Right here, baby," he leaned over her, his face very close to hers and whispered. "Warrior woman, the ancestors got a bone to pick with you, eh?" He stepped back against a woven quilt.

"No—don't go!"

The broad, elderly face of a woman suddenly hovered over her, her honey-colored eyes serene and kind, yet animated. She stroked Moon's forehead with a heavy, soft hand.

"Shhh baby," she said, in a voice like warm honey, "Mama Salt is here, and the Street Priests gonna be right along." With this Mama Salt, still stroking Moon's forehead began humming a singsong tune.

Street Priests?

MoDupe picked up a djembe, the *talking drum,* from the floor then began beating it with the heels of his hand. Along the wall, men wearing dark shades with thick kinky hair appeared. Some held djembes, others myriad-colored rattles, and *sanza.* . . Their music blended with their chanting: "Wo-man. . .Black wo-man. . .Wo-man. . .Ase. . .Ase. . ."

Mama Salt sang, her voice in synergy with them. Now Street Moon could pick out words, fey yet familiar in their melody. *"Sa se pa ou la. Sa se pa ou la nègès,"* This is *yours. This is yours beautiful black woman.* Mama Salt reached behind her and pulled out a pipe and puffed, blowing smoke up and down the length of Street Moon's body.

Street Moon closed her eyes once.

She awoke and found herself in water. She was in the River, leagues below the surface.

I can't breathe!

Swim down.

She headed for the bottom. . . and reached the shore. Street Moon climbed out and stood before a part of the River she'd never seen. The air smelled fresh and clear. And she knew that the Beyond lay ahead, and ahead of this: The fabled *Lush.* A land with real seasons, and moonlight. With clear air, and cities. A land where the Wave couldn't reach her.

Mama Salt appeared to her right in a folding chair, puffing upon her pipe.

"Is this real?" Street Moon asked.

"Yes and no child. This is inside your mind."

"Why are you here?"

To give you a choice."

Suddenly, Street hugged herself. "My pain . . . it's *gone.*"

The elderly woman nodded. "Yes, your agony over Sly's betrayal is gone because it was never real. The Wave magnified what you felt ten times over so that It could use you. When you return it will return, but as healthy grief. Not as an obsession to kill."

"You must decide if you want to return here. Do you understand?"

"Yes. . ." Street Moon said, gazing enrapt at the River.

"When you awaken, you can cross River to the Lush. We can show you how," Mama Salt went on. "Or you can return to The City and join the Revolution— fight beside MoDupe, free as many as you can. Or . . . you can return to the way you were before. Be the City's slave. Its executioner. It's your choice."

"Fight?"

Mama Salt nodded.

"Beside MoDupe?"

Another nod.

"I wanna go back."

Mama Salt arched an eyebrow. "For him?"

Street Moon shook her head. "Naw. For *me.* I was born to do this."

"You'll be a Runner, disconnected from the Wave. Other assassins like you, will hunt you."

"It's what I want."

Mama Salt nodded approvingly. "Then close your eyes."

When she awoke, MoDupe was sitting beside her. He smiled down at her.

"Welcome home, Street Moon. . ."

Welcome to Liberty

by
Howard Night

1.1

Never seen a mess like this and I've seen some really bad waste go down in *Liberty* or the *215* as most call it. D*own the bottom*, but not here.

"How many?" I ask. My left eye is artificial, augmented after a nasty dust up long ago that damaged my Tell. Made it impossible to receive anything through the wave and so impossible to do the job of a *Liberty* police detective. A busted Tell is supposed to mean no chance of survival in the City. So I got it replaced with a cybernetic Artificial Interface Enhancement; an A.I.E. It's not too fancy but it can tap into the wave just like my Tell and it can read the Evidence Techs running report as he updates it. Problem is he's not updating it.

"Uh…sorry…could you get a clearer scan of what's under that joop?" he asks nonchalantly.

I grimace and resist an urge to tell him to go look for himself…because he can't. So, tipping through the 'evidence', I make my way over to the old abandoned joop and peek underneath.

It's harder this time to keep my morning gelba down. "Yea…there's more under here."

"Thought so. Make sure to get at least a ninety percent scan."

"Eat waste," I mutter but forget his name. My A.I.E. records the "evidence" tossed under the old transport which looks like an old Lumbono '69. "Give me an estimate" I ask the Tech.

"Uh...sure...twenty?"

Damn! "Twenty?"

He comes over to the joop then leans down to get a good look for himself now that I've scanned it. "Probably more."

Twenty? I look about the bridge, the long under course that connects *Under the Towers* to the *Market Crossings*. Usually, about now, the morning traffic is starting to get underway. Pedestrians and joops would flow back and forth to whatever business they had but this morning we've blocked it off because not an hour or two ago somebody decided to kill and chop up over twenty people and leave their parts all over the bridge.

For about forty meters there are arms, legs and torsos strewn along the blood smeared, vented road, under the abandoned cars and jamming the gutters. Only things missing are...

"No heads." The E.T. mumbles out. "Haven't found one head, and..."

"Give it time," I say. "There's no pattern here." None my A.I.E. can see. The body parts are spread all over and bunched in clumps at times.

"Sure but," the E.T. stands up and points. "None of them are wearing clothes." I've cataloged twelve different... feet and not one shoe. Seventeen arms and not one sleeve."

He's right. "But the parts weren't just dumped here right?"

"Nope." He reaches out and his arm disappears up to his elbow. After a second he pulls it back and there's a fat gel patty in his hand which he then stuffs into his mouth. I throw him a sneer; if he were actually here instead of virtually I would have smacked that sandwich out of his hands, evidence contamination or not. He sees my look and quickly wolfs down the bite he just took.

"Blood spray clearly indicates the victims were dismembered here...alive."

Like I said; a mess. The bridge doesn't just connect to *Under the Towers* to the *Market Crossing*, there are several on and off ramps leading to other major roadways. Though only one that I'm concerned with; the old and poorly kept ramp leading to *Down the Bottom*...the "Underground", the nastiest part of the *215*. There's no way that this mess didn't start from down there.

I step across the body part ridden causeway, all the while using my A.I.E. to scan the area for more evidence. The ground metal gravel of the road is too porous for finger prints.

...can't get anything in the blood smear either even though a few are clearly foot prints...one set of boot prints.

My A.I.E. scans the print and runs it against the registry but I recognize it easy enough. HE was here. From the congealed blood beneath the print I doubt he was here during the fight. Most likely came after to see what happened here himself. He's usually not this careless when it comes to leaving evidence. Must want us to know, this time, that the *215*'s newest player is getting involved.

The E.T. walks over to me. "There's something else."

"What?" I turn and look to see the E.T. inspecting a particularly bloody foot.

"The bruises on these appendages...the look of the severed ends... I think they were ripped apart, not cut."

Ripped apart? That might mean borg...

...or worse.

Rhodes, Standing in Blood

1.2

Zero raced along the rooftops of Dire Street, feet moving so fast only her toes touched the metal tiling. She was lucky to be so close when the alert went out but knew that she wasn't the only one. The target was painted with another Negs tracker almost as soon as she tagged it herself.

Don't let it be the Celts, she thought, *anyone but them*. She could beat Isla to any runner and could outwit the D.W. Boys easy. She heard Shepard was in Gohelm so she wouldn't have to worry about her pack.

But the Celts were easily the best of them and the most ruthless. They had aspirations of making something more of themselves than just neg running and were willing to do anything to make that happen. Holcomb would agree, if they had left enough of his brain in his head for him to agree with anything.

Her tracker flared with another alert; the target tripped another sensor. Damn…she was right on top of it but the Lords might send out another bounty and that meant any neg in the vicinity not keyed into the first flag would just snatch it before she could.

She leapt when she reached the end of Dire Street, from the top of the Claims building, over the Median Square V-board, to the under hang of the Sun Road causeway. The mirrors of the causeway brought just a little bit of light to the under city of the *215* but this close, even under the road and as early in the morning as it was, she had to drop the shades over her eyes.

Despite that she picked up a heat trail. Footprints… two sets of them, so a pair of runners with only one carrying the Q lock. No problem…but the prints were bare foot…what over the wall?

Might be a borg, Zero thought, or a Faux. Whatever it was it didn't matter; she could handle it.

The heat signature of the footprints was getting hotter

and soon enough she could see a matching heat source just ahead of her on the far side of the causeway. Just one...where was the other runner?

She pulled her harpoon gun from the holster on her right hip and readied a line. It looked fast, whatever it was, and she didn't want it leaping down into the under city where she might lose it.

It hopped off of the causeway onto the zip-rail then rand along the dangerous mass transit tracks. Zero followed but leapt high over the tracks then to the rooftop beyond. Her landing scattered a half dozen pigeons on the rooftop as she rolled to kneeling stance and sighted the runner inside the cross hairs of the harpoon gun. What the hell was it?

It didn't matter, whatever it was it was getting close to a big gap between the *215* north and *215* South, a gap that would let it drop down into the under city.

FWAAANNG! The bolt flew from the harpoon gun trailing ten meters worth of a thick crimson band. A surge of natural adrenalin gushed through Zero as her targeting system registered the hit. An instant after the crimson band exploded into dozens of trailing red ribbons, the ends latching onto whatever they fluttered against; the rail tracks, the structure supports...anything. They stretched as the target struggled to continue running, finding itself not just anchored by the ribbons but being enveloped by the free strands that fluttered onto it.

"GOTCHA!" Zero cried out as the target dropped over the edge of the rail. The ribbons held tight and it swung hard under the rail line, becoming a red streaming pendulum ending with a wriggling, fighting...something...that was naked.

"Whoa!" Zero laughed out loud as she reached the ribbons anchor point midway into a sharp turn along the rail. Long thick strands of ribbon enfolded the target, covering its torso and head. Still she could see the long, very muscular and very naked legs kicking like crazy. Naked like that, it had to be some kind of faux…but her targeting scope read it as having a slightly cooler than normal heat signature. Fauxs usually ran hot.

She holstered the harpoon gun then rotated the forearm guard on her gauntlet until the small thin dart launcher sat just over the back of her hand. Fauxs could be put down by most things that could put down whatever breed it was modeled after but she didn't want to kill it…yet. The darts would inject a potent sedative making it easier to deal with. Adjusting for its kicking, she waited for it to reach the arc of its swing.

Her proximity alarm rang out and she jumped when she saw the distance read less than ten meters…which dropped to zero meters in an instant!

Before she could look up something shot past the runner beneath the rail line. It moved so fast she thought it might have been on a swoop but her gear didn't register an engine…or an engine heat signature.

Careful not to expose herself, she looked over the edge of the rail and saw that nearly half of the ribbons holding the runner to the bridge had been cut. Someone was after her runner!

Quickly she drew her Barron Inc. '72, not the best firearm by a lot but it was ceramic and small enough to get past most weapons sweeps with the shadow tech she rigged into her gear. She'd tripled its stopping power and the rounds could pierce most armor.

The blow came from behind her and sent her over the edge of the zip rail. She lunged out desperately and managed to grab ahold of one of the cut and errant ribbon strands. It stretched and swung her into the fluttering lines that had just been cut from the faux. The bonding agent didn't react to the vilica coating on her gloves and most of her armor, but her equipment packs and straps were snagged enough that she quickly became entangled in her own trap. Upside down and hanging almost parallel to the runner she'd captured; Zero watched her gun drop down into the dark under city.

She ran a targeting check but her systems were all glitch. Something was hacking her ware, ripping through her drives. She looked up but could see little save for the bottom of the rail.

"Hey, spud!" she yelled. It had to be another Neg runner, someone trying to steal her very odd looking catch. She had one arm free but not the one with her dart gauntlet on it and from the way she was wrapped up in her own ribbon she couldn't get to any of her own hardware.

Zero looked back up to the rail. Just peering over, silhouetted by a sliver of light from the Sun road mirrors, was a helmeted man. A runner she did not recognize, not likely working for the Lords.

"I negged it, spud," Zero spat up at him. "Back off!" She opened a rip program in her quickly dying drives and sent it up, hoping to find her attackers systems. In a tenth of a second the rip came back telling her it found; NO SYSTEM DETECTED. She sent another rip from her last remaining drive.

"I work for the Lords, hack-head!" she snapped in as threatening a voice as she could muster. "Don't think they'll like you knocking off one of their negs."

The stranger remained silent but she could see he was examining the ribbons. After another moment he carefully hoisted the strands holding the runner.

She kicked uselessly as the strange runner was pulled up past her. Its top half was completely covered by ribbon but the lower half was exposed. Overly muscular legs, nude, ended in the filthy, grime covered feet that were calloused beyond measure. It had to be a faux, she thought.

Her last rip came back so horribly garbled that it squelched gibberish. "Ung!" she fought against her own bonding tape uselessly. If she could just get her dart gauntlet free she might have a chance. A new Neg runner...likely working for someone other than the Lords...would likely kill her.

Her last drive was failing and her goggles went dark. With her free hand she pulled them off and in the natural light with her own eyes she could see the new Neg runner better.

He was dressed in black leather with green trim and wearing a swoop helmet with a large visor marked with gray, crudely drawn wings. There was obvious armor under the leather jacket; she could see the outline of it at his shoulders. Zero recognized him from rumors that had been floating about in the wave. The Rebel.

He was small, she thought, but clearly strong as the faux runner was drawn up quickly. Soon enough it disappeared up over the top of the rail line. Then it got quiet.

Desperate, she finally opened her com relay and sent a beacon to the Lords...only to hear it squelched by a jammer. Then her last drive finally failed. She looked up again to see the helmeted man looking down on her.

"I neg run for the Lords, spud!" she warned him. "Better back off if you know..."

WHAM! ZARK!

She never even saw what it was he hit her with, he threw it so fast.

Zero, NEGGED...

1.3

The evidence lab is usually under manned due to budget cuts, but because of the number of vics this morning the Captain was forced to call in additional help. So now there's a whopping three Evidence Techs working the case. There are a few 'bots helping but the things are so outdated they can do little more than carry the heavy boxes back and forth.

"Detective?" the E.T. from the crime scene calls me

over. I really should learn his name.

"What have you got?"

"Just some preliminary observations. Look here," he lifts up a pretty bruised and bloody leg. "The heels and toe pad of this foot are heavily calloused. He's been walking barefoot almost exclusively for years if not his whole life."

"So…faux?"

"Likely. Never seen a real with this kind of wear and tear on them; people don't usually last long but you never know."

Hmm? "Can you tell how old it is?"

He nods his head but still says, "I'll have an age after we get the G&C tests processed. Looking at its development I'd say it reached adulthood."

Faux people, bio-engineered quickie clones. They're usually made for some truly disgusting purposes; killing, slave labor…sex. Little more than a monkey brain inside but otherwise they might look perfectly human. There were some that ran through Gohelm a ways back and wreaked havoc on the sex trade business.

Fauxs don't feel pain like people do…unless the designer wants them to. Makes them ideal for hazardous, grueling work. The times I've busted a faux they're almost never clothed.

It usually takes a faux about two Risings to reach adulthood…longer if it's pressed into service earlier. And this one has seen a lot of work…doing what? Where?

"It's the same with them all so far," the tech says. His name is…damn.

"Ok, call me when the G&C is done," and I end the connection. At once the virtual environment around me dissolves and again reality hits me in the face. Instead of standing in the middle of the Evidence Lab I'm sitting in a beat up joop car that has finally arrived at the Nautic avenue rail station. Someone called in a fight, the LPD officer first on the scene reported that they've got a borged up merc in custody. Likely a runner that got negged.

Half the terminal is shut down. Mayor's office will want this cleared up as soon as possible because the shutdown of the bridge *Under the Towers* was already tying up traffic. Police pylons cordon off the north side of the terminal, their virtual banners stream across half the open floor. The inconvenienced commuters seem to be taking it in stride; just another day in the *215*.

"I'm Carr," the uniformed officer is standing just outside the boarding platform. "You Rhoades?"

"Yea," There's a small personal rail car sitting here on the rail instead of a full passenger car. "Where's the perp?"

Carr grins a bit as he climbs into the rail car and gestures for me to follow. "Perp or vic, either really applies. They've got one by the first bend in the track, wrapped in some high level bonding tape."

He starts the rail car and we get moving. I can see the virtual police flare glowing just up ahead of us and around the bend in the track. We're over a bit of a gap in the buildings, an opening leading all the way to *Down to the Bottom*. Sun Road is in view from here and just beyond that by about a kilo down, lay *Under the Towers*. Could this perp be connected to what happened this morning?

There's a hover car floating just by the rail with another group of uniformed officers. SWAT…*215*'s "Top Cops"? Looks like the Mayor is already worried.

We come to a stop and Carr lowers the front shield of our rail car. I hop off and make my way along the tracks until I come to the hover car and several metallic bands latched to the railway.

"SWAT Officer James, Detective Rhoades, here to assist at the insistence of the mayor," the lead top cop announces, telling me I'm right.

"We've met before," she tells me. "At the Bowery drownings last Rising."

"I remember, Sgt. James." I peek over the side to see

the dangling perp who looks to be unconscious. "Didn't want to cut him down?"

"Didn't care to disturb the scene in case there's something here to connect to bodies you guys found this morning."

Somebody's ahead of me. Somebody knows something I don't. "Sure. Let's take a look…"

My A.I.E. zooms in and I go full spectrum. It's a girl, young and borged up alright; high EM readings, dense armor over her vitals… advanced exoskeleton that probably enhances her speed, her leaping ability and…killing. She's got targeting tech and a few obvious weapons.

I send her data into the wave and her image jumps out of the virtual and hangs in space in front of me.

Har Sky, twenty-two Risings, DOA five Risings ago from a Torture/Kill case. Clearly someone bought the meat and resuscitated her not too long after she was down. Tricked her out with all the gear, pulled her Tell and then sold her to someone…likely as a runner.

My A.I.E. picks up blood. Sky is dripping bio-lubricant contaminated plasma so it's not hers. The blood trails off the rail… I peer down into the gap and it leads down into the bottom. Maybe the blood of who ever took her out?

No…there're more footprints in the blood. A quick check tells m they don't match the mercs. One set is barefoot…Damn! Like the vics from the bridge. The other a shoe print…big blocks so it's likely a boot print...comes back as a match for…HIM. He was here too.

Why? He took out Sky and then a faux? Cut it up and leapt back down the bottom?

I look around. No arms and legs here.

James sees what I see. "Those prints are in the D-base, Detective. Looks like the new gang is in on this too."

"The 'Rebel' isn't a gang," I tell her. "All evidence points to it being just one guy."

"Sure," she snorts. "One guy put the Soors down at

Trinity? That's river waste and you know it."

"You got a tracker?" I ask the SWAT commander, ignoring her comment.

"Got an infil with tracking ware."

"Track the blood. Find the body."

James gives a nod to one of her team and in a minute a small hover drone launches into the air and swoops down onto the rail by the blood. It takes a sample and then it flies off down into the gap.

"Figured that blood was hers," the sergeant says.

"Give me the infil ID." She hesitates then posts the ID. A virtual monitor pops up on my right. The infil's POV is displayed so I can see it following a sporadic trail of highlighted blood splotches down towards the bottom and through a crisscrossing labyrinth of alleyways, gantries and piping connecting the lower buildings.

While it's tracking, I hop from the railway and onto the hovercraft. "Lower us a bit, let's get her into custody."

The Sergeant gives the order but then turns to me. "Sure about that? We've got no complaining witness. Might have to let her go."

She's got to be kidding. Quickly I pull up her dossier; Holic James, sergeant, commander of Special Weapons and Tactics, Liberty 215 district 19 through 35. She's been cited numerous times for outstanding performance by her District Chief, the Commissioner and even the Mayor. No citing for misconduct; no community complaints.

She's dirty.

Someone's getting a kickback. Probably from one of the major gangs which mean this runner was running contraband of some kind before she got hit and now her bosses have spent the creds to get her back. That's why she's asking about Rebel.

"She's strapped to the bones with illegal hardware, Sergeant," I tell her. They weren't here waiting for me; they tried to get here first and I just happened to show too early.

"She's going to be processed."

"Your call," she says but I can tell she's sending someone a message through the wave. Dammit, there's a killer on the loose and some on the take roach is gonna help them get away.

It's just a few meters so we're soon right next to Sky. She's wrapped in the metallic tape but not as tightly as I would have thought seeing how completely bonded to the rail it was.

"Her armor," I say out loud. "Her armor is coated with something that this tape can't stick to."

So…I reach out and spin her about a bit. The SWAT team behind me raises their weapons. They may be on the take but they don't trust her either. Borged up mercs are some of the most dangerous criminals.

Trapped beneath the bonding tape is a weapon. It's similarly coated and comes free easily. It's heavy; I have to use two hands just to keep from dropping it. Should've worn an exo but the police standard issue it too damn bulky.

My A.I.E. scans the weapon and brings up its stats… which have got to be wrong. An old Liberty Gear pinning gun; a machinist's tool for building joops. I look closer at it but my A.I.E. finds nothing more. There's scoring and a bit of sloppy wielding. It's been modified to fire something. Runners don't use weapons like these.

"She's a Neg Runner." I say.

"Y-you sure?" the sergeant says.

"The gun must fire the off the bonding tape but it looks like she got caught in her own web." So she was doing the chasing.

They squared off then-her and Rebel-over one of the things from the bridge. He took her out then either snatched the body or continued chasing it.

"The infil lost the trail," the sergeant reports. I look to the virtual POV and see that indeed the infil is circling back. The SWAT leader is still trying to send secret waves. Is she trying to play me? There's no Q box here; the lock box most people in the underworld send their messages in, at least here in the *215*. Might be she wants to beat me to it.

I could send a request through the wave for a set of trackers but it's likely they'll be blocked long enough that someone else will track the body and erase the trail before they even get here. Instead I pull my tagger and "paint" Sky; a virtual flare rises up and locks into the wave. The sergeant won't be able to "lose" her on the way to the precinct.

"No problem," I tell James and move to the hovercraft controls. "I'll track it myself. Call another ride and then take this merc to the lock up."

The sergeant balks. "You can't…I've got orders to clear…"

"Right, sergeant." I smile as I take the hovercraft back up to the railway so they can hop off. "Clear the railway. Now off. Carr?"

The uniform that brought me over is waiting on the mini rail car. "Yea, Detective?"

"You're with me." I may need the back up.

A few of the SWAT team look to James but after a moment she nods and they disembark while Carr hops on. I twist the craft and send it in a nice steep dive down into the gap. About thirty meters down I see the infil hovering just outside of a blood smeared catwalk. I could commandeer the infil and use it to help me track but anyone else with the ID number will be able to monitor me. Don't want that.

I pull my gun and put a hole through it on my way down to the bottom.

Rhodes Headed Down…

1.4

Deep down the bottom, beneath the Towers, far below Sun Road and far from the light of the Sun Tower the Underground was run by the Lords. From the reclamation plant all the way to the dark water spills was their territory and they controlled it despite a number of competing factions. They controlled it because the Lords leaders, two brothers from Gohelm, did not operate like the gangs of old. They had most of the traits of a street gang for sure. They were brutal, maintaining gang membership and territorial dominance through horribly merciless killing. They were corrupt; there was no dark business they were above. They sold purge, weapons, illegal tech and harvested bodies even when the owners were still alive.

Most street gangs flame out. They started strong and fast but that same burst became their downfall as they pushed too far and extended themselves right into the arms of the law or into civil war with themselves.

But the Lords were run with martial precision. Harsh discipline and control of those they commanded and strict, uncanny mastery in their movements, territorial control and business ventures. They started small and expanded not in a flash, but with a controlled and steady growth. Several times the larger gangs of the *215* looked to wipe them out only to find themselves beaten back and on many occasions, eliminated by the Lords of the Underground.

Tone, the older of the two brothers, sat in the garage at W and 80th, the *Mound*, where his small fleet of joop cars and swoop bikes was kept. He sat in the driver's side of a tricked out *Invincible*, hot rod red with the tail streams. His long legs stuck out of the open door as he laid rest of his lithe six foot body across the driver's seat. The worn and beat up leather boots sticking out from beneath the baggy denim jeans he wore loosely about his hips, knocked together in rhythm to driving bass the mod system of the joop played.

"So where is she now?" he asked while running a hand through his knotted and nappy hair. It had been awhile since he'd been able to get it re-braided. Ever since the style shop on 63rd got raided.

He was talking to his brother, Cong, who could have been his twin were it not for the extreme difference in height. Cong barely reached five feet but was just as lean though more pristine in appearance. Sharply squared off hair and goatee, perfectly aligned and extremely expensive custom tailored suit, Cong may have been the "prettier" of the two brothers, but he was also the more feared. While Tone set the direction of the gang it was often Cong who executed the missions…and enemies.

"SWAT's taking her to the lock-up." Cong checked his watch. It was classic, old style and strictly mechanical. With his cyberware he never needed it but he liked to use it to check the time anyway. Like his brother listening to his music, letting it blare throughout the garage instead of listening to it privately in his own head, doing some things in the old ways gave them both comfort.

"Should be there by now."

"Which squad?" Tone asked.

"James' squad."

"Good!" The exclamation came from Red, the third member of the Lords in the garage. Red was nothing like the two brothers. Pale skinned and rotund, the red headed ex-cop sat at by the rear entrance on a mech stool, clearly uncomfortable. "We've got guys in that squad."

.

"Guy," Cong corrected, looking at her. "One man and he's not in position to do anything."

Red was flanked by two very tall men. One golden haired with a wide thick mustache puffed on a fat, handmade cigar. He wore a fancy green vest over a nice dress shirt which contrasted harshly with the worn leather holster and huge sidearm on his hip. Leaning against the wall behind him stood a long, modified sniper rifle. Kodak Cardinal was the best shot in all five wards under the Sun Tower.

The other man was a bit taller and a lot darker. Parrish the Priest wore a long black trench coat and a wide brimmed black hat. The man fiddled with the long set of black beads that hung from his coat and ended in a gold cross.

The Celts, as they were called, were the Lords most successful neg runners and not part of the leadership. Red had found them

"Bullshit," she snapped. "What the fuck is he there for?"

"Eyes and ears," Tone said evenly. Red was a valued recruiter for the Lords; in addition to the Celts she also brought Shepard, so she fancied herself the gang's third leader. Something Tone was only willing to ignore her as long as Red kept the talent coming in.

"The squad leader belongs to the Purple."

"No prob," Cong nodded. "We get a boy thrown in the lock up. A new jack so they get put behind the heavy bars with Zero."

"Jacks just don't come in with the Risings," Red complained. "This ain't worth givin' one up."

Tone kept his voice even despite his growing frustration. "We lost a neg runner this morning 'cause of this shit, Red. I wanna know why."

"Zero was good," Cong added. "We need to get her back."

"Fine," Red grunted as she stood. "I'll set it up."

The Lords, Only Real...

1.5

"Blood's getting thinner," I tell Carr. Figure the runner was killed and the body taken by whoever waylaid the Neg Runner. Means it's being carried quite some ways.

"All that blood on the rail, all of it we've already passed...no way it's alive," he says.

"Not likely. A faux designed to be a runner would need a ton of oxygen and a good supply of blood but fauxs can be manufactured with differing specs. If it was a faux at all."

"Maybe it was bionic," Carr suggests.

We're sitting in a small cavity in between the substructures of two or three condemned buildings. There are virtual warning posts cautioning of the dangerous conditions here. Most of them from the Metal Union, the only group I know that actually refurbishes or scavenges old structures. Didn't know they'd moved this far into the *215*.

At once my Wave link lights up; the Evidence Lab is calling. I put it through audio only. "Rhoades."

"Detective...uh...ok, audio only? Ok, it's me. We've got some really definitive results from the bodies...er...the body parts this morning."

Who's "me"? Damn...the evidence tech. What the hell is his name?? "Go ahead...uh...what have you got?"

He clears his throat again. "Some pretty strange stuff. You should really go virtual and see this for yourself."

I look about the piping and support struts here in the understructure. That runner could be almost anywhere. Especially if it's equipped with some stealth tech.

"Can't right now. Give me what you've got."

"Uh, sure."

I come up on a break between the buildings, a larger cavity where I can see further down into the under city. Not deeper than I've been; it looks like the *bottom* but from above I see structures I've never seen from the street.

There's no sign of runner blood here but my A.I.E. might not catch faint traces that far off.

"There's good news, bad news and some pretty weird news. Which do you want…"

"Just give me your report," There's a thin catwalk spanning the gap over Shadowyunk and I proceed across, peering down trying to catch anything with my sensor A.I.E…

"Sure," he says. "Well, you were right about that Rebel guy. Those are his prints at the scene."

"I already knew that."

"Ok, but you didn't know that he took samples of the blood at the scene."

"What? Are you sure?" Not like a gang or merc to do something like that.

"Yes," the ET says. "Took samples of the blood and I think biopsies of the body parts. It's really kind of cool that…"

"What else?" I snap.

"Uh…ok…uh; we also found trace amounts of dark water coating the surface flesh of the body parts. Enough that we think they must have been near a dark water source for a significant amount of time."

The Dark Water spills, *down the bottom…*the underground…Lords territory. "What else?"

"Um, we were able to rule out it being a quick clone. None of the DNA came back a match from the database and there are natural mutations that only occur in naturally born breeds, specifically human."

"All human?" This is getting ugly. Those were reals; actual citizens that got done? I'm halfway across the catwalk when my A.I.E. catches a slight thermal reading. Not from the tops of the under city buildings below but from the railing of the catwalk I'm on.

"Yup, all human. I guess that would be the bad news," whatever his name says.

"Thought there was too much wear and tear on the limbs for them to be human?"

"There is, which brings us to the really weird news; something showed up in the G&C report that has me thinking."

The thermal reading on the railing is blood, the runners blood, not too old; its thermal was just slightly higher than the railing itself. I reach over and rub the small spot; it's dry and starting to crust over. The blood is splayed out over the railing in tiny little tendrils. It dropped down from high above. I look up; on just a small outcropping above us I can see something moving, fluttering actually. Minimal thermal reading.

"What's that?" I ask Carr, who looks up, shakes his head and shrugs.

"We found what looks to be a custom cocktail." The tech thinks I was asking him. "Some version of a glucocorticoid with TNF binders, mycophenolates and some other possible immunosuppressant drugs that we can't identify."

There's a small service ladder at the end of the catwalk. I make my way across trying to keep an eye on the elbow but there's no movement.

"They were drugged?" I ask.

"No, I mean yes but those are immunosuppressant drugs, used in organ rejection."

Right. Should have caught that. I make my way up the ladder. Slowly because I have my gun drawn and I'm not putting it away. "So they were probably patients coming from a body shop. That means money rich vics, not likely from the *215* or we'd have heard about it."

"Maybe, but the cocktail is custom made like most and so it needs to be adjusted to for each and every body."

"Right." I get to the outcropping. It's maybe a meter wide and I can see the shape of the runner just ahead of me in the shadow. Its thermal is warped; all I can make out are the legs. "So?"

"So, that's what's weird, really weird but I confirmed it by comparing all the blood samples we found at the bridge this morning."

I signal to Carr to keep watch while I check the body. He nods and moves back up the gantry. It only takes me a few steps to reach the thing which I'm now positive is dead. It looks like it had been wrapped in the same metallic bonding ribbons that we found the neg runner, Sky, in but clearly someone has cut most of them free. They cut enough to get at the Q which I figured this runner would have.

And they cut enough to get a really good look at this runner.

"We found enough arms and legs at the bridge this morning for at least twenty-one different individuals," the Evidence Tech says.

"But the blood samples and immunosuppressant drugs," I finish for him…Banks? No… "They indicate that the limbs belonged to far fewer bodies."

"Yes!" he says shocked. "All of the parts we found were from one of only three bodies. It's crazy…wait! How did you know?"

I look down at the runner. I'd expected to see some kind of borg/faux hybrid maybe but what I'm looking at is far worse. The runner has got overly muscular legs, the same wear and tear on the heels as we found on the limbs at the bridge. The legs are not attached to an abdomen but rather to a junction, a muscle ridden meeting point where another set of smaller legs and a pair of small arms met. There was no head, no ass and no mouth that I could see but there were a pair, no, two pair of eyes set into a small slightly raised mound on the…top? On the top of the thing.

"It's not a faux," I tell the tech. And patch him into my virtual feed so he can see what I'm seeing. "I don't know what it is."

"Wow!" he says in fascination. "Whatever it is, it's

made from regular people."

"At least two different people, probably more." That
meant a body shop. One near the Dark Water spills…way
down the bottom.

Rhodes, And the No Body…

1.6

Cong took a careful step to the side, making sure not
to put his foot down on anything that might stain or scuff
the zeal hide of his shoe. He disliked coming to Imaiel's
but time was of the essence so he was forced to brave the
unbelievable squalor of the woman's home.

Room was more like it. While Imaiel had done some
wave trick to get the entire floor to herself, she nonetheless
existed in just the one room at the end of its hall. It was a
small, efficient apartment with a window that looked out
into the blank brick wall of the tenement next door.

Imaiel didn't need a view; she could see nearly
anything she wanted.

Imaiel didn't need the space, her domain stretched on
to infinity.

Imaiel didn't mind the unkempt clutter of her home;
she lived in the wave.

"What about the runner she was chasing?" Cong
asked. He looked down on the dangerously thin woman,
swathed practically in rags that had not been laundered
in…Cong wrinkled his nose; they were so filthy that it was
impossible to tell. Imaiel's hair was stringy and clearly
indicated the woman's extreme state of malnutrition. That
along with her pale uneven skin that just barely stretched
over her frame. Cong would take pity on the woman if it
were not for the smile of overwhelming ecstasy on her face.

"Zero says it fell down here. The Blue Authority

doesn't know." Her voice was a hoarse whisper.

"Down here? Where?"

Imaiel sighed. "Under the railway line at Nautic and Thorn, she thinks."

"She THINKS?"

"Her ware has been wiped. I can't get anything out of it and there's nothing in the wave. All cameras been wrecked. That was you guys, right?"

Cong ignored the dig. "The Blue too?"

"Even more so. They've got nothing on it yet, but I'm not sure. I'm only hooked to Zero through the police cyber division. Her communication underlay is fried."

"Don't take any chance with them," Cong warned. "If they track you in their system…""No worries, Lords," Imaiel slurred. "They're jus' blue cybers. I'm less than a ghost to them."

Cong took another careful step. "Tell Zero to give you her back up drive codes."

There was a brief moment of silence. Imaiel's eyes were closed and her lips parted, moving only slightly as she worked her way through the wave. Cong knew the surfer too well; she was indeed acting as a comm relay to Zero but she was also, almost certainly, simultaneously fishing through the police D-base for her own reasons. Not part of their deal; Cong would have slit her throat if not for Tone. His brother had found the surfer himself and insisted on her value.

"Zero refuses to release hers codes," Imaiel told him.

"Really?" Cong snorted. "Tell her that she doesn't want me to come and get them from her myself."

Again Imaiel drifted off. Cong watched as her eyes darted back and forth. Whatever it was the wave wizard was doing on the side must have been involved. He would come back later and find out.

"She still says no," Imaiel whispered and before Cong could snap she added, "But here's something interesting."

"What?"

"The cops think that there's a body shop here *down the bottom*."

So she was looking through the cops D-base. "So? There are two, but the cops won't find them."

"This one is stitching together runners, runners with no heads but two and three sets of legs. Is that what you're doing?"

Cong took another step, not heeding where his foot came down now. "Where is it?"

"They don't know, but you should dive in," Imaiel whispered. "You need to see what they think ripped apart those bodies at the bridge."

Cong instead turned and walked out of the room and into fresh air of the hall. He brought up his virtual comm and opened a quick pipeline to his brother through the wave. "We got trouble."

His brother appeared in front of him, life size but hazy and shaded in green. The best equipment they could get that could not be monitored was also the most outdated. He quickly relayed the information.

"And Rebel has been at both scenes."

Tone remained so still while digesting the info that Cong almost thought his communication gear had glitched.

"There are only a few places that someone could sneak a body shop in our territory without us knowing."

"There is no place," Cong argued. "We've got the bottom locked down."

"You know the Underground ain't one hundred everywhere."

Cong thought for a moment then nodded. "Got to be down by the bad water. You want us to mess with that?"

"Yea," Tone nodded. "Take some hitters...find the shop. Don't bother with anything else. They're watching there."

"What about Rebel?"

"You see him, you kill him. Tired of that waste."

"On it," and Cong closed the pipe.

    Cong, With the Wave Witch...

1.7

"Look here," whatever his name, the evidence tech, points. The evidence lab surrounds me again while I'm in a joop on my way to the Dark Water spills. The tech pulls a limb out of a freezer box in the actual lab. "This leg was ripped free from body B. Note the bruises and torn skin along the calf."

"Okay." It's a nasty, bruised imprint. My A.I.E. can't analyze the shape as I'm only seeing the image through the wave. "So?"

He points to a small set of parallel bruises. "This is a hand print," he says, turning the leg a bit. "And so is this."

"I see it,"

"These are the prints of whatever it was that pulled the others apart," Kirk? No, that wasn't right. Maybe Kurt? No. Anyway...

"They look normal sized," I notice. "So maybe borg? To have the strength to rip those things limb from limb?"

"I thought so at first but look here." The evidence tech opens a virtual shot of the bridge zooms in on a set of footprints in the splashed blood. "Here are a few more sets of hand prints on the bridge."

"The same?"

"No," The tech...Jack? No. The tech changes the spectrum of the image and the prints emerge from the background clearer. "Do you see the pattern?"

No I don't, but maybe I'm just not looking at it right. The tech pulls the image back a ways and it is familiar but I can't quite see why.

"There's a corresponding pattern I've found with the bruises on the cadaver limbs," he says. Jake? …nope… I should just pop up his damn file!

"What's the pattern? No; I'll look at it later."

"Detective, wait!"

"Not now!" and I mute his connection. The joop car pulls to a stop and before I hop out I don a filter mask. The Dark Water Spills is the bottom of a huge basin where the nasty run off water of a few dozen wards is collected. The mist hanging in the air can be dangerous but there are no virtual hazard warnings…today.

The basin itself is a huge bowl filled with processing gear that rises out of the dark water like black, geometrically perfect, metal stalagmites. The gear doesn't treat the water, it helps collect it and keep the vapor and mist to a minimum. Otherwise the polluted vapor would rise and poison everyone in the *215*. From here the water runs off to the reclamation plants at the far end of the ward. From here to the reclamation plants is referred to as *Down the Bottom* or the *Underground*, the territory of the Lords.

"We should call for back up." Carr says as he hops out of the joop behind me. He's right; there's not a detail assigned down the bottom that has less than three cops on it. Anyone willing to work down here alone is on the take. I should place the call now, for assistance but some roach might tip the Lords or whoever is running the body shop I'm looking for.

But somebody didn't hesitate to stitch parts from reals together to make weird runners. Somebody didn't hesitate to tear them limb from limb on a bridge at dawn. That somebody won't hesitate to kill two cops.

"Call it in," I tell him. "And send a flare up for the current patrol watch."

Carr makes the call through the wave and at the same time lights up a virtual flare. Any cops monitoring the wave will see it clear as day and should, hopefully, respond.

But we've got to get going.

There's bound to be little hidey holes the rogue shop could be tucked away in here *down the bottom*. But this shop doesn't belong to the Lords, so that means it's been hidden even from them. Could be deep below in the under structure below even the under city but with the dark water signature left on the runners skin it should be pretty close to the basin. And that means it's probably in the one of the basins service buildings. And that's not good.

The basin is regulated from an administration building that's filled wall to wall with automated controls for the valves and pumps that move the water down to the reclamation plant. Automated controls built and maintained by those that built the City itself, regulated by those that only the Street Priests have the sacks to talk about. Department regulations are deliberately vague when it comes to crossing the line into the "Watchers" territory; a kind of a "you're on your own" tone is given whenever I've asked about those procedures.

But a body shop needs power and this is the one place they could get it if they're not in league with the Lords. I look at the small building set along the side of the basin. Bound to be bigger on the inside than it is on the outside.

"Let's go." Carr falls in behind hesitantly.

The front is closed up. Like most of the City's processing works, this building is locked up tight. So we work our way behind the Admin building and find a small alley that ends in a set of metal stairs. They lead down to a service door...

...it's sitting open.

"Guns out. Here we go."

It's pitch black behind the door so I set my A.I.E. to infrared. Still not enough light, I pull my flashlight and set it, likewise, to project and infrared beam.

Looks like this is a direct access to the underside of the basin. The doors open to a gantry above the water works. Dark water stink is so heavy in the air that I can smell it through the filter. Worse…there's something heavy in the air that the infrared pics up, it drifts about the room in spots like miniature high tower clouds. Not sure what it is…best to avoid them.

"Bodies…" Carr points down to the lower levels. He's right; there are bodies down there, something in the air…the dark water…is messing with my A.I.E... They're only showing up on thermal intermittently. Crap…half the room is hidden behind those floating chem clouds.

"They're still breathing…I think," I tell him and we move down the gantry to the stairs. Can't see anything in here…the far corners of the room remain dark, even on infrared. The clouds of whatever it is floating through the room drift about, drawing my eye like moving shadows. "Send up a flare for a med wagon."

We get to the bottom of the room and immediately I wish we'd stayed up top. The pumps and control stations are at least five meters tall and make walking the floor like walking a cloudy maze.

"We should wait for back up," Carr suggests nervously.

"Hang in there," but I don't blame him. The longer we stay down here, the deeper we go, the lower our odds at getting out of here alive.

Nevertheless I lead us through the room until we round a corner and find the first of the bodies on the floor. This one is…

"Dead," I tell Carr. Close enough, my A.I.E. picks up his ID from a retina scan. Long rap sheet; he's a thug that's been thrown in lock up for most of his adult life. Works primarily down the bottom for the Lords likely. His life expectancy wasn't much higher than ours are right now but this guy probably didn't expect to go like this; not by bullet or blade, his head has been smashed open.

"Edward Salario, a.k.a. 'Hands'," I tell Carr.

"He's in, was in with the Lords." He moves ahead and peers around the next pump station. "So was this guy."

Another thug who ran with the Lords lays in horribly familiar pieces. Both his legs and one arm have been ripped off. His head is twisted around unnaturally and his heat signature is reading only a little below normal.

"This just happened," I warn Carr. "Stay sharp."

"[SKRZZT!], Detective."

I jump a bit. The damn E.T. never cut the connection. He's been watching the whole time.

"Not now," I snap. He must have overridden the com lines. I don't see him but the audio coming from his end is terrible.

"Detective, you need [SKRZZT!]out of there," whatever his name warns me.

"No shit, uh…"

"The arrangement of the blood prints," he stammers. "The patterns in the [SKRZZT!] indicate a radical design for the attacker."

We're blocked by a wall of the dark chemical cloud. Big and white on infrared, it's really got a deep purple color to it when I turn my goggles off briefly. We avoid it and move around another large control bank then come across another of the Lords thugs, her body twisted around like a rung out washcloth. "What do you mean 'design'"?

Another of the Lords, but her head is so smashed that her eyes won't register for an ID.

"Man, these guys only JUST got done. We should get the hell out of here and wait for back up," Carr is whipping his head back and forth, afraid of an ambush. He's not alone.

"Calm down," I say as firmly as I can manage and waive Carr forward.

"I mean," the ET cuts back in. "That the attacker at the bridge [SKRZZT!] version of the runner you found, only…"

We come around another corner and come up on a retreating dark cloud. It recedes and two rows of dimly lit pods emerge into the infrared light. They resemble medical crèches, each about the length of a human body and with a clouded glass seal on top. Each of these crèches has been smashed open.

"Ugh!" Carr dry heaves. Inside each is a mutilated human corpse. I'm getting no reading on IDs, their heads have been smashed and their Tells removed.

Then my A.I.E. picks up a faint signal from a Q box from somewhere nearby. The chemicals in the room and the heavy machinery are interfering too much for me to lock down its location.

"Hey!" Carr drops to a knee and is peering under the pods. "There's someone here!"

I push past him and see another Lord; hidden behind the pods. My A.I.E. picks his ID right away.

"Cong," the co-leader of the Lords, he's beat up; one arm is broken in two places and the rest of him doesn't look much better but he's alive.

"Cong?" He's jammed down tight in between two of the pods. He's a small man, can't be much more than a meter and a half tall maybe. I can barely reach him the space is so small.

"Uh, can you see these pods?" I ask the tech.

"Detective, those are med-chambers I think," the ET again. "But you really need to [SKRZZT!]…"

"Say what, whatever your damn name is! "Med-chambers?"

"That doesn't [SKRZZT!] now! The attacker is more than [SKRZZT!],"

"Carr, help me pull him out." I can almost reach his leg.

"Still no word on back up, Detective," Carr sounds like he's backing away. "Can't get a signal out here. How are you still getting the wave?"

"Help me, Carr," I grunt. I've got a hold of Cong's ankle. "We'll haul him out of here and wait for back up."

With a suddenness that makes me jump, Cong jerks his leg away from me. I draw back immediately and point my gun at his hiding spot between the pods. Still the ET is practically screaming in my ear.

"...much, much bigger!" he's saying.

"Carr, help me get him out of there,"

"I think I'm getting a thermal sig!" he says. I turn and look to where he's pointing in time to see a slight thermal patch just cooling high above us and across the room. Someone is on the gantry above us...the way we came in, but with the chem clouds floating around, he, she or it could be anywhere.

"Damn...ok, let's circle around and back," I point back the other way when a massive thermal signal slides out of the chemical cloud behind Carr. "Look out!!"

Too late, several arms reach out and grab the patrolman, wrapping around him in a three one-armed bear hugs. A fourth hand reaches from the other side and grabs him by the throat. I raise my gun and try to site over Carr's shoulder, looking for the heads of the attackers but thinking there might not be any. Then Carr is lifted off the ground, a good four meters.

"Freeze!" I belch out hesitantly, and then back pedal as another mass of naked limbs emerges from the dark cloud. Legs; stitched together with bands of flesh and muscle at the tops of the thighs, bottoming out in a group of at least five hard calloused feet. Never in the Risings...

They splay out much like fingers on a hand set to walking across a desk top; spider-like. But the legs bend together and out of the cloud come a second level of legs stitched to the top halves of the first. The entire length bends, sickly, but uniformly, as if one single unit. Like one leg?

The pods come up against my back as I back away. Even more of the thing steps out of the dark cloud, a second leg stalk made of the same number of melded together appendages. Then the entire creature dips out of the cloud.

"Detective," the ET is screaming through the wave connection. "Get the [SKRZZT!]out of there!"

Rhodes, DOWN THE BOTTOM

1.8

I've seen some real waste in the *215*, in *Liberty,* but nothing like what you can find *down the bottom.*

It steps out of the cloud and raises Carr higher into the air. Its legs are made of legs, bound together in flesh, stitched together with tendon and muscle. Its feet are like giant hands with calloused and overly muscled legs for fingers and its hands are much the same with arms for fingers. Its torso is made up of at least three torsos; make that four; that are stitched together almost haphazardly but still arranged about each other to give the whole thing a full range of movement. And its head...

"It's just like the runner [SKRZZT!]," the ET is telling me. "Except [SKRZZT!], obviously."

...is hidden in a crisscrossing mass of arms at the top of its body, only the slightest break in between them giving a shadowy hint that something is watching me from behind them.

"The runner had little more than a Fauxs brain in it. But that thing has got to have a much larger brain in order to coordinate the movement of so many appendages."

A second macabre hand reaches out and grabs Carr by his bottom half, each of the hands tearing into his legs with ugly strength. I raise my gun but have no idea what to shoot.

"Yeeaargh!" Carr screams out as the two hands snap him in half, bending even his exo-armor like it was nothing more than plastic. It tosses him over its shoulder like he was a used gelba stick. It comes for me.

I fire off my gun; it's a fat Sever 82 with the removable barrel cartridge; a powerful gun.

Big splotches of red explode over the things torsos as I hit three straight times but the thing doesn't even notice as it comes at me on those legs of legs. It so...I'm not gonna...

There's a brilliant discharge of electricity followed by a baleful outcry of several voices. I'm blinded by the sharp burst and backpedal into the pods while trying to get away from those hands. But they never come.

There's another burst of electricity followed by another cry of voices but this time they are farther away. The ground shakes with a massive impact and I hear one of the pump control banks fall to the ground. My vision clears slowly and I can see shadows fliting about. The thing is swinging its massive arm about trying to hit something...a man!

"Detective, who is [SKRZZT!]?" He's fighting off the thing with what looks like a stun stick and moving fast enough to keep from being smashed by those massive fists made of arms.

He's not LPD. He's dressed in all black and has a swoop helmet on. It's HIM. I can see the wing design scrawled across the sides of his helmet. The newest faction in the *215* represented by only a single individual; the Rebel.

There's another burst of electricity and the many voiced cry turns into rage filled screams of defiance. The thing reaches into a dark chemical cloud and pulls out a massive disued length of piping and tosses it across the room at Rebel.

Forced to duck away, he slips around another control bank and disappears. Then the thing turns its attention to me.

The arms about its head shift, widening the small opening between two of them giving it the appearance of one massive dark eye, an eye that is looking my way.

The Sever jerks against my palm as I fire before the thing can decide to come at me. But again, the nasty holes my rounds are ripping into it seem not to bother the thing and it rushes at me. I duck and leap, desperately trying to keep away from it but one of its hands is too fast and swats me away.

The hard metal of a pipe control tower smashes into

my face and lights flash across my vision. I fire blindly, emptying the Sever, knowing it has to be on top of me but when I look up the thing is still by the pods, its back to me.

There's the sound of metal ripping and I can see the muscles all across the thing's mixed up body working and twisting as it fights with something. Then there's a pop and it turns quickly, holding what looks to be yet another pod, though smaller, in one of its hands. The Q signal is coming in strong right from that pod.

"That pod is still [SKRZZT!], Detective," the ET tells me. "You can't let [SKRZZT!]with it."

That dark eye peers about the room; from one side to the other and then finally on me. I can almost see something moving in that dark hole. I reload.

Another burst of electricity flares and I see that the thing has been hit by something that's impaled on the folded torso that seems to work as one of its shoulders. As it reaches up with its free hand to pull the thing out the Rebel comes out of the darkness from above and lands in front of it.

The stun stick is gone…no…he's snapped it in two and is now holding half in each hand. Insanely he rushes the thing and begins pummeling it, each strike landing a smaller electrical shock.

But the thing leans back on one of its feet of legs easily and kicks out with the other, forcing Rebel to retreat. The creature takes the opportunity to gather itself and crouches down. After one quick look at me it leaps up, springing off of those near dozen legs into the air and disappearing into the darkness above.

Gone from sight but not from earshot. I can hear it gamboling across the ceiling's support structure and making its way across the room. Through the darkness and chem clouds I can see the random electrical bursts as Rebel gives chase.

"The small pod that thing took," the ET sounds as

terrified as I am. "That [SKRZZZZT!] be what I think [SKRZZT!]. You have to get it!"

One deep breath…then another and I hop up to my feet and give chase.

Rhodes, BEFORE THE BREAKER…

1.9

It takes me too long to reach the staircase and now a nasty purple cloud blocks my path. The fight between Rebel and that thing sounds like it's reached outside now. I can't let them get too far ahead of me.

Despite the fact that I'm wearing a filter I hold my breath as I plunge upward, the exposed skin on my neck and wrists tingle as I pass through but that's all. The chip in the filter doesn't recognize all the components in it and that could be a problem later.

If I'm still alive.

I reach the door leading out of the building but there is a set of stairs leading further up. A quick tap to my goggles and I can see a roof access that's been busted open; a nasty hole roughly the same size as that cobbled together thing.

The stairway feels like it goes on forever. I'm practically wheezing as I reach the top and step out onto the roof. Next time I'm not coming down here without an exo.

My A.I.E. traces the Q and then I see them. They're over the dark water basin, ascending one of the tall processing structures protruding from the foul lake. The thing is still carrying the pod and Rebel is still chasing it.

"If the construct gets to the [SKRZZZT!] above the basin it can use the understructure to disappear!" The ET is still connected to me through the wave.

"What's in the pod?" I run to the edge of the rooftop and look for a way to the processing gear. The basin wall is just beneath me.

"I can't be sure but it's likely [SKRZZT!]"

There's a small dock inside the wall and a network of thin walkways over the water, a small section of which has collapsed into the lake.

"Don't risk the water, Det[SKRZZT!] The fumes above the lake will eat right [SKRZZZT!] your filter!"

I sight the monster with my Sever but it hardly even noticed the rounds before when I was right up on the thing. So I leap down to the dock and almost stumble into the dark water lake.

"Careful, Detective! That close to the water [SKRZZT!] extremely toxic."

"I feel it." I do; the skin around my filter mask and goggles begins to tingle and then burn. Got to get up to the processing gear where I can climb up away from the surface.

There's a rickety section of walkways, made of rusting metal railings and worn rubber ties, that isn't as beaten up as the rest. Stepping as carefully as I can, I run along them to the closest processing framework. Just as I reach the base I hear the static burst of Rebel's stun stick attack followed by that wail of horrid voices.

The processing gear is encircled with scaffolding and stairs that wind their way up its length. As I make my way up I notice the thick leather of my jacket is being corroded by the dark water mist, smoking a bit as it's eaten away.

The scaffolding sways as I scrambled up.

"They're nearing the top, Det [SKRZZZT!]"

"What's in that pod?"

"That thing must [SKRZZZT!"]

"What?"

I can hear the sounds of a fight above me. Rebel must be slowing the thing down but with the limited room up here it can only be a matter of time before it gets its hands on him and breaks him in two.

The processing gear begins to bend as I get closer to the top, arcing smoothly and leveling off a bit. When I get to the top the fight is in full swing.

It stands over Rebel, its macabre stitched together body negotiating the scaffolding of the processing gear with a creepy ease. Rebel is ducking through and around that same scaffolding, trying to stay ahead of it and keep it from reaching the end of the structure.

I slip in closer, raise my gun and target one of the things four backs.

"That won't do [SKRZZT!], Detective!" The ET warns. "Try for its head!"

"It doesn't have a head." Where it should have one there is a raised mound of tightly wound arms. The small gap I saw before is facing away from me. No target but we're coming to the end of the gear; that thing could reach the understructure of the city above and escape.

"The brain is proba[SKRZZZT!] its body! Shoot through [SKRZZZT!]"

Rebel lands another critical strike and the thing screams out again in those echoing voices. With its convulsion, however, it knocks him off of the processing gear with a bone crunching swat. It's so dark up here that I lose sight of him as he tumbles down. There's no time left.

I target its mass of arms that form the hand holding on to the pod, unloading an entire cartridge. The thing wails again and spins around but...drops the pod! Its spider like feet scramble toward me as it advances on me. The dark gap in the arms at the top of its body peers at me hollowly.

My training fails me. I can't get the second barrel cartridge into the Sever before it's on top of me. Its four armed hand reaches out and grabs me in a bear hug. Each hand on each of the arms digs into the leather of my jacket so hard their grip is pinching my skin beneath. My gun arm is pinned, which is probably the only reason why it's not crushing my ribs right now. It lifts me off of the scaffolding deck and swings me over the edge.

That dark gaping hole in that mound of arms atop its shoulders parts a little more, giving it the appearance of an angry dark eyed cyclops.

I twist in its grip, trying to bring the barrel cartridge to my pinned Sever but there's no time. That other hand of arms is reaching for me. It's going to break me in half like so much...

He comes down on us from above somehow, the Rebel, and lands on the thing's torso-shoulder. I hear his scream, muffled by his helmet, as he drives his stun stick down into the mound of arms and let loose another burst.

I can feel the charge myself despite the insulation in my jacket, and shake violently as it passes through me. But the thing gets it much worse; that mound of arms explodes out as each appendage convulses and writhes from the burst, exposing...

"Oh my [SKRZZT!]! Detective, kill it!"

I scream at the sight. Four incomplete heads, each attached to an extended writhing length of patched together neck joints, scream their rage at Rebels assault. None of them are complete; only three have mouths...only two have eyes.

My LPD training finally kicks in and I hear the click of the barrel cartridge collapsing into my Sever. I fight through the convulsing and pull it from my pinned hand with my free one. Still, I'm shaking so bad I can barely target the thing let alone one of those heads but if I hit it, it will drop me down into the dark water.

Doesn't stop me from pulling the trigger.

BOOM! BOOM! The Sever bangs hard and the pressure from those breaking arms is gone. I fall free and try my best to reach out and grab the scaffolding before I fall past the processing gear.

"GOTCHA!" a grip nearly as strong as the thing's snatches my wrist. Rebel hauls me back onto the gear with one heave. We tumble together onto the scaffolding deck and roll until we hit the small pod.

"Here it comes!" he warns. Indeed the thing seems to have recovered from his attack already. It stands on the precipice of the gear; it arms slowly reforming the protective mound over its heads.

Without another word, Rebel launches himself back at it. I run at it as well, raising my Sever and firing until the barrel is empty again.

Rebel throws that stun stick at the thing, which it smacks out of the air before it can connect, receiving one last jolt for its effort. But he doesn't stop; instead of backing off Rebel smashes head long into the thing and sends them both over the edge of the processing gear.

I rush to edge and look down. The thing tumbles, wailing all the way. Rebel is in free fall next to it, curling himself into a ball. The dark water will eat him alive.

Suddenly he extends his arms and legs and there's webbing in between them…a wing suit! It takes a nerve-racking second for his airfoils to catch the wind but just as the thing hits the water; Rebel shoots off vertically and glides over the basin and away into the darkness.

I stare down into the dark water for a long moment before I figure that thing didn't survive. It couldn't survive that.

"The pod, Det [SKRZZZT!]" The ET is still on the line.

"Right," I say and make my way back along the scaffolding to the dropped pod.

"There's a catch [SKRZZZT!] its side panel."

"I'm not opening it!"

"The pod [SKRZZZT!] damaged, Detective," he warns me. "The catch on [SKRZZZT!] only clear the clouded glass."

A virtual flare rises up out of the darkness below; back-up is finally here. Shouldn't hurt to have a look at what that creature wanted so bad.

"What's in it?" I ask and I reset my communication

gear to receive the virtual. "Not another one of those runners?"

The ET appears in a hazy virtual holographic projection. Just seeing him now, his name finally comes to me…no…no it doesn't.

"Of course not, Detective," what's his name says. "It's [SKRZZZT!] spare parts for the Breaker."

"Breaker?"

"It's [SKRZZZT!] calling that thing."

"Spare parts?" I reach and undue the clasp on the side of the pod and a small pink light flashes. "Like another leg?"

"Sadly no, Detective." The top half of the pod then changes color. First to smoky black and then it clears and becomes transparent revealing the interior.

"In all the Risings…"

"I thought so," the ET is shaking his head woefully. "But I couldn't be sure."

"Why didn't you say something?" I snap. "I fired rounds at the thing."

"Like I said; I couldn't be sure."

"What was it going to do with it?"

"Again, like I said; spare parts."

"Where did it come from?"

"Get it back to the lab and we'll [SKRZZT!]. But just looking at it I can say I doubt [SKRZZT!]find out."

"Why?"

"Because it doesn't have a Tell."

No Tell? That's supposed to mean no chance in the City.

I reach down and place my hand on the glass, just over the small baby sleeping in the pod. "Welcome to *Liberty*."

Rhodes, GREETING LIBERTY

Collard Greens, Hummingbirds and Spider Silk

By
Malon Edwards

We come to the stand of Douglas firs with the fallen tree. The stand stretches tall. It speaks with the unseen sky. The fallen tree is massive. It seduces the overgrown forest floor.

So far, the lush code is still within me.

"We're almost there."

Ilo talks to the way we've come. He's my back. I'm his front. He's the only person I'll brave The Beyond with. He's the only person worth running away to The City.

"Do you want to rest?"

I shouldn't have asked him that. I know what his answer will be.

"We can rest when we get to The City."

His voice is pitched low, but it's firm. Like his daddy's. We won't rest long when we get there. If we get there. Perhaps an hour. Maybe two. And then—

Black fur is all up in my face. My claws are out; long-honed instinct. I attempt to block a swipe with my left hand; my forearm fractures. I'm thrown to the forest floor, facedown. My breath is gone. My left arm whispers throe and agony.

And then I hear Ilo say: "Call off your bear, Slim, or I rip out your throat."

*   *   *

"Chile, what y'all want to go bring back Sly Sincere for? Samfang and Kofi already doin' that."

Big Mama Green examined the stems and leaves of her collard green patch. We were in a sun-dappled corner of her Groove Grove. Alto saxophone licks floated down from the treetops. It was a treecode I'd never heard before.

"It's been a while. They haven't returned yet."

I squatted next to her as she picked leaves from the stems of eight different collard green plants. She worked from the bottom up. I could only hear the harvestcode of four of the plants call out to Big Mama Green.

"That's how I know your narrow li'l tail ain't never been to The City."

Big Mama Green sniffed the collard green leaves and smiled, satisfied.

"Excuse me?"

I tried not to twist my mouth to one side. Unlike some of the other young ones around here, I respected my elders. Especially when they had wisdom to impart.

"You heard me. I didn't stutter. The City don't work on your time, my time, or Sly Sincere's time. The City makes its own time. And we all Rise with It."

She looked at the enormous ceramic bowl in my hands.

"I'm ready to rise with It."

I held out the bowl for Big Mama Green.

"Chile, you couldn't rise if The Lush gave you wings."

Big Mama Green placed the collard green leaves in the bowl with the utmost care and stood. Both her knees cracked like rifle shots, dry and loud. She didn't look a day over twenty-five, what with her heart-shaped face, big sparkle-sparkle brown eyes, and smooth, golden skin. That was the Lush love Mama and Daddy wouldn't stop telling me about, morning, noon and night.

"I don't want wings."

I crossed my arms, and then uncrossed them. I didn't want to come off as petulant. Bratty. Ungrateful.

"So, what you want, then?"

Big Mama Green narrowed her eyes at me.

"I've been coming to your Groove Grove since I was three years old, and you haven't figured that out yet?"

I narrowed my eyes right back at her.

"Watch your mouth, gal. You talkin' to grown folk now."

Big Mama Green looked as if she were about to tell me to go cut a switch off the tree.

"I apologize. Sometimes, I get caught up in the greencode."

I dipped my head.

"It's a wonderful thing, ain't it?"

Big Mama Green threw her arms wide, lifted her face to the treetops, and closed her eyes.

"I want to be a sysop. I want to be like you."

I gave her a solemn nod.

"Chile, you ain't got enough hips to be like me."

Big Mama slapped her ample hips with both hands, and laughed, hearty and deep.

"I can, if I listen to the greencode as you do. And with enough Lush love, of course. "

I lifted my chin at her.

"Lush love ain't got nothin' to do with it."

She moved off to pick more collard greens.

"So says the woman who is, what? Eighty-nine years old now?"

I pished-pished before I realized what I was doing. Big Mama Green whirled on me.

"Lush love didn't make Mossberg Slim into what he is today. Lush love didn't make him a sysop. Arrogance did. Stupidity did."

She lifted my chin higher and looked into my eyes.

"I'm not arrogant. Nor am I stupid."

I snatched my face away from hand.

"Chile, keep on talkin' like that, and you gon' find out what you really is."

Big Mama Green tut-tutted something fierce.

"I already know what I am. I'm the next sysop for The Lush."

I folded my arms again, though this time, I was certain I'd taken on a mature stance.

"Mossberg Slim said somethin' very similar to me once. And he had the selfsame look on his face you got on yours now."

Big Mama Green kissed her teeth again.

"And yet, The Lush blessed his code."

My mouth twisted full on to one side this time.

"You call what he is now a blessing?"

Big Mama Green's forehead furrowed with disbelief and concern.

"Yes. He is blessed, as The Lush will bless my journey."

I couldn't help but smile smug.

"Chile, you need to shut your mouth, right here, right now. The Lush got ears, 'specially in my Groove Grove."

Big Mama Green's voice was almost inaudible as she leaned forward to whisper into my left ear.

"Oh, but It already knows. Search the greencode. You'll see for yourself."

I tried to sound confident.

"Oh I done checked it. They don't call me Big Mama Green for nothin'. The Lush done tol' me all your business. And all the juicy 'bout that boy of yours, too."

Big Mama Green leaned back and nodded at me as if she were about to tell me my most unmentionable secrets.

"What does It say?"

I hesitated before I took a step closer and held my breath for her answer.

"It says stay your narrow li'l tail at home, and stay 'way from that boy. He changin' you, and none for the better. He got you in one pocket and trouble in his other."

*   *   *

Now, Big Mama Green gon' tell y'all how things really is 'round here.

Despite what that gal think, The Lush don't let nobody leave. Not you, not me, not nobody. And I been livin' here since Ol' Heck was a pup.

But what about Sly Sincere, y'all say? Well, what about him? He ain't gone. That boy will be back before quick get the news. Just you watch.

See, what some of these people here don't realize is The Lush knows your mind, your heart and your soul. It coded us.

Take that narrow tailed li'l gal, for instance. Her name Jaiyesimi. Means 'let the world rest.' And that hard-headed boy she like so much? His name Ilozumba. Means 'our distant home is forgotten'.

Now, 'tween you, me, and the fence post, they parents didn't choose them names. The Lush put them names in they parents' heads way back when they was conceived.

Sound like some crazy talk, don't it? Y'all sittin' over there thinkin', 'Big Mama Green done ate the wrong mushrooms.' Naw, chile, I ain't trippin'. I'm jus' speakin' the truth. I'm jus' droppin' some Knowledge.

What y'all really should be sayin' is, 'Why would The Lush do that? Why would It put stuff like that in people's heads?'

'Cause It want to. 'Cause It can. 'Cause The Lush knew—even before them two hard-headed chirren were born into this wonderful paradise—that li'l gal would do any and e'rything to become a sysop for The Lush, and that li'l boy would use lies and sweet talk and those beautiful lips of his to convince that li'l gal the only way she can become a sysop is by goin' with him to The City to bring back Sly Sincere. Not Kofi Sincere, not Samfang, not nobody.

All 'cause he feelin' himself.

That boy think he slick, y'all, but don't nobody get nothin' over on The Lush. Jus' ask Big Swole. What was that? Y'all don't know who Big Swole is? That's 'cause we call him Mossberg Slim now.

Big Swole used to be six-foot-eight, three hundred thirty-five pounds. Cut up like a Christmas turkey. He tol' e'rybody he was gon' drag Sly Sincere back to The Lush, and by his ear, no less. So he went into The Beyond, stompin' where he shouldn't have been stompin', and crossed over to the other side of that fallen tree.

Because of that, he wasn't Big Swole no more. My foxtail seeds up his ass made sure of it. Gave him the rot, I did. Made him as skinny as my pinky finger. And The City laughed at him.

Yeah, y'all heard me. The Lush told The City all Mossberg Slim's business.

See, They speak to each other. They share code. They Brother and Sister.

Might have caught some of y'all by surprise with that one. It's all green, though. I can break it down for y'all. I got some time, if y'all got some time.

Ready? Then allow me to get Lateef on y'all for a moment.

E'rybody know The City is the be all and the end all. The City is life; The City is death. The City is in me; The City is in you. The City is here now, was there then, and forever will be.

Ain't no disputin' that.

Now, some of y'all might say, 'How is The City in you, Big Mama Green? You live in The Lush! And besides, you Big Mama Green!'

Well, chile, let me tell you how.

Way back before I was here, you was here, and we all was here, The City existed, and It was aware. It thought, It breathed, It slept. And so did The Lush, beside Her Brother, His conjoined twin 'tached by The River.

Thing is, The City was the one makin' all the noise.

Y'all know what I'm talkin' 'bout, what with the Tell and them Watchers and The Wave, and all that other stuff I don't know 'bout them folk and what they do over there that we don't do over here.

See, now, look at that. There I go again. Look at what y'all done made me do. Y'all got me runnin' my mouth through these sweet, lovely li'l hummingbirds, chirpin' all The City's business. Not that y'all gon' remember none of this code by the time I'm finished, anyway.

But I'm gon' keep tellin' it. Maybe The Lush will fall into a deep slumber one of these days and forget about us all.

Or maybe, more and more of them City folk will start showin' they ass, we'll have an influx of them comin' over here, and there will be too many of y'all for The Lush to mind wipe. Jaiyesimi would like that. She'd have a field day as a sysop, puttin' down all them people who tried to run back to The City. But that ain't neither here nor there right now.

And that's too bad for y'all, 'cause I got some stories to tell. It's all green, though.

So I'm gon' keep tellin' my stories, as long as y'all keep actin' like y'all want to hear them. Maybe one day The Lush will let y'all remember them, so y'all can tell them to your grandbabies.

But 'til that day come, jus' sit back, relax, and listen to this Green-Crowned Brilliant sang.

*   *   *

"Jaiye? Are you all right?"

I feel a snort of humid breath on the back of my neck. I turn over. My left arm is cradled against my ribs. Black bear is still all up in my face, daring me to move. So I don't.

"Talk to me, Jaiye."

I look at the bear. I'm on the other side of the fallen tree.

"I'm too tall for stupid; you're too short for smart."

The bear snuffles. Her eyes twinkle, a deep, verdant green, for just a moment. She's laughing at me. Big Mama Green is probably in her Groove Grove, busting a stitch, as she would say, watching us through the bear, hearing her words come out of my mouth, while she's eating her scrumptious collard greens.

"Don't let a bump on the head make you go all crazy on me now."

Ilo has his left hand around Mossberg Slim's throat. His right hand is crooked like a bird of prey. His long, curved, black claws are poised above Slim's jugular.

"Sounds to me like your girl found some greencode when she was down on the ground there."

Mossberg Slim winks at me.

"I've lost my purity, Ilo."

I reach out a slow, careful hand and stroke the bear's snout. She flares her nostrils, shakes her big, furry head, and sneezes.

"I'm sure you still got enough for the both of us."

Ilo presses his index claw against Slim's mossy throat. A thin thread of blood trickles down Slim's neck to his frail collarbone.

"You done done it, now."

Mossberg Slim grabs Ilo's forearm. Thin, whip-like, sickly-green tendrils blossom beneath Ilo's cheeks. They zigzag across his beautiful dark skin. They creep down to his jaw, to his throat. Ilo stumbles. He lets Mossberg Slim go. His hands scrabble at his now corded neck. He's choking. He's suffocating. His claws try to tear his own flesh. The green rot swells his neck tight to protect against the assault. His claws chip and break, ineffective.

No matter.

I have claws, too.

*   *   *

"I gotta speak fast, 'cause The Lush might change my words and start me lyin'."

Big Mama Green cut the central stems from the collard leaves, stacked the leaves, rolled them lengthwise, and then sliced them crosswise into ribbons.

"You a sweet girl. Your mama and daddy raised you right. You respect The Lush. You honor The Lush. You revere The Lush. You only take what you need when you go out huntin' in The Beyond, and no more."

I raised my eyebrows at Big Mama Green.

"Chile, don't look so surprised. The Lush know. The Lush see. And The Lush only pass on to me what I need to do Its will as a sysop."

Big Mama Green heated olive oil in a deep pot on her stone stove and then added a pinch of red pepper flakes and small slices of bacon. She let the deliciousness fry. The Groove Grove began to smell wonderful.

"Right now, you in The Lush's good books. You pure. You innocent. You a Lush baby through and through. But if you follow that knucklehead boy into The Beyond, past that fallen tree I was jus' tellin' you 'bout, then you lose all of that and make yourself public enemy to The Lush."

I sat back in Big Mama Green's wood-carved chair and spread my fingers wide on her small, smooth kitchen table.

"Now, I know what you gon' say: 'But I love him!'
Maybe you do. That ain't really none of my business."

Big Mama Green grabbed a slotted spoon from a hook
next to the stove.

"But that boy don't love you. I know that for a fact.
He don't love nothin' livin', not even people. What he do
love, though, is adventure. And sneakiness. And deception.
And lies. And fear. And insanity. And disobedience. And
power. And sysop status. But he can't get none of that unless
goes to the other side of that fallen tree—which then makes
it my business."

Big Mama Green turned from the stove for a moment
and kissed the crown of my head. I could feel her warm lips
through my buzz cut.

"So listen to me now, and listen to me good. Don't go
with that boy. You could spread your legs for him in a corner
of my Groove Grove and give up the coochie, and I wouldn't
say boo. But you get on the other side of that tree and try to
leave the Lush with that boy, and Mossberg Slim will put you
down."

She turned back to the stove, and tendrils of her thick,
long loose curls climbed off her shoulders, coiling into a
messy-chic updo. It took me a moment to realize her hair
wasn't hair at all, but vines.

"Now, let me finish puttin' my foot in these collard
greens so you can have a taste, and then take some home to
your mama and daddy."

*   *   *

The bear is gone. The underbrush shows mark of her
lumbering passage: gouged moss, torn ferns. A rake of my
claws blinded her; a swipe across her nose sent her on her
way.

"I tol' Big Mama Green you would choose him over
The Lush."

Mossberg Slim watches as The Lush reclaims Ilo. He's wrapped so tightly with thick vines I can no longer see his once-beautiful dark skin. But I can hear the soft, wet tearing of his flesh as the vines feed.

"I didn't choose Ilo. I chose The Lush. And now, It will bless me with sysop status."

I throw my arms out wide, close my eyes, and lift my face to the sky.

"Big Mama Green was half wrong. You ain't no parts arrogant. You jus' all stupid."

"So says the man once known as Big Swole."

My voice is hushed as I await my blessing.

"Keep on talkin' like that. You 'bout to learn your lesson the hard way."

I tilt my head. Far off, I hear a sound. A scratch-skittering. It sounds like insect legs against the foliage. Hundreds of insect legs. Thousands of insect legs. But I keep my eyes closed and my arms outstretched. I will welcome my blessing, no matter its form.

"You 'bout to learn what I learned too late."

I open my eyes. Mossberg Slim's sunken, disease-ravaged chest is now puffed out with delight, like a bullfrog. He looks to say something more, but then thousands of western black widow spiders swarm me.

They are my blessing. I look to blue sky again and close my eyes. The black widow spiders climb over one another as they spiral my body, wrapping me in their webbing. The silk burns. I want to scream. My mouth is bound. I want to run. My clothes slough off. The silk destroys.

It is not long before the black widows have trussed me from head to foot.

Through my blood-soaked silken gaze, I see Mossberg Slim smiling at me sly.

"See, The Lush never blesses us," he says. "It only blesses Itself."

Hunter's First Rule

By
Gerald L. Coleman

Fué woke to an incessant banging on his door. It made his head hurt. Whoever it was clearly didn't know him. Only a stranger would think it was ok to bang on his door. A quick look at his chronometer confirmed it. His familiars - you didn't really have friends in The City - would know better than to wake him before five *zulu-time*. As he rolled out of bed, Fué corrected himself. You could have friends in The City. It was just incredibly difficult. You see, if friends were anything, they were the people you trusted – people you could rely on. But The City was all angles and hard edges. It was utterly unforgiving and it was always watching. It wasn't the kind of place that lent itself to friendship – not real friendship anyway. Show The City that you cared about something, or someone, and you gave it a handle to grab onto – a pressure point. And believe me; The City knew how to grab hold. It would press until you screamed to be put out of your misery. Fué had seen it. It wasn't pretty.

He did not turn on the lights. Fué wanted to keep his night-sight. It would still be dark outside. The artificial lights on his level would be set to dim, mimicking the time of the morning. Halfway across the room he scooped up his Dha. When he reached the door he pushed up on the *subah* with his thumb, loosening the blade in its black, partec scabbard. He uttered a single word.

"Open." The door slid open with a soft *whoosh.*

Filtch was standing in his doorway, wringing his hands, while trying to look in every direction at once. Fué had been wrong. It wasn't a stranger, just someone who was stupid. Fué grabbed a handful of Filtch's shirt, just beneath his neck, with his free hand, and dragged the thin, small man into his quarters. As the door *whooshed* closed, Fué slammed Filtch into the wall.

"I'm going to assume you have lost your mind, or taken too much glitch. Because it's barely five-zulu and you are pounding on my door like your life doesn't mean anything to you."

He jostled Filtch back and forth, roughly, to drive home the point. "I suggest you give me a reason not to beat you about the head and neck before dumping you down the res-chute. And be quick about it!"

It took Fué a moment to realize that Filtch had been trying to speak the whole time. His hand around the man's neck prevented him from getting a word out. Fué released him. As Filtch's feet hit the carpet, Fué also realized he had been holding the man a foot off the floor. It served the fool right for banging on his door this early in the morning. He took a step back while the man caught his breath. He did not put down his blade or relax. *Hunter's Third Rule? Never drop your guard.*

When Filtch caught his breath, he started talking almost faster than Fué could follow. It had happened the night before, down in the Nine's, across from the Platforms. Some Ret-Cons from the *subs* snatched Azzura off the street. Filtch tried to help but they took her and disappeared. He looked all over the Bazz Ward for Fué but couldn't find him. So he asked around until he found someone who could tell him where Fué lived so he could come and tell him. Fué shoved his Dha blade home in its *sayaddac* with a click.

Fué tried to tell Azzura about The City. But she was too trusting. It had always been that way, ever since he met her at the Drill down by the Platforms. He couldn't believe she was there by herself. Something deep inside told him this day was coming. But he always thought - *nah, that's just my own cynicism talking*. But Fué knew The City. There was nothing soft about it. Sure, people talked about The Lush, but that was a pipedream. The City was always watching. And man, it was patient. The moment you slipped it was there. Not to catch you, but to devour you like it had not eaten in weeks. He should have known falling for someone was stupid. You just didn't do that, not in The City. Once you showed The City a hint of weakness you could be sure of one thing. It was coming for you.

So here was Filtch, glitching in his quarters like a hop-fiend twelve days gone, giving Fué the big bad. They took her last night. They snatched her right off the street. They had an enormous head start. He could have killed Filtch for taking so long to get the word to him. It had taken entirely too long. But he stood there, fighting with himself. He should just throw Filtch out of his quarters headfirst and go back to bed. It was stupid to think you could take something back from The City. It just was not done. When The City took something it was for keeps. Whether your pockets were empty or you had enough credits to live in the Hub, it did not matter. You could be a Magistrate, or strung out on glitch, The City did not care. The City did not give, but it did take away. What it took, you never saw again.

Filtch bounced when Fué threw him out of his quarters. He cleaned up quickly. A hand on the sensor next to his closet opened the door without a sound. His Meg-suit hung there on its steel trellis. It was black, quantum mesh. It took him five jobs to save up enough credits for it. The mesh was soft, and pliable as cloth, but nearly as effective as heavy plate armor. He liked the cross-weave pattern too. A minute was all it took for him to slip into it. His black, calf-high boots were still next to his oversized, leather chair. Fué sat so he could pull them on. With one boot on, he stopped. Filtch had smelled peculiar. The nascent, half-formed scent lingered in the front room. It was long faded, which made it nearly impossible to identify. It was like trying to remember a name that you knew but couldn't quite put your finger on. Fué breathed it in again and grimaced. It escaped him. Shaking his head, he pulled on his other boot.

Finally, he grabbed his black, tech-weave coat. After zipping up the high collar to the top of his neck, he clicked the oval, steel buckle of his black, leather belt in place at his waist. He slid his Dha behind his belt on his left hip. He also clipped a long knife, a sleek hand rayser, and three utility cases onto it. Sliding his rifle strap over his shoulder, Fué left his quarters with two restive thoughts in the back of his mind. He would deal with them when the time was right. He took the gravilift to the ground level in silence.

The City did not give back what it took. But that was the entire reason *Hunters* existed. It was how Fué made his living. His mother had been a former assassin turned Hunter. She had taught him the trade. His left hand absently caressed the hilt of the Dha hanging at his waist. The blade had been hers. Solange True taught him the Rules and Trade. She versed him in turning the Wave and the Tell to his advantage. The only thing she had not been able to do was explain to him just exactly what The City was and how they got here. She lived to see him become a Hunter with a rep of his own. It had made her happy.

If you could find someone with the right skills and the will to use them, sometimes - a very rare sometimes - you could get back what The City had taken. You found yourself a Hunter and you paid them. Fué had retrieved experimental biochips, contraband firearms, and a kidnapped family member or two. Today it was going to be the woman he had begun having feelings for. Because even though The City took her, he was going to get her back.

Hunter's Ninth Rule echoed in his mind, in his mother's voice, as Fué exited his building– *Start at the beginning*. He unlocked the door to his stall on the northern side of the building. Climbing onto his jumpbike, he hit the start button. It came to life with a clean, rumbling hum before rising a few feet off the ground. He checked to be sure he had a full charge before pulling out onto the Ave. Fué didn't even bother to look back to make sure the stall door closed. His mind was focused on the task at hand. If he was going to get Azzura back alive he had to be fast and precise.

It took about half a cycle to make it to the coordinates where she disappeared. Even though it was still early the streets were crowded. The City did not sleep. The artificial lights that mimicked the day were still dim, but the Ward was lit up with a luminescent glow that poured out of windows, off signs, and transports filling the street. Fué shook the feeling that he was being watched. In The City you were always being watched. But today he had an itch between his shoulders that wouldn't relent. He shook it off because he had work to do. A quick, hard sniff got the smell of ion-trails out of his nose. Braking hard, he slid his jumpbike into a parking grid in front of Molls Emporium. After powering down his bike, he waited the half-second it took to touch down onto the ground. Hopping off his bike, he retrieved a datapad from one of the storage compartments on the back.

It took nearly an entire cycle to discover that no one knew anything. Now, sure – normally people didn't want to see anything, even if they had. You couldn't get anyone to speak in the Heap to save your life. Strangely, it was the same way in the Hub. People didn't want to talk. But this was different, especially down here in the District. Shopkeepers were notoriously nosy and loose-lipped. Fué had shown the datapad, with Azzura's image beaming from its screen, to everyone from Ilka at the ticket window of Molls, to Paddic hanging from the serving window of his Zonji Food Truck, down on the corner by Lateef Ave. Not only had they not seen her get snatched but they hadn't seen her at all. It didn't add up. The City might decide what it saw and what it didn't but it wasn't blind. When Fué came up empty, he flagged down a Runner leaving Paddic's food truck with a container of munda, smothered in gallic sauce. Swipe was young, as Runner's went, but he was good. If you wanted to send a message off the grid, he was your man. There were occasions when sending a message through the Wave was warranted, but if you wanted it to stay confidential you used a Runner.

Swipe had black locks hanging halfway down his back. His eyes were covered by misty, blue goggles with a heads-up display. Like most Runners, he was sleek. A brown jumpsuit with hopboots and a burstpack on his back meant he didn't need a jump bike or transport. Fué had no doubt that there were other surprises tucked away on his person. Runners were not helpless. They weren't assassins, but they weren't helpless either.

Swipe had a high voice with a bright disposition. He smiled when he saw Fué. It took him three seconds to burst from the food truck down to where Fué stood next to his jump bike. Swipe landed in a swirl of ion-trail and burst energy.

"Fué! It's good to see you. On the Hunt? Oh yeah, right! Sorry." Swipe dropped his voice and looked around like he was being spied on. Fué tried not to laugh. The young man continued, "Uh … so … uh. What's up?"

Fué just smiled at the Runner. Swipe took one look at his smile and said, "You *are* on the Hunt aren't you?!" The young Runner got even more excited causing his whisper to become a loud faux-whisper. "So what are we doing? Huh? Are we tracking assassins? Are we hunting down nutters? Stolen Tell Tech? Experimental Biowear? Whatever it is I'm so IN!"

Fué held up his hand to get Swipe to stop. "Swipe. There is no *we*. Though it's good to see you. I need you to do a Run."

Swipe looked disappointed for half a second until his mind got to the part where Fué had said that he wanted him to do a Run. His eyes lit up like a nav-screen behind his goggles. The Runner flashed him a bright, winning smile and stuck out his hand. Fué could not help but smile back. The boy's enthusiasm was infectious. Fué handed Swipe the message and told him where to deliver it. When Fué finished giving him coordinates, he had to remind Swipe to remain calm. Swipe's smile seemed to get even bigger, as if that were possible. He shot Fué a salute before blasting off. The boy left nothing but a fading ion-trail in his wake. With a final smile aimed in Swipe's direction, Fué decided to get a drink while he waited.

The Flez was a quaint little café two doors down from Molls. They had really good jawa. So Fué found a quiet table in the back, where he could see all the entrances and exits. He sat there sipping on the dark brew in its tiny cup. *Hunter's Twelfth Rule? Always know which way is out.* He had no idea where Ollo got the beans to grind for the jawa but it was delicious. Fué was on his second cup and halfway through a piece of sweet bread when it hit him. He turned up the cup, gulping down the last dregs of the bitter-sweet infusion. Pushing back his chair, he stood, grabbed the remaining half of his sweet bread, and made his way out of the café. Fué just stood there on the street. As he swallowed the last bit of sweetbread, he pressed his lips together firmly. A deep breath filled his lungs, followed by a grim, resolved, slow exhale through his nose. Maybe it was the conjunction of place and thought. Maybe the smell of jawa had cleared his nose, triggering some kind of sense memory. It hit him like a biosteel wall.

Fué made his way back around to the merchants and shopkeepers he questioned earlier. This time he asked them something different. By his second stop he had his answer, but he kept going. Sure enough, most of the rest verified what he suspected. By the time he returned to the café, two people were standing by his jump bike waiting.

A small patch of anger was beginning to smolder in the back of his mind but that didn't stop him from smiling warmly at Switch. The small, brown woman was a sight for sore eyes. Her smile matched his own when he approached. Switch was a Wave rider, a fractal freak. She had a genius level intellect and knew more about surfing or skewing the Wave than anyone he had ever met. Her thick, wooly hair was pulled up into two enormous puffs. Her brown eyes were a shade lighter than her complexion. She had the face of hollow-mod. Her jumpsuit was blue mesh trimmed in gold. She had tech on her wrist, hanging from her leather belt and likely in a small pack on her back. Her goggles were dark blue, with a tiny antennae sticking up on the right side of the frame. Fué towered over her. She was tiny. He swept her up in a big hug.

After he put her down, he said, "Switch. It's great to see you! Thanks for coming."

Switch straightened the top of her jumpsuit and said, "It's a pleasure to see you again too, Fué. It's been too long." Switch made a half-turn, motioning to the man with her as she said, "You remember Bael, right?"

Fué had to look up to see Bael's face. He was as tall as a Helium Breather. While Switch surfed the Wave for the right price, Bael kept her safe. He was a big bad from the Westside, an enhanced Warrior with a decent disposition. The man's head was clean-shaven like his own, though he was a few shades darker than Fué. Bael also had tattoos up his neck and over one eye. He wore dark, gray, chest armor, blue mesh pants, and black tech boots. Fué also counted a few knives, a blaster, and one mean looking rayser rifle. The large man's grip was firm but not overbearing as Fué shook his hand.

"Nice to see you again, Bael." Bael nodded in response, with a noncommittal grunt for emphasis, before going back to scanning the area for possible threats.

Fué turned back to Switch. "Switch, normally I would invite you into the café for a drink while we caught up, but I'm afraid time is not on our side."

Switch waved off his apology, with an absent hand, as if to say she understood completely. "Not to worry. How can I help?"

So, with Bael watching the street for trouble, Fué explained to Switch what had happened and what he needed her to do. Her eyes narrowed a bit. She pressed her lips together, nodding as he finished. He watched her eyes go up and over in that way people's eyes did when they were thinking over a problem.

Fué had time to look over at Bael, who was still scanning their surroundings, and turn back to Switch before she snapped her fingers, smiled, and said, "I've got it." She tapped the tech band on her arm causing a holographic heads-up display to glow to life. With uncanny speed she began typing on its keyboard. The information passed across the holographic screen faster than Fué could keep up with it. He wasn't sure that he would have understood what he was seeing even if he could. Switch's head moved up and down, and side-to-side, as she scrolled through the information. She disappeared into the computer language of the Wave. It wasn't long before a dot on the screen began blinking. With a squeal of delight, Switch reached into her backpack and pulled out a small data pad. She synced it with her tech band then handed it to Fué. He raised an eyebrow at her.

"It's done," she said. "I found them by locating their I.D. in the Wave then back-traced it to their last known position. I was able to enter a coded geo-tag by tracing their Wave input. Once I tagged their input it was easy enough to attach a data spike to their Tell interface."

Fué just stood there. He was holding the data pad she had just given him in his hand, staring at her blankly. Switch looked from him, to the data pad, and then back at him again. He realized his mouth was open but he didn't know what to say. Switch cleared her throat, took a deep breath, and spoke slowly.

"The data pad has the location. This blinking light is the person you are looking for."

Fué closed his mouth. He looked down at the data pad and sure enough there was a blinking light with a geo-tag. He knew where he was going. He looked back at Switch with a smile.

"Thank you Switch. What do I owe you?"

She was already waving him off. "No, Fué. You don't

owe me anything. I am still trying to pay off the debt I owe you." She unconsciously looked in Bael's direction. Looking back at Fué she said, "So, what's next?"

Fué raised an eyebrow again. He opened his mouth, but Switch cut him off.

"You didn't look close enough at the coordinates of the geo-tag. You are heading for the Tombs. Now, I have no doubt about your abilities. Your reputation is well-deserved. But the Tombs? You are going to need some help."

Hunter's Eighth Rule? Take help where you can get it. Fué smiled and nodded. "Thanks Switch. I appreciate it."

Switch nodded and said, "So, like I said, what's next?"

Fué took a moment to consider everything he knew. The itch between his shoulders, that had been nothing more than a nuisance earlier, was now a full-blown warning bell going off in his head. They had taken her to the Tombs. It had not made sense until just now. Fué let the realization of it wash over him. The pieces had been floating in the back of his mind as individual oddities. They were remarkable on their own, but not a cohesive picture. *They took her to the Tombs.* He nearly laughed. But he didn't. Azzura was in real danger - even more danger now, which he would not have thought possible until this very moment.

Hunter's Fifth Rule? Trust your instincts. So, Fué trusted his. He gave Switch some instructions and then fired up his jump bike. He wove through traffic like he was on autopilot, lost in thought on his way to the Tombs. It took him thirty minutes to make it out of the Bazz Ward and into Sector 43. He could have accessed the Sublevels from his Ward but no one in their right mind would travel that far in the Tombs. That's what they were called. The City went on forever. No one had seen its end, though some claimed to. They were liars. The City was unending. It went up so high it disappeared from sight. It stretched out so far no one knew how many Sectors there were. But The City didn't just go up and out. It also went down. Below the street were the Sublevels. They were called the *subs* and the *Tombs*.

People who went down into the Tombs did not return. The City was uncaring, dangerous, and even nasty. But the Tombs were even more so. The deeper you went into the subs the more dangerous it became. Rooms and corridors were all that existed down there. Some said there were vast chambers too – places where the guts of The City could be found. The Tombs were home to Reavers, refugees, Ret-Cons, and discarded A.I.'s. Fué knew there were gangs down there too. The Scarabs, the Nihils, the 44's and the Scavengers all ran the lower levels with impunity. Some said that every now and then, when the gangs got to be too big or disruptive to be ignored, The Watchers swept the Tombs clean. But Fué didn't know if that was real or not. People disappeared. But there were a hundred reasons for that to happen and none of them named Watcher.

Fué pulled his jump bike into a hollowed out vacant building, a stone's throw from where the coordinates on the data pad indicated. He was in the 99's. The 99th Ward was nearly empty. It looked like the rest of The City but for some reason was mostly abandoned. There were a number of empty buildings that were either falling down or in disrepair. Powering down his jump bike, Fué waited until he felt it touch down before dismounting. He entered his lock code and opened the storage containers, retrieving extra ammo-cartridges and tactical packs. Strapping a tech band onto his wrist, he put on his tac-goggles, and then walked to the grate covering the entrance to the subs. A quick look around, to be sure he wasn't being watched, and Fué pulled up the grate so he could drop into sublevel one. The grate slammed shut over his head. The level was dim but not dark. The lights still worked this far up. The deeper you went into the Tombs the darker it got. The lights rarely functioned in the lower levels. Sometimes it was just disrepair, but other times it was because the people, or things, that roamed the subs broke them.

Fué had synced the data pad Switch gave him with his tech band. Tapping its keypad, he engaged the holographic, heads-up display. And there it was. The geo-tag pulsed softly with a location on the grid of the sub-level. He was going to have to go down several more floors, but the coordinates weren't far. With a deep breath, Fué steeled himself. He reached into one of the utility cases clipped onto his belt. It held a little treat Switch had given him. He clipped it into place on his belt and activated it by pressing the green button on its side. With a soft, low pulse of sound, he knew it was activated. The electro-mag pulse field worked. Every light within thirty paces of him winked out. He stood in utter darkness.

For most people, the darkness is not a welcome place. But Fué was raised by an ex-assassin turned Hunter. She raised him to be unafraid, to make fear such an intimate friend that he could turn it to his own uses. She showed him how to make the darkness his ally not his enemy. So, while there were things in the Tombs to fear, the darkness was not one of them. Fué clicked on a night shield over his goggles. The goggles allowed him to see in the dark and the shield blocked the light his goggles produced so he remained invisible to the naked eye. He moved forward with the darkness like armor around him. He found a stairwell and circled down into the depths of the subs, with the geo-tag leading him twenty floors down. There was no resistance. On sub fourteen, he heard movement in the corridor but whoever it was did not enter the stairwell. Distant laughter floated down to him as he passed the eighteenth level, but he continued to be undiscovered. When he reached the twenty-first sub the readings on the tech band let him know he had reached the right level. Fué drew his blade.

He opened the door slowly and slid into the corridor. The hallway was empty. The electro-mag pulse bathed the entire level in darkness. Fué flitted from one side of the corridor to the other as he made his way down the hall to the last room on the left. That's where the coordinates located his target. He eased up to the door and listened. There was no sound. Fué slid his hand rayser from its holster at his waist. With his thumb he eased the safety off. Rayser in his left hand and his Dha in his right, he kicked open the door, diving into the room with a smooth roll. He came up with his back against the wall on the right side of the room. Just as he did, his electro-meg pulse beeped. The lights flared to life. Fué almost cut himself as he reached up to snatch his goggles off his face with his blade still in his hand. The burst of light nearly blinded him. That's when he heard the laughter.

The man was tall and slender. His mech-suit was dark blue tech weave with well-placed armor plates. His jacket had tan and black fur around the collar. The tech boots were black, with a buckle at the ankle. His name was Spazz and he was a Hunter. His sword hilt stuck up over his shoulder but he was holding a Ramsir 4gen rayser rifle in his hands aimed right at Fué. He glared at Fué out of ice-blue eyes with a broad grin spreading wryly above a square jaw. The pale skin of his face reflected the artificial light of the sublevel poorly.

The room was incredibly large but had obviously been emptied out recently. Dust marks in the floor revealed evidence of relocated furniture. Only a single chair remained in the large, empty chamber. It sat in the middle of the room, three paces behind Spazz, with Azzura strapped to it. She was bound and gagged. When she saw Fué, she struggled uselessly against her bonds. Her muffled shrieks put his teeth on edge.

Spazz chuckled softly. "Well, well, well. If it isn't the great Hunter, Fué True. They call you The Truth don't they? Aren't you supposed to be the big bad? The Hunter who always succeeds? I guess the Street will have to revise the story about you, eh?"

Fué stood, sliding his Dha back in its scabbard as he did. He looked from Spazz, to Azzura, and then past Azzura to the Reavers crowded together at the back of the room. It was a trap. He looked at Spazz.

"What do you want, *Hunter*." He made it sound like an indictment. Slowly, he slid his rayser back into its holster at his right hip. Spazz drank in the moment, savoring it like it was the last bit of savage in the bottom of the glass.

"What do I want? Well, let's see. First, I'm going to kill you. And when she sees that you are no longer a viable option, I'm going to have her. Oh, and I'm going to take your Hunt. It's so large and profitable that I'm going to add it to the other two I've taken. I'm going to have the largest Hunt in The City."

Fué just stood there for a moment. Hunters were solitary creatures. But they did know one another. Spazz had always been a disappointment. He was cowardly and wretched. But since Hunters rarely interacted, he had been allowed to practice the Hunt without interference. Interfering in another Hunter's domain was taboo. Your Hunt, the territory where you practiced as a Hunter, was sacrosanct. You did not Hunt in another Hunter's territory. You did not interfere in another Hunter's business. It did not happen. There were not even stories of it having happened. It was taboo.

"I don't believe you," Fué said.

Spazz's eyes narrowed. "What do you mean?"

"I mean, I don't believe you. You haven't taken over any Hunter's territory and made it yours. And you aren't going to take mine. I know you're stupid, but you aren't that stupid."

Spazz cackled. He tossed his rifle to one of the Reavers behind him and took a few steps toward Fué.

"I'm not stupid. You are. You're stupid for having chased this woman blindly down a hole in the ground. And you're stupid for underestimating me. I ambushed Faelin in the Drells and took his Hunt. I threw Tamerelle off the top floor of Anukoo Tower in the 44th Ward and took her Hunt as well. And now I'm going to do the same thing to you! They will say you went into the Tombs and never came out."

Fué nodded his head once. His voice was surprisingly calm. He spoke so softly that Spazz almost missed it.

"That's what I thought."

Spazz jerked his head back and sneered, "What do you mean that's what you thought?"

Fué sniffed softly and said, "Hunter's First Rule, you fool."

Spazz took a step back. Fué continued.

"I thought it was odd that Filtch would come running to me about something. Then the fool lied about knowing where I live. My quarters aren't a secret. I'm easy to find." Fué took a slow half-step forward and continued, "Worst than that, the idiot didn't have the sense to wash himself before coming to find me. The scent had faded significantly, which is why it took me a few hours to figure out where I knew it from. And when no one could recall seeing Azzura snatched off the street, I realized something was off. But you know what they did remember seeing? The two of you together. Once I made that connection, the rest of it fell into place. I realized that it was the two of you who had taken Azzura and there was only one reason you would have Filtch help lead me to the Tombs."

His voice was heated now. Fué had allowed the anger that had been building all morning to start boiling over.

"But you know what, Spazz. You forgot Hunter's First Rule. Make sure you are never the prey." Fué tapped on his tech band again and said, "Did you get that?"

A voice came back through his tech band. "Yes, we got it."

Spazz's eyes widened. He said, "Who ... who was that?!"

Fué let himself smile now. He smiled a grim smile as he said, "Spazz, you ought to be proud of yourself. You have done something today that I have never seen or even heard of. Once I figured out what you were up to I had Switch search the Wave. She told me about the missing Hunters and the stories surrounding their disappearances. It was easy to check to see if you had increased your Hunt. You were greedy and stupid. So, I had Switch spread the word among the Hunters in the surrounding Sectors. They rendezvoused with her on the surface and she let them listen in on our little conversation." Fué took another step toward Spazz who was looking around the room like he had nowhere to go.

"You know it's taboo to mess with someone else's Hunt, right? You killed two Hunters and have been caught trying to kill a third? Well, guess who is on their way down to this sublevel?"

Spazz yelled at the Reavers, "Kill him! Kill him now!"

Thankfully, the Reavers were basically scavengers – strong-arm brutes, not warriors. Spazz had likely promised them credits to act as his muscle. They were half-crazed nutters who spent their days roaming the sublevels looking for easy prey. They were unorganized, untrained, poorly equipped brawlers. Had they actually been warriors, Fué might have been in real trouble. As it was, he was pushed to his limits by their sheer numbers. There must have been twenty of them, armed with blades, spikes, sticks and makeshift weapons meant to break, bloody, maim and ultimately kill. They swarmed toward him. Azzura was still tied to a chair in the middle of the room, so Fué couldn't use his raysers for fear of a stray blast hitting her. He pulled his Dha free of its scabbard. It was the first thing his mother had begun teaching him. The Way of the Dha. He cleared his mind as they rushed him, purging all thought and hope from his mind. He allowed himself to disappear into the moment. There was no Azzura, no Fué, no life or death – there was only the blade.

Fué spun left. He met a stick, sprouting nails, with fourth position. Pushing up with his sword, he let it pass over his head. He did not stop. He floated through them like a stream through a bed of rocks. He blocked, followed by a thrust – parried and reposted. A cut left followed by a slash to his right, left him twirling back to his center. He moved from a two-handed block, to a single-handed lunge, with economy and fluidity. He could still hear his mother's voice. *The beauty of the movement is in its economic utility.* Fué stopped when he reached the other end of the room.

Turning to look behind him, Fué exhaled slowly. The Reavers lay dead or dying. With a single flick of his wrist, he sent the blood staining his blade flying. The rest, he wiped on the leg of one of the dead Reavers before sliding it home in its scabbard. With another deep breath, he came back to the moment. Three strides took him to where Azzura still sat tied to the chair. He pulled his knife free and cut her loose. She grabbed hold of him, sobbing into his neck. He breathed her in and there it was. This time it was the fully-formed smell of the lilac based scent Azzura was fond of wearing, in all its complexity. What he had smelled on Filtch that morning was faded residue – the faint trace of her perfume having rubbed off onto a man that struggled with her while she was being abducted. Had Filtch taken a shower, the day might have turned out differently. Fué did not know how long he knelt there holding her. It was only when someone cleared their throat that he came back to himself. He gently pushed back from Azzura and stood. She rose to her feet too. He could feel her hovering right behind him, brushing softly up against him.

Fué looked over at the woman who had cleared her throat. It was Zamerra. Tall, with skin as dark as night, and as beautiful as any woman he had ever seen, Zamerra smiled at Fué. To her left and right, six more Hunters stood, causally scanning the room. Hardened men and women of the Hunt looked around the room at his handiwork. Erris Stealth nodded in appreciation. He was a fraction shorter than Zamerra. The man wore feathers in his medium-length halo of black, wooly hair.

"I see that your reputation is well-deserved," he said. Fué gave the man a nod of respect.

Two more Hunters entered with Spazz between them.

Fué looked back at Zamerra.

"Thank you for the heads up, Hunter. We will take care of this filth. Leave him and the rest of this –" she waved her hand in a gesture that took in the whole room, "-to us. You have done enough." She flashed him a big smile.

The other Hunters nodded in agreement.

"He has an accomplice named Filtch who –"

Zamerra cut him off. "Don't worry Fué; we will deal with all of it. Get this woman and yourself to safety. Leave the rest with us. But let's not dawdle. Though we're Hunters, this is still the Tombs."

She was right. They had a victory. But this was still The City. The City knew how to turn a victory into defeat. Just ask Spazz. So, Fué took Azzura by the hand. With one last look at the other Hunters, he said, "Hunter's Thirteenth Rule."

Zamerra nodded, laughed, and said, "Know when to quit."

Fué got to the stairwell and did not stop until he was back above ground, on his jump bike, with Azzura sitting behind him. Know when to quit indeed.

Edge of Innocence

By
Ced Pharaoh

"Mi Azin Alio Na!"

"Mi Azin Alio Na!"

The sounds push and pull like a tide at Night's rise.

"Na!!! NaaaaAAA!"

Omega jolts awake. A chill catches his spine and travels all over. It's not just from the cold.

"NaAAA! Isn Ni Mi Azin, please..please!!"

Screams of distress are clearer, coming through the slit window of his BioEcoTent. He forgot to seal it the evening before. Omega silently scrambles out his shelter. Over the ledge below, he sees two mercs or at least they look the part. Who else dresses in all black, at night, weapons vest exposed holding firearms at the ready? A faint glow emits from their eye and com chip in their neck. Obviously, they're enhanced; but it is the fearful group of children at their feet that grows a frown on Omega's face.

"Nar S?! Nar S?!"

There are three of them. The oldest, or at least the tallest, wears forlorn fibers of blue and grey shredded at the arms and feet. Half shaven head marked with some tat and long blue grey hair hangs down the other side. Wet tracks marked her face from the eyes to her chin. Even facing one of the mercs, her stance is defiant but her knees shake as she shields two other children, one boy and the other a girl.

"Nar S?! Mi Azin! Na!!!"

Omega recognizes the language as a fusion of dialects, but he doesn't understand. The language barrier is broken when the young girl kicks and swings at one of the mercs. He answered with a slap that carried her body backward like a Terra doll. Omega moves without thinking, turning and running to the opposite end of the roof. He leaps out into open air, his body stretching and his hands catching a filter drain pipe that extends to the street. His swinging body circles the pole downward. Padded soles touch the ground, pivot and carry him with speed around the nearest corner, just as more screams pierce the air. His hand is already around the hilt of his blade. One merc in black hears steps and spins around, rifle raised.

SLLAANNG!

Omega's blade slices downward, across the muzzle. Spinning, he ducks with the blade free and clear, a piece of the gun is severed clean off. The blade still in hand, still spinning, the cutting metal bites into the merc's elbow, a soft spot found and he yells in pain.

As he drops his gun, Omega rams him with his head. He falls. Omega turns around and faces the group of children and Merc who slapped the girl.

The second Merc fires two shots but they both go errant, as the older girl rams and pushes him off balance. He shoves her but staggers back. A small bolo hits him in the chest and releases a shocking web of positive and negative energy that dampens his neuro. He falls to his knees in suspended in agony.

"Come ON!!" Omega's hand motions to the frightened girls.

"Let's GO! NOW!"

They didn't budge. Scared witless? Too late! Omega read their eyes and spins just as something black and hard knocks the light out.

*   *   *

The dry smell of rust and dust deaden the air. Stale.

"He's dead weight. Should have dropped him in the River!"

"There was a survey drone in the area. Picked it up on the MAB (Map Aerial Broadcast) Device, so it was too risky. Had the drone picked up his vitals, it would have sent sigs (signals) to MediServices."

"Dead corpses don't talk!"

"Yeah, but our Live bodies do...at least the parts that *are* organic. Our Hire doesn't want any attention, just the delivery of these river rats."

"We make this drop, and our credits add up."

I had no idea what they were talking about. I can barely open my eyes. The pain in my head fires; I swallow bile and a moan. Through slits, I can make out two shapes. Pointing fingers at each other, they are arguing but I can't understand what they're saying. My head explodes with another headache that makes my vision blur and my mind scramble. This time I can't stop from moaning. The Mercs didn't care. The next time I open my eyes, I see the backs of the men leave through a doorway. A metal door slams. The lock tells me I can't get out; if I can even get up.

Wherever *this* is, becomes silent. I hear soft sobs and motion just out of my view. Still hurting while laying on my stomach, I push off with my right hand to shift my body. My blurriness clears up and then I can see two children. I'm not alone.

They haven't noticed or are ignoring me. There are shadows between us but dim illumination of light cast down where we are. Our profiles are well lit.

The larger of the two is sitting and holding her knees to her chin; eyes closed and taking deep breaths. A foot way, legs spread wide in a V, a little girl is playing with a small ball, passing it between her hands. She speaks.

"Monet is hungry!"

"I know...I know...here." The older girl pulls from under her sleeve a small, concealed pouch. I can't see it but she passes something small to Monet, who greedily chews and swallows it.

"Mmm. Ash, That's good. More?"

"That's it for now. Maybe later?"

Monet shrugs her shoulder with no worries and looks down at her small, yarn sack bag. Her fingers fiddle with pieces of dangling colored strands.

The older girl who I assume is Ash comes closer and kneels close to the bag, inspecting it. Her eyes glance at Monet's who is staring at the dangling strands.

"It's ok. Big Sis can fix this," offers Ash.

"No fix. Broken. No fixing us."

Ash pulls the little girl close to her and silent sobs, rock them both. The sound is strangely comforting.

I find the strength to push myself up to a sitting position. My loud groans of strained effort and sharp stabs of pain that made the two girls finally acknowledge me. Their cautious movements are obvious. The youngest slides behind the oldest who also moves in front, shielding the younger; never saying a word to the other and never taking their eyes off of me. The young one, Monet, peers from behind her sister. Ash's stare intensifies, reminding me of a feral beast willing to claw out; to protect her young.

My dry throat croaks, "Peace, Sisters." I sound like I swallowed a pinch of sawdust.

"What did he –?" Monet starts but is cut silent with a hush by Ash.

"Urgg..." clearing my throat, "I am Omega. You two *are* Sisters right?"

Ash doesn't say a word but from behind her Monet, ever the child nods and she and I share a smile. With a slight tilt of her head, Ash's eyes narrow in odd confusion and then spin around to catch Monet, who is quick enough to suppress her smile. Sharp dialect passes between them so quickly, I couldn't understand even if I heard them correctly. They both turn to me.

"Thank you....for trying to save us," offered Ash.

"Uh...yes." My eyes trace around the dim shadows. My vision is a little better now that my mind's clearer. We are in a barren, storage room. "I'm sorry. I'm afraid I didn't do you much good."

"Yeah! You couldn't even save yourself." piped Monet. Ash frowns at her.

The wisdom of children can be harsh.

"But Ash always says trying is better than not." states Monet.

I chuckle, "You are very smart and lucky to have a big sister."

"So, you were not unconscious, just spying in." spits Ash.

I rub the back of my neck.

"No, I have been in and out. Trying to get my strength back. But yes, I heard you two and those river snakes with the guns.

Their fearful wide eyes dart over my shoulder to the door. Their bodies tense and Monet speaks.

"I don't like them. They hurt Ash."

"I'm fine. Don't worry, see?" Ash moves her right arm around in circles with a slight grimace, as proof to her younger sister.

Satisfied, Monet changes subjects. "Call me Monet and her Ash."

"I think he knows that, Mo!"

"OMOASH!"

"What??"

"O," pointing at me. "Mo. Ash." pointing at her sister and herself. "O MO ASH! We're a Family now," she smiles.

"No, we're not! Why did you help us?" Ash asks turning to me.

"You didn't seem like you wanted to go with the Mercs. Do you know why they want you?"

Gently placing her hand on Monet's shoulder, "They're just bad like she says. Slave trade is my guess. I asked but they didn't answer me. We're from the North Ward and we've been looking for a new place to live. We were lost! Then that black cruiser pulled up and I told Monet to run. We didn't want to get snatched again!"

I walk around the room; first testing the locked door and a few small canisters. I turn to Ash.

"Again? What do you mean?"

"Like I said, we were lost but we saw this building. It was a Resort Center. There were a lot of people and children there. They had food and music. A woman asked where we lived and I told her we were lost but we came from the North Ward. She promised to get someone to take us back. Then we heard shooting and these men run in with guns, threatening to kill everyone. Some tried to stand against them but were shot several times. The man that knocked you out shouted for all of the children to come with them. Some were screaming and crying, as about 20 of us were led to a few cruisers and locked in. I held Monet close as the cruiser drove fast. We couldn't see out; there were no windows. We didn't know where they were taking us. I looked around and I asked the boy next to me, did he know what was going on?"

Ash stopped and we both look towards Monet. She is sitting, back to a wall under the strongest beam of light. She was busy digging in her bag, pretending not to listen. I watch Ash's eyes observe her sister and I see sadness. I can see she is more than a sister, more like a mother to Monet. I also suspect that they were probably not as lost as Ash explains. I keep this thought to myself as she continues her story.

"Um...anyway...the boy and another girl told us about groups of armed men, snatching children from their families and taking them away; sometimes even in the light! No one knows why but there are rumors..."

"They want us to go Nutter." a small voice says.

Ash and I look at Monet, who has taken several art tools out of her bag and spread them before her.

"What did she say?"

Ash takes a deep breath, "We overheard one of the Mercs talking about the number of children they were grabbing....and how some would go Nutter, so having a surplus may get them more Credits."

We both shuddered. Nutter was not a cute expression but something to be avoided. Too many Psi skills, if you had any...or if you were into self-maintenance and had the Creds, you could get yourself some enhancements; night vision, extra taste nerves, duo organs...whatever but the Body could only take so much before the Mind goes into a psychosis. Once you're on that path, there's no taking another. You were Nutter! But what did that mean about children? It was illegal for non-adults to have procedures....

"The cruiser came to a stop and the doors opened. Several of us were forced out and that's when some ran. The Mercs didn't but should have known it may happen. They fired in the air and yelled stop. The children fell to the ground and the next moment they got up and turned around. Rocks and stones flew at the Mercs. They were surprised! The children had grabbed handfuls of rocks and were throwing them. The Mercs threatened them and during this, those of us still in the Cruiser, got out and ran. I picked up Monet and ran as fast as I could down a narrow street and around a corner! We heard gunfire and shouts. I put Monet down and we held hands running! There were two more, the boy and an older girl with us but we got separated."

Ash paused and stared at me, "It had been hours and we thought we got away. I guess that's when you saw us."

I took a moment to consider what Ash had just told me. She'd taken the time to step away from me and

Monet. She had her back turned, shoulders slumped and head bowed. I suspected she needed some time to herself. I walk towards Monet and sat down a foot away. She never looked at me but paused with the pencil in hand. I watched the point lower to the page. Monet sketches slowly, lightly across the piece of stained parchment.

"She does that." Monet states, nodding towards Ash, "Sometimes, a lot and sometimes not."

I nod. "What are you doing?"

"What does it look like?" she replies.

I frown but say nothing. Children. I suppose an obvious question to what should be...obvious.

I learn her supplies were given by her older sister, whose full name is Ashla. They found the items during their travels, before they were captured by the mercs. Fully vested in her art, Monet told me the children were forced to part ways with any personal items. It was only when Ashla convinced the merc's leader that Monet would be quiet if she practiced her art. He agreed, threatening a painful punishment if she tried to leave a message to alert anyone. And so, Monet kept her art sheets.

I counted the exposed rocks that lined the floor of our storage prison. I did this twice, as I tried to piece a plan of escape.

"Can I see?" I lean over to Monet.

"No, this one is not done. When it's finished, I will show you."

"I can't wait. What about a peek?"

"No peeking." Monet pulls her sketchbook further away from me.

Walking over to us, Ash says, "She's like that, always sketching but she shares when she feels like it. A very picky artist. You won't get paid for your talent that way."

Never looking up, Monet says, "I sketch for fun and to make the world smile."

ClaKLANG! The noise makes all of us jump. It's the

lock and the door swings open. The first thing we see is a gun nozzle followed by the short Merc.

He motions with the gun, "Get up and move!"

Ash helps her sister gather her drawing tools. "Where are we going?"

The gun rises and points directly at my face. "Move. Now!"

Placing my hand on the girls' shoulders, I guide them in front of me, positioning myself between them and the Merc walking behind me. I don't have a clue what to do, but I could begin by shielding Ash and Monet, if I got desperate. Who knows? Maybe they'd get lucky and find a place to hide and escape. The short Merc directs us through a long, dim lit hall with a low hanging ceiling with pipes hissing steam. The steam adds moisture in the air, which also smelled damp with mildew. I can't tell if we were ground level, above or below.

"Turn right."

We did and there is a doorway that opens to a large room. There on the table is my backpack with all of my personal stuff spread out! I feel sweat on my forehead. My temper rises but there's nothing I can do about....anything. The small Merc sees my expression and laughs.

"You're bugged 'cuz I dumped your bag? It looks like a bunch of junk and garbage."

My eyes take inventory of what's on the table; 2 rolls of different tape, a face shield, some pen torches, goggles, a collage of circuit flashes, a wide black case, tubes of solvent, digi-paper and other items.

"Actually, there are a lot of things here that are very useful." I point to the table, "Like that yellow tube. It's a great cleaning agent for metal and mechanics. Your gun would look like new and fire a lot better."

"Really? Well, after I kill you, then I'll take the time to clean my gun."

"I'm sort of a Techsmith and I know some things

about cleaning, that's all." I quickly add, "All you need to do is squeeze some drops and rub it a little." He grips the gun tighter. "Hey, I'm just trying to keep this friendly, that's all."

The short Merc looks at me and reaches for the yellow tube with his free hand. Using his mouth to unscrew the top, he squeezes not a few drops but an inch trail on the gun. He tosses the tube back on the table and snatches a rag. Keeping the barrel pointed at us, he rubs and the drops quickly foam up.

"What the???"

The foam expands from the exposure to the air and the friction; completely covering the gun. I smile as the foam instantly dries then I rush him. Too in shock to defend himself, I snatch up the black case on the table and swing at his jaw, silencing a mild scream. I imagine the scream was due to the pain he was feeling as the yeast emulsion hardens more. He falls to the floor taken out of his misery. I quickly scan the room and I see the surprised looks on Ash and Monet's face.

"You lied to him, didn't you?" asks Monet.

I stuff my things in my backpack and put it on, "Yeah, I did." I reach for my sheathed blade, gun holster and chest belt.

"What is that??" Ash asks looking closer at the fallen Merc.

"A high sourced adhesive. A few drops would have done it but, of course he didn't listen."

We look down at the nearly covered body frozen in a gray opaque hard plastic. His hand holding the gun had a long, stem extending from it.

"Get back from that. He must have had enough time to squeeze the trigger but the bullet is frozen or moving slowly. We don't want to accidentally get shot. Let's go."

I'm holding my Scout module and turn on the Active Sonar Position Mode. High intensity, ultrasound pulses reverberate to Scout's analyzer, forming a myriad of mapping sequences. I choose the quasi 3D grid which gives me a view of walls and moving objects. I could view the map on the screen but I reroute the image via wireless sync to my goggles that I've put on.

"Can I have this?"

I turn and look at Monet and my eyes go wide.

"NO!" I hold my hand out in protest. "Don't. Do. Anything!"

Ash's head is moving back and forth between me and her sister and instinctively remains calm, sensing my fear.

"Mo listen. Do what our friend Omega says."

"It's a pen, right?"

"Please," I plead while taking off my goggles. "That's a special pen. Not for writing, okay? I'll give you a real nice one."

Monet looks at the both of us and shrugs. "Okay. Why are you so worried? Here."

She passes it to me and I secure the tool to a jacket clasp, tucked away. My hand digs deep into a pocket and I pull out a pen and pencil. Ash looks stressed out. Monet is all smiles, grabbing for the tools and tucks them away in her own pocket.

Looking at the Scout readings and I lead the girls through several doors. We soon enter a much larger room. It looks like a lab for tech operations; horizontal operation platforms with digi-readouts, vertical chambers, unused beds, synapse brackets, pressure gauges, auxiliary pumps, oximeters, plasma bags and more. On several tables and shelves I see raw enhancements, nano-chips and thread spinals. Some are in the open and others are in new boxes or secured in access clamps used as holders for closer observation and repairs.

The floor is littered with debris and discarded or used wires, pieces of paper and blood.

"Keep Monet -"

"AHHHHHHH!"

"-close."

Ash runs by me and I follow around a row of columns. Behind them is a metal operating table. On the table, lies the partially covered body of child; nodes and transmitters are partially visible sticking out of various parts of the body at the temples, chest and arms. Webs of vital sign threads stream across to a console with digital notes of enhancement readings. Blood seeps from wounds, cuts and enhancement stems.

Ash fights to clamp her hands over Monet's eyes to hide the horror and over her mouth to silence her. Ash, herself is looking faint, sickened by the sight while fighting the need to protect her sister versus running from fright.

"By all that breathes! Who...could...do this?"

I have no words. I stare closer at the digital readings and try to access the console. I read the notes and confirm the fear that is crawling up the back of my mind. This child is one of many victims. The Lost Ones, those missing children and now who I believe fully are The Taken. Kidnapped innocents are being subjected to experiments. Unsanctioned, enhancement experiments have been done to children. Why? Based on the notes, the test findings and results the youth don't go immediately nutter from too many enhancements. Some citizens of The City are looking for longevity and more power, by upping their cybernetic and other bio upgrades.

"RooWRoR! Gwawk!!"

"WhoOOWHooOOOWhoOOO!"

An alarm sounds off. The girls fall back against a column and I stagger back. We all stare. The boy on the table moves. One human eye is wide and the other cyber eyes are rotating around in its socket.

"RooWRoR! Gwawk!!"

The boy is gurgling and his body is having a seizure.

"WhoOOWHooOOOWhoOOO!"

He falls still.

"WhoOOWHooOOOWhoOOOooooo.

bbbzzzzzzz..."

I pull a large cable that kills the alarm. Silence. That's when I hear our heavy, hyper breathing. I lean against the electronic equipment and see the Monet and Ash buried in each others' arms. I move to the operating table and cover the still body with a sheet.

Savage.

How else would I describe it?

Stealing the innocent to fulfill quotas.

Enhancement test that strip away the essence.

Failed attempts yield nothing but a shell.

And then what? Discarded and tossed as trash or buried if the cybernetics cause a malfunction or death.

Murder without Merit!

The innocents' lives severed by the laser scalpel's edge.

It doesn't take courage to snatch children. Nothing but heartless resolve and greed; greed to prolong life by sabotaging another's.

I wonder how many would divvy credits to pay for new tech, if they knew children were used to perfect the bio-bonding. Or how many would still do so, despite knowing.

My thoughts are interrupted by Monet's small voice.

"Is that... going to happen...to me...and Ash?"

I look at Monet. Large brown eyes hold mine with anticipation. Pressed lips are tight with determination, standing on hope. I notice Ash has not said a word. She's waiting for an answer with aloofness, likely born from too many promises made and broken in the past. I say to both as I kneel face to face with Monet.

"My Life for Yours."

Her arms swing around my neck and I cradle her gently.

I watch Ash as she sways slightly and nods at me.

"Let's go." I whisper.

We hit the next two hallways at a run. Air is forced through the ceiling and floor vents throughout the building. The sound is everywhere, making it hard to hear anything or anyone!   I motion for Ash and Monet to keep moving. The corridor leads us to an adjacent hall that branches into two different halls.

"Which way?" Ash's rushed voice merges with the sound of the air.

I hold my hand up for silence.

In a harsh whisper, Ash declares, "Death is much better than becoming an experiment. I won't let that happen to Mo."

"It's not."

I focus. My Scout Module has died. Damn! I never got a chance to charge it! Now what are we going to do? My head still aches from the beat down I received from the Mercs and the horrible sight of the young boy. I wonder what his name is. It hurts to think about anything but I gotta ignore the pain. I'm a Psion so maybe I should act like it. There are a lot of citizens of The City with Psi. Some have one Skill, others with two. The more you have, the closer you are to going Nutter. Sometimes, I think I have more than the two.

Breathe.

I hear the deep, anxiety breathes of Ash and Monet. I can feel their tense fear and mine but I must stay calm. This won't work if I'm too tense....yes. Ok, I can sense where to go.

"This way." I head to our right down the hall.

Trailing beside me, Ash asks, "You've never been here before, right? How do you know?"

"I have learned to really trust my Instinct. Most of the times, I'm right."

"Most of the time?"

"Trust me." I glance back at these two remarkable and courageous sisters. Monet winks at me.

We run, dart and pause, listening for anyone. Ash and Monet follow so close behind, that we're almost wearing the same clothes. The next door up looks secure. I have no clue what's on the other side, but ii has to better than what we're leaving behind. I hope. Pray.

A crack beneath the door shows light on the other side but a shadow moves blocking it. I find a pocket on my chest belt. Mini bola in my right hand. The door flies open, I half shield, half push the sisters with my back and left hand behind a wall. The bola speeds from my right hand.

"ARRRRGGHHH!"

The bola must have ignited. I check and then pull the girls with me. On the floor, the Tall Merc, impaled, pin cushioned with hundreds of nano-needles, exploded from the bola at 1/2 mach.

We run outside. Fresh air smells so good! I push the girls ahead of me.

"Where you think you going?!" demands a voice behind us.

I don't hesitate. I don't stop moving. Spinning, my hand grips and finger squeeze the trigger. My gun ignites the air with 4000 psi of compressed air. The body of a third Merc gets lifted, pushed into an adjacent wall; crumpled. Debris falls and I still continue moving.

"RUN!" I scream at the Monet and Ash, but they're well on they're way around a corner of shipping crates. Shouts are coming from within the building. I fire more compressed air at heavy crates behind me and they crash blocking the path. I'm hoping to slow down any more Mercs, so we can get away.

I run around the same corner the girls did. I see a pier in one direction and a path leading off the pier to a beach in another. I don't see any signs of them on the beach. I run along the dock near The River. I see nothing but the edge and something on the ground, flapping from the wind. I walk closer and look down to find a stone on top of a page of art paper.

The River is flowing.

I snatch it up. The image backdrop is The City and the sun. In the center of the page are two girls, one taller than the other with the names, Ashla and Monet spelled under each. A string of hearts extends from the girls to another image...a man surrounded by a heart and underneath him is the word Omega. The River is flowing.

I remember what Ash said to me.

"Death is much better than becoming an experiment. I won't let that happen to Mo."

The River flows...

The Runner's Ball

By
Ashtyn Foster

The Runner's Ball is the closest to participating in the Rising that we runners get. Not being connected to the Wave through Tells can get incredibly lonely. Most of us don't mind it, except during the *only* City-wide celebration. I look at my colleagues and think what made them choose this life. I had no choice, but I'm glad they made theirs.

Due to the feelings of being left out, a century or two back a group of Runner's got together during a Rising and held a party. After that it just got bigger, fancier, crazier, and more dangerous, so much so that we needed to up our security, change the location annually, set up a committee and make it invitation only. It's the most organized we'll ever get as a community.

When you get the majority of The City's former and current Purge users all together in one place, rules and regulations are a must. No weapons, no poisons, any and all grudges are to be forgotten until after the Ball is over. I still don't know where the committee gets all the funding for the gala, but this year they outdid themselves.

The Ball was located in Sector 4, Ward 115. The interior was designed to look like an Opera house from The City's beginnings. Everything was gold and sparkling; we were announced at the top of a wide grand golden marble staircase. Just outside those doors was the Nullifier and "coat check." The Nullifier temporarily deactivated any dangerous implants or cybernetics a citizen may have had in his or her person. The coat check wasn't just for coats. Any weapons not permanently attached to one's person were tagged and locked up. The owner was given a receipt, and then you were allowed to enter the party. Everything was done by robots now, a decade or so ago the newest runners worked the event. Now there are AI-less bots that do everything from check-ins to security. After the first three hours, a shield is placed and no one is allowed in after that. All attendees are free to leave, but if you haven't checked in before the shield is dropped you miss out. This is done to make security easier. With the Rising celebrators practically taking over the entire city, it's safer for us to keep the non-Runners out.

We were halfway down the staircase when an alarm sounded.

"And that makes three." I said happily, holding out my hand.

"You and Kat cheated." Ike said transferring me my winnings.

"Not at all, she owes me too. Katsumi just overestimated how long it would take her to hand over all of her toys."

We bet how many folks would get their hearts stopped by the Nullifier by the time we reached the middle of the stairs. That was the third alarm.

"Well, if her dress wasn't so tight. How do you expect to fight in that thing, Kat? Better yet, how did you hide all those things in your dress?"

Katsumi just smiled. "A lady never reveals her secrets. Eris, honey, do you want your money?"

"Of course I do." I said, spinning around Ike to get to Kat.

Ike just shook his head. "I still can't believe you talked me into this suit."

Katsumi insisted that we dress in the colors of our auras this year. Her kimono was a vibrant red with gold threading. It was impossibly tight and she made four slits in the dress just low enough to not get her arrested. Although this was the Runner's Ball, she didn't have too much to worry about anyway. Her hair was much less traditional, pulled into a side intertwining braid; it fell into loose glossy black curls at its end.

Ike was dressed in the bluest blue tuxedo that we could find. He hated it until he put it on. Then he loved it. He thought for sure with his dark skin he would look ridiculous. He saved the left over fabric and is planning something for it. He hasn't said what. His newfound love of his suit even put him in the mood to design the buttons on his crisp bright white shirt. They each held a different function. It took us hours to braid Ike's thick hair to his head, but all those tiny tight rows looked like dark ocean waves on his head.

My dress was emerald green and shimmery. It had a tight bodice that was programmed to loosen as I ate, danced or just needed more breathing room. The skirt was sweeping and wide. I couldn't wait to start dancing, but as per our tradition, we had to hit the bar first. I reached up to check my hair, I had finally decided on tiny twists close to my head, ending in a curly poof.

"Stop touching your hair, Eris, you look perfect." Kat said. She wasn't even looking at me, she just knew.

"Yeah, we've got drinks to order and compliments to receive."

"You aren't enjoying your new outfit are you Ike, darling?" I asked as we reached the bar.

"Not in the least. But I am here with the two most beautiful runners in the business; I think that should earn me a "Good job man". Excuse me, my fine robot, could I get a Phoenix Fire whiskey and something fruity for my two lovely lady companions?" he asked when the bar-bot finished making its most recent order. It nodded and went to work.

"Thanks Ike." Kat said with a look.

"Hey, add a shot of Dragonfire to those fruity drinks too," he said to the bot. It nodded again.

"Better?" he asked her.

"Thank you." She smiled.

Those drinks couldn't come fast enough. It had been

nearly a month since the incident but I couldn't shake the feeling that something terrible was coming:

Something named Ms. Mya Davenport.

*   *   *

For some reason she loved me, maybe because incredibly we were both born without Tells due to extremely heavy Purge use by both parents. Or maybe because we both valued money over moral failings. I turned a blind eye to the things she did as one of the top bosses in Sector 9 and she kept me in a continual cash flow while still respecting my wishes to be freelance. "Never let any one person hold the key to your financial well-being that isn't yourself" she always told me.

Not that she needed to. I left home as soon as I could. Not because of the drugs; Mama and Daddy went straight as soon as they found out I was coming. I left because they couldn't afford me and all my siblings that came after. They loved being parents but forgot how to work. They did what they could, but I promised myself I wouldn't live like that. They were poor but happy; I was not. So I took my birth defect and became a runner. Two of my brother's became Street Priests, all three of my sisters took "respectable" positions as teachers and my youngest brother was regrettably in Ward 215.

Ms. Davenport's story was similar to mine but she turned to a life of organized crime. She was too good at it not to be. She was charismatic, cool-headed and terrifyingly smart which also made her terrifyingly dangerous. She built a legitimate cybernetics company around her crime business. Everything that came out of Dove Cybernetic Inc., was in some way or another a brain child of hers.

I had been on a routine job for her. Deliver her message. Wait for the response. Then deliver it back to her. It used to be dangerous, but now everyone knew that if anything happened to me they'd wake up to their beds on fire. And that was if she in a hurry.

I landed on the roof of her building that day and played the recorded holo-message from Boss Morimoto:

"Good evening Ms. Davenport." He bowed with some pain and smiled even though I knew it hurt to do that too. Her boys had worked over the entire clan pretty well. It barely turned my stomach to see that much violence, but it still did, so I took that as a good sign.

"It is always a pleasure to do business with you. I spoke with the other bosses and we unanimously decided that having you head our sectors is the most profitable, wisest and most innocuous choice. All big moves will now go through you for approval and your generous offer of allowing us to keep sixty percent of our earning was most gracious. The Bosses of Wards 352, 356, 359 and I await your orders." Boss Morimoto bowed and again and the recording ended.

The whole sector was hers now. Whether it was bought, won or begrudgingly given the entire Sector was now property of Ms. Mya Davenport. And due to her allowing the other Bosses to keep their titles and not redistributing the areas, it could take years, even decades for the Watchers to realize what she'd done.

She knew she had won. She had this smile, this grin that couldn't have been human. A smile that folks say she designed herself and was then surgically implanted by her top doctors. It was the type of smile that said "You are wrong and I am right and if you do not see things my way I have very slow and painful ways to make you understand." She gave me this smile now. My heart stopped.

"Pay her."

Vincent walked towards me. I reached for my gun.

"Seriously child, I would never harm you. Not so long as you continue to stay useful to me." And there it was, the catch. S*tay useful.*

Vincent transferred the funds to me and I left.

Ms. Davenport's affairs were no longer my business after I got paid. Or at least that's what I thought.

I never should have taken that damn detour.

I flew over the buildings trying to get some semblance of freedom. Knowing that she owned everything in Sector 9 didn't make me feel safe. It made me want to move. I hovered in front of the Dove Cybernetics Inc. sign wondering if I could make myself, Ike and Katsumi disappear when I heard a crash. Normally I would say "It's none of my business" and move on, but not that night; that night I decided to see what was wrong.

I turned off my jets and dropped to the rooftop closest to the commotion. Thanks to my armor and runner's experience I managed to land softly. Not that it would have mattered. It was a four against one fight. Even if that one was a cyborg, those were Ms. Davenport's men. After non-stop physical training and some of the best, most likely *the* best enhancements in The City, it was hard to be a match for them. I was, because I insisted on going through the training if I was to work for her even part-time. Katsumi absolutely was because her uncle is a master at swords and martial arts. And Ike has so many gadgets; he doesn't need to be as good at fighting as he is.

This man they had cornered though….it looked as if they already beat him bloody pretty well.

"Get back here Sphinx. You can't hide from us," one of them taunted.

"How could she think she could get away with this? People are going to find out! Everyone will know what kind of monster Mya Davenport really is. The entire city will find out!"

He knew was a dead man. I wasn't sure why he was delaying the inevitable by rattling on, but I was intrigued. What was so terrible that he felt he had to tell the entire City? What was so inconceivably heinous that this man was about to be assassinated in the street by four overpowered thugs, in order for it to not get out?

It appeared that I wasn't to know the answer. Before Sphinx could get out anymore dead man walking rants, the men descended upon him and began beating and tearing at him. I saw his cybernetic arm go skidding across the alley.

I was about to leave (there are some things that even I can't stomach) when I heard a shout.

"BOMB!"

I dove behind a nearby vent and my armor automatically increased its protective percentage. I may have been high above the fighting but a bomb is a bomb. Three of the four didn't stand a chance. They were nothing but silhouettes on the pavement and walls. The fourth, the one who'd done most of the talking had sense enough to throw up a shield. His hands were burned the worst; I could see a metal skeleton underneath charred skin. He didn't even blink. It's as if he didn't feel the pain at all from being blown up. I would have thought he was a robot had I not seen red blood dripping off his fingers. He looked at the aftermath of the explosion and grinned. Then he walked away, most likely to get a cleaning crew.

I should have left then, but Sphinx wasn't as dead as he should have been. Most of his artificial skin had been burned off, his actual skin was crispy and he had shrapnel everywhere else. And if he was still alive I had to know what was worth dying like that for.

I jumped down off the building using my jets to help me land. I didn't say anything; I just stood over him.

"I know you..." he coughed "You're Mya's girl. Don't worrying; I'm dying."

"I can see that. I want to know why." I wasn't about to argue that I wasn't *hers*, the man didn't have much time left.

"Your boss is up to nothing good. I don't know how much you know, but it goes so much deeper than that. She's too smart to try to take over The City. The Watchers would stop her, but her ambition may as well be that big. She's starting her own army. That's why she needs the other Bosses. She needs their men for fodder and testing."

"Testing?"

"She's cloning them. All of them. She's trying to become immortal."

"That's insane."

"Then why were they trying so hard to make sure they killed me?" His voice was soft. I could tell he wasn't going to make it much longer. "Ask her how old she is. She won't be able to tell you and you won't be able to find it. The record of her birth is a fake. She has to be stopped."

"Stop," I said gently. "Stop talking."

I knelt and then put my hands on his bloody head and scanned him. All of Mya's dirty secrets came flooding to my mind. I had never scanned a single living thing that so willingly pushed all of their thoughts into my mind.

After I stopped, he grabbed me, "You can't let her do it. She trusts you. You have...you have to stop her." And then he was gone. And not a second too soon. It sounded like the Cleaners were coming. I jumped on the wall and scaled it as silently as I could.

I hadn't seen Ms. Davenport since that night. I told her I wasn't feeling well and that I wanted to try to let nature run its course before taking any scientific routes. She knew it was a lie. She always knew when someone lied to her. But she let it go. For now.

*　　*　　*

Now weeks later at the Ball I'm trying to forget. I'm dancing and drinking and laughing. It nearly worked.

Then the shooting started. The shield had come down; we thought we were safe in our party palace. She broke through. The chandelier came crashing down. She'd defiled the Holiday. Some of the Purgeheads wanted to fight. But all of our weapons were locked up and they had theirs in their hands.

"EVERYBODY GET OUT!"

I didn't move. I knew what she wanted. The rush of the others flooding past me running and screaming, flying or crawling; they all wanted to escape with their lives once they saw Mya Davenport.

She'd come for me herself. Even those who first thought of taking on this brazen group of thugs thought better of it when they realized to whom they belonged. Everyone wanted to keep their skin.

When the crowd had dissipated that only left Kat, Ike, and I.

"Get out you guys. I won't have you dying for me."

Ike was fumbling with his shirt, and Katsumi rounded on me. Her back was to the danger at hand. "We will not leave you to the likes of her. Not on your own."

"Your friends are loyal to you. I hope more loyal than you were to me." Her voice was as smooth as silk and gentle as a summer breeze, and I had never been more terrified in my life.

"Ms. Davenport, I never told anyone what happened or about you. Just let them go."

"You are in no position to make demands, requests or even ask questions. I should simply destroy you here and now. Erase you from the fabric of this place."

She took a breath to continue, and then Katsumi's wakizashi came bursting through the chest of several of her thugs. And she laughed.

I had never heard her laugh before. Kat was so distracted she missed catching her sword and it just hovered above her head, dripping with blood, waiting for her to take hold of it. Ike stopped messing with the buttons on his shirt.

"How marvelous Isaac! I must pick your brain on how you programmed it to return to its master. Whether you're alive or not when I do it depends on Eris." She said all of that with her smile on her face.

Before we could react the rest of our gear and weapons

came zooming in overhead, the blades slicing through the henchmen and the guns cocked themselves ready to fire. I grabbed my tanto from the air as it came at me, and the first gun that came within reach.

"How cute. They're going to try to fight," she said still smiling. "Destroy them. But leave enough for me to use later."

With that we were swarmed. Sphinx was right; she was building a clone army. There was no other was to explain how many men rushed into the ballroom.

"Are you guys sure you want to do this?" I asked them.

"Eris, if you ask us that one more time, we may just come to our senses and stay here and fight by your side." Ike said.

Katsumi took her blade from the air and assumed her fighting stance.

They all charged at once. At some point I was separated from my friends. Diving into the fray, I lost sight of the two people in the world willing to die with me.

One of the henchmen swung a clawed hand at me, I back flipped to avoid it and sliced open the belly another, dropped to one knee and shot the clawed one in the head.

I was nearly back to Ike, who was not only taking out Mya's clones with the guns in his hands; he had also programmed the guns we weren't holding to fire at anything without our DNA signatures.

Kat was using one goon she dismembered as a shield. She was grinning. She'd often spoke of wanting a warrior's death. Being a Runner made that difficult...until now. In this once sacred hall, she'd found an opponent who was just as good with a blade as she was. The others backed away giving them room to fight.

Her adversary was dressed in all black. He was lithe and moved like water. He swung a few feints to test her reflexes. She answered each with a slash of her own, testing him out. I wanted to watch to make sure she was okay, but I was busy with problems of my own, mainly my lack of bullets and I was unable to get to a new gun.

As another clone came forward I dislocated his shoulder, then wrapped my arm around his neck and snapped it. Luckily this one had a gun. Shooting is a lot faster at opening a path than trying to slice one open.

I had just gotten back to Ike when we heard it. Katsumi. Her wakizashi was sticking out of her opponent's back. She twisted the blade and tore it out of his side. As he fell away we saw that she had a deep gash across her abdomen. She dropped to her knees and was about to be overrun. Ike immediately took off to aid her.

I turned to look at Ms. Davenport. She was still smiling. I raised the gun in my hand and fired. The bullet bounced off a force field she was wearing and embedded itself in the wall. I turned and ran to Katsumi. Ike had all available firearms ready to shoot leaving us in a semi-protected circle.

"Eris…"

"Shhh, it'll be okay. Don't talk." I said. "Ike, please tell me you can do something." I looked up at him, the tears were flowing.

"I can save her." That was not Ike.

I hadn't even noticed when the noise had stopped let alone when she had walked up beside me.

"Eris…no…" Kat tried to sway me from a decision I'd already made.

"Ms. Davenport, I will pledge myself to you if you stop this and save her. Whatever you want whenever you want, just let them live."

She closed her eyes to savor her victory.

"Isaac, put down your toys and collect the bleeding child. Gently now; she's already going into shock. Yuri!"

She snapped her fingers and one of her goons came forward. "Collect Ms. Eris."

Yuri walked up, jabbed me with something and my world went black.

When I woke up I was in an all-white room with an IV in my arm. I yanked it out and got off the bed. The wall across from me looked like a mirror, but it was a glass wall looking into a pitch black hallway. I only knew that because as I got closer the hallway began to light up. I heard heels walking down the ceramic tile floor.

She knew I was awake. She must know everything about me now. I stood with my feet planted, ready to demand to see my friends. But I wasn't ready for who came to see me.

"Hello Eris. I trust you've been comfortable."

I gasped and took large steps backwards, before falling to my knees.

My clone had come to visit me.

The Score

By
Chanel Harry

Nia

This city is my home. Hell, it's the only home that I have ever known. This city is so big that it can swallow you whole if you let it. Everything and everyone can consume you; just like it did me and my sister Dia. Dia; how that name breaks my heart sometimes. My twin, my other half; we shared everything with each other and we had always been together since our parents disappeared. But she didn't share that she was leaving to be with Mark Malum, best known as "The Politician". Damn, do I hate him; luring Dia away from here, showering her with promises of a better life or so he says.

The Heap is where we live and where our hideout is based. Being the leader of a small organization has its perks. It also brings unwanted attention by watchers and of course The Politician

Dia, the only family that I really have left in this city. Just thinking about her gone makes tears form.

"Nia, I got some good news for ya." Laarz said, interrupting me from my thoughts and easing my stress a bit.

"What is it?" I asked with a smirk, knowing that Laarz had some good news for me. He's always reliable and he's my right hand man. I couldn't ask for a better stand in while Dante was in the Distal Correctional Facility, the most heavily guarded prison here in the city. The love of my life, the only man I had been with since we were children; always playing together by the River with Laarz and Dia.

Dante and I started The Collective when we were teenagers around the time my parents disappeared. It was also around the time when The Soors were taking advantage of those that lived in the Heap. Robbing us of our creds, destroying businesses, doing anything they could to bring down the old gang of The Heap. That was when Dante had his plan to get back what was stolen from us, give back to our people. We have been doing what we can to keep everyone safe from The Soors and anyone that tried to get in our way. However, Dante was sent to Distal and now it's just me who runs The Collective.

Laarz was my man of business, my first mate. He was also my bodyguard, standing at six feet four weighing three hundred and ninety two pounds. His huge frame would scare anyone he came across. However, his gentle face and demeanor was a part of his true nature.

"I have some info about The Politician's next campaign appearance," he informed me. "It will be around p.m. downtown three days from now. I'm sure Dia is going to be there."

Laarz put the campaign ad in front of me; there was The Politician's face. Even though I hate to say it he was definitely handsome. I could see why Dia would fall for him. But beyond that brown skin and chiseled features, that man was nobody she should be with.   Reading his famous campaign slogan, "*MY WAY IS THE ONLY WAY*", I thought what an arrogant man he was. Malum was trying to become the new director of the Southside. Corruption was his game; I have no idea how someone who was a former Papi and Pusher of Purge could be allowed to run for Southside. I guess anything goes here in the Southside.

"Thanks a lot Laarz," I said grinning at him. He grinned back knowing that I had some sort of plan concocting in my head. I did have a plan but I was pretty unsure of how that plan would work. The rest of the gang came inside our dimly lit hideout laughing and chatting about the latest job I assigned them to. I didn't have to ask them how the job went. I already knew that my gang always made me proud and Dante too. Damn, my heart went heavy thinking about my man. This sentence wasn't long but a girl could use a break and some male attention. At least Dia was getting that attention! I chuckled at this thought.

"Hey y'all I'm about to call it a night. Lock up when y'all leave." I said, grinning back at them.

Alright boss lady have a good night." Laarz said with his gentle booming voice. My crew waved back at me as I closed the warehouse door. I started up the street. The Heap, this side of the city, wasn't the worst but it wasn't the best. I've seen a lot go down here. Pleasure borgs roamed the streets at night looking to please anyone that they could and I mean anyone. Watchers everywhere, watching everyone who lives down here, making sure we don't get to ahead of ourselves.

Tonight is just like all nights. Everyone's out clubbing, pushing purge, doing them, nothing new here. Even though that was the case I always made sure to stay strapped with my Zentec Beast in my waist holster, attentive and alert like all the other nights. But on this night, walking on Gola Avenue, I felt again like someone was watching me. Someone or something lurking in the shadows. I walked faster towards my apartment clutching my pistol grip ready to draw it out if need be. Looking out the corner of my eye I could have sworn I saw a shadow in the alleyway following me very swiftly.

"There's nothing like that; you need to relax." I said to myself. I let go of my gun and made it to the end of Gola Avenue. I was almost to my apartment without any trouble. I saw my block; An Boulevard. My neighbors were outside hanging out talking to borgs and some Helium Breathers that lived in the area. I was home free, away from that shadowy feeling that's been stalking me for a week every time I walked home.

"Hey Nia, on our way home I see?" Axel, the Helium Breather said. I gave him dap as he handed me cold *Fressho Freeze* drink.

Helium Breathers are 7 feet tall highly intelligent humanoids. They live amongst any species here in the city and they are really friendly. They all wear rigs on their heads that produce...well Helium. Axel lived next door to me with his with wife and two children. He and his family always opened up their home to me and Dia ever since our parents disappeared. He taught me everything I know when it comes to combat. Good old Axel; I was forever indebted to him and his family.

"Yeah Ax, another day another...well you know." I said as I took a sip of the Fressho Freeze. I eyed the male pleasure borg that was standing next to Axel. Maybe I should use his services after all. I was kind of lonely. Nah, I couldn't do that to Dante. I shook that thought out of my mind and stared straight ahead.

"Any news on your sis?" Axel asked, interrupting my lustful thoughts abut Dante. "Has she at least called?"

I took another swig of the drink and sucked my teeth. "She called me this a week ago, saying that I needed to drop this whole warrior act and chill out. She said I need to let her live her life the way she wants to."

"Ooh that's bad. I can't believe Dia would get in with a man like Mark Malum. He used to be a real chump around the Southside," Axel said.

"Yeah, she just doesn't know that it's not safe for her to be out there," I said. "I know that life and that life ain't worth nothing without having your peace of mind. I need to get her away from him before he drags her down with him."

Axel nodded then bobbed his head to the latest club banger by Mr. Thought Crime.

I shuddered, feeling that feeling again. Someone was definitely watching me. All I can see is my neighbors outside doing what they usually do. It was something different, something dark. I knew that I was not going crazy.

"Whoever this is has to wait because I have bigger fish to fry." I mumbled to the lurking shadow in the far corner of the building's end. I opened my apartment building's front door and headed upstairs to my house. I went inside, turned on the lights and breathed a sigh of relief. I made it home another night without anyone trying to kill me. I opened the fridge and took out a wave meal and put it in the waver. A poor existence indeed; living alone in a lavish apartment, Dante and Dia gone, no one to talk to except my gang. Is this life? This cannot be. I looked at Dante and I's photo that hung on the living room wall. He was handsome with his smooth caramel skin, and tall but muscular frame. I took it down and kissed it.

"I love you, honey." I said. The ritual I always did every time I came home. I heard the waver beep and went to get my wave meal and a drink from the fridge. I turned on the teleborg to see the local news. Of course nothing but the usual was on, the same old crime and Malum making it known to the Southside that he was coming for his next campaign speech. I rolled my eyes as I chewed my food. I turned up the teleborg to hear his redundancy.

"So, Mr. Malum, tell us about your Southside debut tomorrow." The Reporter asked. The Politician smiled one of his usual Cheshire grins as he held my sister Dia's hand. She was smiling too, that damn fake smile of hers.

"I will be speaking about some ways that we can clean up the Southside and take the gangs off the streets. The Heap has one of the most elusive gang in the heart of the Southside. I know doing this will make that section of The Southside more livable." Malum said. He looked directly at the camera and smiled. It was as if he knew I was watching. I looked back at him and grinned. I wonder if he indeed knows of my plan to get back my sister.

"Yeah, you keep on thinking that," I mumbled to the screen. Dia looked a bit uneasy when he mentioned The Heap. I can tell by my twin's face that she was a bit worried about me. I watched as the reporter kept talking to Malum, nothing of importance really. Not until she mentioned me and Dante's name.

"I know you have a mission to fight gangs in the Southside, however, what is your plan against The Collective?"

the reporter asked. I scanned the screen both Malum's and Dia's facial expressions. Malum had a disdainful yet cunning look on his face as the reporter mentioned my name while my sister's uneasy look was more elaborate in her face.

"My mission is simple; go in and get rid of the new leader of The Collective. I know she is watching this broadcast right now, and I just want to say; I'm coming for you." The Politician looked directly at the camera and smiled again.

"Well, you heard it first from the new candidate for the Southside. Thank you, Mr. Malum for speaking with us today. That's all for now, I am Jay Lawson with The City News."

The teleborg changed to the next program, my favorite soap opera. However, I didn't need to watch this time. I had quite a dilemma and a triumph on The Politician and his plans. First I needed to get to my sister. I didn't need her to be in any danger because of this. I knew The Politicians motives; he was using her to get to me.

That feeling disrupted my thoughts again, that weird feeling of someone watching and lurking. It was the shadow again. I held my Zentec Beast and cocked it back just in case someone it was one of The Politician's henchmen trying to get at me. I stayed still and so did the shadow. The shadow writhed then came into focus, taking the shape of a man. I still could not make out who he or it was.

"Who the hell are you and what are you doing in my apartment?" I asked, ready to blow whoever it was away. The shadow said nothing as it stood still. I sighed and shook my head.

"I have to be paranoid". I said out loud. The shadow disappeared when it heard my voice.

"Am I tripping this hard?" I asked myself. Again I was confused; was I seeing things? Maybe I wasn't; maybe my imagination wasn't running wild. Someone was definitely watching me. I could think of no one but The Politician. He probably sent the Shadow people of legend after me. To calculate my every step so that he can make his move on me and my gang. Damn! I've been outwitted. This shadow man will have to be exterminated soon. I can't have my plans thwarted by miniscule things. I have three days' time to get rid of this shadow man.

*   *   *

I was never a morning person; I always dreaded the daylight. However, I always loved the way the Sun Tower looked high in the sky gleaming on every living thing in this city. I got up and did my daily duties; bathed, brushed my teeth, let loose my curly shoulder length hair and looked in the mirror at my birthmark. This was no ordinary birthmark; under my right eye I had two marks. My mother always said I was kissed by our ancestors. She said that it was the eye of Horus. She said this eye would help me see things that could not be seen. My Mother was right in this revelation. With this eye I acquired many Psi abilities, four senses other than my five. I can control the languages of my target's mind, reducing their ability to talk. I can create mental barriers in my mind which helps resist any infiltration or manipulations. Reading emotions is another psi ability I possess; that is why I was able to read Dia's and Malum's emotions. Lastly is awareness. I am so hypersensitive to other biological life that is around me. That is why I was aware that the Shadow man was watching.

Yes, this eye is very handy when it comes to my profession. My mother always said that Dia and I were special and that we were highly favored by the ancestors. Dia had the eye also but it was on her left eye. However she had one ability and that was to predict. She has the enhanced ability to estimate and predict the outcomes of events around her as they unfold in real-time. Also, updating those predictions and the information changes, Dia was very useful to us when she lived in the Heap; she helped with many of our jobs.

Staring in the mirror I begin to wonder if Dia already

knew my plan. Does she know that I am coming for her in three days? Does she know that there is a shadow man following me? I wonder if she'll try to warn me about the impending danger that I will probably face from the Shadow Man. I sighed and walked out of the bathroom and got dressed in my usual skin tight latex outfit, with the black combat heels I like. Pure warrior attire was always my style. I kissed Dante's picture and left our apartment to head over to the hideout. On the block, my neighbors were outside doing the usual. Some were getting ready for work; some were sitting outside enjoying the morning light of the Sun Tower.

"Good Morning, Nia." Axel's daughter Lexx shouted. She ran up to me and gave me a hug, almost killing me in the process with her tall stature.

"Hey, Lexx." I said trying to breath. She put me down and smiled.

"Do you want to play Yorks and Watchers with me?" She asked. Her smile was so huge and sweet. One day I wanted to have children...one day when this is all over.

"Sorry, but I have some things to take care of. But after I'm done I would love to play Yorks and Watchers," I said with a smile. Lexx returned it and went back to her stoop to play with her brother.

I walked to the hideout, relieved that the daylight would keep the Shadow Man at bay for me to walk in peace. Today was one of those days that most of my crew spent at home with their families.

I usually came here during the day to make sure everything is up to par with the jobs. As always it was empty, dark and dismal in our hideout. It was basically an abandoned building, like most of the buildings here in The Heap. Dante always liked to keep it simple and make sure that we kept a low profile. All it had was a couple of tables with guns on them, a room for the things we got from the jobs, chairs, and a couple of teleborgs that we can watch The City News.

I pulled the string to turn the light on above my desk.

I sat down and saw that my computer droid was blinking. I turned it on to see that I had a message from none other than my twin sister. I pressed the message button.

"Sis, it's me. Look I'm not going to stay long, but Mark is doing a meet and greet down in the Southside today. I will be there and I want to see you. I don't want you to do anything that you'll regret because he's heavily guarded. Nia, I want you to hear me out and I want you to let me finish what I am going to say to you when we meet. I will be in front of the River. I love you and I hope you come."

The computer droid ended the message and turned off. I sat at my desk stunned and wondered if I should go. Could this be a trap? Or maybe my sister really did want to see me and tell me what was on her mind? Once again questions that might go unanswered. I had only one way of finding out. I had to meet her. I looked around my dark office just thinking about this opportunity to make my move on The Politician. Even though I could take on his bodyguards alone, I wasn't going to do anything reckless.

Thump! Someone was here.

I pulled my knife from the inside of my boot. Listening, ready to kill whoever was. It was dark but I couldn't see; all I heard was footsteps. I got up from my desk and followed the footsteps towards the back door. It was dark there too.

I felt a cold chill run down my back; it was as if something was trying to engulf me. It was the shadow man again. This time I was ready to kill him at no costs. He came to me so easily; I guess he didn't know that I was coming for him.

I felt him closer to me now, agile; I moved aside and did a roundhouse kick on him which brought him down instantly.

He fell to the floor and I quickly put my knife to his neck. His shadow left him and I could see his whole face now. Wow! This guy was beautiful! I tried not to blush at his face. I kept my facial expression the same; trying not to let him know what I was thinking. I used my psychic abilities to barricade my mind from him. I didn't know really what the people of the shadows were capable of. He stared at me first in bewilderment, and then gave me a look of blankness. It was as if he was trying not to let me read his emotions, even though I could not. I stood looking into his deep brown eyes.

"Who are you and why are you following me? Are you working for The Politician?" I asked sternly, holding the knife closer to his throat.

He was silent for a minute still looking knowingly into my eyes.

"I came to give you something and also to warn you." he said.

"Warn me about what?" I asked looking deeper in his eyes, trying to read him, trying to see.

"Don't go to the downtown meet and greet today. It's a trap set by Malum. He knows your love for Dia will be your undoing," The Shadow Man said. I sighed and put my knife away and helped him up.

"That was one powerful kick," he said. I didn't know whether it was a joke or not because he remained expressionless. I was in no laughing mood even though I could feel the laughter forming.

"Just who are you anyway?" I asked putting the knife back in my boot. He looked at me in awe as if he were trying to find the right words to say.

"Name's Ososi; I've been tracking you for a while now. Reasons that you don't need to know just yet. All I have is this warning to give you and the real facts about your sister," he said arms folded, leaning against my desk. Indeed he was beautiful to look at but he was the enemy for now.

"Ok, spill the info." I said.

"Your sister is with The Politician of course but she is with him for reasons that are different than what you think they may be. I have the real info as to where The Politician's next plan of action against you and The Collective will be. I am sure you think in three days' time The Politician will be doing his campaign speech here in the Southside, but he has a plan to get you and your whole group wasted. An ambush if you will. He's also trying to kill Dante. Malum's plans for Dia are not well ones neither." He replied.

Ososi handed me a piece of paper with some writing on it. I looked in his eyes once again to try and read this Shadow man. Who was he and where did he come from? I couldn't dwell on this right now, this information was most important to me. Ososi didn't smile and kind of caressed my hand.

"I don't flirt with strangers." I said sternly. He turned his back to me and left with the darkness.

I stood there waiting for something, anything to happen. Ososi had to be right; Dia wouldn't just meet with me on a whim like this. Not the way The Politician had her under his finger. My mind was racing and trust issues began to arise. Ososi was a shadow man but why do I feel that he isn't lying. He would have no reason to deal with me and my plight, so he couldn't be my enemy.

This wretched Politician was smarter than I thought he was. He is definitely using Dia against me. Our bond would be our undoing, but for what? What was his personal vendetta against me and my twin? Could it be more than his lust for her or something more?

I played with the paper between my fingers. I didn't want to read it, nor did I want to know what The Politician had in mid for Dia. For the first time in my life I felt helpless. I felt like I couldn't do anything to protect her neither. I mulled over the thought of asking Ososi for help but I didn't know if he would be willing to help me do something like that. I had to help her. She was my twin after all.

I unfolded the piece of paper; I was shocked as to what it said:

"Tonight infiltrate The Heap, try not to draw attention to yourselves and bring The Collective scum bitch to me."

The note was anonymous; it must have been to one of Malum's henchmen. Ososi was useful to me after all. Without him I wouldn't have known this information. I smirked at the thought of knowing The Politician's next move.

I went over to the weapons table and loaded my Zentec Beast. I was ready for whoever would come at my door. I decided that I would call an old friend of Dante's to help with the impending ambush. Wyse, the bouncer at Club Ooze and also Laarz's cousin. I needed all of the muscle I could get.

I haven't had a battle in so long and I was ready to draw some blood. I turned on my computer droid and sent my message to my crew and Wyse. Minutes later I got the signal that they were on their way ready to protect me and what Dante built at any cost. My riders, my crew, and my friends we were not going to let The Politician have the last word. I cocked my Zentec Beast and waited patiently for my crew before the ambush started. Tonight would be the night I would get even with Malum and get my sister back. However, I'm going to deal with these low lives first.

Dia

"Please get this man off of me" I thought to myself as Mark hugged me. I loathed this man with everything in me. I loathed him for many reasons; he killed my parents. I was tipped off by one of his old secretaries. Mark killed them, in a deal gone bad when he was a teenager. Apparently, he was sent to kill them because his former boss thought they were the people that owed him creds from purchasing Ooze. My parents weren't like that; they were a loving pair whom would never harm anyone or anything in this wretched city. They were kind to it but the city wasn't kind to them. Neither was it kind to my twin sister and I. Growing up in The Heap; one of the worst sections in The City, we never had a chance. There was a reason I was with him, a reason that even my sister couldn't fathom. I was going to exact the revenge against Malum for everything that he put us through.

Of course Malum didn't know that we were the little twins that were orphaned because of him. However he will know soon enough. I had the psi ability to predict I know the turnout and I cannot wait to spring it on him.

He let go of me and gave me a kiss. I braced myself for the sound of his voice. I hated everything about this man.

"The interview went great don't you think?" he asked. I know Nia saw this interview and I know that she would be plotting and so would he. I forced a smile.

"Yes, it went good." I said flatly. He looked at me as if I was on something. I wonder if he knew what I was thinking; Malum had no Psi abilities so he was of no use. He grabbed me by my arms and looked deep into my eyes.

"Aren't you on my side?" Malum asked sternly.

"*No I'm not on your side, I am on mine.*" I thought to myself. Trying not to let him see what I was thinking in my face.

"Of course baby, that's why I'm here." I said trying to be sweet. He sighed, relief overcame him. Malum was like putty in my hand. I knew that I would become his downfall, and I was ready to get my revenge. Malum let go of me and sat down on the chair. He looked down at his papers in his desk. Looking at Nia and Dante's file; he smirked. My disdain for him grew now; his vendetta against my family was nothing compared to the vendetta I have in store for him.

I slowly walked out of his office and made my way to the elevator. I needed to get my plan in motion and the first thing was to see Ososi the Shadow Man. He didn't know me but I knew he had a thing for Nia because I saw this in my prediction. I know that he would be perfect to help us. While my sister would be occupied with Malum's ambush while I would get rid of him myself.

I sent a signal to Laarz through my computer droid, letting him know that there would be an ambush tonight. I know that he and the rest of The Collective crew will do anything to protect my sister. My computer droid pinged and it was Laarz letting me know that he and the crew were all in the clear and ready to fight back.

I took my Zentec out of my purse; my sister wasn't the only one who could handle a gun. I was going to kill Malum myself. Getting off the elevator and out into the streets, I made my way to Ososi's place. I needed to convince him to help me and Nia.

It was raining here in the city, the perfect tone to set off what I am about to do for my sister and I. Ososi didn't reside too far but he was in the shadows. Getting to his place would be easy for me; hopefully The Politician doesn't have his usual henchmen following me. I was definitely in the clear.

I made it to Ososi's place near the sun tower. I was apprehensive. I wasn't scared but I wasn't the bravest like Nia. I didn't know what the shadow man might do to me. It had to be done though; I needed this revenge for my family and Ososi would help us. I knew this for a fact because he would do anything to protect my sister. I entered his building, my palms sweating and ready.

Nia

The whole crew was with me, ready to get Malum's men. To my surprise Laarz, Wyse and the rest of my crew were already tipped off that Malum's men were coming to attack. Laarz said that he didn't want to tell me, but I knew that my sister had a hand in tipping us off.

We all were in position around our warehouse. Every second felt longer than it should. We heard footsteps; my heart raced and my finger held steady on the trigger of my Zentec Beast. Laarz and Wyse were in position on the rooftop while me and the other members were ready in the corners of the hideout.

"We're inside," one of Malum's men whispered in his ear connector.

I looked at the men from my corner and saw that there weren't many but enough to take us out. Their weapons were state of the art, bought with citizen's campaign money.

His henchmen walked around scoping the hideout; I didn't want to wait any longer. I signaled my men to commence the attack. We stormed them, shooting them down left and right. Laarz and Wyse battled as well; I could hear it going down on the rooftop over our blasting weapons.

"Laarz keep them occupied. I'm going for my sister." I said into the communicator.

"No, it's too risky. What if she's not there?" Laarz read back.

"I've got to big guy. This is my only chance." I said back.

"Affirmative, boss lady. We've got it covered." Laarz said.

I sprinted out of the warehouse knowing that my crew had it under control. I climbed into the hover car then sped downtown to Malum's office to get my sister back. Rain began falling as I raced through traffic. This omen wasn't going to stop me. I prayed to the River that this day would come and finally it was here.

Once I reached my destination I hurried out the car then made my way towards Malum's office on the third floor. The rain fell harder, thunder crashing in the sky. I broke in the door; the lobby was dark. The front desk was empty. Usually his secretary would be here pounding away at the keyboard always looking sinister. However, she wasn't here and I could use this to my advantage. No one could alert The Politician now. I strolled in the lobby with my Zentec Beast in my hand. I felt a bit cocky.

"Come on out you son of a bitch! I know you're here!" I shouted, making sure he heard me.

"I'm here to bring my sister back home where she belongs!" I shouted again as I made my way to his office. I made a mad dash for the staircase so that I could get to Dia and Malum faster before he had any time to think. Opening the third floor staircase door, I reached his corridor. So this is where Malum lived. The carpet was velvet and there were ficus trees standing in the corner. It was obvious Malum used the creds donated to his campaign to live a lavish lifestyle.

I treaded down the hallway making sure the area was clear. I kicked down his office door and scoped it out. No one was there. Rain and wind gusted around me, blowing files from his desk. I grabbed one of the files; it was a file on Laarz and my crew. Malum was scheming to get my whole crew sent to Distal. I ripped up the files and left the office. As I reached back to the hallway I saw a shadow. I pointed my gun at it and then the shadow dispersed to reveal Dia.

"Dia, thank the River!" I said running, up to her then hugging her tight. She hugged me back just as tight. I looked at her as if I was looking in the mirror.

"Nia, you can't stay here," she said, a blank look on her face. "This is something that I must do on my own." What does she mean that she has to do this alone? She cannot be serious.

"You're coming back with me and that's final," I said. I know who gave us the warning, the Shadow Man."

"Ososi," Dia said. "His name is Ososi."

"That doesn't matter," I replied. "The Collective is dealing with his men right now, so once they are done Malum will be finished and you won't have to be with him any more."

I pulled her hand but she didn't budge, she looked down at her feet.

"He's on the roof now Nia, I have to kill him for what he did to you and I. He took the people that were most important to us and I have a score to settle," she said.

I looked at her as if she was crazy I didn't know what the hell she was talking about. What score and what people? That's when it dawned on me.

"Our parents...he killed them when we thought they disappeared," Dia said. "He took them from us; I saw when he killed them. That's why I was with him; that's why I waited. For revenge; for the vow that I took when he killed them with no mercy. You see sister; I have to do this alone. You will only be in my way." She turned away from me and went to the staircase to get to the roof.

"WAIT!" I shouted, following here up the stairs. Dia was always a fast runner and at times I thought I would never be able to catch her. She was always running away...

We made it to the roof and like she said Malum stood in the rain, his suit drenched. I looked at Malum straight in the eyes; he smiled and winked at me. I aimed my Zentec Beast at him. Dia looked at me and shook her head no. But I couldn't listen to her now.

"Is what my sister said true? Did you kill Jamal and Shadia Sabine?" I asked, my hands trembling with rage. Malum looked at Dia then back at me, the smile never leaving his face. He walked toward me as the wind blew increased. I kept my gun aimed at him, ready for any move he made.

"That was then, this is now," he crooned. "Your sister loves me and she always will. You and The Collective on the other hand are just another gang that I need to get off the streets."

"And besides they were just Ooze abusers anyway," he said chuckling. That's when Dia lost it. She pulled out a small Zentec and shot The Politician in his chest. He stood there stunned for a moment and I stood there my mouth open.

"Di-ahhh, Ho-w c-could you? I-I gave you e-everything," he stammered, holding his chest as he gazed at her. He dropped to his knees, trying to keep the blood in. Dia walked over to him and knelt down and hugged him.

"But you took everything already. Goodbye." Dia said. That's when she took her gun and shot him through the temple. All I saw was his blood being washed away by the rain and Dia looking at me. The score was settled; we hugged each other and that's when I knew that in the end she had saved me. I was the one she wanted to protect from danger.

"Thank You," I said.

"Now it's time to get Dante out of Distal," she whispered.

"Yes, back to how things used to be." I replied. I called in on Laarz and Wyse to make sure that everything was ok, and it was. They demolished Malum's henchmen. No one was lost on my end. My sister and I might be held accountable for this by The Watchers but we didn't care. As we walked off the roof, my marked eye began to burn. It was a sign that it wasn't over. But at that moment, I didn't care.

Darkest Light

By
Natiq Jalil

Anything goes in The City.

I don't see that as a problem. In fact, I'm counting on it.

I stand on the balcony of my building, staring at the glaring light of the Sun Tower, loathing its intensity. You see, I'm built for the shadows. That's where I'm comfortable. And soon, this whole goddamn world will be as I like it.

I look down at the people at street level, scurrying around like ants, playing their parts, oblivious to the darkness that already exists here. They think they're so much better than those who live in other wards... the wards untouched by the Sun Tower's unnatural light. I can't wait to uproot their simple lives. I know the day will come when *They* will emerge from the shadows. I will watch them scream and beg for their lives. It's laughable the way they always offer up their creds in exchange for their lives, like digital wealth is really worth anything. Their lives are worth even less. I take their lives *and* their creds, every single time.

For the ones who manage to cling to their lives after losing them, the world will become theirs. Only those who survive the process will realize the gift I bring them. Problem is I'm the only one to have ever survived it. I am the exception to the rule... the deviation. I don't expect very many to become as I am, so in a way, I guess my plan is a second Culling, of sorts. My father carried out the first.

The Culling that my father led took place 20 years ago. With him at the leader, thousands of "Believers" across 30 wards were slaughtered. Over a thousand by his own hands. Believers are those gullible, unfortunate masses who have been convinced there is a way out of the City. They claim there is a Paradise right outside the borders where there is free sunlight, green grass, and trees. Some people will believe anything. But the thing about naïve stupidity is it spreads. My father did the City a service by killing the weeds at the root. He became a legend that night. He became the monster under the bed and in the shadows that never went away, but was never there when you turned on the lights.

That's how I remember my father before the Watchers took him. It's interesting that I became exactly that. I guess the sins of the father run deep.

During the Culling, the Sun Tower became the epicenter of a night of death like no one had ever witnessed before. Not that anyone really remembers much of anything before then, anyway. All anyone remembers anymore is The City, and the infectious fear that invaded even the wards that were untouched by the Culling. That was the birth of the taboo that no one escapes, except through death.

I am proof of that being untrue. Death is no escape.

My father raised me to believe that The City was everything. He'd risen to heights that caused envy in those around him by brutality and cold calculation. It was because of his ruthless nature that he'd been given command of The Left Hand, the group that watched and dealt swift "justice" to those who dreamed of escape. Those who hoped. I am definitely my father's son.

With the death of my father and myself, The Left Hand was dissolved and *They* began to fuel the fear that kept The City breathing. Funny how the politicians and corporate heads can't even imagine that *They* are in my hands, now. And that *They* are coming for the light.

I feel the air shift behind me, which distracts me from my thoughts. I know who it is without even having to look. It is *Her*. She is always watching me. She has been fascinated by me since before I died so long ago. She brought me back to life using her own body. She suffused me with her own shadows.

In a way, I'm very similar to a Shedder. I come back

when I die. But unlike a Shedder, I come back as myself. Well, maybe that's not completely true. I seem to come back more powerful... more in tune with the shadows... less human than I was before. Another difference is I don't need a bunch of tech to come back. The shadows take care of that, themselves.

They, the Shadow-Touched, have a shadow ceremony every year. Every year, when the Sun is at its weakest, *They* die again. Some do not come back. Those who do are stronger, darker than they were before. She is perhaps the most powerful. That is probably why she was able to bring me, a human, back from the dead. That is probably why she was able to shatter my illusions to dust on a shallow wind. Now, it is *She* who lives an illusion. An illusion where I am the center of her world and destined to be *Hers*, always.

Our thoughts share a faint connection. Due to that connection, she is now uneasy, and watches me constantly. She feels that I am pulling away from her. Her own illusion is fading away, revealing a reality she'd rather stay blind to. The dark fantasy of her mind is being torn asunder, and for the first time, she feels powerless. She watches on, her denial waning, as the one thing she ever desired for herself slips through her fingers.

That's why the worst sin of the Shadow-Touched is the sin of Belief.

Though I want to be detached from it all, to pretend that she isn't my concern, my bond to her won't let me. It forces me to acknowledge her feelings on a deep level, close to whatever's left of my soul. Honestly, it's a bit disturbing. But it is something I cannot run from. Truth be told, it is my fault, though not intentional. It happened without warning. It happened so subtly that I didn't notice. She, however, did notice. And nothing has been the same since. I imagine it never will be, again.

That is why I am trying to stay squarely focused on the goal. I keep hoping that she will be comforted by my single-minded pursuit of the shadows and stop monitoring my thoughts and emotions for subtle shifts in attention. I hate to admit it, but it happens more than I'd like. The simplest, most inconsequential things stir the surface waters, and all I can do is watch the ripples spread out of my control. Moments like this, when I'm pondering how meaningless life is. When something in the back of my mind responds by recalling that fateful meeting in the middle of the night. My mind betrays me. It recalls the unique scent, the sharp bite of tempered steel at my throat, the fiery eyes and the way they looked though me, and the way my heart beat faster under the intense scrutiny. Moments like these are the ones that make things hard. Moment when thoughts of Nia Sabine enter, unbidden, to my mind.

I felt the moment when she latched on to the stray thought, so I acted without pausing.

"Vivian," I call out into the seemingly empty room. "Come out. I know you're there."

She seems startled by my voice cutting into the silence, but recovers quickly. I turn to face where I know she will appear. We are too connected for me not to know.

She steps from the shadows into the dim light of the room in the unintentionally seductive way that she always does. All curves and shadows, long legs and lashes, elegance and deadly intent... it's impossible to not be attracted to her. She catches the tail end of my observation, and softens a little, pleased that I am affected by her. Emboldened, she saunters over to my side like her curves own the reality that clings to them. She is a woman who is always aware of her surroundings, and how she can use them. The shadows of the room obscure parts of her, while the dim light plays on others, adding beautiful depth to her golden brown skin. Her long hair, impossibly thick dreadlocks, seems to melt into the darkness behind her. The deep red of the markings above her left eye add to her allure. To me, the markings look kind of like a fancy way of writing the letters V-V-N. That's why

I call her Vivian. The Shadow-Touched have no need for meaningless titles. Since I'm an outsider, new to their ways, they've allowed me this one lingering human attachment.

Sometimes, I think that she watches herself through my eyes, exerting a certain amount of control over a certain part of me. I'm pretty sure of it, in fact. She doesn't realize that it has put her at a disadvantage. Her manipulations can only force me to lust. Nia however, didn't have to play such games to inspire... what?

I quickly shake away the thought and focus on what's in front of me. She is feeling some kind of a way again.

"What are you thinking about?"

This is not a question. This is a demand. A dare. If I'm honest, she will be angered. If I lie, she will be angered. Avoidance will also call down her anger. So I do them all.

"I was thinking about how meaningless it all is," I began. "All of it. Them. Us. The City. The world. All of it. Meaningless."

Her shocked confusion at my answer was strangely satisfying. I told the truth, lied, and avoided, simultaneously, throwing her off balance and delaying her wrath. I feel the touch of her mind as she tries to hold onto her anger, but that cerebral part of her that has helped her survive for so long kicks in. I understand this part of her better than she does. It is instinct to her. To be in the present at all times is her nature, and I weld her nature like a knife. Her need to figure out the immediate enigma kicks in. Her curiosity wins. I am her deepest curiosity.

"Wh-what do you mean?" she stammers. She realizes, with no small measure of self-loathing, that she has already lost this round.

"I mean that everything is meaningless," I begin again. "Those people down there, for instance. They have built up philosophies that place them squarely in the center of the universe. Each one of them is so sure of their importance. None of them could ever imagine that *We* are coming for them. That they are not likely to survive what *We* have in mind for them. And that *We* don't give a shit, either way.

"Then there is *Us*. What makes Us think We are so important? We can't even get out of this damned City. Here we are, seeking to wrest control of something that, for all we know, means less than nothing. Like birds and squirrels fighting over breadcrumbs, laying our lives down, we die from wounds we earn for the sake of something we believe worthwhile. Something bigger than ourselves. When we step outside of ourselves, however, we are faced with the fact that what we fight and die over are nothing but crumbs.

"We live and die to feed our denial of this fact. We create gods and religion, science and philosophy, all so that we can feel like we matter. Truth is this universe was not made for us. There is no "god" sitting in the clouds watching us with love. No deity created the universe just so we would have a place to exist. That's all bullshit.

"The truth that we deny is that we are simply a side effect... an insignificant consequence. We want so badly to have meaning, that we ignore the order of things. We didn't come first. The universe did. The universe wasn't built for us. We just happen to adapt to it. Life isn't some grand miracle. It was an inevitability that couldn't be avoided. And it ends just as quickly as it begins.

"You've seen into the shadows. You know that once the spark of life fades, it is just gone. That's why you had to work quickly to bring me back, right. You knew there would be nothing so romantic as an afterlife, or reincarnation, where we could magically meet each other in the future. No destiny. That's why you risked it all. Because all there is in existence is the current moment. And once the moment passes, you never get it back."

I spew all of this out without taking a breath, my voice rising and falling like tides. I actually feel exhausted. What started out as simply a way to avoid a discussion about a woman I planned to never see again, turns out to be something much more crucial to me. I realize, with a start, that this is what I truly believe. Vivian realizes this, too, and doesn't know what to do with it any more than I do.

"You really believe this?" The sincere shock and surprise in her tone color these few, simple words with such heaviness.

"Yes. Yes, I do." What more could I say?

"But you didn't feel this way when you saw her." She says this with no condemnation in her voice. Somehow, this was heartbreaking to me. "I felt the shock of that moment. That moment when you met her eyes, I saw them just as clearly as you did. She ripped your reality apart. She ripped mine apart, too. Since the day we first bonded, I knew you'd struggled to make sense of the world. I knew you struggled to find your place in it, to find a reason to exist. I wanted to become that for you. I felt it was my responsibility since I'm the one who awakened the shadows within you. Nothing I did worked. But the moment you saw her, everything changed. I felt the light ripping away the shadows. And for the first time ever, I felt fear. You did this to me! She did this!"

She was yelling, now. Panic was in her eyes. Looks like I hadn't won this round after all. I stand there helplessly as she continues.

"In a moment, she became everything to you that I wanted to be. And when you are not around her, you slip into the melancholy you are in, now. You'd finally started to feel comfort in the shadows. Now, they are sinister to you, again. You hesitate now, where before, you were all action. What do you think happens when the Others notice? I've been protecting you while you run off to watch her from the shadows. Don't think I hadn't noticed. Because the moment *They* realize that your head isn't in the game like it was before, They will *end you*. And I won't be able to stop it."

With that, she melts into the shadows, leaving no trace of her presence. She leaves so quickly the silence deafens me. The bitterness of her last words leaves me numb and empty.

Her words bring the shadows crashing in on me. Everything she said was right. Every word she said mirrored thoughts that I'd had. I realize that the reason I only watch from a distance... the reason I continually battle with myself... why I convince myself to stay away from her is because of my own sense of self-preservation. Because *They would end* me. And everything would be for nothing.

Even the Shadow-Touched have things they revere... things they feel were greater than themselves. Even the Shadow-Touched have a couple of labels they use. The Others. They are the leadership, the strongest, and the least affected by such trivial things as emotion and attachment. They spend their time thinking, calculating, planning, implementing, and communing with Shadow. They are the ones closest to the essence of darkness and cold. Their only attachment is to their goals. Everything else is expendable. Anything that doesn't fit perfectly into their plans is quickly and mercilessly destroyed and discarded.

This realization, that my feelings could betray me... that my saviors will hunt me down relentlessly... that I will cease to exist without accomplishing anything... terrified and sobered me. I now know that in order to live, I will have to cut her, the silent woman with the penetrating eyes, out of my life. The immediate regret I feel is knocking the wind out of me. There is a pain in me that I do not understand. She was never even mine, so why do I feel such loss. In this moment, I feel overwhelmed. I feel like the universe has abandoned me. The loneliness is crushing me with its terrible weight. I feel like I am dying again.

So I decide to do the only thing I can do. I will kill the rest of me that is affected by her. I will kill my emotions. I will focus only on revenge for the death of my mother, father, and myself. I will focus only on the cause. I will rededicate myself to the shadows, and never again seek out Nia's light.

I sit down in the lotus position, as I've been taught, and begin the arduous task of emptying myself. I let go of the warmth I feel when I think of my mother. This attachment is probably the hardest. I loved and hated her with everything I had. She was the sweetest and bitterest of my memories. It was for her sake that I'd sown the seeds that would eventually destroy my family. For her, I'd become a shadow, even while alive.

My mother had been a master of the high society social circuits. Politicians and corporate heads, well-to-do families, nobodies with strong ambition, they all came to her when their influence wasn't enough. She used her smiles and beauty like a sword. And I was her constant companion, learning all that she had to teach. I remember how she would smile down at me... how she said looking at me was like looking at herself. I think it was around that time that a part of me started hating her. I hated being her little ornamental accessory for her parties and events; a decorative hand mirror she carried around in her jeweled purse to remind her of her own magnificence. She fed and thrived on the confidence I gave her. And I began a slow descent into darkness. And her brilliant light couldn't reach me there.

My mother was light; I was her shadow. By the time I was ten, I'd already learned how I could help endeavors reach fruition. I began with kids my own age, the sons and daughters of the rich and powerful. I'd drive them into corners they'd have to stain themselves to escape. I forced them to commit crimes that could ruin their families. Then, I kept their secrets. I became their best friend in the worst way. I eventually used the same methods on adults, all of whom where the movers and shakers of the City. Including a certain young Politician who'd had his eyes on my mother, and was sharpening a blade to use on my father.

I'd thought I was smarter than them all, and individually, I probably was. However, having too many enemies became my undoing... and my whole family was killed as a result.

I was killed.

Very patiently, I let go. I let emptiness fill the space where my mother once existed.

I let go of the unrequited love I feel as I think of my father. I'd once convinced myself that I'd hated him, but deep inside I knew it wasn't true. Truth was I'd hated myself. I'd hated that I'd looked so much like my mother. I was like a twin of her, all beauty and grace. Nothing manly. My father once said that it would've been better if I'd been born a girl, since I insisted on being pretty. I'd resented him for that. I had no choice in the matter. I hated myself for not looking like him. For not being him.

So what I'd lacked in physical manliness was compensated for with intellect, cold calculation, and ruthless ambition. Using that networks I'd built up at my mother's events, I'd learned secrets that furthered my father's goals. I spied on his enemies, I made allies with the beneficial, and I destroyed anyone who stood in his way. In that way, I became useful to him.

I don't think he noticed at first. I'd grown used to his coldness toward me, and had given up on that ever changing. But one day, that changed. It was the night before we were killed. The Politician had come over. He'd been arguing with my father. I'm not even sure what the argument was about. But I had dirt on him. And he knew it. And he knew what I'd done to those who'd become enemies of my father. You see, the one thing I had in common with Mark Malum, The Politician, was that we were both in the business of keeping secrets.

That night, the night before I was killed, I'd heard my father yelling at someone from outside of his room. I recognized the other voice and was immediately filled with anger. Boldly, I stepped into the room, and watched the Politician's face pale... quite the feat for someone with such dark skin. In just five words, I'd sent Mark Malum fleeing from the room, humiliated, outclassed, and defeated... by a fifteen year old. What were the words, you ask? Simple...

"Do we have a problem?"

Mark Malum knew those were the words to announce my next target. And he knew that it wouldn't be long. What I didn't know was that the humiliation he'd felt was deeper than I could have imagined. I didn't know that his sense of self-preservation was stronger than mine. I had no idea that he'd strike first. But I think my father did.

For the first time ever, I saw a panic-stricken expression on my father's face as he looked back and forth between me and the fleeing Politician. I watched his face as some realization formed in his mind. Then I watched his face soften into an expression I'd never seen before. That night, for the first time ever, my father introduced me proudly as his son to others. The night, he had dinner together with my mother and me. That night was a night that I'd wished would last forever. That night...

...was my last.

I let go of the imaginary brother I relied on to alleviate my loneliness. As I think back, I realize I was a really lonely kid. The estate we lived was huge and required a staff of well over a hundred people to maintain it. I was treated like a little prince, given whatever I asked for. The staff never questioned me. I was like a parent and they the obedient child. Problem was, I was a child. I was a child who ordered around adults. When I was really young, before I'd learned to become useful to my parents, I'd rarely ever seen them. The maids would dress me up like a doll and lock me away in my room with whatever entertainments they could find. I guess that it was natural that I'd eventually invent a playmate.

So vivid was my imagination, so deep were the lies that I told myself, that even I started to believe them. By the time I was ten, being carted from one event to another with my mother, I built up a new layer of resentment toward my parents. I hated them for completely ignoring their "other son". Of course, I was too much of a coward to ever bring it up to them. I was too in love with being useful. So, to make it up to my "brother", I'd sneak him out of his lavish prison to accompany me in my business dealings.

Looking back, I must have appeared quite insane. When cornering someone for my later use, I'd openly discuss what I would do to them with my "brother". That was probably the reason so many of them complied with little or no trouble.

I remember how my "brother" smiled at me on the last night, as I told him about the dinner with our mother and father. I'd made a promise to him that night. I promised him that one day soon, I'd make sure he was acknowledged by them.

I remember the night I died, as I lay there in a pool of my own blood, my father and mother motionless beside me, Mark Malum laughing not too far away, having drinks with so many others I foolishly believed I'd controlled, and thinking, at least my brother escaped. Even in death, my mind had been clouded by delusion.

Sitting alone now in my empty room, I recalled all of this, and let it go. I ignore all warmth I can feel with my senses. I let all the pain wash over me and disappear.

That's when it happens. That's when I feel the shadows start to creep in. That's when I feel the biting cold of darkness sink into me, like tendrils of ice reaching toward my heart. Every moment that passes brings the death of another part of me. I try to welcome it, but it is not easy.

It feels like an invasion into the deepest core of me. Its shadows scrape away my humanity with surgical precision, with no tenderness or compassion. It brutally strips away my sense of honor and decency. This is the first time the shadows have penetrated this deeply. In my determination to rid myself of the emotions that would make me an enemy to my new people, I'm becoming a vessel to the shadows.

Now, I feel almost empty. I can barely recall my mother. I can barely recall my father. I only see darkness. And the darkness becomes deeper as it spreads toward the only light that is left in me. The shadows have leeched away all warmth from my skin. I can feel my cold breath as I continue the methodic and controlled breathing I've been taught. This is what invited the shadows.

Almost distantly, I feel Vivian. I realize that the part of me that feels affection toward her is starting to fade, also. With the decrease of emotion, my thoughts and focus become clearer, and I can hear her thoughts clearly amongst the millions of voices in the darkness. She approves of my actions. She feels I am doing the right thing. The shadows have penetrated so deeply that this knowledge means nothing to me. I feel her expectation. I feel her excitement building as I am consumed, and only the tiniest speck of light is left inside.

That's when I catch a glimpse of life through her eyes. She is proud of my progress. None of *Them* have ever gone this deep, not even the Others. I realize that it's not that *They* are devoid of emotion, they simply practice a suppression of emotion. She is in awe of my power, right now. She feels that with me as a weapon, there is no one who can stand against Them. Then I see through her eyes for the first time. And I feel her intentions. She has seen through my eyes before.

She is on the move. And she is not alone. She is with her brother, Him. Little Killer, a young girl I rescued by accident some time ago, is with them. So are several others. At least 20 of Them. They are moving quickly. So fast, that no one else would be able to see them.

I see a familiar building in the distance. It is a building that I've visited many times before. It is the hideout of Nia Sabine and her merry band of thieves. Though I still feel detached and disoriented, and though the shadows are steadily devouring the last of me, curiosity rears its head.

Why are they there?

As if the universe heard my question, Vivian's thoughts and emotions answer. In her jealousy and anger, she has spoken with The Others about Nia Sabine, and convinced Them of a threat. They are there for assassination. Vivian's thoughts are clear. She will kill anyone who gets in her way. Her intent is deadly. Calculating. Cold. Vivian is using the shadows to see inside the compound. Nia Sabine is settling down for the night. She is totally unaware of the danger she is in. She is thinking of her sister. She is thinking of the Politician. She is feeling guilt over a stray, but powerful emotion. She is thinking about… me?

Really?

I feel the shadows inside me pause. They seem hesitant about the last of the light within me. I realize, that I am completely cold inside except for one thing; one emotion specifically for one person… Nia. The woman I'm killing myself trying to forget.

She doesn't see them coming. If nothing is done, she will die. She will die without saving her prodigal sister. She will die without knowing her own heart. She will die bitterly and slowly, cursing the day she met me. Vivian doesn't plan to do this quickly. Her murderous intent won't allow her to.

That's when the shadows stop. They stopped just short of their goal of complete emptiness. Oddly, however, they don't try to force the issue. The shadows seem to protectively fold around and embrace that last ember of light. Distantly, I realize why. Purpose. For the shadows, that last ember of light is the purpose they will strive toward, the ambition they will pursue.

In the hazy twilight of my dimly lit room across from the Sun Tower, I finally move. I stand, emptied of all emotion except one. I am empty of all desire, except one. I am now a killer with one anchor to reality. And these bitches are on their way to kill her.

With no distractions or emotional conflict left to me, my path is clear. I open my eyes and see my cold breath fogging in front of me. The shadows I cast are so deep; you can see stars in them. I feel every shadow in The City, including the ones attached to Vivian. And that is where I focus. She feels my intent just a moment too late.

In an instant, I am in front of her. She is moving so fast that she can't slow down fast enough. Her momentum carries her straight to me. I feel nothing as I remove her head from her body. Her startled gasp is abruptly cut short. Her body seems to fall to the ground in slow motion. Blood and shadows pour from her neck and stain the ground beneath her. Her head dangles pathetically by her hair, which is held tightly in my grasp. There's a shocked expression carved onto her face. She knew she fucked up.

The others also have a delay reaction. I collect three more heads before they come to a halt and surround me. With the exception of Little Killer, everyone looks confused and livid. Wrath was in their eyes, and retribution was in their stance. Little Killer looked scared.

"Soso?"

Her voice trembles as she speaks the name she always calls me. She has doubt in her eyes. Confusion. I'd brought her, a little girl, into this crazy world of death and shadows. She'd already been insane enough to acclimate to it well, but the thought of one day facing me, the one she admired most, had never crossed her mind. The man I was moments ago would have hesitated.

That man is gone, now.

With little more than a thought about how I'd like them to the die, it is done. The shadows rippled, and then quickly shaped themselves into spear-like points. In a fraction of a moment the three who'd been inching their way toward me from behind were impaled. I felt a slight rush as the shadowy spears lingered, and realized that my shadows were devouring theirs, leaving their lifeless bodies in a truly humanlike state.

That was new.

Up until now, I'd struggle to mold my shadows into different shapes, and nothing useful ever came of it. And stories of the fabled Shadowy Devourer were myth and legend among the Shadow-Touched. No one actually believed in it.

Yet, here I was, molding shadows like a beast, and gobbling them down whole.

The Shadow-Touched are similar to the stories children read about werewolves, except these beings were part shadow, not wolf. The Shadow-Touched are weakest during the daylight hours and during a full-moon. At this moment, in mid-afternoon with the sun blazing overhead, I feel like I could take over the world. If this is me at my weakest, I can't wait until nightfall.

Looks like I'm not the only one who has realizes this.

Their leader, the one called, HIM, and who I've called my brother since I'd been reborn, is seething with anger. I'm sure that I've seen this anger somewhere before, but it doesn't worry me. Even if I had the capacity to worry in my current state, I don't think I would. I can't afford to worry right now.

He is looking at the bodies on the ground… the heads in my hands… the shadows taking sinister form around me, the three human bodies looking utterly pathetic just lying there. I watch the emotions play across His face. He wonders why I do this. He feels betrayed. He wants vengeance for His sister. He wonders if He can take me. With a slight feeling of déjà vu, I speak words I haven't spoken in a long time.

"Do we have a problem?"

I watch Him determine that I cannot be taken with such a small force in daylight.

"Ososi. You have made a serious mistake. You've seriously fucked up. You do realize that we will come for you, right?"

He almost screams the last words.

Unmoved by his threat, I answered truthfully. Logically.

"You won't have to come for me. I will come for you. Realize that you will now flee to the shadows… shadows that I control. How long do you think it would take for me to hunt you to extinction? An hour? Half an hour? Five minutes? I think you might want to let this one go. I only killed those who attacked me or attempted to harm Nia. I will not harm anyone who doesn't cross those lines. Approach either of us again, and your head will be next. "

Unceremoniously, I tossed four heads at his feet. The wet sound they made as they hit the ground and bounced over to him was kind of disgusting. Vivian's face seemed to look right at him.

Little Killer couldn't take it. She ran a few feet away, and then threw up. I've seen her do some cruel things to living creatures, including killing people, and there are times when I thought that maybe she was one of those people born completely fucked in the head, but apparently, even she has limits. She paused just long enough to get it all out, then continued, slowly and bewilderedly, in the direction they'd come from. HE doesn't even notice her departure.

With hatred, pain, betrayal, and death in his eyes, He gives me one last look; a glare that promises my end. He fades into the shadows first. Then the others. They leave the dead behind.

Just then, I feel something behind me. I turn and see Nia approaching. At least, until she sees me. She stops dead in her tracks. Her beautiful face distorted by horror. I'd never even considered what I might look like, now that I've given myself to the shadows.

She starts to turn and flee, but abruptly stops. Slowly she turns around and intently looks at me, as if searching for something. I am tempted to walk toward her. Without even meaning to, I take a step forward. Reflexively, she almost turns away and runs, like a deer sensing danger and leaping into the forest. I can sense her fear through her shadow. She is tense and every nerve in her body is screaming at her to run. But she is stubbornly resisting. She sees something in me. I don't think I'd appreciated the strength of this woman until just this moment.

She is staring at me with those eyes that see through me. These are the same eyes that captivated me from the beginning. Despite her fear, despite her fight or flight instincts on overdrive, she takes a hesitant step toward me. Then another. Until finally, she is standing before me. She looks up at me with an expression I can't define. And finally, she speaks.

"Ososi?"

She said my name. The spark of light inside me responds, vibrates, and pulses through the shadows. I can speak. I just nod. Once.

She looked around at the dead bodies lying around. I quickly deepen the shadows so she doesn't see the heads. I also become aware of the fact that we are being watched. Little Killer didn't wander off far. She is watching, peeking from around a corner. No time to worry about her. Nia is right in front of me, and I don't know how to explain.

"Ososi? What happened to you? Did you do all of this? Why?"

There is no condemnation in her voice. Not sure if she is in shock, or she really believes that I'd only do this for a good reason. I have to say something. She is the only purpose I have left and maybe my only connection to my humanity. No knowing it will make a difference, I decided to just tell the truth.

"I did this. All of it. You were in danger. They would have killed you. No longer the Ososi you knew. All shadows now. To protect you."

She's taking it all in, but I can tell it is a bit much. Her carefully controlled expression is starting to crack around the edges and I can see the beginnings of tears in her eyes. She's having a hard time even looking at me. What kind of monster have I become?

I can tell there is a part of her that wants to run away screaming, but she hasn't moved from that spot – neither forward nor backward. I have to do something, but I don't know what. Then, a thought occurs to me.

Using every ounce of control I have, I focus on the

little bit of light left within me. I carefully peel the shadows away, allowing the light to once again take form. What happens next, I never would have imagined. In my mind, I'm thinking, that if I can invite the shadows in, I can probably uninvite them. And to a certain degree, that is what happening. What I don't expect is for my body to split into two separate forms.

In bewilderment, I watch as the face and body I've come to know as my own slumps forward and into Nia Sabine's arms, the weight knocking her to the ground. She seems almost as startled as me.

Now I have a new question, and it is quite perplexing. If I am me, still thinking these thoughts, but my body is over there, still breathing, though unconscious, and in the arms of the woman I want to protect, then what do I do? Who and what am I? The Ososi in here arms, is he human? Is he the real me? If so, then am I even needed?

Distantly, I hear a voice. I think it is addressing me. I'm having a hard time focusing on it as I finally notice my own shadowy hands, seemingly formed of black fire. I realize that I am completely formed of shadow. How can this be?

"Ososi!" Hearing my name rips me from my thoughts. Nia is speaking. Is she speaking to this me or the one in her arms? She is looking in my direction, so can I even dare hope that she'd still call me by that name?

"Ososi, I'm not sure what's going on, but thank you. Thank you for protecting me. Thank you for giving me a chance. I promise I will keep your body safe until you return for it." With that, she carefully stood up and began dragging the Ososi I'd always been toward her hideout.

She'd actually thanked me. Why? Is that body even mine anymore? And what is to become of this me?

A gentle touch on my hand wakes me from my darkening thoughts. I look down to see Little Killer looking up at me. She seems hesitant, but not afraid.

"Soso?"

She still calls me that. Even when I'm like this. Abruptly, she lets go and runs over to the nearest body. She lifts the torso, grabs firmly at the armpits then starts pulling it toward the shadows.

"Soso," she says, breathing heavily, "Help with this. We need to go before *They* come back?"

"We?"

The question slips out before I can stop it. She intends to come with me? Even now? This confirms that she really is fucked in the head.

"Can't I?"

She looks hurt that I'd consider separating from her. I now notice the shadows that make up my body are rippling. It seems there was one more little sliver of light inside, and it was for this one. I guess a little crazy company is better than no company, at all.

"Sure," I say, "Though I don't know where we are going to go?" The only place I can think of, right now, is the hotel room near the Sun Tower. Guess I'll figure it out from there. I help Little Killer move the bodies while I think about our next move. I look over at Nia's hideout. As long as the other "me" is there, Nia will be in danger. I don't know whether the other Ososi will still be able to control shadows, so best to be safe. I plan to come back later and take him somewhere far away from her. Hopefully, she will understand.

I take on last look at the bodies we've hidden. The dead here are not forgotten or forsaken. I know this. They plan to have my blood for this (or whatever it is I bleed). That's fine with me. I am uncertain on the possibility of taking all of Them down. There is too much about my new bodies that I don't know. Most likely, I won't survive. But I promise myself one thing... that they will experience abysmal loss and pain before they kill me. They will lose their desire to assassinate Nia. There is no uncertainty in that.

How High the Moon

By
B. Sharise Moore

"If I say hit me with another 20 volts, I mean hit me with another 20 fucking volts!"

She watched her brother glare in her direction through heavy lids and returned the look with a scowl.

He cleared his throat. "You can't handle it Street. I know you think you can, but..."

In an instant, the barrel of a 22 mm sonic shotgun tucked in the small of her back kissed his temple. "Do it or die."

With blinding speed, Night Moon pulled his own weapon, a laser hidden in a leather holster beneath a bulging bicep. They stood in silence, each poised to pulverize the other's skull. "If you wanna sizzle that's on you, but remember who I am, Street."

She winked and lowered her weapon. "True. But I still need those volts. Work with me."

Night put his piece away and shook his head. "You may be bat shit crazy, but we're cut from the same cloth; know that." He kneeled beneath a nearby table, his muscular frame bathed in florescent pink light. The floor below was littered with sockets, plugs, and parallel squares. "I got a free 12 volt line," he said through clenched teeth. "You're already at 88." He motioned toward her arms donned in silver cuffs from elbow to wrist. "We don't know how those new upgrades are gonna react to the juice either. They're still fresh."

Street Moon rolled her eyes. Before stripping down to her thermal suit, she pulled her fro into a tight knot and stuck her big toe in the steel tub. Once she found a degree of comfort, she slid inside, adjusting her neck and shoulders against the edge of the basin. Night poured the Ooze over his sister's torso, feet, and thighs. She closed her eyes and waited. Nothing. "I got this. Gimme some juice!"

He exhaled before immersing the plugs in the basin one by one. Her eyes rolled. A back alley purge was the perfect marriage of Ooze and electricity. Naked metal streaming with live current rippling through lavender sludge. It was the most intense orgasm she'd experienced. Some injected, which was good enough for a decent trip, but since its accidental discovery, she preferred the electric bath. It made her toes curl like no man ever had.

"Sis, this could fry you. The suit can only protect but so much."

She dismissed him with a hand and focused on the intensifying tingle. It was time. Time to float, to trip, to feel good, to forget.

Pulse: 88 beats per minute. Blood pressure: 110 over 80. Respiration: Shallow; 14 breaths per minute.

The old man's vital signs scrolled across the lens of the scope attached to her thermo sensory crossbow. According to the readout on her cuffs, the target was in exceptional health. Her full lips stretched into a tight smile. Sixty somethings were hard to come by in the City. Around these parts if the poverty and stress didn't kill you first, a Watcher's grip, or a stray bullet was as likely as the sunrise.

She squatted atop the building with her back to a flag post. The night shrouded the City like a cloak with a smattering of silver stars. From where she crouched, she could make out the River in the semblance of a crystal snake, the Heap, an eyesore that looked more mountain than landfill, and the flickering lights of the Southside. She imagined the Lush was somewhere out there as well. Sly had described it as a limbo, neither here nor there, but a place of color and healing. The greens were greener and the sky was the most brilliant blue anyone could imagine. Sometimes Sly referred to it as beyond the beyond. "It's either me or those kills babe. You gotta choose," he'd said. His last words ricocheted inside her skull like a wave crashing to shore. Her lip twitched.

She retrieved a suction cup the size of a thimble from a shoulder pocket in her leather vest and pulled. A sleek black rope inlaid with biosteel appeared, wire thin and strong. She notched the wire along with an arrow in her crossbow then loosed it in the direction of the building in front of her. When it caught, she tugged and attached the other end to the base of the flag post creating a zip line. With ease she swung the bow square across the line, grabbed hold of the ends, and propelled her weight forward. There was a noticeable chill in the air that gnawed at her bare scalp and ear lobes. It was then that she realized how much she missed her fro. But when it came time to choose between her hair and her high, bald was best.

Once she descended to a two foot wide landing and regained her footing, she retracted the wire, secured her bow across her shoulder blades, and scaled the wall like a shadow. She climbed another ten feet before hoisting herself on the roof and through one of the open skylights. She hung there for a moment while her eyes adjusted to the light. The space was spectacular with its stone pillars, large, leafy plants in clay jars, plush chairs, ebony bookshelves lined with volumes of leather bound books, a twisting circular staircase, and shiny black marble floors. The man lived like a king in a palace in the middle of the City. Perhaps wisdom had its rewards after all.

Thunder rattled a chandelier and a bolt of lightning lit up the massive room. She landed to the floor without a sound while keeping her eyes fastened to her target asleep in an oversized wicker chair. Kneeling beside him, she retrieved the bow and notched an arrow not more than an inch from his temple. With the next crackle of thunder the man's eyes flew open. In an instant he was on his feet with an old Smith and Wesson aimed between her eyes. She didn't flinch.

"Come on Street, you could've knocked on the door... maybe sent a message with a borg or contacted me through your brother like any normal person." His nostrils flared as he peered over the gun barrel.

In the old days the mere thought of penetrating the lair of the Learned Order of Street Priests was a death wish. He got a few consolation points for the quick response, but clearly the old man had lost a step. Aging sucked.

Street Moon squinted through the darkness, the old man in her crosshairs. "I got a rep Lateef. Can't have nobody runnin' round here sayin' Street Moon's soft." She nodded in the direction of the weapon. "We good?"

He shook his head. "We ain't good 'til you stand down."

"Ain't gonna happen."

"Well, looks like one of us won't be making it outta here alive."

"Trust and believe I never cock my piece without loading it. The Knowledge Lateef I knew always kept one in the chamber. You slippin'."

His eyes narrowed. "There was a time when no one would dare break in the lair of a Street Priest. There's a code." He lowered the shotgun.

"Things change," she shrugged. "Besides, your skylight was open. I saw it as an invitation."

She tugged at a thin wire and the bow collapsed into a lightweight ebony baton concealed in her leather boot.

"The bald look...becomes you. Brings out your eyes." He glanced at her silver cuffs. "Didn't think you were the type to upgrade. They look like they cost a pretty penny."

Her response was a lengthy exhale. Though she'd never admit it aloud, she was winded. The priest wasn't the only one who'd lost a step. She helped herself to a chair, ran a palm over her naked scalp, and retrieved her trusty 22.

Knowledge Lateef smoothed the lapels on his burgundy suit jacket. She noted the crow's feet clawing at the edges of his dark brown eyes as well as the shocks of gray ravaging his mustache and beard. Wiry thin, yet deceptively strong and distinguished, Lateef was the quintessential elder. He wasn't above being murked though. No one was.

"A little feedback on your entrance if I may." The man formed a tent with his thumb and fingertips beneath his nose. "Your stealth is nonexistent and your breathing sounds labored. What would you attribute that to?"

She ignored the question. "I need something from you Lateef."

"Need or want?" His eyes shifted toward her weapon.

"A database of human scalpers. As soon as possible."

"Most of the human scalpers are dead, Street."

"Most, not all."

He smiled. Bits of gold glimmered through his full lips. A pair of tortoise shell spectacles hung on the tip of his long, pointed nose. When he spoke he peered over the frames like a professor delivering a lecture. "But you're an assassin," he raised his brow. "You need your Tell. It helps with identifying your kills."

Blah blah blah. Street rolled her eyes. Everyone in the City was born with a Tell, a sub-dermal organ that connected citizens to the Wave so they could be Watched. She knew all about how much it meant to her "occupation." Still, she was willing to rid herself of it. She needed to hear herself think. A permanent Tell removal would allow that. "This ain't just about my Tell, Lateef." Her voice caught in her throat, dry and brittle.

He walked across the room to light a tall candle. Slowly the den brightened to reveal thin clouds of smoke meandering throughout the room. Frankincense. She could pinpoint that scent anywhere.

"Sly," he shook his head. "This is all about Sly isn't it?" He nodded in the direction of the open skylight and the weapons attached to her person. "You gotta give me more than that Street. Where does the scalping come in? Scalpers remove the Tell and you're in love with a man who's married to another woman. I don't see the connection."

She crossed her long, sculpted legs. "I've been doing some research. The thing that holds love, it's like..." she fumbled for the words. "...a desire at the soul level. If I can locate a scalper who might be able..."

He cut in. "Impossible. Won't work."

She leaned forward, her palm resting firmly on the gun. "Who said this was a choice, Lateef?"

"You're suggesting a rare procedure...one that hasn't been done before. It's not wise."

"I didn't ask what was wise. I need a database of scalpers. Now."

His wide eyes narrowed into slits. "I'm more valuable to you alive; otherwise I'd be dead already."

She relaxed her shoulders.

"Making threats won't get you any closer to a scalper, Street. Cut the shit. I may be old, but I'm nobody's tool."

She grit her teeth. "Fine. But I make the terms."

Lateef nodded. "I wouldn't expect anything else."

Street Moon rose from her chair and began counting on her jeweled green polished nails. "*One.* No questions. No attempts at mind tricks or influence. *Two.* Once we're there you're gone. No sticking around to watch the procedure. *Three.* You take this to your grave. What happens there stays there."

"Fair enough. But I have a term of my own."

She sucked her teeth.

"Trust."

"Trust?" She scoffed at the old man, sat, and crossed her legs again. "Assassins trust no one."

"I beg to differ. There was a time when you trusted, loved..."

"True. And that's what landed me here. I respect your wisdom Lateef. You know things no one else does. But trust... nah I don't trust anyone farther than I can throw them."

"You're arrogant Street. And because of that, you'll never be happy. Ain't that much purging or scalping in the City. I know love and loss Street. I know the hurt you're feeling. It's a constant gnaw…like a dog got a hold of your soul and won't stop chewing. But you can't cut off your nose to spite your face. Have you talked to your brother about this?"

She tensed at the mention of her brother. Little did he know, Night Moon was the last person with whom she wanted to share her heart break.

Street and Night Moon were orphans in the 215 district. Their biological parents were unknown though the rumor mill linked them to everyone from Bridget the Bard and Mama Smokes to The Purple and Tillian Drew. No one could really explain their escape from 215, but it was as simple as this: one day they were there and the next they weren't. For that, she was grateful.

Street and Night's closeness in age ignited a seething sibling rivalry. When Night made the decision to become a Kill for Hire at fifteen, it was only a matter of time before she'd do the same. Of course he hadn't had a clue that she'd tagged along on those first few missions. She recalled how she watched his every move, how he became one with the scenery to escape detection, the way he used silence as a weapon. They'd spent the last fifteen years attempting to outdo one another in terms of skill, style, and number of kills in a day, week, or month. The Moon assassins were blood sport elites; no one did it better. Other than Night Moon, Sly had been the only man she'd allowed herself to trust and admire. Perhaps this was why he'd been so difficult to shake.

"Nope." She didn't think it was necessary to tell Night Moon anything. Besides, she wanted to murk Abeekay and Sly herself. Night would have their heads at her feet by sunrise.

"Follow me."

She did so wordlessly. Together, they climbed the

circular staircase, up an additional two flights of stairs, and finally through a hall lined with ticking clocks and mirrors. As they approached the end of a long corridor, Street Moon prepared to stop. Instead of doing the same, Knowledge Lateef walked briskly through the wide mirror in front of them and into a pyramidal shaped room. She followed, itching with curiosity.

"These are the City's archives." He turned to face her. "What happens here stays here." She nodded.

Three of the four angled walls were lined with handwritten notes, photographs, and pages torn from old newspapers and books. The wall directly ahead of them held a three dimensional living map of the City. The River ran silvery smooth, tiny clouds surrounded the Apunu hives, and buildings appeared and disappeared into nothingness. Tiny dots represented humans, borgs, and others who made up the City's eclectic landscape. She turned her attention to a squat, granite pillar in the room's center. A golden globe the size of a melon hovered just above it.

Knowledge Lateef stepped toward the pillar and snapped his fingers. "Iset the Protector." His voice echoed throughout the room, bouncing from the walls.

The globe began to take shape as if it were being sculpted with human hands. A tuft of thick hair sprouted from a head with wide, questioning eyes and rounded features. Once the face on the globe was fully formed, she recognized her immediately, a Runner for whom she'd still had an open contract. The head spoke.

"Teacher. It's been too long. What can I do for you?"

The Street Priest wrinkled his brow. "I need a scalper. There's someone here who wants to get rid of her Tell."

The eyes on the floating head grew wider. "Another brave one. Let's meet."

"Not that simple," he paused. "She wants a soul scalp. There's a jones in her bones she can't kick."

The head was silent for a moment. "Rare. Extremely

rare. But there's someone here who may be able to pull it off."

"She's tainted."

Street Moon's mouth twisted as she began to protest.

Knowledge Lateef raised his two fingers to his lips.

"How so?" the head asked.

"Blood sport. She's one of the elites."

"The Rats aren't fond of assassins Lateef. This is a tall order. One wrong move and she'll be eliminated."

Street Moon blinked in surprise. It was obvious this Runner bitch didn't know who she was. She folded her arms and ran her tongue across her teeth.

Knowledge Lateef turned to Street Moon, his eyes questioning. She nodded to proceed.

The semblance of Iset addressed Lateef. "Bring her in."

No one willingly visited The Heap. It was a sticky soup of heavy air and mile high stockpiles of rubbish. The stench alone was enough to make anyone gag upon arrival. She bent over and took in shallow breaths.

"Almost there. Hold on." Lateef's words were muffled through his mesh mask.

Street held her abdomen and stumbled forward into a long, looming shadow. The priest led the way through the labyrinth of garbage. "Be vigilant. The Heap is home to Rats, killers, and spies. They won't harm me but you have no friends here; remember that." He patted the bulk of his sawed off as it dangled from his belt. She gathered herself, and immediately drew her bow. "You believe this is gonna work huh? Free you from your obsession."

She didn't answer, focusing instead on making her way through the ginormous maze.

"It's been years Street. Not months, *years*. Sly married Abeekay years ago."

She scoffed. "It's hard for me to love. And when I

do..." She lowered the bow and let go of a heavy sigh. "I stalk them Lateef. I watch them, follow them. I listen to their conversations. I listen to them...fucking. I want them dead."

He stopped in his tracks and offered a concerned glance. Street Moon bent beneath a winding bridge of rubber tires and red rust steel. A hive of buzzing insects with golden pincers and solid silver wings hovered in the hazy sunset.

"Her name was Igbo...brilliant, funny, fine. She had me from the moment I saw her. This was before I was a priest. I was young then...probably twenty-five or so. We were the same age. Igbo was a scalper. I didn't know at first. She kept it from me. But even if she'd told me I probably would have fallen for her anyway. She was just that good." His eyes glazed over as they made their way through the path of garbage and stink.

"The Watchers got her one day after she'd done a Scalp. I saw the whole thing accidentally," he sighed before continuing. "I had flowers...I think they were white lilies. Igbo loved lilies..." he paused a moment to think. "Oh and I had on a new suit that cost a month's worth of savings. I heard the yelling before I could knock on the door," he turned and held her stare. "There's a certain scream that comes from a person being taken by a Watcher. It'll make your stomach turn and your bowels weak. I watched them take her through the window," he paused. "Ever see a Watcher take someone?"

His voice was a whisper. Street Moon slowly shook her head and looked on with sad, serious eyes.

"It looked like they were snatching the soul right out of her." The priest motioned as if he were pulling an invisible string from the sky. "It looks like the skin is being sucked away. Like the spine's been replaced with a zipper and the flesh and blood are squeezed from the inside out," he paused as they approached a sideways leaning building covered in solar panels and trash. "It's the soul that makes you whole. It gives you form and shape...not these organs and bones." He pointed in the direction of his torso, arms, and legs. "After they snatched it, she was a puddle on the floor. The light had left her," he focused on the doorway in the distance. "She was cold...formless. I didn't eat for weeks."

"I'm sorry Lateef," she whispered.

"No need. Igbo was a revolutionary. She loved freedom and believed the people deserved that much."

Street Moon felt the hairs on her neck bristle. A second later they were surrounded. They stood back to back weapons drawn. Surrounding them was a gang of men and women dressed similarly in a hodgepodge of black mesh, bright orange cloth, and black leather. The circle around them parted and in floated a thickset woman with heavy thighs, elaborate neck and arm tattoos, and orange braids. The exposed skin that hadn't been tattooed was a deep golden brown with eyes to match. Street immediately took note of her shoes. *Kicks: one of the City's most powerful and unassuming weapons.*

Lateef lowered his sawed off and motioned for Street to do the same. She refused, choosing instead to keep the woman in her crosshairs. Knowledge addressed the newcomer.

"Iset. Thank you for having us."

"Teacher," she bowed. "Ain't aged a day since we last saw one another," her lips spread into an easy smile. He extended his arms as she floated into his embrace. Her expression hardened. "Street Moon." Iset circled while studying her closely. "Please stand down."

She answered with a scowl.

Nonplussed, Iset folded her arms across her ample chest. "You will only be asked once."

Street glanced at Lateef who gave her the go ahead and lowered her bow.

"Good. Take her down."

She felt the dart seer into the vein in her neck before she could react. Her vision split in two, then three, and more. She swayed and fell to the ground.

Street Moon awoke naked on a canopy bed of down feathers. She shifted as her eyes fluttered open. Everything in her sight line was a bluish hue. Then came the soft, otherworldly kisses. A pair of full lips and a warm tongue inched their way from her toes to shins, thighs, waist, and breasts. She inhaled as the familiar scent of persimmons tickled her nostrils. *Sly.* It had been so long since she'd held his deep brown eyes in her gaze and allowed her palms to cup his chin. He'd grown a goatee since she'd last seen him. It was different, yet perfect still.

"Street...I have to tell you..."

Uninterested in words, she put a finger to his lips. At this moment, she only cared about consuming every inch of him. It had been far too long. She threw her head back, receiving his tongue as it traveled toward her navel and beyond. Her breath hitched as they tumbled over the softness of the sheets, vying for dominance and pleasure. She gazed in his eyes, took his fingers in her mouth, and nibbled on his chest just as she'd done numerous times before. Their shared desire grew white hot and feral as he called her name, grabbed hold of her thighs and buttocks, and stroked her spine with an index finger. Her cuffs became slick from the sweat dripping from his abdomen. She moaned as he wailed. A tear slid down her cheek as she watched him shudder in her position from above.

"I love...I love you Street Moon," he stammered. His eyes rolled. With one hand she massaged a rock hard nipple on his chest as his teeth chattered. Lost in the rhythm of their desire, she used the other hand to grip his throat. Basking in her own pleasure, she watched his eyes bulge. The sound of her thighs and buttocks slapping against his torso was an aphrodisiac. She watched as he wheezed, struggling to pry her grip from his neck. Even the strength of Sly Sincere was no match for her recent upgrades. *Money well spent.* Her climax extended through several seconds. His body fell limp after a final, violent quake. Street Moon wiped away the tear on her cheek and stopped another from rolling down her chin. When she climbed down from her position, she leaned over his lifeless body and whispered in his ear. "That was the best death anyone could ask for."

"She can't hunt what she believes she's already killed. The implanted memory will take hold and make her think the murder was real. No one will be able to tell her otherwise. It's the only thing that will bring her peace." Iset and Knowledge Lateef stood at Street Moon's bedside in a sterile, makeshift lab.

Lateef stroked his chin. "And what's the next phase?"

Iset cracked her knuckles. "What's left of her Tell will be removed."

"Will there be pain?"

"No, but the dreams she has will be potent."

"Good. Who will be performing the procedure?"

"She's well studied and anxious to dive in. She's new to the profession."

The sound of a door opening on its hinges interrupted them. In walked a woman with dark brown skin and shoulder length white-blonde locs. She was tallish, solidly built. Lateef stared at the woman in shock.

Iset smirked. "Abeekay Sincere, I think you know Knowledge Lateef."

The City Mole

By
Alan Jones

The singing. I remember the singing most of all.

The first of the month was next week and once again all I would be able to say was, "I ain't got it." But I knew that my landlady couldn't wait for me to slip so she could put my black butt out on the street, and I for one, more than anyone I knew, surely didn't need to see any deputies at my door. I knew I shouldn't have messed with landlady, but it was late, I'd had a couple of brews and well, you know. Anyway, I found myself needing a payday, with a quickness. So, I decided to check out The City want-ads. Here's what I found.

"Wanted: Food tasters. 40 credits a week."

For some Cartel boss, most likely. Nah, that's a sucker bet for folks living on the street. I wasn't that desperate, not yet anyway.

"Wanted: Research subjects for an exciting new human enhancement drug. Must sign waiver. 200 credits."

Yeah, right. Like I need an extra eye or run the risk of some body part turning green and falling off. No thank you.

"Wanted: Mole Removal. 5000 credits."

Hmm, this ad has been running for weeks and each week they offer a little bit more. 5000 credits would cover my expenses for the rest of the year, plus some. I knew moles were crafty, but for 5000 credits, its days were numbered. I'm a strong dude. Back in my previous life I laid rail and asphalt. I know how to dig a hole and I always keep my hammer and pick axe nearby. What could go wrong?

So, I go to the address in the ad, and it's a freakin' sewage treatment facility. I walked up to the little trailer sized office and out stepped the short bald guy who runs the place and his secretary, a lovely young lady with flawless brown skin, wearing a clinging knit skirt. I have a real weakness for clinging skirts. She smiled at me and I smiled back. The boss man, who I noticed had his hand on his side-piece, gave me a look.

"Popeye, over here!" he shouted. "You're here for job in the ad, right?"

Having regained my focus I answered him, "Yes, I am. My name is John H."

"John H, what?" he asked.

"Just, John H," I replied.

"Okay, whatever. My name is, for the purposes of this here arrangement, Chuck. And this here is Carla."

I was happy that her name wasn't Sharon. I haven't had the best success with women named Sharon over the years. But a "Carla", I can certainly deal with a Carla.

Chuck, who reeked of Ooze, opened his pie hole again.

"Look, John, it's real simple. The City has a mole problem. The mole is in the sewers causing havoc. You climb down through that there manhole and bring me back one dead mole and I'll give you five grand. Carla will give you a disposable tracker to track the critter. It's really just a cheap preset spectrometer that glows brighter the more concentrated the mole pheromones become. Also, Carla will provide you with both a disposable jumpsuit and gas mask. You'll want to be done before the suit or gas mask turn totally black. Questions? No, then just follow Carla and she'll get you taken care of."

As Carla strolled towards the trailer and I followed, she spoke to me over her shoulder.

"You may have noticed, but clearly his Karma is soiled."

No, I was distracted and hadn't noticed, not that I was in tune with such things anyway. Carla continued.

"The Collectors will be here any day now. That's why he's a little trigger happy. You're pretty much his last hope to get paid before they arrive."

Puzzled, I said "I don't know much about them, but they don't take cash do they?"

Carla replied, "No, they don't take cash and even if they did, no one ever sees them until it's too late. Folks say that they're really renegade Watchers impatient for justice. But none of the living has ever seen them. Chuck is hoping that getting rid of this mole will win him some standing with the higher ups and somehow they'll protect him. But he just doesn't get it. By taking the contract from The City he just sped up his day of Collection. And they are just one of his enemies. He's in deep hock to The Cartel loan sharks, and their patience is running thin. Basically, he's a dead man walking, he just hasn't accepted it. So, I suggest that you whack this mole and get back up here with a quickness if you want to collect."

"So, he's really a bad dude, huh?"

"The worst," she said.

"So, why are you here?"

"He's a grade A sociopath, but he's my uncle and I'm the only family member that will have anything to do with him. So, yes, why am I here? Well, even a bad man needs someone to escort him to the gates of hell."

At this point you may be asking, "Doesn't John H realize this is a shady situation?" Well, yes he does and did. From the escalating reward offers in the paper, to the nervous fat man calling himself "Chuck" checking for Collectors around every corner, everything about this situation figuratively and literally stunk. And while I really did need the money, it was more a case of temporary insanity. The kind you get when a pretty woman asks you to follow her. I know as surely as the stars do shine, that these skirts will someday be the death of me.

Once I had my gear, Carla and the fat man led me to the entry point of the underbelly of the beast known as The City. I descended the metal stairs a hundred feet down to the main sewer line. Of course, the cheap bald guy gave me a very cheap flashlight, which I quickly tossed in favor of my own personal night vision goggles so seeing in nearly complete darkness was not a problem for me. The stench was so strong that even through the gas mask that I was taken aback by the odor. It was some unadulterated uncut funk down there. Once I touched bottom I stood in a sluggish sewage stream destined for the uptake pipe about seventy five yards downstream. And still, even at that distance, I heard some of the most disgusting sounds every experienced by mankind. So, I decided to try my luck upstream first. As I turned, I noticed immediately that my spectrometer began to glow ever so slightly. The mole's scent was riding downstream with the poop.

As I was strolling I noticed something shiny which had washed up on the side. It was a bracelet. I thought it might be gold or possibly platinum, but in the darkness it was hard to tell. I secured it in one of my outer pockets and kept moving.

I followed the sewer line about a hundred yards until it reached a fork. There I tried each option to see which would cause the spectrometer to glow the brightest. But when I stepped into the second tunnel my confirmation was more than visual. I could also hear a faint but consistent scratching sound. I knew right off that it wasn't the sound of machine against rock. In my past life I became very familiar with the sound motorized excavation equipment. No, this had the subtle tones of manual labor. Yet it was still odd. I continued forward, passing tributaries from office buildings and residential complexes, until through my goggles I saw movement. As I crept forward, I slowly removed my rail hammer from my back. Getting closer I realized that the movement was debris falling from rather large hole off to the side. It appeared as though someone was actively expanding one of the existing tributaries and pushing the residue out. But this was no hole for a mole, it was far too big. It had to be at least six to seven feet in diameter and the sound I was hearing was definitely coming from it. So, of course being the dumb fool that I was, I decided to climb up into the hole to take a look. The tunnel was sloped at about a forty degree angle, which would had made it a very difficult climb, had the sides been smooth. But the sides were very irregular and allowed me very good footing.

Amazingly, the hole was even darker than the sewer lines leading to it. So dark in fact that I could see very little. Then all of a sudden the scratching noise stopped. Instinctively, I stopped my ascent. Then, no more than a second or two later, seeing nothing but sensing movement, I came face to face with two beady eyes set back from a long snout. I let out a "What da...", but before I could finish my exclamation, the creature bum rushed me, pushing me rapidly back down the hole and out into the tributary. Standing quickly, I could see the deal, regardless of how unbelievable it might have been. This was indeed a mole, but as it stood I could see that it was about eight feet tall and at least five or six hundred pounds. Immediately, I pulled my rail hammer from my back and swung it into the gut of the beast.

The mole flinched just a bit and then struck me with one of its talon laced paws knocking me into the stone side wall. And just as I was regaining my feet I heard, "That was a mistake!" Stunned that the animal spoke I hesitated for just a second, which was just enough time for the beast to strike me again, knocking me out cold.

Sometime later I awoke and I found myself hanging upside down from the roof of the mole's den. I could see my tools over in the corner far out of reach. Dazed and groggy, I saw the mole with its back to me, sitting at a desk lit by a very dim light, going through some papers. I was in a bit of pain still, but I managed to speak.

"So, you talk?"

"Duh..."

"Okay, yeah, but there certainly has to be a story here."

I looked up; my feet and legs were wrapped in some sort of adhesive goo which literally had me stuck to the ceiling.

The mole spun around in its chair to face me, "Yes, I get that. I'm the product of one of experiments carried out by a few of The City scientists back in the day before everything went dark. Actually, I was born human. The plan was to equip humans with night vision through gene therapy. So, the night vision thing worked quite well, but I'm not quite human anymore either."

Then I dared to ask, "So, what was your name when you were human?"

"My name was and still is, Sharon."

"Damn, damn, damn..." I said silently to myself, but to her I said, "That's a pretty name."

She rolled the humongous chair she was sitting in towards me before speaking, "Aw, that's nice of you to say, but I'm still gonna eat your ass for dinner tomorrow. "

Choosing to ignore her comment for the moment, I continued on.

"So, what's up with all this ruckus you're kicking up down here? They're taking out ads up there looking for folks to take you out."

Sharon the mole turned her head slightly as she focused mostly on her papers again.

"Ruckus? Where you country fed? This ruckus I'm kicking up is me tunneling into the offices and residences of the powers that be in this hell hole. I know their secrets. I know why they won't come down here themselves. I know why the city went dark; I know how the new would-be rulers plan to relight The City in their own image. These new posers keep sending you suckers down here because they're are afraid that I'll rat them out before they can carry out their plans. But I could give a rat's butt about their plans."

"So, what is it that you want?"

Sharon answered, "I want to find out where the Contractor and his engineers have gone. Some of his engineers were the very ones who made me. Only they can make me human again. I found a roster with contact information for most of the former leaders and many of their homes and offices still exist. So, I dig into these dwellings looking for clues. Some of the basements of these structures have City related documents dating back hundreds of years."

I saw an opening so I went for it, "Wow! See, you and I are really the same."

"Really? How so, Jethro?"

"Well, my situation is also a product of the Contractor. See, I signed up to do construction work on this huge secret project. So, the day I'm suppose to start work, I show up and all they tell me and the others to do, is to shower and then to step into a capsule. There were rows and rows of them, so I picked one and stepped in. Well, when I woke up, which seemed like just the next moment for me, I found myself in the wastelands on the outskirts of The City. So, like you, I'm still trying to figure out what happened."

Okay, that last part was a lie. For a month or two, I did, but I didn't see the point in looking back. My daddy taught me that, but you know women, they always want closure, so I played along like I did too, so that maybe she'd feel some kind of bond with me.

"Poor baby, you woke up with all your parts? Look, I know your type and I know what you're trying to do!"

Slightly offended, I asked, "My type? What do you mean?"

"You're one of those love-them-and-leave-them kind of guys. I've had my fill of guys like you."

"Damn." I thought. It might be true, but she don't know that. I fixed my face and continued on.

"Sharon, I'm sorry. Maybe we got off on the wrong foot. I'm sorry that I swung my mallet at you."

I continued to talk, but she said nothing as she continued to pour through the latest batch of official looking documents she'd acquired. She was done with me. I finally got the message and turned my attention elsewhere. I curled my body up and pulled at the sticky stuff which held me, but to no avail. Then I remembered the bracelet I'd found earlier. I unclasped my pocket and quietly pulled it out. At first I thought that maybe I could find a sharp edge on it or somehow twist it into something I could use to free myself. But as I touched the bracelet with my then exposed hand (my gloves had been on when I first picked it up), I immediately noticed a change. It was a change in my vision. At first, I thought that maybe there was something wrong with my night vision goggles, but as I slid them away from my eyes, I saw that wasn't the case. While in contact with the bracelet could I not only see the room in low light, I could also see subtleties and previously unseen aspects of everything in the room. I could see through walls as easily as one could see a hill in the distance. I could also see that the goo wasn't contiguous, but was rather like plastic wrap that had been woven around legs and feet attaching them to the ceiling. And most importantly, I could see exactly where this wrapping ended. So, after sliding the bracelet onto my wrist, I slowly curled myself up again in the darkness and scraped my fingernails against the goo until I felt the outer layer loosen. I glanced back at Sharon the mole, and then proceeded to unwrap the layers of goo from around my legs and feet. As I finished my task, I flipped my body right side up then dropped to the floor. But just as I did, Sharon spun around in her chair. Knowing how fast she could move, I darted for my pick axe. I grabbed the handle just as Sharon was upon me, but the bracelet revealed to me a vulnerable spot right above her snout and my aim was true. I drove the sharp end of the axe into that weak spot as I sprung from the wall and leapt into her. I pulled axe out of her as I went one way and her body fell the other way.

As I stood there, I felt some kind of way. Yes, I was glad to be alive, extremely so, but I can honestly say that I felt bad for Sharon. Like so many others in The City, she had been subjected to a hell not of her own making, a hell which ended abruptly at the blade of a stranger. On the other hand, it had been a quick death, unlike the one her previous victims had suffered through. Then again, like me, they had all come to kill her. All this thinking made my head hurt, so I decided, as always, to keep it moving. No way was I gonna drag her body back through the sewers and up that raggedy set of stairs back to the treatment plant. So, I decided that I'd just cut off her paws as proof. And if I needed the whole body to claim my reward, I'd come back with a cart or something to roll her to an exit point.

After I found a large knapsack to carry her paws in, I realized that I had no clue where I was. The mole had dragged me some distance to her lair. And the spectrometer was of little use leading me back to exit point. But then as I stood there contemplating my next move, I heard it. I heard the singing. Somehow, I knew that I should follow the singing. A faint echo at first, the closer I got to its source, the clearer the singing became. I followed the melodious tones until I reached the stairwell I'd descended into this smelly pit. As I climbed, I thought I saw shadows above me, but I wasn't sure since the day had passed and it was now night. As I continued to ascend towards the angelic vocals, I looked up when I was about ten feet from the opening and saw a face glance down and then recede. Reaching the manhole, I tossed my bag out first and then maneuvered my large frame through the portal. Once through, I stood to see Carla smiling at me.

"That was you singing, wasn't it?"

"Yes, it was. I thought you might need some help finding your way back." Carla said still smiling.

"Did you do that for the other guys who took this job?"

"No."

"So, why for me? How did you know I was coming back?"

Giving a wink, Carla replied, "I have a sense for such things."

Just then the boss man, "Chuck" walked up. Seeing him, I emptied the knapsack revealing the massive mole claws.

The squat man seemed to be impressed and a bit relieved, "Great job, Brutus."

"It's John, John H." I corrected him.

"Yeah, whatever. Carla here will take you to get cleaned up. When you're done come see me in the trailer and I'll pay you your money."

I was a bit surprised that he didn't ask me more details about what I'd found. But I paid it no mind, as I followed Carla to the detox shed. Once in the shed, I stripped down to my skivvies and stepped into a tub as Carla brought me fresh towels. While I was sitting in the tub Carla knelt down behind me and began to assist me bathing. All this was brand new to me and caught me a little off guard. Sensing my reaction, she explained, "Relax. You were down there too long and the toxin soaked through your gear. So, we need to make sure that this solution is applied to your entire body, even those areas that you can't reach."

"Okay." I said. Then amazingly I thought for a moment before asking, "So, you guys don't want to know what I found out down there?"

"Nope." Then seeing that I wasn't satisfied with the sparseness of her reply, Carla sighed, laid down the wash rag and removed her gloves. Then after she dipped her hands into the water, she began to wash my back, neck and scalp with her bare hands. And as she touched me, felt her in my mind speaking to me clear as day.

"Do not say a word; there might be Watchers in here. Look John, I have this ability to read the mind of anyone I touch and I'm taking a huge chance revealing myself to you this way. But you need to know that this mole hunt was never about the damage being done to the waste system, it was about all the data that the mole was collecting. My uncle and I pretend like we don't know, so that when the powers that be start erasing their tracks they won't come looking for us. So, if you value your life and ours, you'll keep your mouth shut."

Mentally, I replied to her, "So, what you're telling me is that from this point forward, I'll need to live life on the low, right?"

"Yes, but as an unlicensed plumber, that's nothing new for you, is it? The pipefitters union is itching to bust a cap in your behind aren't they?"

"Yes, plumbing is not my first choice. Actually, I'm a rail man by profession, but that's a lost art here. But my daddy was a plumber, and he taught me how to lay pipe and that's what I do to make ends meet."

Carla removed her hands from my scalp for a moment, breaking our connection and giggled just a bit. Then placing her hands back into my lathered hair, she continued, "Well, I must commend you being able to survive off of the grid for the last three years like you have."

"What choice do I have? As an undocumented resident what else could I have done? I can't really stick my head up, much less get licensed. Should I go to this Lush place I hear folks talking about?

"No, and it's better that you don't know why."

I pondered for a moment as she scrubbed my back. "So, tell me, have you ever read your uncle's mind." I asked.

Carla answered, "No, I never have. He doesn't want me knowing about all the bad things he's done. But by reading the minds of those who know him, I think I have a pretty good picture of the life he's lived."

Finishing up, Carla was about to stand, when she noticed the bracelet on my left wrist. She reached over my shoulder to touch it. Instantly, her eyes rolled back in her head. Instinctually, I turned to her and pulled her face into my chest to hide her reaction from any prying eyes which might be in the room. Eventually, Carla's breathing slowed and I dared to pull back just enough to see her eyes. Reengaging me psychically, she said, "Surely, the City's secrets entombed below are of great value, but this is the real prize. The history of all existence is within that bracelet!"

"What do you mean?" I asked.

"What it reveals depends on who wears or touches it. For you it revealed what you needed, what you could handle. It allowed you to see through walls and through fibers. For me, an intuit and priestess, it revealed so much more!"

"Girl, you tripping. I'm going to throw that robe on and go get my money. Then, I'd like to take you to dinner." I told Carla.

Carla smiled as she handed me a towel. "I'll just clean up in here and meet you outside. We'll need to stop to get you something decent to wear in public first. By the way, while touching the bracelet I could see that we're alone in here."

Carla was the real deal. In the brief time that she touched me she could see everything about me, but I, perhaps without her fully knowing, saw who she truly was. As beautiful as she was on the outside, she was even more beautiful inside. In the three years since my awakening, I'd not met anyone like her. She had a kindness of an age long since passed. For the first time in my adult life I'd met someone I'd like to make my wife.

I stepped out of the shed and walked towards the boss man's trailer. Since he was expecting me, I didn't see the need to knock, so I turned the knob and opened the door. What I saw next is something that I will never forget. Seated and apparently frozen, at his desk was Chuck, but surrounding him I could see three figures. They appeared as flames to me standing about seven feet tall, with each one extending a flare which rested upon Chuck. I realized that these were the renegade Watchers known as the Collectors. I hesitated for a moment before I realized that I needed to play along if I wanted to live. So, I called out, "Chuck, are you alright?" I gathered my courage and walked closer to him so that I could wave my hand back and forth in front of his face, and I pretended to look for a reaction from him. I noticed a stuffed envelope on his desk and figured rightly that it must be my reward. So, I picked it up and stuck it into one of the front pockets of the robe I was wearing. I did all of this with no obvious regard for the flaming pillars in the room. They truly did not know that I could see them.

Having my money, I turned to exit the trailer, but before I could leave I heard one of the Collectors speaking in a frequency which no mortal could hear, "That's one of the workers that the Contractor hired but never activated."

Then I heard a second Collector say, "Most of them are hardworking and harmless."

The first Collector replied, "Yes, they are, but this one is an asshole. That's why he's on our list."

I nearly fell out on the spot, but I managed to reach for the door knob and turn it. Thankfully, I thought, none of them could see my face. As I pulled the door back I heard the third Collector say, "It's a shame what this man's enemies will do to that young lady. The City needs more like her, but we dare not interfere in Cartel business, at least not yet."

As I stepped through the doorway I realized what they were saying. In the yard between the shed and the trailer I saw these winged beasts holding Carla fast. They saw me coming out of his trailer and growled, "Tell the fat man, we're taking back our collateral. If he pays quickly, he can have her back alive, otherwise..." The two of them began to laugh, as they flapped their wings and began lifting Carla into the air. Oddly, Carla, who could be formable, was not fighting back, but instead she simply had the strangest look on her face. Then it struck me. That fat bastard had taken out a loan with the Cartel loan sharks using Carla as collateral.

I called out, "But Chuck, the fat man is dead." They didn't hear me, or at least they didn't bother to process what I was trying to say. These kinds seldom do. So, I ran toward them and leapt as they ascended with Carla. I grabbed for Carla's right foot, but came down with her shoe.

The two beasts continued to cackle as they flew away. One called out, "Just pay the money. It's not complicated." In that moment I would have given everything I had to purchase Carla's freedom. But I had no idea of how much they wanted or how to contact them. In time I would come to know all these things and much more. Thus did the pursuit of Carla's song revealed itself as the real journey of my life.

I learned two lessons that day. First, I realized that I'd gladly suffer any consequence, be it from the Cartel, Collectors, Watchers, or whomever, to get Carla back. But also on that day I learned the real truth about the City. It's not a place of refuge, but rather a place where dreams go to die. It's a graveyard of hope, filled with the walking dead, of which I was one.

Washed Pure, Washed Clean

By
Ray Dean

The mind numbing quiet of Ben Willard's rooms was broken by grumbling voices. Stretching the tired muscles of his back, Ben pushed back from his desk and stifled a yawn.

"Just come on in instead of arguing outside my door."

The door remained closed for a moment longer before the handle twisted open. Peering in from the hallway was one of his River Rats, her hair bound back from her face as he had requested. Her hesitation was worrisome; she was good at what she did, devoted and loyal, so her tight expression caused him no small amount of concern.

"Come, Aysi, don't hover."

She did what he asked and entered, but she pushed a younger boy ahead of her.

After her second prod at his shoulder he jumped ahead of her, turning away from her hand. "Leave me be, Aysi." He glared at her before lowering his eyes to the floor at the Ben's feet. "I didn't want to come, sir."

"Well," Ben leaned forward in his chair, hoping to get a good look at the child's face, "I know Aysi and if she brought you here then there is a reason for it."

"I told her we shouldn't bother you."

"Bother me?" He turned to Aysi, his patience running short. "Why don't you just tell me what this is about?"

She reached for the boy's arm, but he shrugged away, pulling his arm tight to his body with the opposite hand. With a huff she set her hand on his shoulder and wouldn't let him pull away, jerking his sleeve up toward his shoulder. "Noah's hurt."

Ben's mood turned in that moment. His frustration became concern. He moved closer, hunching down a bit to minimize his sheer size and put himself as near to eye-level with the boy as he could manage.

"Hold still." He could see by the stone-like set of the boy's jaw that he felt this was a thing to suffer through.

Hurt. Aysi said the boy had been hurt, but looking at the crusted wound on his bicep Ben wondered if he'd been poisoned. Reaching his hand out he touched the top of the wound and felt the scratch of ruined skin against the tip of his finger.

"Where did you get this, Noah?"

The boy hunched his shoulders up around his ears and glared sideways at Aysi. "UpRiver a bit. Someone left a bunch of containers near the River. I wanted to move them away."

The other child chimed in. "They were dripping something into the water. Noah moved them away to a disposal center. While he was carrying them he got some on his shirt."

Noah sighed loudly. "She took away my shirt, threw it into the bin!"

"It was burned through with the liquid from the drums... straight through to his skin! Of course I threw it away." Her anger rolled away like a tide. "Please don't be mad at me, Noah. I worry about you."

Noah blinked away his own sudden onslaught of tears and reached out to squeeze her hand. He barely met Ben's concerned gaze. "I'm so sorry, sir. I told Aysi I'd be fine. She didn't have to tell-"

"Aysi," Ben silenced the excuse and beckoned the girl forward with a crook of his finger; "I'll have you take a message for me."

She stepped forward, her chin tilting up a little bit as she moved in close enough to touch. His size was enough to frighten the littlest among them and his voice, the booming echo that sometimes rumbled around in his chest had startled some of the adults. Ignoring her fear, for she did an admirable job of the same, Ben scribbled a note on a sheet of paper. Folding it into a packet, he picked up a bit of wax from the same box and melted it over the blue flame of his lamp. The two children watched in curious wide-eyed expressions as he dabbed the wax on the paper and pressed the pad of his thumb in the middle. "Take this."

Aysi took the missive in her hands with a gentle touch; as though she worried she'd crease the document.

"Where?" She stepped closer when he beckoned her, leaning to hear the words he let fall from his lips.

"Take this to Ife."

He knew she heard him at the sharp intake of her breath and the sudden flutter of the makeshift envelope she held. "Yes, sir." She backed away from him slowly. Once clear of any obstacles she dashed for the door, leaving Noah standing in the center of the room by himself.

Ben noticed the waver in the boy's posture, the flinch of a muscle in his cheek as he struggled to stand straight and at attention.

"Come, Noah, tell me more about this place UpRiver."

It took little prompting for the boy to speak. Ben was his leader and he would obey for that reason alone, but it took a few minutes for him to relax and spread in longer stretches of words. Noah was eager to please, but while he insisted he suffered only from the wounds on his skin, his energy flagged quickly and he soon fell asleep on a pallet that Ben had made in the center of the room.

While the youngster slept, he pondered his next course of action. He'd changed their schedules the last few months, sending out pairs of the little ones during the odd hours, hoping to keep their larger, older, more intimidating Rats for peak hours where troublemakers were wont to stir, but Ben could see they would have to change their schedules... They had discovered a new threat and now if they wanted to protect The River and his children, he would need to adjust his methods and venture out of his self-imposed confinement and once again, wade into the River.

Word of Ife's impending arrival had spread quickly through the streets and curiosity drew nearly a score of Rats to the hall. They had all heard stories of her power, but few had seen the legendary Techsorcist with their own eyes.

The room hushed when the door swung inward, bringing the odd wind of the River with it. A chilling brush at such a late hour would normally send people scrambling for cover, searching out a source of heat to hover near. Instead, they stayed in their places, afraid to disturb the approaching tremble of footsteps moving across the plascrete. Even the littlest Rats kept mum without anyone needing to hush them or tell them to mind their manners. Most of them disappeared into the shadows finding safety in the silence of light.

Ben waited just inside the doorway, letting the neon lights spill in like overflow, sparkling of the layers of clothing he wore to stave off the cold. He waited in his own pensive silence with his eyes trained on the outside world for the first elusive glimpse of the Techsorcist.

She was a ripple of darkness beneath the shadows, a shimmer within the neon that sparked and sparkled as if life fairly breathed with magic. And there she was. Soft strides marking even intervals of the ground with no sound beyond the heavy beat of his blood pumping through his ears.

With a start he realized she was standing before him, waiting for a word of greeting.

He was a spokesman, a man of fine voice, and a leader of multitudes, yet in her petite presence he struggled for his thoughts and stumbled over his words. "We-welcome, Ife."

She smiled and nodded, hiding her eyes from him for a moment. But when she raised them again he felt a tremor of energy roll over him and her eyes, he was almost certain it had been a trick of the light, a reflection of something behind him that flickered like fire. "And I find you well, Ben Willard?"

The sound of his name, spoken from her lips, nearly drowned him in sensation. And he wondered if it was only his weakness that reacted in that manner or if she entranced everyone.

"So I am, Ife. It is not for me that I have asked you to come to The River."

Her laughter trembled through the room, leaving more than a handful of the assembly gazing at her in wonder. "Let me see to the boy and we will speak later."

Noah barely stirred earlier when Kato and Tau moved his pallet to the center of the room. Ben opened the panel in the roof that let in the most light and cleared a few of his books and tablets from the floor so that there would be enough room for Ife to work.

Ife whispered as she moved. Her hands lifted from her sides, one at a time, removing one sandal and then the other, giving them over into eager hands. It left her feet bare as she moved about the room, treading the same oblong circle of plascrete over and over.

The light danced over her features, glazing the planes of her face with silver and white. Ben lost count of the number of times she circled, but she traveled enough to paint the bottoms of her feet a shade darker with dust and had displaced the rest from the ground beneath her delicate strides.

She closed the distance to the side of the pallet a moment later, so quickly that none would be able to swear they had actually seen her do it. Lowering herself to her knees, she placed her hands on Noah's head, smoothing the furrows that pain wrought on his young skin. She traced the pattern again, returning to the highest point of his forehead each time. "The water... like life," she began, "begins..."

She trailed her fingertips down the sides of his face to his shoulders. "Those that protect the River take on such responsibility with such eager hearts and find much weight on their shoulders."

Ife drew her hands a scant few inches down his arms and stopped when he flinched away from her touch. She worked free the toggles of his shirt and accepted help from Ben to remove the garment from his body.

Since the boy had let him view the wounds on his body over an hour earlier, they had seeped again, drying against the fabric like glue. Together they were forced to pry the fabric clear of his body. The motion removed some of the injured skin from his body and tears leaked from the corners of his eyes.

"Sore," he complained as he opened his eyes to see his tormentors. "Stop."

"I am here to help," Ife's voice was gentle, but it was her eyes that mesmerized the boy. "Be calm, Child of the River".

On the other side of the pallet, Ben wondered if the child saw the same sparkle of magic in her eyes, like water shot through with electricity.

And so Noah calmed, his eyes watching her in fascination like the others that had come to witness the healer. He watched her and his body lost the tension that pulled at his shoulders. He sank deeper into the pallet and his hands were soft against the dark pile of cloth beneath him.

Reaching to her side, she lifted a canteen that had been shrouded within the soft folds of her clothes. Lifting it higher, she pulled the long strap free of her neck and held it out toward Ben.

"I would ask your help."

Lowering his larger frame down beside her, he ignored the pain in his knees from the hard plascrete ground and took the container she offered with a reverent nod. When she put the container in his hands he felt the heavy slosh of something liquid within, changing the weight and balance of the container, but he held it securely. "What do you need?"

She held her hands out to him, cupped together like a waiting vessel. "Pour The Water into my hands."

He heard the heavy import of the word in her tone. The Water. He knew then that the container held a measure of the River in its confines. The Techsorcists were known to use the waters of the River in their magic, but he had never seen such a feat. When he laid his hand on the cap and gave it a twist the room stilled again. All of the eager observers leaned closer to see what would happen next, but the absence of sound told Ben that they were all holding their breath.

And if he was honest about it, he did the same as he tipped the container a fraction of an inch at the time, unwilling to accidentally spill any of the precious Water.

Ife lifted her hands higher and there it was. A sudden spill of silver into her hands, the Water lapping at her skin with a gentle swish of motion. The silver seemed to glow blue like the fire he'd seen in her eyes and he stopped the flow when she nodded.

Turning, she held her hands close to her body, looked into the Water, and she spoke.

No. Ben fought to make sense of the actual sensations he was feeling. Ife didn't speak so much as she sang. Her voice stirring the Water with ripples of sound, stirring it into a froth of movement, ripples that curled against her skin like a living creature climbing up a wall toward freedom. And freedom... is what she gave it.

The water fell when she opened a crack in her cupped hands, pouring like a trail of silver down onto Noah's arm.

Ben feared for the boy as he saw the Water course over his wound, but there was no flinch of movement, no arch of pain in his small body. The river of silver fire that licked at his skin seemed to illuminate the sores, swell and shift around them like waves around rock piles, yet its touch seemed soothing.

He meant to hold his tongue. Meant to watch and keep quiet. So when his lips parted he was as shocked as the rest of their audience. "What is happening?"

Ife's voice washed over him, silencing his worries. "Let the Water do its work."

And work it did, for the water washed over his

wounds, breaking away parts of the ruined flesh and revealed soft new skin beneath. She offered her hands to Ben again and he carefully filled them with more of the Water.

Again, she poured it over his arm, washing more of his flesh free of ruin and pain. She let the power flow through her hands and over his wounds. The process continued over and over until the last few droplets of Water fell into her hands. They glimmered and seemed to disperse into a mist, rising from her hands to illuminate her face.

Ben could find no words capable of expressing the image that shimmered before him. Ife was light itself. And when she rose from her knees and stepped into the sandals that helpful hands had set before her, she held her hand out to Ben. She waited for him to move, but the larger man found himself stuck on his knees, his hands holding on to the container as if his skin was metal and magnetized.

"Ben?" He saw her lips move and watched the way they formed the sound. "Ben?" She leaned down and took the container from him, fitting the top to its base with practiced ease. When she slung the strap over her head and settled it on her shoulder, crossing her slight form to lay it against her hip, she offered Ben her hand.

Her eyes watched him carefully, sparkling with soft laughter. "Do you need my help as well?"

His only answer was to gain his feet and slowly let go of her hand, watching the gentle motion as it fell to her side. "Thank you."

Ife looked down at young Noah, resting peacefully on the pallet. "He needed my help, Ben." She raised her eyes to meet his. "He will not be the last. There are those who would ignore the sanctity of the River, Ben... you cannot allow this desecration to continue. If it does... if we cannot keep the Water clean it will be disastrous."

He felt her fears wash over him in a rolling wave of disquiet. Rocking back on his heels he reached out a hand to brace himself until he could stand on his own.

"We will do what is needed. I promise you, Ife. We will protect the River."

She smiled, turning her gentle gaze on the roomful of River Rats. "And I will protect you as well... all of you. The Water," she promised them, "will wash you clean."

When the room had emptied, the curious satisfied, and Noah removed to his own room with the others of his age, Ben sat alone staring at the pool of light centered on his floor. He saw the circle of steps, her soft tread across the ground. He heard the tender music of her voice in the safety of his ears. He felt the shudder of power rushing over him from an unseen source. He remembered Ife and her gentle promise, but he could not seem to recall exactly what was done or said during her visit.

Had he been mesmerized like the littlest ones who had walked away in a dazed shuffle? Or had he simply been washed clean of the memory by the power of her Techsorcist magic? The answer escaped him, rushed past his mind in the heavy current of his worries. He had made her a promise to continue their work and he would.

Drawing a tablet free of the stack on his desk, Ben began to devise a new schedule of patrols and new methods that would keep the River free of contamination. He had his warning in the pain and suffering of young Noah. He would not allow such danger to sweep through their ranks. He would protect them with his life.

Dreamer's Recall

By
Jeff Caroll

1

"Stay down!" yelled the voice from his wrist computer. "There are four gun droids at the end of the corridor. Once you get past them you have a clear path to the escape pods."

As sirens sounded and "security breech" echoed throughout the ship, energy gun blaster fire hit the inside of the doorway he crouched against. Two security droids shot at him from 20 feet down the corridor, pinning him down. On the other end of the corridor was the occupied control room; behind him was the storage room with no exit. The only way for him to get out was to get past the security droids then to the docking bay where a small shuttle waited.

There was nothing else he could do. It was a man up moment. If he got caught and taken into custody with the Skyport plans he had just stolen his reputation would be destroyed.

"Arm my gun with one coat electro plasma pellets," he said into his wrist com. Coating the pellets would allow the pellets to bounce once before they would stick on something.

He turned then put his back to the wall opposite from the security droids and in the line of fire. As he rotated he shot two pellets. The projectiles hit the wall behind the security droids, bounced back then stuck to each of the droids.

"Yes!" he said. He covered his face with his arm; seconds later the droids shook as voltage pulses fried their circuits.

As he ran past the disabled droids his wrist computer said, "I'm glad I don't have to go against you."

"You don't have to worry about that, you're my side kick," the man said as he climbed into the transport shuttle and opened the bay door leading to space.

Once in the comfort of the stars he loaded the coordinates to his command base. As he raised the throttle the sky went blank.

*   *   *

"Solar. Hey Solar, wake up! It's time to get up."

The voice was followed by the slap of syntho pillow which knocked him off the side of his sleep shelf. Solar fell onto his shaggy carpet and opened his eyes. To his surprise he was in his apartment, not in the drive seat of a transport shuttle. He recognized his Refresh room right away, the thin red line tracing the edges of his roof a dead giveaway. The smooth curved furniture and bright colors were much different than the silver metal of the sky ship corridor walls.

"Solar, you better wake your butt up and start your morning preparation."

Solar shook his head and took in two lungs full of air. He rolled over to see whose voice called to him.

"Essence," he said. "What are you doing here so early?" He pushed himself off the floor then walked to his com screen. "What is today's rush? I'm sure you have something to get excited about."

She ambled over to his food processor and typed in Monday first meal high energy. "Just another good day in the City. You got to be happy about that. Now come on get yourself together so we can get to work before everybody else."

"You're here so early you just need to move in with me. All I gotta do is move these chairs and put the hologame table in the first room. I could make this a couple's room." Solar smiled and picked up his breakfast juice as soon as his processor finished blending it.

"I'm comfortable on the 75th floor," Essence said. "You only live on the 324th so once I get to the central lifts it takes me 10 minutes to get here. This is good for us now. If I decide you're worthy of getting hitched to then I'll tell you how I want to rearrange this man crib. But don't worry because we might have to move. I like looking at the River. The water is calming and this apartment is in center building. I need a view. You could have com screens on every wall and I still would prefer a view of the River. Even if you had lava ceilings it would not be enough to get me to stay here."

"Ah, it's a lava inspired emotion ceiling and it is what's trending. Now, how did you get in here without me hearing you?" Solar took a big gulp of his drink. He quickly raised eyebrows and smirked.

Essence punched up a juice for herself and snatched it up as soon as the processor beeped. "I didn't have to sneak in, you were sleeping hard again. Please don't try to tell me you were having one of those things you call night visions."

"How did you know?" Solar took another big swallow of his juice. "I don't care if you believe me or not. This one was real groovy. I had a mean real hip, can you dig what I'm saying? You know I never took any Ooze or any drugs. So you gotta believe me when I tell you. It was like I was there in a small night sky transporter or something. I could talk into my hand."

Essence frowned. "Okay, see I just can't. You aren't making any sense. A dark sky flying ship? That makes no sense. Why would anyone want to fly into darkness? That just seems stupid. Maybe you used so much Ooze in your life when you were young that you can't remember you used to use it." Essence drank her juice. "Just finish your morning prep and I'll wait for you in your other room."

"Essence, why you gotta treat me like a square? You know I'm as cool as they come. So, don't throw me into some crazy box just because I have night visions."

"Just go do your prep," Essence said.

2

The central cafeteria of the office 47 building was packed with day shift lunch and Solar was still thinking about his night vision. He felt the confidence of the guy he was in the dream flowing through him. Walking with his meal tray back to his table his body had swag to it. Many of the female workers took notice; Solar took notice of them as well. As he sat down at his table to wait for Essence he picked up on a conversation between to two girls sitting nearby. The girls spoke low as if they didn't want others to hear them.

"Yes, they called them dreams and everyone had them," one of the girls said softly.

"I can't believe you went to Dreamers Recall. That's so unlike you. You're so reserved. Those sleep stories must have been killing you. I'm glad it helped you," said the other girl.

"Well don't tell anybody because I don't want people to think I'm different. They say dreams aren't bad but why don't you ever hear about people having them? I don't know, I just think it's strange. I'm only going to these meetings because I think they will help me get rid of them."

The other girl looked over at Solar and smiled and he smiled back. She turned back to her friend and said "Well I think it's funny how somebody who doesn't like animals has dreams of being an animal doctor."

Solar replayed the conversation over and over in his head the rest of the day without telling anyone, not even Essence. That evening the two of them had drinks at The Lounge, a small bar near the education center of the City. Inside was long bar and no stools just chase lounge chairs and cushion love seats spread about, a pleasant contrast to the small cubicles they sat in all day at work.

They shared the night dancing and enjoying the City's night people. Afterwards they walked along the River, gazing into its flowing blueness. The neon lights and florescent billboards made a dazzling spectacle as they bounced off the water. Cars moved in programmed precision down the streets and crowds of people filled the walkways along the sides. The hum of hover bikes and soft vibration of shuttle buses provided a rhythmical soundtrack.

"Isn't this beautiful?" Essence said. "It's like we live hologram. All of these lights and people around us. How could you imagine living anywhere else? Look at the dark sky with the trail of moving stars. Looks like it's just a big reflection of the City down here. I mean if the big stars were the buildings then the smaller stars that move back and forth are the transportation. Even up there loves the City. You know what they say; imitation is the sincerest form of flattery."

Solar listen to Essence make her case for him to stop having what he discovered were dreams but he couldn't shake the effect they had on him. Knowing he wasn't the only person having them was mind blowing. To also know that there was an entire group of dreamers was too much for him to handle.

"What if there was life out there? Another place like here?" Solar felt the stupidity of his comments as soon as the words left his mouth and he laughed as soon as finished saying them. "Wow, that is crazy. What am I thinking? I know the sky is a ceiling. Hell I have a ceiling in my apartment. I'd make more sense talking about talking building that can fix itself."

"Well there are those people who do believe that the sidewalks fix themselves," Essence laughed along with Solar. "And if you started talking like that I'd have to say goodbye."

"Trust me I'd take myself to the Watchers on my own." Solar smiled and gave Essence a hug. "I'm glad you can laugh with me about this. I was feeling real crazy today, like I was all alone. Then I heard some girls talking at work today."

Solar felt a flash of anxiety wondering if he should

destroy the moment by telling her more stories about his night visons. He quickly played out the scenarios in his head. If he told her she might start counseling him again and if he backed up and waited for another opportunity he would continue with the progress of the evening's romance. So, the choice was simple.

"Oh yeah," Essence said with a curious tone. "What were they talking about?"

"Um, well it seemed that one girl was coming to the other girl with something she couldn't tell anybody else and the other girl listened to her. After the girl told her what was troubling her she thanked her friend for letting her share her feelings. And you listening to me talk about my night visions was really nice. That's why I love you." Solar push the braids from Essence's face and gave her a big wet kiss.

"Let's go back to your place so I can enjoy looking at that lava ceiling while you make me see colors," Essence grabbed Solar's hand and pulled him across the middle of the street. She waved a cab and led him into the back seat. They made out all the way to Solar's front door.

Later that night while lying in his bed Solar's mind drifted again. This time he was climbing into a shipping container. A man in a similar uniform gave him a shot in his arm.

"This will lower your heartbeat so you will pass the scan as the container is loaded into the ship."

The man looked at his wrist com and looked back at Solar. "It should last about three hours. Good luck and bring back those plans. This is your last mission before a three month break to see your family."

"Family?" The thought woke Solar up. He sat up in the bed and looked around dazed, half expecting to see the inside of a ship rather than the ambiance of his ceiling screen.

3

Solar's quick movements startled Essence and soon after his jolt from sleep she sat up. "What's happened?"

She wiped sweat from his forehead. "Why are you breathing so hard? Did you have another vison?"

"No," Solar mumbled. "I mean yeah. Sort of I guess."

"Well that's it! I'm taking you for a check-up. This ain't right."

"Remember those girls I told you about?"

"Yeah what do they have to do with your visions?" Essence batted her eyes. "Were they in your vision also?"

"No, nothing like that," Solar caressed the side of Essence's cheek. "You're the only girl for me." He smiled and gave her a kiss.

"Okay, you had me scared," Essence said and leaned back to listen.

"Well, I told you what happened but I didn't tell you what they were talking about. The problem the girl was having was..." Solar felt the comfortable enough bring up the dreaded subject again and paused a little before he continued.

"Was what, man? Come on, I hope it is juicy."

"She was having night visions like me." Solar released a big exhale.

"Here you go again," Essence said. "I'm going to pray to the Contractor for you. Maybe he can fix you like he fixes the buildings around here."

"Essence, please. I thought I could trust you," Solar wiped his face and cleaned his eyes. "She said she went to a group where they help people. She said they are called dreams and the name of the group Dreamers ReCall."

"Well that's all very good for her but I think it's a waste of time. What do we need dreams for?"

"Come on really. You can't be that closed minded."

Essence got out of the bed and marched over to his holoscreen. She turned it on and pointed to the images of the

City. "See this is the real world. See the beautiful buildings. Look at the shuttle tubes. They can take you all around the City without going outside. If you want to fly around take the Metro Shuttles but the sky is flat. There's nothing up there."

"Well, I am not causing myself to dream. And I don't even believe what I'm seeing. You act like I want to have dreams." Solar yelled. He felt himself overheating and something inside him calmed him down. He walked over and looked Essence in the eyes. "I don't like having these dreams. Just be patient with me."

Essence smiled and gave Solar a tight hug as tears rolled down both her and Solar eyes.

"Whatever you're going through I'll be there to support you."

Later that night Solar found himself alone while Essence visited a cyber spa. Everyone had their addictions and good rub down as only a cyborg could provide was hers.

Solar hailed a City cab and jumped in. The driver, a young hippy chap with multicolor hair twists, face tattoo and a nose ring turned and looked over his shoulder toward Solar.

"Welcome to Kofe's Cab, where will I be taking you this fine evening?

"I'd like to go to the Westside," Solar said.

"Wait did you say the Westside, really? Would this be your first time?"

"I don't see why that would be any of your concern. Can't a guy travel to the Westside of the City if he likes?" Solar said.

The driver lowered the forward throttle of the cab then eased into traffic.

"Look buddy I not busting your balls or nothing but you hardly look like a Westsider," said the cabby. "I'll take you anywhere you pay the fare but I'm just saying."

Solar realized what he was wearing. All his clothes matched and his hair was evenly trimmed. The driver was correct; he wasn't prepared for his journey.

The cab cruised down the illuminated streets of the main district of the City, twisting and turning and passing under places Solar hadn't seen in a while.

"Thanks," Solar said as he watched the lights come to an end as the cab pulled down a dark street.

"We're here," the driver announced. "Anywhere in specific you want to be dropped off?"

"This is fine. Thanks," Solar answered quickly. Solar looked at the meter as it flashed the final fare. He handed the credits to the cabby, added a little extra for a tip. The cab driver counted the credits and noticed the tip. He slid the door back open and lend over the passenger's seat.

"Look buddy be careful. Thanks for taking a human driven car service. So many people taking these robot cabs, you dig? Take my ID number and call me when you want to come back. Remember my name; Kofe. This is the best cab in the City."

Solar had all night to hang out but he remembered the girl mention the Dreamers meeting only lasted a few hours. He had no idea what a Dreamers ReCall meeting place would look like plus this was his first time coming to the Westside. He had only seen images of it on the news reports. It was just as it looked. Dark and dirty. There were no lights, no big store signs flashing, only ragged streets and graffiti covered walls. He saw only a few people walking down the streets. The buildings looked old and run down.

He had no time to be a tourist so he kept a brisk walking pace. The people he passed were vastly different from the central city folk. They were mostly human; most sported wild haircuts with tattoos and piercings everywhere on their visible bodies. They clustered together on the corners of the streets and in the doorways of buildings. Solar hurried by, avoiding eye contact. He noticed an older lady pulling a food cart ambling toward him who was also averting her eyes. Despite their efforts their eyes met; he saw the fear in her brief stare. Solar remembered news report of all the rapes and murders that took place in the Westside. He recalled the names of the gangs; the Lords, the Cartel and the Soors. There was one more He struggled to remember. Then it came to him, York. That was the fourth gang. He wondered whose turf he was on. He realized he really hadn't thought his trip through. He figured he would walk two more blocks and if he didn't see another marker he would turn around.

Just as he started to turn around a well-dressed Helium Breather walked past him. The Breather towered over him and was even dressed. He stood out like a sore thumb but he walked like he knew where he was going. Solar figured with all of the crime and unsavory people the last non-human he would see would be a Helium Breather. Solar decided to follow the gentleman.

The Helium Breather turned down a street two blocks from where Solar began following him. Scribbled on the wall were the words, Dreamers come here'. He saw the man walk through the door of a rundown building. As Solar approached the building he saw the words 'Welcome to Dreamers ReCall' written over the door.

Solar watched from far enough back not to be seen but close enough to make out what was happening. When the door opened bright light shined out casting a shadow of the man on the sidewalk.

He had arrived. Now, he would find the answers to his confusion. The Dreamer's ReCall people would help him. Or would they? Could it be true or was this just a hoax or a scam? He had heard of those. How people talked about traveling through the River to some sort of place they called The Lush. It was stupid to believe in something like that. His dreams were real and that's all he knew. So, he had to finish his journey.

A man dressed in a loose fitted white gown opened the door then held it open as the man Solar was following walked inside. Solar took a deep breath and decided to be as daring as the man he dreamt about in the Sky ship. As he walked toward the building he began to have doubts. What was the worst that could happen? Would they laugh at him? Would his dream not stack up to the others in the meeting? He had to find out.

So with a little hesitation Solar approached the door. The man saw him and held the door open for him.

"Welcome," he said in a deep, comforting tone.

A woman met him in the hallway then led him into a large bare room with pockmarked plastcrete. There were about 25 people sitting in a circle. He only saw a couple of helium breathers; everyone else was human. Some of the human were dressed similar to him, other garbed in more casual clothes. One person had a face tattoo and looked like a member of a Westside gang.

As soon as Solar and the gentleman before him sat down the man who had held the door entered the room then stood before them. The woman who escorted him to the meeting circle walked over to the man then stood beside him.

"I would like to call this Dreamer's ReCall meeting to order," said a black man with a trimmed gray beard. He stood up from a seat in the circle of people. "Peace, Dreamers."

A few people in the group responded "Peace."

The man continued. "I'd like to welcome all of our returning participants. If you haven't shared your dream I hope you'll bless us with your story tonight. And for those good people who have lucked up on our lovely support group, please don't feel pressure to share tonight. We know you still can't believe this is real. Hell, many of you still don't even understand what you are having. So sit back and enjoy. Tonight you will feel more normal than you have ever felt in your life. This is a 100% Watcher free environment."

Everyone in the room laughed, including Solar. The bearded man grinned.

"Well we can't guarantee that but we do say what's said in DR or Dreamer's ReCall stays in DR," he said. "Now, let's get to sharing those dreams. Who's up first?"

Before the host could get back to his chair two people stood up. One was a white man and the other the girl Solar had seen in his cafeteria who indirectly told him about the meeting. He was hoping she told her story.

"Well, hello everybody," said the girl from Solar's office building. "Oh, I'm sorry. Peace Dreamers."

The group responded, including Solar.

"Peace Dreamer."

"I need to let you all know I'm a little nervous," the woman said. " My name is Kelendra and I work in Office Building 47 where I sit in a little cubical for eight hours. My job is boring but my dreams are much different. For the past few months I have been dreaming I was some sort of animal doctor. However, the animals I worked on were not any animals I've ever seen. The funny thing is if you know me I hate animals. My dreams are very fun. They are so much fun I feel like they are real and that I do love animals. Now, if that 's not strange enough the place where I work on the animals has windows which are clear but there's nothing to see. It's just black. A few white dots but all black. I wonder if that is how the inside of my brain looks. Well that's it. I'm an animal doctor dreamer. Thank you for listening."

The gray bearded man stood up as soon as Kelendra sat down. "That was beautiful sister. Now as we do with all who share their stories we invite you to meet with us. We don't have much but we do like to give those dreamers generous enough to share their stories with us a little something. So, my sister dreamer Kelendra, please follow the sister over there." The man extended his arm out and pointed to the girl who had led Solar into the room.

Solar followed Kelendra with his eyes hoping she would recognize him but she never made eye contact as she walked through the same door Solar had entered. The group applauded as she walked out of the circle.

The next person sharing a dream began talking

immediately after Kelendra walked out of the group. Solar listened to his dream and few more dream stories afterwards. Just as with Kelendra each dream teller was escorted out the door. The meeting ended with the same man who welcomed them to the meeting thanking them for coming and invited them back to share their stories.

When Solar got back to his apartment he was eager to sleep and start dreaming. He didn't even wait for Essence to come home. Not long after he closed his eyes he was back in his uniform.

This time Solar stood beside a box in some sort of loading bay. There were all sorts of cargo lifts and boxes in the room. Another man dressed in the same uniform was talking to him.

"Okay you got everything?" the man spoke with authority and confidence. "Okay Faazon, this is probably going to be your easiest assignment. You're lucky you have leave coming up. Three hours into your flight the crew will be in cryosleep and the robots deactivated. First thing you need to do when you wake up is disable the door to the sleep cabin. Then you must find an open port. Plug in and download the plans. Once you download the plans the alarm will sound. If you have disabled the door the way you did in the test run it will buy you enough time to get back to this bay and into one of the transport pods."

"What about the robots?" Solar asked.

"You have electro plasma rounds in your gun. They have the regular delays so you can time their release. You could bounce these bullets off a wall and still have them stick to a robot. I also gave you a few incendiary rounds just in case they piss you off. Once you are in the transport turn off the tracking and activate you comm-link." The man pointed to what Solar had thought was a wrist computer. "It should take us about an hour to pick you up."

The man pulled out a long tube then looked over his shoulder. Solar held out his arm and the man pressed the tube to Solar's wrist. Solar felt a sting and the tube hummed for a few seconds. The man pulled the tube away.

"Okay, you're good. Now hurry up and climb in so I can secure the box and make it look like produce. You should already feel light headed. In a moment your vitals will be undetectable and you'll scan as a big piece of meat."

Solar felt the humming crawl up his arm then all around his body. His vision blurred: He took a deep breath to gain a little more composer. He climbed into the box then sat against the side. The man slid the lid over the top.

After the lid closed Solar could barely open his eyes. He could still hear but even his hearing was muffled.

"Hey, I'm scanning you and I'm getting nothing," the man voice echoed from outside of the box. "You're dead buddy. Have fun."

The next morning Solar was bursting with excitement as he awoke before Essence. When she opened her eyes, he had her Breakfast drink waiting for her.

"Good morning," Solar grinned from eye to eye as he stood over Essence. "Today is a glorious day."

Essence took a deep breath as she sat up and took the glass from Solar. "Wow, this is a surprise."

"Well, I just found out I'm normal. Can you dig it? Last night while you were getting your rejuvenation I went to one of those Dreamer's ReCall meeting. It was amazing."

"You did, did you?" Essence sat up on the edge of the bed.

"Totally did. It was way out on the Westside but the people there were from all over."

"Did you see the girl from work?"

Solar waved his arms and moved as he spoke. "Sure did and she told her dream. She dreamt she was an animal doctor in a room that looked down on the City. Another guy told a dream where he was running on the sky ceiling. It was funny but I understood his dream. In fact I understood everyone's dream stories. The coordinator said that only less than one percent of the twenty million people who live in the City are able to have dreams. But even with all that I didn't tell my dream."

"You punked out," Essence laughed. "You don't have to explain. I'm just impressed you went all the way over to the Westside by yourself."

"I wanted to listen to see how it was before I shared my dream. I'll share mine next time."

"I'm so happy for you. I can't lie I was a little scared. It seemed like it could have been some gathering of weirdoes or a recruitment meeting for the River Rats. Man, I'm not spending my life with some River worshiper. I was thinking I was going to have to take you to a Street Priest and get you a spiritual cleansing." Essence finished her juice.

"I want to go back. You should come with. You know even though you don't have dreams it's still fun listening to all of the different dreams."

Essence paused for a moment to think about her week. "Well, I have a busy week. I got school every night. Plus tonight I will be in a group lab. I won't see you until the morning. I can go this weekend."

"Cool beans, you'll come with me Friday night. I can't wait to tell my dream."

As soon as it was lunch hour Solar made a mad dash to the Cafeteria. He looked for his new friend, Kelendra. He walked each of the four food stations but she was no where to be found. He took a plate of food and Essence found him on line.

"Wow, you got here early," Essence said.

"I was looking for the girl."

Solar started to woof down his food as he began to get inpatient. He wanted to introduce himself and thank Kelendra. Even though she didn't intentionally tell him about Dreamer's ReCall it was because of her he learned of the wonderful place. She opened him up to a new world so the least he could do was buy her lunch or maybe a week of lunches.

"You still thinking about your dreams?" Essence asked.

"Yeah, but don't say it so loud." Solar spoke in a low voice and didn't look at Essence. He continued to search the room for Kelendra.

His prayers were answered. He saw the girl who Kelendra spoke to the previous day stepping off the food line.

"Excuse me Essence, that's her friend." Solar jumped up then walked over to Kelendra's friend. He didn't even wait for Essence to say okay before he walked off.

"Hello," Solar said quickly, startling the girl. Solar immediately read her surprise and readjusted his approach. "Pardon me. You don't know me. I heard you and your friend Kelendra talking yesterday about a place called Dreamer's ReCall."

As soon as the words Dreamer's ReCall came out of his mouth the girl's facial expression changed. She went from listening to pushing passed him.

"I know we can't talk about so loud but I went to the meeting last night."

The girl stopped and turned back.

"Yes, and I heard Kelendra tell her dream. I wanted to thank her."

The girl put her food tray down and stepped close to Solar. "Well good for you but I haven't heard from her. She said she was going to call me after she got back but I haven't heard from her. She probably met a man. She ain't even at work today. So you may see her before I do."

Solar stood dumbfounded.

"Okay. If you see her my name is Solar and I work in the claims department."

That night after work while Essence was away at a dance class Solar got the irresistible urge to go to Dreamer's

ReCall. His dream finally made sense and he wanted to tell it. He remembered what he told Essence. She wanted him to wait until the weekend to go back the Dreamers ReCall but he figured she wouldn't know if he went. Maybe he would just listen and wait until the weekend to tell his dream.

The thoughts were overwhelming and the next minute he was in the back of Kofe's cab on his way to the Westside.

The meeting had already started by the time Solar arrived. The gray haired man was still welcoming people. This meeting had more people. There had to be at least fifty people and more of every species. This was an audience to tell a dream to. The room had a feeling of electricity to it. Solar felt like he belonged, surrounded his dreamer brothers and sisters.

He looked for Kelendra but she was nowhere to be found. There wasn't even anyone in the crowd with a face close to hers. Maybe she was absent. Maybe she had so much fun telling her story she wanted to skip a meeting. Who knew?

Solar's wandering speculation was cut short by the end of the gray haired man's address.

"That said do we have anyone who has a dream to tell?"

Solar could not help himself as his hand rose without him thinking about it. He was ready whether he knew it before he got there or when he woke up that morning. Telling his dream was his destiny and it was something which could not wait for Essence. The weekend was too far away.

"Okay I got one fella ready to tell his dream and boy he's got an amazing smile," said the gray haired man. "So, what's your name young dreamer?"

"My name is Solar."

4

Solar began his dream story with excitement. Everyone listened and clung to everyone he said. It was just like he'd imagined. He was a dreamer.

"My dreams came to me in a mixed up order," Solar began describing his dream. "Every night when I would fall asleep I would dream I was fighting robots on some sort of sky ship. Over time my dreams started to connect and I learned I was on a secret mission to steal a set of plans for a great weapon in the sky."

Solar took in the eyes and ears from the crowd as he spoke. They were his family. They respected him. He had to please them. He couldn't tell a boring story to his new friends.

"In my dreams I was a spy and fought robots. Can you dig it? I had strength and confidence. How cool was that?" Solar paused and the crowd responded with a loud applauds. He still did not see Kelendra but he continued.

"After I put my dreams together I had accomplished my mission and had fun doing it. My name was Faazon and I had a family. I am nothing like Faazon but it was fun being him. It was real easy. I know it sounds stupid but after I learned to embrace my dreams I have tried to be more like the character in my dreams. When I first heard about Dreamers ReCall I was scared to come but I just imagined I was secret agent Faazon and I mustered up the courage to come all the way out here to the Westside."

As Solar brought his story to an end the man with the gray hair stood up and spoke.

"Good story my young brother and by all means we are all family. Dreamers, give it up for Solar for his excellent dream story." The man with the gray beard tdirected Solar to the lady standing by the door the same way he had directed Kelendra.

Solar enjoyed his applause as he turned and waved

to the audience before started walking out of the dreamer's circle. He looked toward the lady, excited about what would be waiting for him. The celebration for first time dream tellers had to be something spectacular. Kelendra had to still be partying.

The gray haired man lowered arms signaling the audience to lower their voices and get ready for the next dreamer.

"We celebrate each and every one of our dreamers in our private VIP room. Hopefully, every one of you here will share your dreams with us."

The next dreamer was just introducing herself as Solar walked out of the room.

*   *   *

Essence awoke still tired from working so late at lab with her team. She always believed that humans couldn't slack off too much or a cyborg would replace you. So she got used to going to work tired. She dragged herself up to the 324th floor to the front door of Solar's apartment. She buzzed his door alert; she was too tired to jimmy his lock and break in. She laid up against to wall for a moment to rest and that short rest turned into ten minutes. Something was odd; the blast of confusion gave her the energy to break into Solar's apartment.

Essence looked all around Solar's apartment but he was gone. In fact the apartment looked just how she left it when they went to work the day before. She couldn't believe Solar had left for work without her. It was odd but maybe he had a dream and wanted to run into the girl he met before work. She couldn't imagine any other logical explanation.

When Essence arrived at work she called Solar's work phone. There was no answer. She called his department head and the lady said she had not seen Solar. Essence searched at lunch in the cafeteria; no Solar. She spent the rest of her day looking for him. She missed her lab meeting and explained things to her partners. She filed a missing person's report with the City police.

Two weeks later while Essence was posting up missing person posters in the City's south side miles from where she and Solar traveled someone recognized Solar.

"Excuse me miss," said a Fudokiht man with a high pitched voice. "I just saw that guy."

Essence dropped her stack of posters at the man's words. It didn't matter they came from a Fudokiht whom she didn't like too much. They were a hairless apelike species who thought they were better than humans. It was hard for her to let one of them help her but this was her first lead and finding Solar was too important.

"Really. Are you sure it was him?"

"Well, I have a knack for human faces, as disturbing as they are, and I know that smile anywhere," the apelike man boasted. "I just saw him ordering a super combo at that fast food spot on 63rd street." The Fudokiht man pointed down the street. "If you hurry up he might still be there."

Essence wanted to stay there and give the Fudokiht a piece of her mind but she was more interested in seeing if he was telling the truth. She was also confused as to why Solar would be eating at a fast food station.

Since Essence was on 60th street she only had a few streets away. She quickly dodged through people on the street as she made her way to the fast food place where Solar was just seen.

It was a Quick Burger and it was packed. As soon as she opened the door she had half the faces in the fast food joint scanned. Solar sat near the window in the back of store. Essence couldn't believe it; the ape man was right. Solar didn't look injured at all. He had a slightly different haircut and different clothes but it was him. She was sure of that much.

"Oh my God Solar it's so good to see you!" Essence

said as she ran to him. "Where have you been? And how come you didn't call me? I have been looking for you and putting up posters for two weeks."

Solar looked into Essence's eyes. "Who are you?" he said. "I think you are mistaken."

"Mistaken?" Essence laughed. "What? Solar why are you buggin?"

A woman put her hand on Essence's shoulder and stepped in between Solar and Essence. She looked at Essence and sat on Solar's lap.

"What seems to be the problem Alexis?" the woman asked Solar.

Essence mouth fell open as her once boyfriend dismissed her in a way she had never imagined. There was no way Solar could have been living a double life. She was with him every day for three years.

"I have no idea," the man who looked like Solar said. "Miss my name is Alexis Adobe and this is my wife Solange. Perhaps you are confusing me with your friend."

Essence was now really confused. "I'm sorry I must be confused. I've just been looking for my boyfriend and I...I," she struggled to say the word. "I thought you were my boyfriend."

The couple gathered their things and walked out of the restaurant. Essence buried her head in her palms and cried.

The Verdict

By
Balogun Ojetade

Judge Ngozi Edochie's disapproval was etched upon her face.

Bola looked from the judge's scowling visage – rendered twice its actual size by the M-Screen mounted on the wall before her – to defense attorney Akindele Ogunseye, who gazed up at the Judge with a boyish grin that nearly stretched to his ears. It was a look that made Bola want to slap him. And if he wasn't the City's most accomplished defense attorney and darling of the three most active – and powerful – non-mundane cultures in the City, she probably *would* have forcefully removed the taste from his mouth long ago.

She understood how he endeared himself to the Fudokiht – he had gotten the docile Sweepers higher pay and better treatment along with the other citizens charged with keeping the City clean; and she could possibly see how the business-minded Apunu, with their monopoly on Ooze, would even find a shark like Akin useful, but love from the Helium Breathers? Now that was a conundrum if there ever was one. Those brutes only respected Warriors – skilled thugs like them – and Bola doubted Akin had ever even broken a fingernail, let alone pick up a weapon.

"And Mr. Ogunseye, you tell your client that from now on, he is to attend every session of his trial without fail, or his bail will be revoked!" The Judge barked.

"Of course, Your Honor," Akin replied.

"We're done for the day," Judge Edochie declared, slamming her gavel down upon her desk with a bang that made Bola flinch.

Bola, who had arrived a little late to the proceedings

– too much Ooze the night before a case was not the wisest thing she had ever done, but it *did* relieve the stress of the case – was pleased that the Judge had decided not to reprimand her. Not willing to tempt fate by lingering any longer than necessary, she quickly packed away her notes and darted toward the exit.

"Prosecutor Bayo," Akin called behind her when she was in the hall.

Bola turned to face him. Her face was a mask of stone. "Defense Attorney Ogunseye."

She nodded, whirled on her heels and resumed her stride.

"So," Akin began, falling into step beside her. "I thought it might be nice if we went out for drinks sometime, to celebrate my inevitable victory."

"You're going to lose this one, Akin; you *do* know that, right?" Bola replied.

"Yup," Akin said. "Vobua's as guilty as sin and you've got the evidence to prove it. That deadly Fudokiht, who killed his poor, bullying, tyrannical, cyber-modded bastard of a boss, is going to jail – where a respectful team of surgeons will dissect his brain and tear out his Tell for recycling; then he'll be incinerated, of course, denying his family their traditional burial rites. That's reason enough to celebrate, isn't it, prosecutor?"

"Vobua ripped off that man's arms and beat him to death with them," Bola replied. "I know the Fudokiht *look* innocent with those big, cat-like eyes and they *act* like loveable morons, but they are really quite cunning; quite intelligent. Not to mention they possess the size and strength of a gorilla."

"Only in the face of danger," Akin said.

"Or *perceived* danger," Bola replied. "Your client saw danger where there was none and tore a man to shreds because of it. He has to pay for that."

"You don't really believe that, do you?"

"It doesn't matter what *I* believe," Bola said with a shrug. "Only what the judge and jury belive."

Akin laughed. "Why so cold, Bola?" You're not still mad about the transcripts, are you?"

Bola glared at him. "The evidence I presented was sound…and more than enough to put Vobua away. It shouldn't have been excluded, but once again, you worked your damn magic on the judge. I'm starting to believe you're some type of Psion with mind control powers!"

Akin laughed again. "Of course the evidence was sound – Vobua did move the body a few feet, like he was going to try to cover up his crime, but changed his mind for some reason – but you found and introduced it *way* too late; too late to present in this trial. Judge Edochie agreed."

Akin wrapped his arm around Bola's shoulder and pulled her to him. He brought his lips close to her ear and whispered "And if I had mind control powers, you would have given me some years ago."

Bola gritted her teeth. "Go away, Mr. Ogunseye."

"See you tomorrow, Ms. Bayo," Akin said, flashing that wide, boyish grin Bola hated so much.

*   *   *

Detective Talionis leaned against his car, sipping hot vanilla chai tea from his stainless steel thermos.

"…eleven…twelve," he said between sips, counting the 'borgs and cyber-enhanced people leaving the court house he'd arrested during his forty years as a cop.

"And thirteen," he said as Bola approached him.

"Oh shut up, Lex, you old bastard," the young attorney giggled, flushing slightly as she avoided his gaze.

The old cop laughed. "Everybody's got a past."

"Yeah, but most of us don't have *histories*"," replied Bola. "Where's Zipporah?"

Talionis shrugged. "We traded jobs; she gets to play

bodyguard for the 'borg who witnessed that big ass Fudokiht kill his asshole boss while I do escort duty."

Lex opened the front passenger door of the sedan. "Hop in."

"What do you know about escorting?" Bola asked.

"Less than you, I bet," he answered.

"*Shut-up, Lex!*" Bola said, slapping him on the shoulder. "No one could even *afford* my goodies. What I mean is that when I took this case – and I'm the only prosecutor who was willing to, I might add – they told me that if there was ever anything unusual about my escort – specifically if someone I was not expecting showed up – I should run back inside and have the bailiffs shoot whoever followed."

"Good thing you know me, then," Lex replied.

"So I'll ask them to shoot to wound," said Bola.

"Hilarious," Lex said dryly. "After I'm done dying from laughter, can I take you home?"

Bola smiled and slipped into the passenger seat.

*   *   *

"So how's the new turbine treating you?" Cheez asked as he took a sip of Ooze.

"Pretty good," Hercules replied. "I'm still a little stiff, though, but the power it gives is *way* beyond my old engine. Thanks, for the hook up."

Hercules raised his mug to his lips, his broad shoulders creaked. "I'm due for a servicing."

"Those titanium bones gotta stay oiled, Herc'," Cheez said. "Too much discomfort will drive you nutter and then Detective Father Time's old ass will come a-huntin'."

Cheez nodded toward Detective Talionis and Prosecutor Bayo, who stormed toward them.

"Shoot him!" Bola demanded. "Right now, Detective Talionis!"

"Is this about the Ooze?" Cheez asked, taking another sip of the purple liquid from his plastic cup. "Because current research indicates that a cup of Ooze a day promotes…"

"In the face, please, Lex," Bola said, interrupting him.

"My name's Bennett…and I ain't *in* it," the detective said, shaking his head.

"Kill your star – and *only* – witness and Vobua walks," Cheez said. "So, I will enjoy my Ooze anywhere I damned well please; and right now, I am pleased to get high in your lobby with your doorman."

"You're a rat," Bola said. "A dirty 'borg rat. That must be why they call you Cheez."

"Squeak, squeak," Cheez replied. "And rats don't actually like cheese. An edumacated girl like you should know that."

Bola locked eyes with Cheez, glaring madly at him.

Cheez smiled. "Arguing with you is one of the few worthwhile diversions I've had since turning prosecutor's witness.

"Where are your guards?" Detective Talionis inquired.

Cheez shrugged. "Wondering what's taking me so long in the loo?"

"Back inside," Lex ordered.

"But…" Cheez protested.

"Find them; apologize to them," Detective Talionis said.

"Yeah, whatever," Cheez replied.

Cheez gulped down the remainder of Ooze, tapping the bottom of the cup to dislodge every syrupy drop.

Detective Talionis hooked his fingers into Cheez's armpits and yanked him onto his feet.

"Hey!" Cheez gasped.

"Go!" Lex shouted, pointing toward the elevator.

Cheez scurried to the elevator and then placed his right palm on a panel to the left of it. The elevator door slid open and he hopped in. A moment later the door closed and the elevator rose with a low hum.

*   *   *

Knock on the door; show your face in the monitor. Don't smile, don't frown, look bored.

The door opened; Kullin stood in the doorway smiling.

"What's up?" he said.

Smile, force it.

"Nothing much, I have to talk to Cheez."

I'm going to kill you.

"This late?" Kullin asked.

"What, did I disturb your beauty sleep?"

Kullin laughed.

He's waving me through. Good. Damn, Cheo is here, too.

"What's up, Cheo?"

Cheo grunted, throwing his hand in the air. He went back to watching *Ninja Borgs*, his favorite M-Screen series.

He isn't paying attention. Good.

"Through there?"

Kullin nodded.

Walk to Cheez's room; go through the open door; shut it behind me.

Cheez sat bolt upright on the bed, his eyes as big around as dinner plates.

He's surprised to see me. He looks worried. Good.

"What the hell?" Cheez gasped. "What are you doing here?"

"My job. Now, shut up!"

He's studying me; weighing the situation. He's not as dumb as he puts on.

"You're in danger here; I'm going to get you to safety."

"Danger from whom?" Cheez asked "From what?"

"Kullin, Cheo, I don't know who else. Vobua broke free from his cell an hour ago. He's making a move."

"He can't, he…"

"He knows you're being held in a safe house. The Fudokiht are the Sweepers for this building. You sneak out of the flat all the time; you think they don't know you're here? You think they didn't tell Vobua?"

Cheez buried his face in his hands. "What do you need me to do?" He sighed.

Smart boy, Cheez.

"You're a hacker…don't deny it. We've known since day one. Can you get into the building's mainframe?"

"Do fat boys in turtlenecks sweat rivers?" Cheez replied with a smirk.

""I'll take that as a yes. Disable the cameras; wipe the whole night. The less these guys know about how and when you escape the better."

Cheez went to work, his fingers dancing upon the keys in his bed's headboard. After a few minutes, he leaned back on the bed and smiled smugly.

"It's done," he said. "Easy as pie."

I've got him, now, arrogant fool.

"Follow me."

Kullin's stuffing his face with pizza. Cheo's still into that dumb ass show. Hmm…Cheo's going bald; the track lights reflect off his scalp. I'll aim for that shiny spot. This City Slicker mini-machinegun barely has any recoil.

Cheo's head exploded, peppering the walls, floor and M-Screen with flecks of grey, pink and red.

Kullin yanked his Zentec "Beast" from his shoulder holster and pointed the big pistol at the attacker. "Drop it, drop it now!"

Ah, Kullin. So predictable. So old. The City really

needs younger detectives. Oh, well, time to die Kullin.

Kullin squeezed the trigger of the "Beast" in rapid succession, firing a volley of deadly lead.

Damn it, he shot me! Shot me again! Quicker than I thought. Hurts, hurts bad – gotta stay on feet. Advance.

Kullin's jaw fell slack. "What...impossible!"

A gaping hole erupted in Kullin's chest as several bullets from the attacker's gun met their mark.

"Holy shit! You...you killed them!" Cheez cried.

"No kidding, Captain Obvious. Now, come on!"

Cheez trotted across the room, hot on the killer's heels.

"Shut the door behind you!" The killer commanded.

Cheez grabbed the door's handle and gave it a tug. The door closed with a soft click.

Cheez is getting used to following orders. He wants to survive. Good.

The killer sprinted down the hall with Cheez huffing and puffing close behind him. The killer stopped at the end of the hall and pointed toward a round, steel door in the wall.

"Get in."

"Um...no!" Cheez shouted. "You know what that is?"

"Keep your voice down! Yeah, I know what it is – it's a garbage chute; people throw their garbage down to the disintegrator, where the energy from the disintegrated trash is used to power the building. I had it turned off, so you'll land safely in the garage. Someone will meet you down there."

Cheez smiled and climbed into the chute.

"Hey, thanks!" Cheez said. "I owe you one."

"More than one. I'll see you soon; you can repay me then."

Cheez released his grip on the side of the chute and vanished into the darkness.

Silly Cheez.
The power is still on.
The disintegrator is on.
Bye-bye, Cheez.

*   *   *

Bola stared at the carnage, her face a pallid gray. The bodies of Kullin and Cheo had been taken away, but the violence was inscribed in crimson.

"What the hell happened here?" she sobbed.

Lex placed a firm hand on her shoulder. "Prosecutor Bayo, the shooter emerged from the back room. Kullin was shot four times in the abdomen at close range and Cheo was shot once in the head. Both died on the scene. Kullin's gun had been fired three times. One round is lodged in the wall. The other two must have hit whatever Kullin was aiming for, but the only blood here is from Kullin and Cheo. One person left shoe prints in the blood splatter; the imprints match the brand worn by Cheez. Multiple sets of prints were found on the doorknob. The only set of prints not overlaid by any others belongs to Cheez."

Bola crossed her arms behind her back and drew in a breath. "So, Cheez came out of his room with a weapon. He murdered Kullin and Cheo, and then ran. Is that what you're telling me happened here?"

Lex shook his head. "It doesn't make any sense. Cheez hated non-mundanes. From what I could tell, he *wanted* to take down Vobua."

Bola sighed. "He wasn't supposed to be a goddamned gunslinger either; the son-of-a-bitch was a hacker, not a wet-worker. And where the hell is Zipporah?"

"I pulled her out of here yesterday evening to help me punch a nutter 'borg's ticket early this a.m. We were staking out his place all night. If I didn't need her, she'd be gone, too."

Lex's eyes widened and his eyebrows rose on his furrowed brow. "Damn!" he growled, slamming his right fist into his left palm.

"What is it, Lex?" Bola asked.

"He set us up," Detective Talionis replied. "That rat bastard and that Fudokiht set us up! Cheez was never going to testify; he was a plant. Vobua knew he screwed himself when he moved the body. He was going down. He gave us Cheez to make us jump the gun! We built our case on Cheez's testimony. Without him, Vobua's going to get acquitted. He gets a clean slate and we're the ones who gave it to him!"

Lex paced back and forth, his face twisting into a scowl. "I'm gonna kill Vobua, then, I'm gonna find Cheez and blow his head clean off his shoulders."

"You will do nothing of the sort," Bola said, taking him by the arm and leading him from the room. "You're worth a hundred Vobua's and a *thousand* Cheez's."

"Then what are we gonna do?" Lex sobbed. "Kullin; Cheo…I've worked with those guys for damned near twenty years. They were like family. Damn…their families…we gotta tell 'em."

"Shh," Bola whispered, laying her head on Lex's massive chest. "I'll think of something. We'll still get him, ok? We'll still get him."

*   *   *

"And those are the facts as they stand?" Judge Edochie asked, her image projected onto the large screen from some undisclosed location.

"Yes, Your Honor," Bola said. She peered over her shoulder to gauge the reactions of Akin and Vobua, it was a sign of weakness, but she had to know. Akin looked concerned; Vobua was doing a good job of looking perplexed.

"Hmm," Edochie said, rubbing her finger across her bottom lip. "Any comment, Mr. Ogunseye?"

Akin stood. "Well, Your Honor, as the prosecution's main witness umm...refuses to testify, I'd like to request a recess in order to prepare final arguments."

"That is completely...!" Bola started to protest.

The judge silenced her with an upraised had. "It *is* pushing the limits of the law to request a recess this late in the trial, Miss Bayo. I know that." She turned her head toward Akin. "As do you, Mr. Ogunseye. However, I will allow it considering the circumstances. The court will adjourn for two weeks while the detectives conduct a thorough investigation into the disappearance of the witness. Dismissed!"

Bola bolted out of the courtroom.

"Miss Bayo, we need to...."

She didn't even stop when Akin called her name. Detective Talionis was, once again waiting at his car. This time, she slipped into it without any complaint or comment.

"So we've got time?" Lex asked.

"Two weeks," Bola replied.

The detective swerved into traffic. "Good," he said. "I'll try to find evidence that Vobua had something to do with Cheez's disappearance."

"If you don't, I'll try to convince the Judge that Cheez was a puppet of the Fudokiht. If I can, I *may* be able to get a retrial."

*   *   *

A knock on Bola's front door roused her from sleep.

She slid off the living room couch and lumbered, half-asleep, to the door. She checked the monitor. It was Lex. She opened the door.

"Hey, Lex. What ya got for me?" she asked.

"I've got nothing," he replied. "What about you?"

Bola shook her head. "There are just no grounds; not even shaky grounds. There's nothing at all. Akin is going to win this one, damn it! And you could have called, Lex. It's one in the damned morning!"

Lex shrugged his shoulders. "I needed to get out. To clear my head. You're up now, so walk with me."

"Whatever," Bola said, slipping on her jogging shoes. "You better buy me a chai while we're out."

"Deal," Lex replied.

In silence, the pair walked to the elevator.

"We haven't got the cameras back working yet," Lex said. "Whatever the hell Cheez did to them, none of our guys have been able to fix."

Bola grunted, Lex could tell she wasn't listening, but he continued anyway. "He might still be here, you know. He would sneak out on occasion, but it's impossible that he has evaded our search this long with absolutely no clues left behind. Unless it's something else."

The elevator dinged open and Bola walked inside without giving any sign that she had heard Lex. Shaking his head the detective moved to follow, but then froze.

"Lex?" asked Bola, as the elevator doors slid toward each other.

Just before the doors slammed shut, Lex shot his hand between them. The doors slid apart.

Lex squinted and shook his head, as if trying to shake off a terrible migraine. He stared at Bola, unblinking.

"Lex...?" Bola began, and then the words died in her throat, choked by some invisible, strong hand.

Lex had drawn his gun.

"Lex, what are you doing?" Bola croaked. "What's

wrong?"

"It was you," Lex sighed. "You took this case when no one else would. *You* built the case on Cheez. *You* brought forward the only evidence we had at the wrong time and got it dismissed."

"So, you're arresting me, then?" Bola sighed.

"No," Lex said. "You know the law too well. You'll manipulate it somehow and get away with murdering some good guys. I'm sorry Bola; I owe them and their families more than that."

"Please, Lex," Bola cried.

"How much did the Fudokiht pay you?" Lex asked, tears welling in the corners of his eyes. "How much did they pay you to kill Cheez? How much to murder my friends?"

"Obviously, not enough."

Lex fired twice, hitting Bola square in the chest.

Bola staggered backward, her back crashing into the rear elevator wall. She roared, a frightening din born from pain and fury and then sprang forward, slashing with her now extended iron claws.

Lex slammed the heel of his left foot into Bola's kneecap.

Bola collapsed onto her haunches on the floor of the elevator, writhing in agony; wailing in pain.

"They never reinforce those kneecaps enough," Lex said, shaking his head.

He fired his gun once more. Bola's head rolled into the far corner of the elevator as her body collapsed before him.

The elevator dinged. The doors closed.

*   *   *

"And this court finds the defendant, Vobua, not guilty of the crime of murder."

Judge Edochie slammed her hammer onto her desk.

The giant, ape-like Fudokiht clapped his massive hands and then wrapped his arms around defense attorney Ogunseye, hugging him tightly while being careful not to crush the man.

Vobua sauntered out of the courtroom smiling almost as broadly as Akin, who walked beside him.

"Want to have a drink with me to celebrate?" Akin asked.

"Nah," Vobua replied, shaking his large, bald head. "My rides here," he said pointing toward a black sedan parked across the street from the courthouse. "I'm going home and enjoying a good night's sleep in my own bed."

"I definitely understand that," Akin said. "Some other time, then."

"Of course," Vobua replied.

Akin waved and walked off.

Vobua strode to the car awaiting him.

Lex slid out of the car and ran around to the passenger's side. "I'm Detective Lex Talionis and I'll be your escort home."

"This is so nice of the City, taking care of me like this," Vobua chuckled.

"Oh, yes, sir," Lex replied with a smile. "It's the least we can do to repay you for your trouble…the *least* we can do."

Move

By
ZZ Claybourne

"They never see me. Not even Knowledge Lateef. I walk into anyone's space, eat their food, watch them argue, love, or a lot of times die. I am a Ghost. My name is Sightline. I am a telepath for hire."

The first beat:

They thought by now they'd mapped every visible meter of The City, every crag, every cistern, every hightower, every launch point, but instead of sticking flags as markers they might as well have stuck bodies. There were people everywhere. Staying Ghost took a toll, but Miradeen preferred it. Everywhere she looked: a massive, pensive Fudokiht, their apish figures moving slowly but feline eyes always darting; an Eensa, like her, mostly tall and lean, mostly dark, bartering all over The City and forever tinkering. If not tinkering, fighting. If not fighting, fornicating. In many circles a mixture of all three. *Humans* they were if someone wanted to insult them with myth knowledge. Few still ambulatory had ever insulted Miradeen Lau 'Coo. All humans, no matter their color, sex, or City affiliation, were *Eensa*. Every child of the world, no matter the species, was taught three undeniable words. As far as Miradeen knew, it was the only unified thought The City possessed. Nigerian Space Agency. The Eensa had been the first to live in The City. Bits of old records had survived, more legend than anything now.

But the powers hadn't found everything. Not yet.

Miradeen's grip tightened on the whipsteel. The thin filament instantly hardened outward into a pole no thicker than a *cheksaa's* tail.

There was one group that no one, not Eensa, Fudokiht,

or even the helium-breathing Kempa Protectorate, saw on a regular basis: the Apunu, their insect heads and plated bodies constantly clicking as they moved. Her first menial job inside an Apunu hive had nearly driven her mad with the noise.

Devils, as that old piece of whipsteel of a man known as Knowledge Lateef too indiscriminately said. *Devils of the biomimetic salvation.* The Apunu provided (excreted, Miradeen reminded herself; words were important) the *Ooze*. For all his care, Lateef could be amazingly unwise at times. The City had its Watchers, and the Apunu had theirs. There was no wealth in The City that didn't start with the Apunu.

Miradeen, unlike Lateef, was of the opinion that if you were a wealthy devil, you were simply a devil all along.

Wealth also made one incredibly stupid, as the security of the Apunu hive she was leaving attested. Getting into a Fudokiht's nursery had been harder.

She wedged the whipsteel into the fingernail's-width base of the garbage shaft's door. A tap on the steel's end flattened and expanded the filament, forcing the unprotected door enough for her to roll out. Falling, she gave the command to her bodysuit to seal before sluicing into the thick muck of Apunu secondary waste. She waited till her feet touched bottom, then allowed her body to angle forward before pushing out one slow step at a time. There wouldn't be a harvester for this waste for another half cycle, not like the regular Ooze harvests. Nobody ever thought to secure their waste; nobody.

Slogging through Apunu shit was slow going, but she had allowed plenty of time on the bomb for detonation.

*   *   *

"You're not as smart as you think you are," said the woman massaging the kinks from Miradeen's shoulders, her sinewy dark fingers merging into perfect invisibility against Miradeen's cobalt skin. "The Watchers will track your pattern."

"There is no pattern."

"Just because we got rid of our Tells doesn't mean we're invulnerable."

"Since we practically died doing so I think we get leeway," said Miradeen. This was an argument that came up frequently as the war solidified from idea to inevitability.

She didn't want the edge of worry in Tanight's voice cutting into the day's victory.

"I'm not as good at Ghosting as you are," Tanight said, bending till her forehead rested on Miradeen's hairless crown.

Miradeen craned her neck around. "You worry too much, Ms. Two Five Eight. A hit of Ooze will smooth that out of you."

"Not funny."

"Not meant to be. How long did it take the Instant to come up with a story for the explosion?"

Tanight, small but wiry and hard as whipsteel, sat on Miradeen's lap. "They were saying it had nothing to do with anything before the first Watcher formed," she exaggerated, but only slightly.

"That, my dear, is where the pattern forms. The more they say nothing is happening, the more people know something *is*." She played a finger over the familiar adulthood scars on Tanight's forearm.

"What do you get out of being pattern master?" Tanight said, holding Miradeen at the chin so the woman had to look at her. She wasn't interested in the way Miradeen feinted issues by using empathic communication.

"This is an old issue, love," said Miradeen.

"But a necessary one."

"One I wish you would stop asking," said Miradeen. Miradeen gently eased her off her lap and stood with her, pushing her to the table where their plates of vegetables remained warming. "Until someone else steps in, I do the job. There isn't a better telepath for hire in The City."

"So you say," said Tanight, taking a seat.

"So I say," agreed Miradeen.

*   *   *

The pulse:

Tillian Drew didn't bother with information coming through the Instant. When you were Tillian Drew you already were the news. A phase-shift bomb in an Apunu hive that didn't do much damage was the latest story he was ignoring, no matter that it sent a message directly to him.

"You corralled Lateef and those other freaks?" Drew asked, meaning the Techsorcists. A lumbering blue body shouldered past him toward a replenished plate of *myloum* the table delivered.

"Not his way," said Tk'weiJatkatl. The ancient Fudokiht gingerly picked the largest of the soft fruits and popped it whole into its mouth. Freckles on its grey-blue chest turned a deeper blue as the blessed nectar reached its ribbed tongue.

"Not what I asked, Honored Guest," said Tillian.

"Are you broadcasting this meeting to interested parties?" asked Tk'weiJakatl. It spoke the old tongue, that low pastiche of words from all species that was best left to the fanatical Soors. Tk'weiJakatl sat very slowly and softly on the floor. Very few Fudokiht found Eensa furniture of any use. "Are you positive it was not No Name?"

"I've been assured it was not," said Drew.

"An explosion...in an Ooze collection point...and Tillian Drew does not know the why of it?" Tk'weiJakatl snuffed and closed its eyes, an open sign of disrespect.

Tillian grunted back. "My chief of security sits and eats fruit."

Tk'weiJakatl snuffed again, louder this time. It opened one eye and closed it.

Rattling a Fudokiht served no useful purpose. Both sat quietly, waiting upon the other. Tk'weiJakatl thick, sonorous voice issued first.

"I have teams amidst the Street Priests, Ward 215. I have agents within the Apunu Rise—and I say this for the benefit of Queen Q'b—there is nowhere I am not." At this Tk'weiJakatl did something few Fudokiht tried: a smile, each of its sharp, serrated teeth jutting out, its feline eyes narrowing and "going dark," as children called it, the pupils immediately dilating to fill the entire eye. It looked as though one were facing death's harlequin.

He smiled directly at Tillian Drew.

*　　*　　*

The return:

The bones of the ships sometimes soared skyward several stories. The largest, Last Grasp, threw claws of twisted metal and active power cores into the very breath of The City, blending into the atmosphere's haze nightmares that kept most away. The City allowed scavenger runs to parts of the ships, although none had been necessary for hundreds of years. The parts that were forbidden…remained forbidden. Watchers, if you had enough of the Ooze in you, knew your intentions. And who wasn't pumped full of Ooze now? For all its "therapeutic" properties, the Ooze guaranteed no one ever tried to journey. But Miradeen saw the sky. It was right there! Stories, however, about Watchers forming from the thinnest layers of dust along hulls and deck plates were not false. The records were quite clear on this. Species were allowed to cannibalize their own and the ships of others, but in the known history of The City not a single ship had attempted escape. Low-orbit jumps for supply runs near the Zero Point were as far as anyone thought to go.

Yet no one knew why they didn't want to go anywhere, but they knew Ooze was readily and plentifully supplied. The City, in perfect symmetry with its inhabitants, could not thrive without Ooze. The Hammer Foundation and the Apunu had quickly realized that, forming the strongest economic and social cartel in the world. Ooze, Inc. Mainlining Ooze to destroy the genetic Tells implanted inside every single being by The City was punishable by Watcher death; ingesting it in approved quantities and methods was encouraged to the point of religion. So few people even knew how to properly mainline the thick, purple liquid that corporal punishment might as well have been moot; folks died anyway. Knowledge Lateef was one who knew. It wasn't something he broadcasted. It was something Miradeen "accidentally" picked up from his mind. She tried staying out of the minds of those she respected, but things slipped.

Waging a war, especially a one-mutant war, required knowledge. These trips to the Bones weren't safe, even for her, but they were necessary. The mimetic filaments of her suit kept her well-camouflaged, even from hypersensitive Apunu eyes, not that they ever bothered scavenging anymore. Modifiers would come out from time to time, looking for hardware as though jewelry shopping, adding tiny bits of Eensa, Fudokiht, Heliums, or what was barely left of the massive fingers coming out of the Apunu world ship, to their body tech.

The Apunu ship's main core threw blue light into the three-kilometer long gash the ship gouged into the surface on its collision long ago. The track was dubbed "The Blue Nile" though no one remembered where that came from. Radiation, the skewed blue lighting, walking untracked by and untethered to The City...all these were disorienting enough, but the worst of the Nile: its Watchers. In this track they assumed the shape and characteristics of the Apunu, and she'd seen enough archival footage of the Apunu/Eensa Actions to know a group of Apunu engaged in a hive kill was a death few deserved.

She sighted ahead. The boneyard was under the influence of The City's night cycle. She waited for Tanight's signal.

The excited buzzing inside her temples got her on her feet and running. She was fast and quiet. She stopped and started at random intervals, weaving erratically through the Nile. Patterns of any kind, even out here, were giveaways.

She and Tanight communicated in blips of impressions too fast to generate potential Watchers. Miradeen passed Tanight without even glancing her way. She ran until wedging herself into a fissure in the wall of the Nile ravine. She waited a random interval.

Tanight Dasch felt the buzzing and raced out. When she reached a stopping point she waited to be sure of no Watchers, and then signaled Miradeen. They continued in relay until both stood at the base of the Last Grasp. A black shaft led downward into the innards of the derelict. Tanight and Miradeen briefly butted the heads of their suits together.

There are no Watchers inside. The shared thought bolstered them. They jumped.

*   *   *

The fool:

When Sightline was needed she seemed to know, and she appeared.

"The wards are getting sloppy," said Tillian Drew. Anything in his office would have kept her fed her entire juvenile street apprenticeship. "Bombing the Apunu. I need you to wipe a few targets."

"Payment has been tendered?" she asked. They payment system she'd set up seemed simple on the surface. It was as pocked, twisted, and complex as an Apunu hive beneath, with the added protection of her blocking the transactions from the minds of her clients. Embezzlement was rampant among The City's elite. And expected.

Tillian Drew nodded.

"Targets in mind?" Miradeen asked. Drew tapped his temple. "Then I was never here." She pulled the targets from his mind then wiped herself from his memory.

She went Ghost and left, and while she did so Tk'weiJakatl, in its roost home within the Drew Enclave, regretted knowing as much about The City as it did; regretted having to befriend people it planned to kill. As such even those not born were already victims. Tillian Drew had a son. Tk'weiJakatl knew, as it savored another myloum, it would be best for Drew's son if that son never bred.

It stared out the bubble of its roost. The City stretched forever and yet was a simple thing to one attuned. A minor bomb in an Apunu facility sowed no discord. Machinery moved. Lives moved. The Fudokiht being extremely long-lived, it didn't do to live a life along an unpredictable, rocky road.

It sat to meditate on its City.

*   *   *

Death:

"Night, he wants the Street Priests erased."

"You're not going to do it."

"No. But this…without the Street Priests what would life become?" Miradeen paced, brow furrowed, hands needing to feel her whipsteel.

"You suddenly care?" said Tanight. "Common life?"

"As much as I ever. You doubt me?"

Tanight drew a deep breath. "Wipe Tillian."

"No," Miradeen said, although the idea had occurred to her. "Not there yet."

"But…"

"Not there yet." Miradeen laid her hand on Tanight's cheek. "Not till they come after me. Things need to be done."

"And when they come after you?" Tanight hated feeling as though she'd fallen in love with a god.

"By then it'll be too late."

*   *   *

The heart beats:

Knowledge Lateef, a gaunt man who expertly wielded the angles of his narrow face and sharp goatee like the blade of a knife designed to show distaste, razored a frown across Miradeen's forehead.

"Why would Drew blame Street Priests?" he said.

"Just know they may be coming for you," said Miradeen.

"No one is that foolish. We *are* The City. There's no war."

"There's always war, Lateef. Especially when things are quiet. Especially as days go by."

Lateef considered this. He knew this woman had ways that not even he, as leader of the Street Priests, could sway.

"The City is dying, Lateef," said Miradeen.

"Social tides, girl. Ebb, flow."

"I mean literally, teacher! You of all people know the life that lives under your feet. Don't tell me you haven't felt a change."

They were in an empty space. Even so, he glanced. "Do not speak of the world's sentience to others." His eyes glared from the mech lenses of his ancient spectacles.

"I will not."

"Tell me."

"It poisoned itself bringing us here. Here and there, repairs aren't appearing. You've noticed it. Radiation levels along the Blue Nile have steadily increased. It's not absorbing it. It can't keep up. The cores of the Last Grasp alone will likely last the next thousand years. But Ooze is more plentiful than ever."

"Leave the Ooze to us," said Lateef.

"Everyone is sick, teacher. Most of the people in this world are born dead."

"Poetry." Lateef regarded the small, dark woman.

She did not usually show the skin of her entire face. It was flawless, dark as the universe. Lateef knew The City dreamed. He had touched its dream once in meditation. Fear kept him from attempting to do so again. Through this, Lateef knew the universe. "And you?"

"I was born alive."

*   *   *

War:

A year passed. In that year, 3 more bombings, each a larger degree than the last. Gangs and governing factions targeted one another. Micro-wars erupted throughout The City, different from the wars of the common day in one regard: everyone was swinging blindly. Assassins, flush with assignments, became economic drivers. An underground meme cropped up among the Modifiers regarding this deadly notoriety: *Life is good when you're killing people.* Miradeen hated it but paid it no mind. The strands of the web were plucked, the spiders in motion. She was able to Ghost for longer periods of time with less stress. Tanight too. Evenings out being invisible while Mechs, AIs, drones, Eensa, six-legged *Chi* priests, and everything else that gave The City its length and breadth, had become very necessary for the two.

Along the River, where it was warm and pavilions dotted stretches, they walked directly in the paths of others, projecting reasons for The City's life to go around them rather than the other way around. The insectoid Chi priests, out in force prior to their hibernation, skittered around the feet of Bigs and clicked the words of salvation with their claws. There was a melody to their clicking, not like the Apunu's accidental noises. Miradeen slowed to listen to a group of three trying to convince a huddled blue group of Fudokiht to learn with them.

Miradeen paid no mind as Tanight veered toward a *Fooloy* stand, its multiple metal arms working in unison to make sure none of the sweet melons burned or stuck. Seared fooloy was Tanight's weakness. Tanight went Solid, sending out an impression to all in the vicinity that she had always been there. It would have been easy enough to remain Ghost and take the fooloy but Tanight Dasch was no thief. She would stay Solid only long enough to complete the transaction.

One of the Fudokiht seated on the ground amongst the skittering priests viewed Tanight. It smiled. Something was wrong with the timing. Its teeth had shown before Tanight had. Miradeen's ears immediately clogged and her throat tightened. She scanned for danger even as she moved and reached for Tanight.

"We have to go," she hissed for Tanight's ears only. "The big one, sky blue over there. It knew. Let's go."

"We're being followed?" Tanight barely believed it.

Miradeen cursed herself. Eyes were everywhere, but she hadn't met a race yet that could see through her Ghosting, and she'd Ghosted many Fudokiht. But patience was the hallmark of all Fudokiht, slow to anger or offense, but when moved past their tolerance, deadly. All this time...

"Ghost as deeply as you can and meet me," said Miradeen. She went Ghost and ran. Tanight, the same. They had rendezvous points set up throughout The City. The one nearest the River pavilions was two kilometers away by way of several hellish enclaves and non-Apunu sewage lines. Miradeen kept her mind off worry by keeping her mind blank. Her limbs moved via automatic pilot and pre-programmed directives. Tanight would be where she needed to be. It was that simple.

It was that simple. It...

Damnation's bloodied edge! cracked through Miradeen's discipline before she whipped it back inside. She raced through a home of Albino Eensa preparing to settle for the family meal. This home opened into a Kempa helium reserve: a huge, dank industrial area generally deserted save for scheduled maintenance Mechs rolling and tromping the metal grounds. From there, the wetlands of the Perch, then a small pocket of water that connected with a fissure in the wall of The River's bank, some 12 meters underwater. The fissure was barely wide enough for the women's bodies to traverse. Miradeen had widened it at key points using whipsteel and laser; a tunnel led from it to an underwater cave outfitted with illegal stealth mech and psionic diffusers of her own invention. There were similarly-outfitted pods within that would take them the remainder of their escape back to their Dead Zone in their area of the world so protected it didn't exist.

Tanight would be there, in that cave, waiting. She was always the faster of the two.

The Fudokiht had smiled at Tanight.

Out of consideration for others Fudokiht didn't smile often. It was a terrifying sight, and had come to be known as extremely self-serving...

Miradeen stopped.

We're giving them exactly what they want! Tanight, stop! she blared mentally. She ran harder, Ghosting through homes, yards, and businesses. When she reached the deserted fissure point Tanight was nowhere to be seen. Nothing was out of place, no one visible, nothing moving. *Night?*

The current floated something outward, away from the bank.

Miradeen's mind flared, blinding and paralyzing her to the spot. Her Ghosting wavered.

A shot seared through her mech suit, damaging too many circuits for the suit to instantly repair the area. Blood barely registered; the heat of the blast had cauterized its own wound. She whirled, directing a mental blast outward, frying the concentration of the assassin's link with his mimetic suit. He shimmered into view a thousand paces from her, standing on a *shaver* which he kicked into hover mode and raced toward her. This was open ground.

But he wasn't firing.

She crouched. The whipsteel was instantly a staff in her hands, both ends tapered to fine points.

She rammed the staff into the ground and flipped herself to the top of it just as the first Watcher formed from the ground, its combination of mech and soil constantly roiling until humanoid enough to reach for her even as the ground itself was pushing against the whipsteel, forcing it out. She swung her body quickly, taking herself and the steel backwards. The ends of the steel flattened into scythes. She slashed the Watcher in half and didn't give a second a chance to form, hitting the scrambler on her hip that effectively destabilized all mech and neurals but her own in a wide radius, gifts of the ship graveyard. The shaver went down. The assassin somersaulted nearer her, rolled quickly to a standing position, and fired from two hands, but without his mech she was already in his mind, twisting her body a second before he fired so that the red flashes passed her harmlessly. From his mind she picked the weak points on his purple and black body armor and Ghost-advanced so quickly his left hand falling to the ground surprised him; the right joined it. The whipsteel pierced the flexible siding of his armor the moment his arms spasmed upward a second, the point bumping against his back armor. She yanked the whipsteel out and grabbed his head before his body hit the ground. There was nothing left there.

She raced to the water and dove. The body hadn't floated far. There were only minutes before another Watcher would be able to appear. She sealed Tanight's suit over her lover's head, sealed her own, held tight to Tanight, and submerged.

* * *

Lords:

Tillian Drew and Tk'weiJakatl hadn't said anything consequential the entire time she watched them. Neither had shown any indication they knew she was there. She wasn't worried about Drew. He was nothing but money. The Fudokiht, though, she'd seen enough times via the Instant as Drew's mouthpiece. Tk'weiJakatl got her full attention. She watched it for any sign of psionics, any tell whatsoever. The Fudokiht were now enemies. One did not go to war without first staring an enemy in the face.

"Ward 215 has figured out how to breach the Vertigo Gate," said Tk'weiJakatl. Slowly. Everything about the muscular blue mass was slow torture. "Three to date."

"What has it affected?" asked Drew.

"Nothing."

A considerable amount of time had passed since Miradeen had squeezed through passages dragging the weight of the only reason The City had provided to survive her earlier youth.

"I suggest," continued the blue giant, "having additional Ooze sent to the Soors. Let us foster fighting between the gangs for it."

"There's already too much fighting in 215," said Drew.

"Necessary," said Tk'weiJakatl.

"It'd be like wasting myloum on vermin. Anything else to report?" There had been no bombings or issues the past quarter cycle. The City turned, The City moved, The City grew.

Tk'weiJakatl remained silent.

"I need to see my son now," Drew said, dismissing this session. Tk'weiJakatl rose and left. Absolutely no indication it knew she was there.

Miradeen did the same, knowing two things: Tillian

Drew was a fool; the Fudokiht security chief was not.

*   *   *

Time:

The untouched land she found showed the distant light of the Last Grasp just over the tips of a craggy buttress. She had seeded the area with enough micro-mechs programmed to appear as Watchers that no one would possibly stumble on it. Everything was not yet known, and so much that was known, forgotten. Not every stretch plotted, or if plotted, no longer useful. Not marketable. Not profitable. One of her last runs into an Eensa ship she found a book in a highly damaged database. A book of myths that she barely understood. But one line hit her. It was the first thing she whispered when Tanight she came out of her coma, because Tanight loved archaic phrases.

"For the wages of sin is death, but the gift of god is eternal life."

She now roused Tanight. She had not felt alone since finding another like herself; had known no reason under Tanight's soul not to be fearless.

I will give this world eternal life or topple it to the ground. "Love?" She ran a hand over Tanight's hair, the last time she would do so for a very long time. Tanight had fallen asleep in Miradeen's lap as the two watched their section of The City slide toward night. "Night?" she whispered.

"Yes."

"I need you very much."

"I know," the other murmured, still medicated, a vial of Ooze on the table beside them.

Miradeen opened her mouth to speak, found herself about to cry instead, and closed it. Their skins merged into one another under the wan light. Tanight now preferred the evening cycles to be open to the sky. Miradeen did not let her know that the sky, in this instance, was a live image of outside on a large indoor screen. This space was completely encased, shielded, and buried in such a way as to appear a part of the landscape.

A home waited for Tanight among the solitary Helium Breathers after convincing several of them that Tanight was a warrior recovering from recent battles. The Breathers worshipped warriors.

She kissed Tanight on the forehead. "I'm giving you the universe, Night." It was a promise to Tanight. It was a command to herself.

Tanight was empathic enough to know her friend's intent but too weak to protest. Ever since they had found one another in the most squalid Eensa region as starving outcasts, both surviving by being quiet, being smart, Miradeen Lau 'Coo's voice had been the one thing promised her in a raging sea of minds.

Miradeen kissed the smooth, dark forehead again, each kiss an erasure.

"Why are you doing this?" Tanight's voice was low, barely audible.

"Because I'm the only one who can."

*   *   *

Flatline:

The space among the Breathers lacked no amenity that would call attention to itself. There were feeds in key points, micro mechs that would come together to record, transmit, then disperse when needed. There were weapons hidden, of which Tanight remained unaware. Hidden weapons except for one: the whipsteel, cleaned of all DNA markers, displayed above the doorway of the interior the customary way among the honored of the Helium Breathers.

"This is home," Miradeen said to Tanight.

They stood hand-in-hand, arms crossed, facing one another without looking at either.

"There are too many who have no idea what the sky is," said Miradeen. Tanight held her hands tighter. "There's more than what's beneath our feet. I'm giving all of us the sky, love."

Tanight's tears flowed quietly and steadily.

"They almost killed you, love. As a message to me," said Miradeen.

Tanight closed her eyes and held her head back, hoping to slow the tears. She loved Miradeen Lau 'Coo and would not now cause her pain.

"Will I know you again?" she asked, drawing Miradeen closer.

"I promise."

She went Ghost, wiping the last bit of herself from Tanight's mind, watching her only friend—her *life*—go blank then restart with the implanted notion that she was hungry and had been about to prepare a meal. She passed Miradeen for the cabinet; certain she had dried myloum leaves. A soup. Real soup, prepared minus any mech aid. Finding the leaves, Tanight muttered, "I wonder how long this will take?" and for a moment Miradeen thought she was talking to her.

She wanted to kiss the back of Tanight's neck. She wanted to smell her skin and hear the rustle of her fingernails across her hair.

Ghosts don't touch, ghosts don't feel, ghosts don't live.

Ghosts remain silent and invisible until the world is ready.

The Cityzens

(In alphabetical order)

Jeff Carroll
Dreamers Recall

Jeff Carroll is a writer and a filmmaker. He is pioneering what he calls Hip Hop horror, Sci/fi and fantasy. His stories always have lots of action and a social edge. He has written and produced 2 films, Holla If I Kill You and Gold Digger Killer which won BEST Picture at the International Hip Hop film festival. He has published 3 books the novelization to Gold Digger Killer, Thug angel Rebirth of a Gargoyle and It Happened on Negro Mountain. His short stories have appeared in both The Black Science Fiction Society's anthology and their magazine. He writes out of South Florida where he lives with his wife and youngest son.

Jeff Carroll is also the author of the non-fiction book The Hip Hop Dating Guide. When he is not writing Sci-fi stories he enjoys speaking on Healthy Dating to college and high school students everywhere and goes by Yo Jeff.

Please connect with him on Facebook, Instagram, Twitter and his blog http://hhcnf.blogspot.com/

ZZ Claybourne
Move

Zig Zag Claybourne is the author of the acclaimed short story collection Historical Inaccuracies, two novels, and the new sci fi adventure The Brothers Jetstream: Leviathan.

Gerald Coleman
Hunters' First Rule

Gerald L. Coleman is a Philosopher, Theologian, Poet, and Author residing in Atlanta. Born in Lexington, he did his undergraduate work in Philosophy and English at the University of Kentucky before completing a Master's degree in Theology at Trevecca Nazarene University in Nashville. His most recent work appears in, Pluck! The Journal of Affrilachian Arts & Culture Issue 9, Drawn To Marvel: Poems From The Comic Books, Pine Mountain Sand & Gravel Vol. 18 and he is the author of the scifi/fantasy novel When Night Falls: Book One of The Three Gifts. He is a co-founder of the Affrilachian Poets. You can find him at http://www.geraldlcoleman.co or follow him on Twitter @Iconiclast.

Milton Davis
Knowledge

Milton Davis is a research and development chemist, speculative fiction writer and owner of MVmedia, LLC, a micro publishing company specializing in Science Fiction, Fantasy and Sword and Soul. MVmedia's mission is to provide speculative fiction books that represent people of color in a positive manner. Milton is the author of Changa's Safari Volumes One, Two and Three. His most recent releases are Woman of the Woods and Amber and the Hidden City. He is co-editor of four anthologies; Griots: A Sword and Soul Anthology and Griot: Sisters of the Spear, with Charles R. Saunders; The Ki Khanga Anthology with Balogun Ojetade and the Steamfunk! Anthology, also with Balogun Ojetade. Milton Davis and Balogun Ojetade recently received the Best Screenplay Award for 2014 from the Urban Action Showcase for their African martial arts script, Ngolo. His current projects include The City, a Cyberfunk anthology, Dark Universe, a space opera anthology based on a galactic empire ruled by people of African American descent, and From Here to Timbuktu, a Steamfunk novel.

Ray Dean
Washed Pure, Washed Clean

Ray Dean was born and raised in Hawaii where she spent many a quiet hour reading and writing stories. Performing in theater and working backstage lead her into the delights of Living History, creating her own worlds through writing seemed the next logical step. Historical settings are her first love, but there is something heady about twisting the threads of time into little knots and creating new timelines to explore. There are endless possibilities that she is just beginning to discover.

Malon Edwards
Collard Greens, Hummingbirds and Spider Silk

Malon Edwards was born and raised on the South Side of Chicago, but now lives in the Greater Toronto Area, where he was lured by his beautiful Canadian wife. Many of his short stories are set in an alternate Chicago and feature people of color.

Ashtyn Foster

Ashtyn Foster has had a deep love of literature since she was two and has been writing since she was six years old. She loves telling stories, whether they be her own through words or others via the stage. SF was engrained in her at an early age while watching the Star Trek TV shows and Batman movies with her parents. She thanks them for their gift of aliens, space/time travel and superheroes and to her best friend for teaching her the true meaning of deadlines, as well their love and support.

Otis Galloway
The City DJ

Otis Galloway has an insatiable wanderlust. He started out in Bermuda, and then subsequently left there for Worcester, Massachusetts. After that, a move to Boston, then after collecting ex-wife#1, a move to the West Coast, with stints throughout California, in San Francisco, Albany, Berkeley, Palm Springs, Los Angeles and San Diego. After collecting ex-wife #2, he decided to stop collecting ex-wives (because they're expensive) and instead returned to his first love, collecting music.

Otis currently lives and works in Glasgow, Scotland. He is working on his first book, which is nonfiction and very sweary. Occasionally he is known to put together quite a decent DJ set.

Keith Gaston
The Man with No Name

Keith Gaston was born in Detroit, Michigan. After earning a Bachelor's in Computer Science and two Masters degrees, he decided to pursue his passion of writing. D K Gaston is known for writing books in different genres that are filled with action and adventure. He writes mysteries, crime, thrillers, and speculative fiction. He has written over a dozen novels since 2007 and shows no signs of slowing down. D K Gaston is a devoted husband and father residing in Michigan. He is currently working on his next novel.

Chanel Harry

Chanel Harry is an up and coming science fiction, fantasy and horror writer that hails from The Bronx New York. "The Score" is her first work that will be published in the anthology. However, she is in the process of working on her debut novel "Fire Lady: Tales of the Soucouyants.

Natiq Jalil

Natiq Jalil is a self-taught, emerging visual artist who specializes in watercolor, acrylics, oils, and digital media. He focuses his work on human form and emotion, and often includes organic shapes and written words in pieces. Though originally from Montgomery, AL, he has lived all over the US, including Denver, Pittsburgh, and most recently New York City. He has sold work to many businesses and private collectors throughout the world, including Italy, South Africa,

South Korea, Sweden, Japan, UK, and various states in the US. There is also a documentary in production centering around the paintings he completes on the subway trains of New York City.

Though he is finding success in visual arts, Natiq also considers himself a storyteller. Much of his success in visual arts is due to the fact that he easily recants the individual stories of each of his visual works. He is a lifelong fan of sci-fi, fantasy, manga, and anime, not to mention an avid reader. He writes short stories of urban speculative fiction in his spare time, and hopes to pursue his writing in addition to fine art as a career. His short story in The City is his first published written work.

Valjeanne Jeffers
Street Moon's Revolution

Valjeanne Jeffers is a graduate of Spelman College, and a member of the Carolina African American Writer's Collective. She is the author of Voyage of Dreams; Immortal; Immortal II: The Time of Legend; Immortal III: Stealer of Souls; The Switch II: Clockwork; Immortal IV: Collision of Worlds; Mona Livelong: Paranormal Detective; and Colony: Ascension.

Her fiction has been published in Pembroke Magazine; Steamfunk!; Griots: A Sword and Soul Anthology; Genesis Science Fiction Magazine; PurpleMag; LuneWing; Griots II: Sisters of the Spear; Possibilities, and The City (in press). Book I of The Switch II: Clockwork was also nominated for the best e-book novella of 2013 by the eFestival of Words; and her short story Awakening (from Griots I) was published as a podcast by Far Fetched Fables. Valjeanne is co-owner of Q&V Affordable Editing. Preview or publish her novels at: www.vjeffersandqveal.com

Alan Jones

Born and raised in Atlanta, GA. Alan attended Georgia Tech and Ga. State, obtaining his MBA from the latter. In addition to writing on the student newspapers at these institutions, Alan worked as a columnist for The Atlanta Tribune. Alan continues to write and his latest work, Sacrifices, is available on Amazon.

When not writing, Alan, a former Wall Street Consultant, currently works as an Oracle Business Software Consultant.

Brandee Laird
Glitch

Brandee Laird is a warrior-poet from Seattle, WA, USA. She is a dedicated parkour athlete, one of the founders of the 501(c) 3 non-profit organization Parkour Visions, and acts as the Coaching and Curriculum Director of their Seattle facility. She lives her life exuberantly and with the intent to write it down, constantly collecting experiences and ideas from the world around her. In the daytime you can generally find her in the parkour gym or in the trees, or frequenting the urban shadows at night.

Kai Leakes
Free Your Mind

Born in Iowa, but later relocating and raised in Alton, IL and St. Louis, MO, Kai Leakes was a multifaceted Midwestern child, who gained an addiction to books at an early age. The art of imagination was the very start of Kai's path of writing which lead her to creating the Sin Eaters: Devotion Books Series. Since a young child, her love for creating, vibrant romance and fantasy driven mystical tales, continues to be a major part of her very DNA. With the goal of sharing tales that entertain and add color to a gray literary world, Kai Leakes hopes to continue to reach out to those who love the same fantasy, paranormal, romantic, sci/fi, and soon, steampunk driven worlds that shaped her unique vision.

You can find Kai Leakes at her website: www.kwhp5f. wix.com/kai-leakes.com

Edison Moody
Cover and interior artist

I strive to illustrate the imagination through knowledge and research. As I study the natural, civilized, and invented worlds, the more powerful my paintings become. Other than painting I spend a great deal of time thinking of new ideas about society, technology, characters and culture. I love just as equally to hear the original ideas of others. Feel free to check out my website at www.edisonmoody.com

B. Sharise Moore

Published author, poet, certified educator, and budding screenwriter B. Sharise Moore is a New Jersey native and graduate of Rutgers University. At present, B. Sharise is working on the completion of a short film based on her collection of short stories, Djinn and Tonics, to be published later this year.

Howard Night
Welcome to Liberty

Author of "The Serpent Cult" and Head Writer of Dark Universe: Interregnum Speculative Fiction Books, Howard Night loves setting his characters in warped versions of his hometown of Philadelphia and neighborhood; Mt. Airy. His next novel, King's Bounty, set in the DARK UNIVERSE will be available summer 2015.

Balogun Ojetade
The Verdict

Balogun Ojetade is an author, master-level martial artist in indigenous, Afrikan combative arts and sciences, a survival and preparedness consultant, a former Communications and Asst. Operations Sergeant in the U.S. 7th Special Forces Group (Airborne) and a priest in several Afrikan spiritual traditions.

Balogun is Master Instructor and Technical Director of the Afrikan Martial Arts Institute, which has branches in the Unites States, England and Ghana, West Afrika and Co-Chair of the Urban Survival Preparedness Institute.

He is the author of the bestselling non-fiction books Afrikan Martial Arts: Discovering the Warrior Within and The Afrikan Warriors' Bible and eight novels, including the Steamfunk bestseller, MOSES: The Chronicles of Harriet Tubman (Books 1 & 2); the Urban Science Fiction saga, Redeemer; the Sword & Soul epic, Once Upon A Time In Afrika; a Fight Fiction, New Pulp novella, Fist of Afrika; the gritty, Urban Superhero series, A Single Link and Wrath of the Siafu; the two-fisted Dieselfunk tale, The Scythe and the "Choose-Your-Own-Destiny"-style Young Adult novel,

The Keys. Balogun is also contributing co-editor of two anthologies: Ki: Khanga: The Anthology and Steamfunk.

Finally, Balogun is the Director and Fight Choreographer of the Steamfunk feature film, Rite of Passage and co-author of the award winning screenplay, Ngolo.

Ced Pharaoh
Edge of Innocence

Ced Pharaoh was born and raised in Chicago, Illinois. A lifelong bookworm; his earliest favorites were comic books/graphic novels, mysteries (Encyclopedia Brown, Sherlock Holmes etc.), thrillers, poetry, non-fiction biographies and sci-fi/fantasy! Ced has a blog, 360BEYOND where he highlights indie artists and other creative ideas. Also, he has written several comic book scripts for indie publishing companies that are slated for release.

Ced is working on his series, The Legacy Chronicles and in 2012 he published the collection of dark fantasy poetry, Watch The Shadows: The Legacy Chronicles Book 1. He is busy working on the novel, Urban Mage | The Legacy Chronicles Book 2 slated for 2015.

K. Ceres Wright
Mission: Surreality

K. Ceres Wright is the author of the cyberpunk book, Cog. Her short stories, articles, and poetry have appeared in Hazard Yet Forward; Genesis: An Anthology of Black Science Fiction; Many Genres, One Craft; 2008 Rhysling Anthology; Diner Stories: Off the Menu; and Far Worlds. Contact her on Twitter: @KCeresWright

CPSIA information can be obtained
at www.ICGtesting.com
Printed in the USA
LVHW03s2317150618
580966LV00001B/40/P